THE BOURNE DECEPTION

By Robert Ludlum

The Bancroft Strategy
The Ambler Warning
The Tristan Betrayal
The Janson Directive
The Sigma Protocol
The Prometheus Deception
The Matarese Countdown
The Cry of the Halidon
The Apocalypse Watch
The Scorpio Illusion
The Road to Omaha
The Bourne Ultimatum
Trevayne
The Icarus Agenda
The Bourne Supremacy
The Aquitaine Progression
The Road to Gandolfo
The Parsifal Mosaic
The Bourne Identity
The Matarese Circle
The Holcroft Covenant
The Chancellor Manuscript
The Gemini Contenders
The Rhinemann Exchange
The Matlock Paper
The Osterman Weekend
The Scarlatti Inheritance

Written by Eric Van Lustbader

Robert Ludlum's™ The Bourne Legacy
Robert Ludlum's™ The Bourne Betrayal
Robert Ludlum's™ The Bourne Sanction

Also by Eric Van Lustbader

NICHOLAS LINNEAR NOVELS

Second Skin
Floating City
The Kaisho
White Ninja
The Miko
The Ninja

CHINA MAROC NOVELS

Shan
Jian

OTHER NOVELS

First Daughter
The Testament
Art Kills
Pale Saint
Dark Homecoming
Black Blade
Angel Eyes
French Kiss
Zero
Black Heart
Sirens

ROBERT LUDLUM'S™

THE BOURNE DECEPTION

A NEW JASON BOURNE NOVEL BY

ERIC VAN LUSTBADER

Doubleday Large Print Home Library Edition

GRAND CENTRAL PUBLISHING

NEW YORK BOSTON

This Large Print Edition, prepared especially for Doubleday Large Print Home Library, contains the complete, unabridged text of the original Publisher's Edition.

Grand Central Publishing
Hachette Book Group
237 Park Avenue
New York, NY 10017

Printed in the United States of America

Grand Central Publishing is a division of Hachette Book Group, Inc.

ISBN 978-1-61523-119-5

This Large Print Book carries the
Seal of Approval of N.A.V.H.

**For Jeff,
who started it all with one
simple question.**

Prologue

Munich, Germany/Bali, Indonesia

I speak Russian well enough," Secretary of Defense Bud Halliday said, "but I prefer to speak English."

"That suits me," the Russian colonel said with a heavy accent. "I'm always happy to speak foreign languages."

Halliday gave the Russian a sour smile in response to his jibe. It was well told that Americans overseas only wanted to speak English.

"Good. We'll get this done faster." But instead of beginning, he stared at a wall full of very bad portraits of jazz greats like

Miles Davis and John Coltrane, copied, he had no doubt, from press photos.

After seeing the colonel in the flesh he had begun to have second thoughts about this meeting. For one thing, he was younger than Halliday had imagined. His blond hair was thick, without the slightest wave, and cut short in the style of the Russian military. For another, he looked like a man of action. Halliday could see, beneath his suit, the play of muscles as now and again they bulged against the cheap material. He possessed a peculiar stillness that unsettled Halliday. But it was his eyes—pale, deep-set, unblinking—that truly unnerved the secretary. It was as if he were looking at a photograph of eyes rather than the real thing. The bulbous, veiny nose only served to intensify their implacable peculiarity: It was as if there was no one home, as if the soul of the man did not exist, leaving nothing but a monolithic will, like something ancient and evil Halliday had read about in an H. P. Lovecraft story when he was a teenager.

He trampled the impulse to get up, walk out, and never look back. He had come all this way for a reason, he reminded himself.

The smog that choked Munich—the same precise shade of filthy gray as Karpov's eyes—perfectly mirrored Secretary Halliday's mood. If he never saw this miserable excuse for a city again it would be too soon for him. Unfortunately, here he was in this godforsaken, smoke-clogged subterranean jazz club, having stepped out of the back of an armored Lincoln limousine onto tourist-infested Rumfordstrasse. What was so special about the Russian to bring the American secretary of defense forty-two hundred miles to a city he despised? Boris Karpov was a colonel in FSB-2, ostensibly the new Russian anti-drug enforcement agency. It was a measure of the FSB-2's meteoric rise to power that one of its officers was able to get a message to Halliday, let alone entice him out of Washington.

But Karpov had hinted that he could deliver something Halliday wanted very much. The defense secretary might have been wondering what that might be, but he was too busy trying to figure out what the

Russian would want in return. There was always a quid pro quo to these deals, Halliday knew only too well. He was a veteran of the political infighting that perpetually surrounded the president like a Kansas dust storm. He knew full well that quid pro quos could be painful to accept, but compromise was the name of the political game, whether it be domestic or international.

Even so, Halliday might not have taken up Karpov's offer had it not been for his own suddenly tenuous position with the president. The shockingly abrupt fall from power of Luther LaValle, his handpicked intelligence czar, had shaken Halliday's power base. Friends and allies alike were criticizing or second-guessing him behind his back, and he had to wonder which one of them would be the first to sink the metaphorical knife into his back.

But he'd been around long enough to understand that hope sometimes arrived in seemingly unpleasant forms, like a bed of nails. He was hoping Karpov's deal would provide the political capital that would at once restore his prestige with the president and his power base within the multinational military-industrial complex.

As the trio on stage opened a box full of noise Halliday once again mentally reread the file on Boris Karpov, as if this time he'd find some further information—anything, including a surveillance photo, no matter how grainy or out of focus, of the colonel. No such photo existed, of course, no more intel than the four threadbare paragraphs on the single sheet of paper watermarked TOP SECRET. Because of the administration's dismissive relationship with Russia, the NSA had limited knowledge of the workings inside the Russian political system, not to mention FSB-2, whose actual mission was highly covert, far more so than the FSB, the political inheritor of what had once been the KGB.

"Mr. Smith, you appear distracted," the Russian said. They had agreed on using the pseudonyms Mr. Smith and Mr. Jones in public.

The secretary's head swung around. He was profoundly uncomfortable underground, unlike Karpov who more and more seemed to him like a creature of the dark. Raising his voice to be heard over the rhythmic clangor, he said, "Nothing could be farther from the truth, Mr. Jones. I'm just taking in with a sightseer's bliss the particular atmosphere you've chosen."

The colonel chuckled deep in his throat. "You have a droll sense of humor, yes?"

"You have me entirely."

The colonel laughed out loud. "We'll see about that, Mr. Smith. Since we do not even know our wives, it seems unlikely we should know our . . . counterparts."

The small hesitation had Halliday wondering whether Karpov was going to say *adversaries* instead of the neutral word he'd chosen. He didn't bother to wonder whether the Russian was aware of his political position, because it didn't matter. All that concerned him was whether the deal about to be proposed would help him.

The trio lurched into another tempo, the secretary's only clue that they'd segued into another selection, and he hunched forward over the too-bitter beer he'd hardly touched. No Coors in this joint. "Let's get on with it, shall we?"

"Without delay." Colonel Karpov placed his hands on his golden forearms. The knuckles were scarred and yellow with calluses, which made them look as ridged as the Rockies. "I know, Mr. Smith, that I don't have to explain who Jason Bourne is, yes?"

At the name Halliday's expression hardened. He felt as if the Russian had sprayed him with Freon. "Your point?" he said woodenly.

"My point, Mr. Smith, is this: I will kill Jason Bourne for you."

Halliday didn't waste time in asking how Karpov knew he wanted Bourne dead—there had been enough NSA activity in Moscow the last month when Bourne was there to make it abundantly clear to a deaf, dumb, and blind man that he was targeted for termination.

"Very magnanimous of you, Mr. Jones."

"No, sir, not magnanimous. I have my own reasons for wanting him dead."

At this admission the secretary relaxed slightly. "All right, let's say you do kill Bourne. What do you want in return?"

There was in what anyone else might be termed a twinkle in the colonel's eye, but to Halliday, who was still trying to get the measure of him, it seemed as if someone had walked over Bourne's grave. Death had winked at him.

"I know that look, Mr. Smith. I know you're

expecting the worst—a high payment. But in exchange for you giving me license to take Bourne out with full immunity against the consequences of collateral disturbance or damage, I want you to eliminate a vexing thorn in my side."

"Whom you can't terminate yourself."

Karpov nodded. "You have me entirely, Mr. Smith."

The two men laughed at the same time, but their tones were absolutely different.

"So." Halliday made a tent of his fingers. "Who is the target?"

"Abdulla Khoury."

The secretary's heart sank. "The head of the Eastern Brotherhood? Christ on a crutch, you might as well ask me to assassinate the pope."

"Assassinating the pope would do neither of us any good. But killing Abdulla Khoury, well, that's another matter entirely, yes?"

"Of course, yes. The man's a radical Islamic maniac as well as a menace. Right now he's holding hands with the president of Iran. But the Eastern Brotherhood is a worldwide organization. Khoury has many friends in very high places." The secretary shook his head with a good deal of vehemence. "Attempting to terminate him would be political suicide."

Karpov nodded. "All this is unquestionably true. But what about the Eastern Brotherhood's terrorist activities?"

Halliday snorted. "A pipe dream; rumors, at best. No one in our secret services has ever found a scrap of reliable evidence that it has ties to any terrorist organization. And believe me, we've tried."

"Of this I have no doubt, which means that you didn't find any evidence of terrorist activity in Professor Specter's residence."

"There's no doubt the good professor was a terrorist hunter, but as for allegations he was anything more . . ." Halliday shrugged.

A sudden smile wreathed the colonel's face, and all at once an unmarked manila envelope was on the table between them. "Then you'll find this of particular value." As if maneuvering his queen into checkmate position, Karpov slid the envelope over to Halliday.

As the secretary slit open the envelope

and scanned the contents, Karpov continued. "As you know, FSB-2 is primarily concerned with international drug trafficking."

"So I've heard," Halliday said drily, because he knew damn well that FSB-2's purview was much wider than that.

"Ten days ago," Karpov went on, "we initiated the final phase of a drug bust in Mexico, one we'd been working on for more than two years because one of our Moscow *grupperovka*, the Kazanskaya, has been searching for a secure pipeline as it moved into the drug trade."

Halliday nodded. He knew a bit about the Kazanskaya, one of Moscow's most notorious criminal families, and its head, Dimitri Maslov.

"We were entirely successful, I'm pleased to say," the colonel continued. "In the final sweep of the dead drug lord Gustavo Moreno's house we confiscated a notebook computer before it could be destroyed. The information you're reading now was printed out from the hard drive."

The tips of Halliday's fingers had gone cold. The printout was dense with figures, cross-references, annotations. "This is a money trail. The Mexican drug ring was financed by the Eastern Brotherhood. Fifty percent of the profits went to buying weapons, which were transshipped to various ports in the Middle East by Air Afrika Airways."

"Which is wholly owned by Nikolai Yevsen, the world's largest arms dealer." The colonel cleared his throat. "You see, Mr. Smith, there are powerful elements in my government aligned with Iran because we want their oil and they want our uranium. Energy trumps everything else these days, yes? And so, vis-à-vis Abdulla Khoury, I find myself in the awkward position of possessing evidence implicating him in terrorist activities, yet unable to act on that evidence." He cocked his head. "Possibly you can help me out."

Calming the thundering of his heart, Halliday said, "Why do you want Khoury out of the picture?"

"I could tell you," Karpov said, "but then, regrettably, I'd have to kill you."

It was an old joke, and a stale one, but there was again in the colonel's pale, implacable eyes the eerie twinkle that chilled the secretary to the bone, and absurdly it occurred to him that Karpov might not be joking. This was not a theory he was eager to pursue, so he made his decision quickly.

"Terminate Jason Bourne and I will use the full might of the American government to put Abdulla Khoury where he belongs."

But the colonel was already shaking his head. "Not good enough, Mr. Smith. An eye for an eye, this is the true meaning of quid pro quo, yes?"

"We don't assassinate people, Colonel Karpov," Halliday said stiffly.

The Russian snickered unkindly. "Of course not," he said drily, then shrugged. "No matter, *Secretary Halliday*. I have no such compunctions."

Halliday hesitated but a moment. "Yes, of course, in the heat of the moment I forgot our protocols, Mr. Jones. Send me the entire contents of the hard drive and it will be done." Bracing himself, he stared into those pale eyes. "Agreed?"

Boris Karpov gave a sharp military nod. "Agreed."

When the colonel exited the jazz club, he located Halliday's Lincoln and Secret Service bodyguards arrayed along this block of Rumfordstrasse like tin soldiers. Walking in the opposite direction, he turned a corner, fished inside his mouth, and removed the plastic prosthetics that had changed the shape of his jawline. He grabbed the veiny bulb of his latex nose and pulled it and the actor's putty off, removed the gray-colored contact lenses, stowing them in a plastic case. Himself again, he laughed. There was a colonel in FSB-2 by the name of Boris Karpov; in fact, Karpov and Jason Bourne were friends, which was why Leonid Danilovich Arkadin had chosen Karpov to impersonate. The irony appealed to him: Bourne's friend proposing to terminate him. Plus, Karpov was a strand in the web he was spinning.

There was no danger from the American politician. Arkadin knew full well that Halliday's people had no idea what Karpov looked like. Nevertheless, even if his Treadstone training had taught him never to leave anything to chance, there was a very good reason why he had become the visual approximation of Karpov.

Anonymous within the swirl of passengers, he boarded the U-bahn at Marienplatz. Three stops and four blocks later, at the specified location, he found a perfectly nondescript car waiting for him. As soon as he climbed in, it took off, heading toward Franz Josef Strauss International Airport. He was booked on the 1:20 AM Lufthansa flight to Singapore, where he'd catch the 9:35 AM flight to Denpasar in Bali. It had been far easier to trace Bourne's whereabouts—the people at NextGen Energy Solutions where Moira Trevor worked knew where the two of them had gone—than to steal Gustavo Moreno's laptop. But he had a number of men inside the Kazanskaya. One of them had been fortunate enough to be in Gustavo Moreno's house an hour before the FSB-2 bust went down. He absconded with the incriminating evidence that would now plant Abdulla Khoury six feet under. As soon as Arkadin shot Bourne dead.

Jason Bourne was at peace. At long last his grieving for Marie was over, the guilt lifted from his heart. He lay side by side with Moira, on a *bale*, a huge Balinese daybed with a thatched roof, supported by four carved wooden posts. The *bale* was set into a low stone wall to one side of a three-tiered infinity pool that overlooked the Lombok Strait in southeast Bali. Because the Balinese were aware of everything and forgot nothing, after the first day their *bale* was set up for them each morning when they arrived for their pre-breakfast swim, and their waitress would bring without being asked the drink that Moira loved most: a Bali Sunrise, consisting of chilled sour orange, mango, and passion fruit juices.

"There is no time but time," Moira said dreamily.

Bourne stirred. "Translation."

"Do you know what time it is?"

"I don't care."

"My point," she said. "We've been here ten days; it feels like ten months." She laughed. "I mean that in the best way possible."

Swifts darted like bats from tree to tree, or skimmed the surface of the highest pool. The muted crash of the surf lulled them from below. Moments ago two small Balinese girls had presented them with a handful of fresh blossoms in a bowl of palm leaves they had woven by hand. Now the air was perfumed with the exotic scents of frangipani and tuberose.

Moira turned to him. "It's as they say: On Bali time stands still, and in that stillness lie many lifetimes."

Bourne, his eyes half closed, was dreaming of another life—his life—but the images were dark and murky, as if seen through a projector with a faulty bulb. He'd been here before, he knew it. There was a vibration from the wind, the restful sea, the smiling people, the island itself to which something inside him resonated. It was déjà vu, yes, but it was also more. Something had called him back here, had drawn him like a magnet to true north, and now that he was here he could almost reach out and touch it. Yet still its secret eluded him.

What had happened here? Something important, something he needed to remember. He sank deeper into his dream of a life lived on the edge of yesterday. In the dream he roamed across Bali until he came to the Indian Ocean. There, rising out of the creaming surf, was a pillar of fire. It rose up into the clear blue sky until its tip touched the sun. As a shadow he went across the sand, soft as talcum, to embrace the flames.

He awoke, wanting to tell Moira about his dream, but for some reason he didn't.

That evening, on the way down to the beach club at the foot of the cliff on which the hotel was perched, Moira stopped at one of the many shrines strewn around the property. It was made of stone, its haunches draped with a checkered black-and-white cloth. A small yellow umbrella shaded the upper part; onto it had been laid a number of offerings of brightly colored flowers in woven palm leaf cups. The cloth and the umbrella were signs that the local spirit was in residence. The cloth's pattern had a meaning also: White and black represented the Balinese duality of gods and demons, good and evil.

Kicking off her sandals, Moira stepped onto the square stone in front of the shrine, put her palms together at forehead height, and bowed her head.

"I didn't know you were a practicing Hindu," Bourne said when she was finished.

Moira picked her sandals up, swung them at her side. "I was thanking the spirit for our time here, for all the gifts Bali has to offer." She gave him a wry smile. "And I was thanking the spirit of the suckling pig we ate yesterday for sacrificing himself for us."

They had booked the evening alone at the beach club. Towels were waiting for them, as well as frosty glasses of mango *lassi*, and pitchers of tropical juices and ice water. The attendants had discreetly tucked themselves away in the windowless auxiliary kitchen.

They spent an hour in the ocean, swimming back and forth just beyond the curling surf line. The water was warm, as soft on the skin as velvet. Across the dark beach, hermit crabs went about their sideways business, and here and there bats could be seen winging in and out of a cave at the other end of the beach, just beyond a finger of rocks, part of the western half of the crescent cove.

Afterward they drank their mango *lassis* in the pool, guarded by a huge grinning wooden pig with a medallioned collar and a crown behind its ears.

"He's smiling," Moira said, "because I paid homage to our suckling pig."

They swam laps, then came together at the end of the pool overhung by a magnificent frangipani tree with its buttery white and yellow blossoms. Beneath its leafy branches, they held each other, watching the moon move in and out of gathering clouds. A gust of wind clattered the fronds of the thirty-foot palms that lined the beach side of the pool deck, and their legs went from pale to dark.

"It's almost over, Jason."

"What is?"

"This." Moira wriggled her hand under the water like a fish. "All of this. In a few days we'll be gone."

He watched the moon wink out, felt the first fat drops on his face. A moment later, rain goosefleshed the skin of the pool.

She put her head back against his shoulder, deeper into the shadow of the frangipani. "And what will become of us?"

He knew she didn't want an answer, wanted only to taste the thought on her tongue. He could feel the weight of her, her warmth through the water, against his heart. It was a good weight; it made him drowsy.

"Jason, what will you do when we get back?"

"I don't know," he said truthfully. "I haven't thought about it." But he wondered now whether he would leave with her. How could he when something from his past was waiting for him here, so close he could feel its breath on the back of his neck? He said nothing of this, however, because it would require an explanation, and he had none. Just a feeling. And how many times had this feeling saved his life?

"I'm not going back to NextGen," she said.

His attention returned fully to her. "When did you come to that decision?"

"While we were here." She smiled. "Bali has a way of opening the path to decisions. I came here just before I joined Black River. It seems to be an island of transformations, at least for me."

"What will you do?"

"I want to start my own risk management firm."

"Nice." He smiled. "In direct competition with Black River."

"If you want to look at it that way."

"Other people will."

It was raining harder now; the palm fronds

clashed against one another, and it was impossible to see the sky.

"That could be dangerous," he added.

"Life is dangerous, Jason, like anything governed by chaos."

"I can't argue with that. But there's your old boss, Noah Petersen."

"That's his ops name. His real name is Perlis."

Bourne glanced up at the white flowers, which now began to fall all around them like snow. The sweet scent of frangipani mingled with the fresh smell of the rain.

"Perlis was none too happy with you when we ran into him in Munich two weeks ago."

"Noah's never happy." Moira snuggled deeper into his arms. "I gave up trying to please him six months before I quit Black River. It was a fool's game."

"The fact remains that we were right about the terrorist attack on the liquid natural gas tanker and he was wrong. I'm willing to bet he hasn't forgotten. Now that you're encroaching on his territory you'll have made an enemy."

She laughed softly. "You should talk."

"Arkadin's dead," Bourne said soberly. "He took a header off the LNG tanker into the Pacific off Long Beach. He didn't survive; no one could."

"He was a product of Treadstone, isn't that what Willard told you?"

"According to Willard, who was there, Arkadin was Alex Conklin's first success—and his first failure. He was sent to Conklin by Semion Icoupov, the co-head of the Black Legion and the Eastern Brotherhood until Arkadin killed him for shooting his girlfriend."

"And his secret partner, Asher Sever, your former mentor, is in a permanent coma."

"We all get what we deserve, in the end," Bourne said bitterly.

Moira returned to the subject of Treadstone. "According to Willard, Conklin's aim was to create a superior warrior—a fighting machine."

"That was Arkadin," Bourne said, "but he escaped the Treadstone program back to Russia, where he got up to all sorts of mayhem, hiring himself out to the heads of various Moscow *grupperovka*."

"And you became his successor—Conklin's success story."

"Not if you poll CI's directorate chiefs," Bourne said. "They would shoot me dead as soon as look at me."

"That hasn't stopped them from coercing you into working for them when they needed you."

"That's all over with," Bourne said.

Moira had just decided to change the subject when the power failed. The lights in the pool and within the open-air beach club itself winked out. The wind and the rain remained swirling in the darkness. Bourne tensed, tried to move her away so he could get up. She could sense him questing in the darkness for the source of the outage.

"Jason," she whispered, "it's all right. We're safe here."

He moved them through the water from where they had been sitting to the other side of the pool. She could feel his accelerated heartbeat, his heightened sense of awareness, of waiting for something terrible to happen, and in that instant she was given an insight into his life she'd never had before.

She wanted to tell him again not to worry, that power outages happened all the time on Bali, but now she knew it would be useless. He was hardwired for this kind of reaction; nothing she could say or do would change that.

She listened to the wind and the rain, wondering if he heard anything that she didn't. For an instant she felt a stab of anxiety: What if this wasn't a simple power outage? What if they were being stalked by one of Jason's enemies?

All at once, power was restored, causing her to laugh at her foolishness. "I told you," she said, pointing to the smiling carved pig spirit. "He's protecting us."

Bourne lay back in the water. "There's no escape," he said. "Even here."

"You don't believe in spirits, good or evil, do you, Jason?"

"I can't afford to," he said. "I come across enough evil as it is."

Picking up on his tone, Moira at last broached the subject closest to her heart. "I'm going to have to do some heavy recruiting right off the bat. It's certain we'll see a lot less of each other, at least until I set up my new shop."

"Is that a warning or a promise?"

He couldn't help noting that her laughter

had a brittle edge to it. "Okay, I was nervous about bringing it up."

"Why?"

"You know how it is."

"Tell me."

She turned in his arms, sat straddling him in the dimpled water. The rush of the rain through the leaves was all they could hear.

"Jason, neither of us are the kind of people . . . I mean, we both live the kind of life that makes it difficult to hold on to a steady anything, especially relationships, so—"

He cut her off by kissing her. When they came up for air, he said in her ear, "It's okay. We have this now. If we need more, we'll come back."

Her heart was gripped by joy. She hugged him tight. "It's a deal. Oh, yes, it is."

Leonid Arkadin's flight from Singapore arrived on time. At customs, he paid for his entry visa, then walked quickly through the terminal until he found a men's room. Inside, he went into a stall, shut the door, and latched it. From a shoulder pack he took out the bulbous latex nose, three pots of makeup, soft plastic cheek inserts, and gray contact lenses he'd used in Munich. Not more than eight minutes later, exiting the stall, he went to the line of sinks and stared at his altered appearance, which was once again the very image of Bourne's friend, the FSB-2 colonel Boris Karpov.

Packing up the case, he crossed the terminal, out into the heat and the dense texture of humanity. Climbing into the air-conditioned car he'd hired was a blessed relief. As the taxi exited Ngurah Rai International Airport, he leaned forward, said "Badung Market" to the driver. The young man nodded, grinned, and, along with an armada of kids on motor scooters, promptly got stuck behind an enormous truck lumbering toward the Lombok ferry.

After a harrowing twenty-minute ride during which they overtook the truck by dodging oncoming traffic, played chicken with a pair of teenagers on motorbikes, and almost ran over one of the thousands of feral dogs on the island, they arrived on Jl. Gajah Mada, just across the Badung River. The taxi slowed to a crawl until the seething crowds made further forward progress impossible. Arkadin paid for the driver to hang around until he was ready to be picked up, exited, and went into the tented market.

He was immediately seized by a score of pungent odors—black shrimp paste, chilies, garlic, *karupuk*, cinnamon, lemongrass, pandan leaf, galangal, *kencur*, Salam leaf—and raised voices selling everything from fighting cocks, their plumage dyed pink and orange, to live piglets trussed and tied to bamboo poles for easy transport.

As he passed a stall filled with wide-mouthed baskets of spices, the proprietor, an old woman with no upper lip, dug her claw-like hand into a vat of roots, held a palmful out to him.

"*Kencur*," she said. "*Kencur* very good today."

The *kencur*, Arkadin saw, looked something like ginger, only smaller. Repelled by both the root and its hideous seller, he waved away the *kencur* and pressed on.

It was to one of the pig stalls he headed. Halfway there, he was stopped by an insistent tapping on his arm, like the dry scratch of a chicken's foot. He turned to see a young woman holding a baby in her arms, her eyes beseeching while her brown fingers continued to tap his arm as if it was all they were good for. Ignoring her, he pushed on through the crowd. Aware that if he gave her anything, he'd be immediately besieged by a multitude of others.

The middle pig dealer was a wide man, squat as a frog, with glittering black eyes, a moon face, and a pronounced limp. After Arkadin spoke the specified phrase in Indonesian, the man led him back through the ranks of trussed piglets, their bodies quivering, their terrified eyes staring straight ahead. In the shadows at the rear of the tent were two stacks of hogs, gutted, skinned, ready for the spit. From the belly cavity of one the man drew out a Remington 700P, which he tried to palm off on Arkadin, until Arkadin refused enough times for him to go on to Plan B, which turned out to be precisely what Arkadin wanted: a Parker Hale M85, a super-accurate bolt-action, heavy-barreled rifle. It had a guaranteed first-round-hit capability up to seventy-eight yards. To this, the vendor added a Schmidt & Bender Police Marksman II 4-16x50 rifle scope. The price for both seemed a bit high even after some vigorous bargaining took it down from the stratosphere, but this close to his prey he wasn't in any mood to nitpick. Besides, he was getting top-of-the-line product all the way. He got the pig man to throw in a box of full-metal-jacket .30-caliber M118 cartridges and called it a success. He paid and the dealer broke down the rifle, boxed it and the scope into a hard-sided case.

On the way out, he bought himself a bunch of milk bananas, and ate them slowly and methodically as the taxi made its painfully slow way out of Denpasar. Once on the highway, their speed increased dramatically. The lack of heavy traffic made it easier to get around the trucks that clogged the road.

In Gianyar he saw an open-air market on his left and told the driver to pull over. Despite the bananas—or perhaps because of them—his stomach was growling for some real food. At the market, he ordered a plate of babi guling, roast suckling pig, and, served on a broad vivid green banana leaf, lawar, coconut and strips of spiced turtle. Its sauce of uncooked blood appealed to him particularly. He rent the succulent meat of the piglet between his teeth, swallowing quickly to take another bite.

Because of the clamor of the market, he

periodically checked his cell phone. The longer he waited, the greater his tension, but he needed to be patient because it would take some days for his man to be sure of Bourne's comings and goings. Still, he was uncharacteristically on edge. He put it down to being this close to Bourne, but that only caused him more discomfort. There was something about Bourne that had gotten under his skin, that had become an itch he couldn't scratch.

In an effort to control himself, he turned his thoughts to the recent events that had led him here. Two weeks ago Bourne had thrown him off the side of the LNG tanker. It was a long way down into the Pacific, and he had prepared himself by turning his body into a spear, keeping it perfectly vertical so that when he hit the water he wouldn't break his back or his neck. He went in feetfirst, the force of the fall pushing him so deep the world fell into twilight and he was gripped by a terrible chill that worked its way into his bones before he'd even begun his double-kick upward.

By the time he broke the surface, the tanker was a blur, steaming toward the docks at Long Beach. Treading water, he swiveled his body around as a submarine captain might swivel his periscope to get the lay of the land, as it were. The vessel nearest to him was a fishing trawler, but until it was an emergency, he wanted no part of it. The captain would be bound to report rescuing a man overboard to the American Coast Guard, which was precisely what Arkadin didn't want: Bourne was sure to check the records.

He felt no panic, or even concern. He knew he wouldn't drown. He was a powerful swimmer with great endurance, even after his exhausting hand-to-hand fight with Bourne aboard the tanker. The sky was blue, except where the brown haze hung over the shore, stretching inland to Los Angeles. The waves lifted him up and swept him into their valleys. He kicked to maintain his position. Now and again curious gulls wheeled overhead.

After twenty minutes his patience was rewarded. A sixty-foot pleasure craft hove into view, moving at about four times the speed of the trawler. Soon it was near enough to him for him to begin waving. Almost immediately the boat altered course.

Another fifteen minutes and he was on

board, wrapped in two towels and a blanket because his core temperature had dropped below acceptable levels. His lips were blue and he was shivering. The owner, whose name was Manny, fed him some brandy and a chunk of Italian bread and cheese.

"If you excuse me a minute, I'll get on the horn with the Coast Guard, tell them I've picked you up. What's your name?"

"Willy," Arkadin lied. "But I wish you wouldn't."

Manny made an apologetic gesture with his meaty shoulders. He was of middle height, red-faced, balding. He was dressed casually but expensively. "Sorry, pal. Rules of the road."

"Wait, Manny, wait. It's like this." Arkadin was speaking English with a native's Midwestern twang. His time in America had served him well on many fronts. "Are you married?"

"Divorced. Twice."

"See there? I knew you'd understand. See, I'd chartered a boat to take my wife out for a nice day, maybe head over to Catalina for drinks. Anyway, how was I to know my girlfriend stowed away on board. I'd told her I was going fishing with the guys so she thought she'd surprise me."

"She did surprise you."

"Shit," Arkadin said, "did she ever!" He finished off his brandy, shook his head. "Anyhoo, things got kinda wild. I mean all hell broke loose. You don't know my wife, she can be a real queen bitch."

"I think I was married to her once." Manny sat back down. "So what did you do?"

Arkadin shrugged. "What could I do? I jumped overboard."

Manny threw his head back and laughed. He slapped his thigh. "Goddammit! Willy, you sonovabitch!"

"So you see why it'd be so much better if no one knows you picked me up."

"Sure, sure, I understand, but still . . ."

"Manny, what's your line of work, if I might ask?"

"I own a company that imports and sells high-end computer chips."

"Well, now, isn't that something?" Arkadin had said. "I think I might have a deal that could net both of us a boatload of money."

Arkadin, finishing the last of his lawar at

the Gianyar market, laughed to himself. Manny got two hundred thousand dollars, and through one of his regular business shipments Arkadin received the Mexican drug lord Gustavo Moreno's laptop in Los Angeles without either the FSB-2 or the Kazanskaya being any the wiser.

He found a bed-and-breakfast—what the Balinese called a home stay—on the outskirts of Gianyar center. Before he settled down for the night he took out the rifle, put it together, loaded it, unloaded it, broke it down. He did this twelve times exactly. Then he pulled the mosquito netting closed, lay down on the bed, and stared unblinking at the ceiling.

And there was Devra, pale, already a ghost, as he had found her in the artist's apartment in Munich, shot by Semion Icoupov when her concentration was diverted by Bourne entering the room. Her eyes searched his, looking for something. If only he knew what.

Even this evil demon of a man had his vanities: Since Devra's death, he had convinced himself that she was the only woman he had loved or could have loved, because this fueled his desire for one thing: revenge. He had killed Icoupov, but Bourne was still alive. Not only had Bourne been complicit in Devra's death, but he had also killed Mischa, Arkadin's best friend.

Now Bourne had given him a reason to live. His plan to take over the Black Legion—in order to complete his revenge against Icoupov and Sever—wasn't enough, though his plans for it were large and far ranging, beyond anything either Icoupov or Sever could conceive. But he craved more: a specific target on which to vent his rage.

Beneath the mosquito netting he periodically broke out into a cold sweat; his brain seemed to be alternately on fire or as sluggish as if it had been submerged in ice. Sleep, already barely known to him, was now out of the question. But he must have fallen asleep at some point because in the darkness he was gripped by a dream: Devra, holding out her slim, white arms to him. Yet when he entered their embrace, her mouth yawned wide, covering him with spewed black bile. She was dead, but he could not forget her, or what she caused in him: the tiniest fissure in the speckled granite of his soul, through which her mysterious light had begun to trickle, like the first snowmelt of spring.

Moira awoke without the feel of Bourne beside her. Still half asleep, she rolled out of bed, crushing the flower petals they'd found strewn there on their return from their evening at the beach club. Padding across the cool tile floor, she slid open the glass doors. Bourne was sitting on the terrace that overlooked the Lombok Strait. Fingers of salmon-colored clouds drifted just above the eastern horizon. Though the sun had yet to appear, its light shone upward like a beacon beating back the tattered remnants of night.

Opening the door, she went out onto the terrace. The air was rich with the scent of the potted tuberose sitting on the rattan desk. Bourne became aware of her the moment the door slid back, and he half turned.

Moira put her hands on his shoulders. "What are you doing?"

"Thinking."

She bent down, touched his ear with her lips. "About what?"

"About what a cipher I am. I'm a mystery to myself."

Typical of him, there was no self-pity in his voice, only frustration. She thought a moment. "You know when you were born."

"Of course, but that's the beginning and the end of it."

She came around in front of him. "Maybe there's something we can do about that."

"What d'you mean?"

"There's a man who lives thirty minutes from here. I've heard stories about his amazing abilities."

Bourne looked at her. "You're kidding, right?"

She shrugged. "What have you got to lose?"

The call came and, with an eagerness he hadn't felt since before Devra was killed, Arkadin climbed onto the motorbike he had ordered the day before. He rechecked a local map and set off. Past the temple complex at Klungkung, right at Goa Lawah, the thruway dipped down closer to the ocean on their right. Then the modern four-lane highway vanished, leaving him back on a two-lane blacktop. Just east of

Goa Lawah he turned north, heading along a narrow track into the mountains.

To begin with," Suparwita said, "what is the day of your birth?"

"January fifteenth," Bourne replied.

Suparwita stared at him for a very long time. He sat perfectly still on the hard-packed earth floor of his hut. Only his eyes moved, minutely, but very quickly, as if they were making complex mathematical calculations. At length, he shook his head. "The man I see before me does not exist—"

"What do you mean?" Bourne said sharply.

"—therefore, you were not born on the fifteenth of January."

"That's what my birth certificate says." Marie had researched it herself.

"You speak to me of a certificate of birth." Suparwita spoke slowly and carefully, as if each word were precious. "Which is a piece of paper only." He smiled, and his beautiful white teeth seemed to light up the dimness. "I know what I know."

Suparwita was a large man for a Balinese, with skin dark as mahogany, perfect, unblemished and unlined, making it impossible to guess his age. His hair was thick, black, and naturally wavy. It was pushed back from his forehead by what seemed to Bourne to be the same crown-like band the pig spirit wore. He had powerful-looking arms and shoulders without the usual Western over-muscled definition. His hairless body looked smooth as glass. He was naked from the waist up; below he wore a traditional Balinese sarong of white, brown, and black. His brown feet were bare.

After breakfast, Moira and Bourne had mounted a rental motorbike and headed into the lush, green countryside, to a thatched-roof house at the end of a narrow dirt path in the jungle, the home of the Balinese holy man named Suparwita who, she claimed, could find out something of Bourne's lost past.

Suparwita had greeted them warmly and without surprise as they approached, as if he had been expecting them. Gesturing for them to come inside, he had served them small cups of Balinese coffee and freshly made fried banana fritters, both sweetened with palm sugar syrup.

"If my birth certificate is wrong," Bourne said now, "can you tell me when I was born?"

Suparwita's expressive brown eyes had not stopped their mysterious calculations. "December thirty-one," the holy man said without hesitation. "You know our universe is overseen by three gods: Brahma, the creator, Vishnu, the preserver, Shiva, the destroyer." He pronounced Shiva as all Balinese did, so that it sounded like *Siwa*. He hesitated a moment, as if unsure whether to proceed. "After you leave here you will find yourself at Tenganan."

"Tenganan?" Moira said. "Why would we go there?"

Suparwita smiled at her indulgently. "The village is known for double *ikat* weaving. Double *ikat* is sacred, it provides protection from the demons of our universe. It is woven in three colors only, the colors of our gods. Blue for Brahma, red for Vishnu, yellow for Shiva." He handed Moira a card. "You will buy a double *ikat* here, at the best weaver." He gave her a hard look. "Please do not forget."

"Why would I forget?" Moira asked.

As if her question did not merit an answer, he returned his attention to Bourne. “So you understand completely, the month of December—your birth month—is ruled by Shiva, the god of destruction.” Suparwita paused here, as if out of breath. “But please remember that Shiva is also the god of transformation.”

The holy man now turned to a low wooden table on which was set a series of small wooden bowls, which were variously filled with powders and what looked like nuts or perhaps dried seedpods. He chose one of these pods, ground it in another bowl with a stone pestle. Then he added a pinch of yellow powder and dumped the mixture into a small iron kettle, which he set over a small wood fire. A cloud of fragrant steam perfumed the room.

Seven minutes of brewing passed before Suparwita took the kettle off the fire and poured the liquid into a coconut shell cup inlaid with mother-of-pearl. Without a word, he handed the cup to Bourne. When Bourne hesitated, he said, “Drink. Please.” His smile lit up the room again. “It is an elixir made of green coconut juice, cardamom, and *kencur*. Mainly, it is *kencur*. You know *kencur*? It is also called resurrection lily." He gestured. "Please."

Bourne drank the mixture, which tasted of camphor.

"What can you tell me about the life I can't remember?"

"Everything," Suparwita said, "and nothing."

Bourne frowned. "What does that mean?"

"I can tell you nothing more now."

"Apart from my real birth date, you haven't told me anything."

"I have told you everything you need to know." Suparwita cocked his head to one side. "You aren't ready to hear more."

Bourne was growing more impatient by the second. "What makes you say that?"

Suparwita's eyes engaged Bourne's. "Because you do not remember me."

"I've met you before?"

"Have you?"

Bourne got to his feet, pent-up anger erupting from him. "I was brought here for answers, not more questions."

The holy man looked up at him mildly.

"You came here wanting to be told what you must discover for yourself."

Bourne took Moira's hand, pulled her up. "Come on," he said. "Let's go."

As they were about to step out the door, the holy man said in a casual tone: "You know, all this has happened before. And it will happen again."

That was a waste of time," Bourne said as he took the keys from Moira.

She said nothing, climbed on the bike behind him.

As they were heading back down the narrow dirt path the way they had come, a compact Indonesian man with a weathered face the color of old mahogany on a souped-up motorbike broke out of the forest ahead of them, coming straight toward them. He drew a handgun and Bourne spun them around, then headed farther up into the hills.

This was far from a perfect place for an ambush. He'd taken a look at the local map and knew that in a moment they'd break out of the trees onto the terraced rice paddies that surrounded the village of Tenganan.

"There's an irrigation system that runs above the paddies," Moira said in his ear.

He nodded just as the terraced quilt of vivid emerald green appeared, sparkling in the brilliant sunlight. The sun blazed down on men and women with straw hats and long knives bent over the rice plants. Others walked behind teams of plodding cows, tilling sections of the paddies where the rice had been harvested, the remains burned off so that other crops—potatoes, chilies, or long beans—could be grown, ensuring that the rich, volcanic soil wouldn't be depleted of minerals. Still other women, their posture ramrod-straight, transported large sacks balanced on their heads. They moved like tightrope walkers, negotiating the sinuous, narrow margins between the paddies, placing one foot carefully in front of the other.

A sharp crack caused them to bend low over the motorbike, even as it brought the heads of the workers up. The Indonesian had shot at them as he'd broken through the last stand of trees bordering the paddies.

Bourne veered off, treading the fine, serpentine line between the rice fields.

"What are you doing?" Moira shouted.

"We'll be entirely out in the open, nothing but sitting ducks!"

Bourne was nearing one of the paddies where the stalks were being burned off. Smoke, pungent and thick, rose up into the clear sky.

"Grab a handful as we pass by!" he called back to her.

Immediately she understood. With her right arm tight around his waist, she leaned to her left, scooped up a handful of burning rice stalks, flung them backward. Released, they flew into the air, directly in front of their pursuer.

While the Indonesian's vision was momentarily obstructed, Bourne veered back to his right, following the winding edge through the labyrinth of the paddies. He had to be careful; the smallest miscalculation would plunge them down into muddy water and densely packed plants, rendering the motorbike useless. Then they really would be sitting ducks.

The Indonesian took aim at them again, but a woman was in his way, and then a pair of cows, and he put his handgun away, needing both hands to negotiate the trickier path Bourne had chosen.

Cleaving to the outside of the paddies, Bourne took them up the hill, past terrace after terrace, some filled with brilliant green rice plants, others ashy brown following the harvest. A haze of aromatic smoke drifted over the hillside.

"Here!" Moira said urgently. "Here!"

Bourne saw the abutment of the drainage system, a five-inch ribbon of concrete on which he needed to drive the motorbike. Waiting until the last moment, he turned sharply to the left, running parallel to the terraces, which were laid out below them in a dizzying pattern, like hieroglyphics, immense and mysterious, carved into the hillside.

Due to his size and that of his motorbike, the Indonesian was able to close the gap between them. He was no more than two arm's-lengths behind them when Bourne came upon a worker—an old man with spindly legs and eyes the size of raisins. In one hand he held one of the fat-bladed knives used to harvest the rice, in the other a clump of freshly sliced raw rice. Seeing the two motorbikes approaching, the man froze in astonishment. As he passed, Bourne snatched the knife out of his hand.

Moments later Jason spied a rough wooden plank that crossed over the irrigation streamlet into the jungle on their right. He went over it, but as he did so the half-rotten board cracked, then splintered just as the front wheel bit into the dirt on the other side. The motorbike slewed dangerously, almost spilling them into the densely packed trees.

Their pursuer revved his motorbike, made the leap across the span left by the ruined bridge. He followed Bourne and Moira down a steeply sloping path, filled with rocks and half-buried tree roots.

The way grew steeper, Moira held on tighter. He could feel her heart hammering in her chest, her accelerated breath against his cheek. Trees flashed by frighteningly close on either side. Rocks caused the motorbike to rear up like a bucking bronco, forcing Bourne to fight to keep it under control. One mistake would send them plummeting off the path, down into the forest of thick-boled trees. Just when it seemed as if the trail couldn't get any steeper, it turned into a series of rock steps, down which they clattered and bumped with heart-stopping speed. Moira, risking a glance over her shoulder, saw the Indonesian, bent low over the handlebars of his motorbike, intent on overtaking them.

All at once the natural stairs gave out and the path resumed, this time at a more bearable pitch. Their pursuer tried to aim his handgun, but Bourne slashed a stand of bamboo with the knife he'd taken from the old man, and the thin trees came crashing down across the path. The mahogany man was forced to jam the gun between his teeth. It took all his skill to keep from veering off into the looming forest.

As the path flattened out, they whizzed past small shacks, men wielding axes or stirring pots over fires, women with babies in the crooks of their arms, and the ubiquitous feral dogs, thin and cowed, which shied away from the racing vehicles. Clearly they were on the outskirts of a village. Could it be Tenganan? Bourne wondered. Had Suparwita foreseen this chase?

Soon thereafter they passed through a stone archway and entered the village proper. Children playing badminton outside the local school stopped and stared as the bikes flashed by. Chickens scattered, squawking, and huge fighting cocks dyed pink, orange, and blue were so agitated they overturned their wicker cages, in turn disturbing the cows and calves lying in the center of the village. The villagers themselves, emerging from the walled compounds of their houses, ran after their precious fighting cocks.

Like all hill villages, this one was built on terraces, much like the rice paddies: swaths of packed earth and scraggly grass interspersed with stone ramps that led to the next level. Running down the center was a wall-less structure used by the elders for town meetings. On either side were shops, part of the living compounds, selling single and double *ikat* weavings. Catching sight of the first of the weaving shop signs through the chaos of running feet and animal sounds, Bourne felt a chill run down his spine. So this was, indeed, Tenganan, the village of Suparwita's prediction.

In the chaos that had erupted in the village, Bourne cut a line of washing, which undulated in the air like a scaled reptile, before fluttering in their wake. Skillfully guiding the motorbike through a narrow alley, he doubled back the way they had come.

Risking a glance behind him, he saw he'd failed to lose the Indonesian; he came roaring at them unabated, unfazed by the downed laundry. Bourne with a burst of speed lengthened the distance between him and his pursuer enough to make a sharp U-turn, reversing course to make a run past the small man and out of the village. But once again, the Indonesian seemed unsurprised, almost as if he were expecting this tactic. He pulled up, drew his gun, and fired, forcing Bourne to whirl the motorbike back the way he had been going, even as a second shot passed just wide of his left shoulder. Bourne kept going in the only direction open to him, continued on over the bumpy packed dirt and stone ramps, away from his dogged pursuer.

Leonid Arkadin, lost in the dappled shadows of the forest, heard the roar of the engines over the measured chanting that came from inside the walls of the temple over which, from his position, he had a perfect view. He raised the Parker Hale

M85 so the stock fit comfortably to his shoulder and sighted down the Schmidt & Bender scope.

He was calm now, his anxiety replaced by a curious and cunning fire that burned away all thought extraneous to his purpose, leaving his mind as clear as the sky above him, as still as the forest within which he was nestled like an adder in a tree, waiting patiently for its prey. He'd planned well, using the local Indonesian as a hunter will use a beater to stalk the prey, moving it ever closer to where the hunter has hidden himself.

All at once a motorbike emerged into the temple clearing, and Arkadin breathed deeply as he centered Bourne in his sights. And in that moment the outline of Bourne's body became keenly defined, like vapor condensing into the poisoned nectar of revenge.

Bourne and Moira broke out into a perfectly still clearing in which were set three temples—a large one in the center, two smaller ones on either side. There was no sound except the rhythmic throb of the motorbike's engine. Then, hearing chanting from inside the walls of the center temple, Bourne pulled up.

In that moment Arkadin, settling himself on the nearly horizontal branch of a tree, pulled the trigger, and Bourne was blown backward off the motorbike. Moira screamed.

Throwing aside the rifle and drawing a wicked-looking hunting knife with a serrated blade, Arkadin jumped to the ground and raced toward the kill site in order to slit Bourne's throat and ensure his death. But his progress was impeded by a herd of cows. Following them were women with offerings of fruit and flowers on their heads, and behind them came the town's children in a ceremonial procession, moving toward the temple. Arkadin tried to get around them, but one of the cows, disturbed by his frantic movements, turned in his direction. It shook its long, sharp horns and at once the procession froze as if in midstep. Heads turned and all eyes were on him, and with one last look at Bourne's bloody body, he vanished back into the jungle.

The celebrants rushed toward Bourne, spilling their offerings across the sparse grass where he lay on his back in the dirt.

He tried to get up, failed. Moira knelt over him, and he pulled her down so her ear was against his mouth. Blood had soaked the front of his shirt, and now trickled darkly into the earth.

Book One

1

Three Months Later

In an upper-class suburb of Munich, two young bodyguards with gimlet eyes and holstered 9mm Glocks in their armpits flanked a thin, hyperactive man as he emerged from a house. An older man with dark skin and grave lines reaching down from either corner of his mouth, like mustaches, emerged from the shadowed refuge to briefly shake the hyperactive man's hand. Then the three men trotted down the stairs and entered a waiting car: one of the bodyguards riding shotgun, the other one with the hyperactive man in back. The meeting had been intense but brief, and the engine was already running, purring like a well-fed cat. His mind was filled with how he was going to structure the debriefing he would give his boss, Abdulla Khoury, on the rapidly changing face of the Turkish situation as it had just been outlined to him.

The newborn morning lay drowsing, barely awake, and utterly silent. The trees, well manicured and leafy, dappled the sidewalks in inky shade. The air was soft and cool, as yet innocent of the harsh sun that would turn the sky white in a few hours' time. The early hour had been deliberately chosen. As expected, there was no traffic to speak of, just a young boy at the far end of the block teaching himself to ride a bicycle. A sanitation truck lumbered around the corner at the opposite end of the block, its huge brushes beginning to spin whatever dirt there might be on the nearly immaculate street into the truck's belly. Again, the sight was utterly normal; the residents of this neighborhood all had pull with the municipal government, and they were proud of the fact that their streets were always the first to be cleaned each day.

As the car gathered speed, making its

way down the street, the huge truck turned so that it was sideways to the oncoming vehicle, blocking the road. Without an instant's hesitation the car's driver threw the vehicle into reverse and stepped on the gas. With a screech of tires the car shot backward, away from the truck. At the sound, the boy looked up. He was standing, straddling the bike, appearing to get his wind back. But at the last moment, as the oncoming car neared him, he reached into the bike's wicker basket and drew out an odd-looking weapon with an unnaturally long barrel. The rocket-launched grenade shattered the car's rear window and the car burst apart in an oily orange-and-black fireball. By this time the boy, hunched over the handlebars of his bike, was pedaling expertly away, a satisfied smile on his face.

Just past noon that same day, Leonid Arkadin was sitting in a Munich beer hall surrounded by oompah music and drunken Germans when his cell phone buzzed. Recognizing the caller's phone number, he walked out into the street, where it was slightly less noisy, and grunted a wordless greeting.

"Like the others, your latest attempt to destroy the Eastern Brotherhood has failed." Abdulla Khoury's ugly voice buzzed in his ear like an angry wasp. "You killed my finance minister this morning, that's all. I've already appointed another."

"You misunderstand me, I don't mean to destroy the Eastern Brotherhood," Arkadin said. "I mean to take it over."

The response was a harsh laugh devoid of all humor, or even human emotion. "No matter how many of my associates you kill, Arkadin, this I assure you: I will always survive."

Moira Trevor was sitting behind her sparkling new chrome-and-glass desk, in the sparkling new offices of Heartland Risk Management, LLC, her brand-new company, occupying two floors of a postmodern building in the heart of Northwest Washington, DC. She was on the phone with Steve Stevenson, one of her contacts in the Department of Defense, being briefed on a lucrative job her new company had been hired to do, one of half a dozen that had rolled in over the past five weeks, and simultaneously running through sets of daily intelligence reports on her computer terminal. Beside it was a snapshot of her and Jason Bourne, the Bali sun on their faces. In the background was Mount Agung, the island's sacred volcano, up whose spine they had trekked early one morning before sunlight kissed the eastern horizon. Her face was completely relaxed; she looked ten years younger. As for Bourne, he was smiling in that enigmatic way she loved. She used to trace the line of his lips when he smiled like that, as if she were a blind woman able to glean a hidden meaning with her fingertip.

When her intercom sounded, she started, realizing she'd been gazing at the photo, her thoughts wandering back, as they often did these days, to those golden days on Bali before Bourne was gunned down in the dirt of Tenganan. Glancing at the electronic clock on her desk, she gathered herself, finished up her call, and said "Send him in" into the intercom speaker.

A moment later Noah Perlis entered. He was her former handler at Black River, a private mercenary army used by the United States in Middle East hot spots. Moira's firm was now in direct competition with

Black River. Noah's narrow face was more sallow than ever, his hair flecked with more gray. His long nose swept out like a sword-stroke above a mouth that had forgotten how to laugh or even smile. He prided himself on his keen insight into other people, which was ironic considering he was so heavily defended he was cut off even from himself.

She gestured at one of the contemporary chrome and black-strap chairs facing her desk. "Take a seat."

He remained standing, as if he already had one foot out the door. "I've come to tell you to stop raiding our personnel."

"You mean you've been sent like a common messenger." Moira looked up, smiled with a warmth she didn't feel. Her uptilted brown eyes, wide apart and inquiring, betrayed none of her feelings. Her face was uncommonly strong or intimidating, depending on your point of view. Nevertheless, she possessed a serenity that served her well in stressful situations such as this one.

Bourne had warned her even before she set up Heartland almost three months ago that this moment was going to come.

Something inside her had been looking forward to it. Noah had come to personify Black River, and she'd been under his boot heel for too long.

Taking several steps toward her, he plucked the framed photograph off her desk, then turned it to gaze down at the image.

"Too bad about your boyfriend," he said. "Got gunned down in a stinking village in the middle of nowhere. You must have been broken up."

Moira had no intention of allowing him to upset her. "It's nice to see you, Noah."

He sneered as he replaced the photo. "*Nice* is a word people use when they politely lie."

Her face held its innocent expression, a form of armor against his slings and arrows. "Why shouldn't we continue to be polite to each other?"

Noah returned to stand with his fingers curled hard into his palms. His knuckles were white with the force he used to make his fists, and Moira couldn't help but wonder whether he wished he had his hands around her neck rather than hanging at his sides.

"I'm very fucking serious, Moira." His eyes engaged hers. Noah could be a scary individual when he put his mind to it. "There's no turning back for you, but as for going forward in the way you have . . ." He shook his head in warning.

Moira shrugged. "No problem. The fact is, you have no people left who meet my ethical requirements."

Her words had the effect of relaxing him enough to say in an entirely different tone, "Why are you doing this?"

"Why are you asking me a question to which you already know the answer?"

He stared at her, keeping silent, until she continued, "There needs to be a legitimate alternative to Black River, one whose members don't skate at the edge of legality, then regularly cross over."

"This is a dirty business. You of all people know that."

"Of course I know it. That's why I started this company." She rose, leaned across her desk. "Iran is now on everyone's radar. I'm not going to sit back and let the same thing happen there that's happened in Afghanistan and Iraq."

Noah turned on his heel and crossed to

the door. With his hand on the knob he looked back at her with a cold intensity, an old trick of his. “You know you can’t hold back the flood of filthy water. Don’t be a hypocrite, Moira. You want to wade in the muck like the rest of us because it’s all about the money.” His eyes glittered darkly. “Billions of dollars to be made off a war in a new theater of operations.”

2

Lying in the dirt of Tenganan, Bourne whispers into Moira's ear. "*Tell them* . . ."

She is bent low over him in the dust and the running blood. She is listening to him with one ear while pressing her cell phone to the other. "*Just lie still, Jason. I'm calling for help.*"

"*Tell them I'm dead,*" Bourne says just before losing consciousness . . .

Jason Bourne awoke from his recurring dream, sweating like a pig through the bedsheets. The warm tropical night was clouded by the mosquito netting tented around him. Somewhere high in the mountains it was raining. He heard the thunder like hoofbeats, felt the sluggish, wet wind on his chest, bare where the wound was in the latter stages of healing.

It had been three months since the bullet struck him, three months since Moira followed his orders to the letter. Now virtually everyone who knew him believed him to be dead. Only three people other than him knew the truth: Moira; Benjamin Firth, the Australian surgeon whom Moira brought him to in the village of Manggis; and Frederick Willard, the last remaining member of Treadstone, who had revealed Leonid Arkadin's Treadstone training to Bourne. It was Willard, contacted by Moira at Bourne's behest, who had begun reconditioning Bourne as soon as Dr. Firth allowed it.

"You're damn lucky to be alive, mate," Firth said when Bourne had regained consciousness after the first of two operations. Moira was there, having just returned from making very public arrangements for Bourne's "body" to be shipped back to the States. "In fact, if it weren't for a congenital abnormality in the shape of your heart, the bullet would have killed you almost instantly.

Whoever shot you knew what he was doing."

Then he'd gripped Bourne's forearm and flashed a bony smile. "Not to worry, mate. We'll have you right as rain in a month or two."

A month or two. Bourne, listening to the torrential rain come closer, reached out to touch the double *ikat* cloth that hung beside his bed, and felt calmer. He remembered the long weeks he'd been forced to remain in the doctor's surgery on Bali, both for health and for security reasons. For a number of weeks after the second operation it was all he could do just to sit up. During that syrupy time Bourne discovered Firth's secret: He was an inveterate alcoholic. The only time he could be counted on to be stone-cold sober was when he had a patient on the operating table. He proved himself to be a brilliant cutter; any other time, he reeked of *arak*, the fermented Balinese palm liquor. It was so strong, he used it to wipe down his operating theater when he occasionally forgot to refill his order of pure alcohol. In this way, Bourne unlocked the mystery of what the doctor was doing hidden far away from everything: He'd been canned from every hospital in Western Australia.

All at once Bourne's attention turned outward as the doctor entered the room across the compound from the surgery.

"Firth," he said, sitting up. "What are you doing up at this time of night?"

The doctor moved over to the rattan chair by the wall. He had a noticeable limp; one leg was shorter than the other. "I don't like thunder and lightning," he said as he sat down heavily.

"You're like a child."

"In many ways, yes." Firth nodded. "But unlike many blokes I met back in the bad old days, I can admit it."

Bourne switched on the bedside lamp, and a cone of cool light spread over the bed and lapped at the floor. As the thunder rumbled closer, Firth leaned into the light, as if for protection. He was carrying a bottle of *arak* by its neck.

"Your faithful companion," Bourne said.

The doctor winced. "Tonight, no amount of liquor will help."

Bourne held out his hand, and Firth handed him the bottle. He waited for Bourne to take a swig, then took possession of it.

Though he sat back in the chair, he was far from relaxed. Thunder cracked overhead and all at once the downpour hit the thatch roof with the bang of a shotgun. Firth winced again, but he didn't take more *arak*. It appeared that even he had a limit.

"I'm hoping I can convince you to throttle back your physical training."

"Why would I do that?" Bourne said.

"Because Willard pushes you too hard." Firth licked his lips, as if his body was dying for another drink.

"That's his job."

"Maybe so, but he's not your doctor. He hasn't taken you apart and stitched you back together." He finally put the bottle down between his legs. "Besides, he scares the bejesus out of me."

"Everything scares you," Bourne said, not unkindly.

"Not everything, no." The doctor waited while a crack of thunder shuddered overhead. "Not torn-up bodies."

"A torn-up body can't talk back," Bourne pointed out.

Firth smiled ruefully. "You haven't had my nightmares."

"That's all right." Bourne once again saw

himself in the dirt and the blood of Tenganan. "I have my own."

For a time nothing more was said. Then Bourne asked a question, but when the only answer forthcoming was a brief snore, he lay back in the bed, closed his eyes, and willed himself to sleep. Before the soft morning light woke him, he had returned, unwillingly, to Tenganan, where the heat of Moira's cinnamon musk mingled with the odor of his own blood.

Do you like it?" Moira held up the cloth woven in the colors of the gods Brahma, Vishnu, and Shiva: blue, red, and yellow. The intricate pattern was of interlocking flowers, frangipani, perhaps. Since the dyes used were all natural, some water-based, others oil-based, the threads took eighteen months to two years to finish. The yellow—the personification of Shiva, the destroyer—would take another five years to slowly oxidize and reveal its final hue. In double *ikats* the pattern was dyed into both the warp and weft threads so that when it was woven all the colors would be pure, unlike the more common single *ikat* weaving in which the pattern was only in one set of threads, the other being a background color such as black. The double *ikat* was part of every Balinese home, where it hung on a wall in a place of honor and respect.

"Yes," Bourne had replied. "I like it very much."

He was about to go into the surgery for the first of his two operations.

"Suparwita said it was important I get a double *ikat* for you." She leaned closer. "It's sacred, Jason, remember? Brahma, Vishnu, and Shiva together will protect you from evil and illness. I'll make sure it's near you all the time."

Just before Dr. Firth wheeled him into the surgery, she leaned even closer, whispered in his ear: "You'll be fine, Jason. You drank the tea made from *kencur*."

Kencur, Bourne thought as Firth applied the anesthetic. *The resurrection lily*.

He dreamed of a temple high in the Balinese mountains while Benjamin Firth cut him open with little hope of his survival. Through the carved red gates of the temple rose the hazy pyramidal shape of Mount Agung, blue and majestic against the yellow sky. He was gazing down at the gate from a great height and, looking around, he realized that he was on the top step of a steep triple staircase, guarded by six ferocious stone dragons, whose bared teeth were easily seven inches long. The bodies of these dragons undulated upward on both sides of the three staircases, creating banisters whose solidity appeared to carry the stairs upward to the plaza of the temple proper.

As Bourne's gaze was drawn again to the gates and Mount Agung, he saw a figure silhouetted against the sacred volcano, and his heart began to pound in his chest. The setting sun fell upon his face, and he shaded his eyes with one hand, straining to identify the figure, who now turned toward him. At once, he felt searing pain and pleasure.

At that precise moment Dr. Firth came across the curious abnormality in Bourne's heart and began to work, knowing that he now had a chance to save his patient.

Just over four hours later, Firth, exhausted but cautiously triumphant, wheeled Bourne into the recovery room, adjacent to the surgery, that would become Bourne's home for the next six weeks.

Moira was waiting for them. Her face was pale, her emotions retreated from her flesh, curled into a ball in the pit of her stomach.

"Will he live?" She almost choked on the words. "Tell me he'll live."

Firth sat wearily on a canvas folding chair as he stripped off his bloody gloves. "The bullet went clear through him, which is good because I didn't have to dig it out. It is my considered opinion that he'll live, Ms. Trevor, with the important caveat that nothing in life is certain, especially in medicine."

As Firth took the first drink of *arak* he'd had that day, Moira approached Bourne with a mixture of elation and trepidation. She'd been so terrified that for the last four and a half hours her heart had hurt as much as she had imagined Bourne's had. Gazing down into his near-bloodless but peaceful face, she took his hand in hers, squeezing hard to reestablish the physical connection between them.

"Jason," she said.

"He's still well under," Firth said, as if from a great distance. "He can't hear you."

Moira ignored him. She tried not to

imagine the hole in Bourne's chest beneath the bandage, but failed. Her eyes were streaming tears, as they had periodically while he was in surgery, but the abyss of despair along which she had been walking was folding in on itself. Still, her breathing was ragged and she had to struggle to feel the solid ground beneath her feet, because for hours she was certain it had been about to open up and swallow her whole.

"Jason, listen to me. Suparwita knew what would happen to you, and he prepared you as best he could. He fed you the *kencur*, he had me get the double *ikat* for you. They both protected you, I know it, even if you won't ever believe it."

Morning broke in the soft colors of pink and yellow against the pale blue sky. Brahma, Vishnu, and Shiva rose as Bourne opened his eyes. Last night's storm had scrubbed off the film of haze that had built up from the burning off of the rice stalks in the hillside paddies.

As Bourne sat up, his eyes fell upon the double *ikat* that Moira had bought for him in Tenganan. Holding its rough texture between his fingers he saw, like a flash of lightning, the silhouette standing between him and Mount Agung, framed by the temple gates, and wondered anew who it could possibly be.

3

The cockpit of the American passenger airliner, Flight 891 out of Cairo, Egypt, hummed contentedly. The pilot and copilot, longtime friends, joked about the flight attendant they'd both like to take to bed. They were in the final stages of negotiating the terms of a thoroughly adolescent contest that would involve her as a prize when the radar picked up a blip rapidly closing on the plane. Responding in proper fashion, the pilot got on the intercom and ordered all seat belts fastened, then took the plane out of its pre-planned route in an attempt at an evasive maneuver. But the

767 was too large and ungainly; it wasn't built for easy maneuverability. The copilot tried to get a visual fix on the object, even as he raised the Cairo airport control tower on the radio.

"Flight Eight-Niner-One, there are no scheduled flights that close to you," the calm voice from the control tower said. "Can you get a visual fix?"

"Not yet. The object is too small to be another passenger plane," the copilot responded. "Maybe it's a private jet."

"There are no flight plans posted. Repeat: There are no flight plans posted."

"Roger that," the copilot said. "But it's still closing."

"Eight-Niner-One, elevate to forty-five thousand feet."

"Roger that," the pilot said, making the necessary adjustments on the controls. "Elevating to forty-five thou—"

"I see it!" the copilot cut in. "It's traveling too fast to be a private jet!"

"What is it?" There was a sudden urgency to the voice from Cairo. *"What's happening? Eight-Niner-One, please report!"*

"Here it comes!" the copilot screamed.

An instant later disaster struck as the mighty metal fist hit the jetliner in a blinding flare. An immense explosion disjointed the fuselage as a beast pulls its prey limb from limb, and the twisted, blackened remains plummeted to earth with breathtaking speed.

Deep beneath the West Wing of the White House, in a spacious room made of steel-reinforced concrete eight feet thick, the president of the United States was in a high-level security meeting with Secretary of Defense Halliday; DCI Veronica Hart; Jon Mueller, head of the Department of Homeland Security; and Jaime Hernandez, the new intelligence czar, who had taken over the NSA in the wake of the illegal waterboarding scandal that brought down his predecessor.

Halliday, a ruddy-cheeked man with dark blond hair combed straight back, a politician's sly eyes, and a perfect Crest smile, seemed as if he were reading from a script he might have prepared for a Senate subcommittee. "After months of arduous prep work, judicious bribes, and discreet probing," he said, "Black River has at last made first contact with a group of dissident, pro-Western Iranis." Ever the showman, he paused, looked around the highly polished table, making eye contact with each person in turn. "This is blockbuster news," he added unnecessarily, and, with a nod to the president, "something this administration has been searching for for years, because the only known Iranian dissident group has so far proved impotent."

Halliday was at his most eloquent, and Hart thought she knew why. Though his stock had risen because of the death of Jason Bourne, for which he had agitated and for which he'd taken credit, Hart knew Halliday needed another victory, one that was more wide ranging, that could be exploited by the president himself for political capital.

"At last a group we can work with," Halliday continued with unbridled enthusiasm as he handed around the fact sheet prepared by Black River detailing dates and places of meeting, along with transcripts of clandestinely recorded conversations between Black River operatives and leading members of the dissident group, whose names had been redacted for security reasons. All the conversations, Hart saw, underscored both their militancy and their commitment to accept aid from the West.

"They're unquestionably pro-Western," the secretary of defense said, as if his audience required a verbal guide through the densely worded pages. "Moreover, they're preparing for an armed revolution and are eager for whatever support we can supply."

"What are their real capabilities?" Jon Mueller asked. Mueller had that typical ex-NSA mien of a soldier with a thousand-yard stare. He looked like a man who could break a body with the same nonchalant ease he'd crack a wooden matchstick in two.

"Excellent question, Jon. If you turn to page thirty-eight, you'll see Black River's detailed assessment of the training preparedness and arms expertise of this particular group, which both rate eight out of ten on their proprietary rating scale."

"You seem to be relying a great deal on Black River, Mr. Secretary," Hart said drily.

Halliday didn't even look at her; it was her people—Soraya Moore and Tyrone

Elkins—who had brought his man, Luther LaValle, down. He hated her guts, but Hart knew he was too canny a politician to let his animosity show in front of the president, who now held her in high esteem.

Halliday nodded sagely, his voice carefully neutral. "I wish it were otherwise, Director. It's no secret that our own resources are already at their limits due to the ongoing conflicts in Afghanistan and Iraq, and now that Iran is on our radar as a clear and present danger, we're obliged to outsource more and more of our far-flung intelligence gathering."

"You mean the NSA is. CI created Typhon last year specifically to handle more of the Middle East field intelligence," Hart pointed out. "Every Typhon field agent is fluent in the various dialects of Arabic and Farsi. Tell me, Mr. Secretary, how many NSA agents are similarly trained?"

Hart could see the color rising up Halliday's throat into his cheeks, and she leaned forward, further inflaming an intemperate outburst from him. Unluckily for her, the meeting was interrupted by the burr of the blue telephone at the president's right elbow. The entire room fell into a tense silence so absolute that the discreet sound had the resonance of a pneumatic jackhammer. The blue telephone brought bad news, they all knew that.

With a grim expression, the president pressed the receiver to his ear, listened to the voice of General Leland over at the Pentagon who briefed him, even while he told his commander in chief that a more detailed document would be on its way to the White House by special courier within the hour.

The president took all this in with his usual equanimity. He was not a man to panic or to take precipitous action. As he cradled the receiver, he said, "There has been an air disaster. American Flight Eight-Nine-One, outward bound from Cairo, was taken out of the sky by an explosion."

"A bomb?" Jaime Hernandez, the new intelligence czar, said. He was slim and handsome, with calculating eyes as dark as his thick hair. He looked like the kind of individual who counted the wontons in his soup to make sure he wasn't being short-changed.

"Are there any survivors?" Hart asked.

"We don't know the answer to either

question," the president said. "What we do know is that there were one hundred eighty-one souls on that flight."

"Good God." Hart shook her head.

There was a moment of stunned silence while they all contemplated both the enormity of the calamity and the terrible repercussions that might very well ensue. No matter what the cause, a great many American civilians were dead, and if the worst-case scenario were to come true, if those American civilians proved to be the victims of a terrorist attack . . .

"Sir, I think we should send a joint NSA-DHS forensics team to the crash site," Halliday said in a bid to take charge.

"Let's not get ahead of ourselves," Hart countered. Halliday's words had energized them out of their initial shock. "This isn't Iraq. We'll need the permission of the Egyptian government to send our troops in."

"Those are American citizens—our people blown out of the sky," Halliday said. "Fuck the Egyptians. What've they done for us lately?"

Before the argument could escalate, the president held up his hand. "First things first. Veronica is right." He stood up. "We'll reconvene this discussion in an hour after I've spoken to the Egyptian president."

Precisely sixty minutes later, the president reentered the room, nodded to those present, and sat down before addressing them. "All right, it's settled. Hernandez, Mueller, assemble a joint task force of your best people and get them on a plane to Cairo ASAP. First: survivors; second: identify casualties; third: for the love of God ascertain the cause of the explosion."

"Sir, if I may," Hart interjected, "I suggest adding Soraya Moore, the director of Typhon, to the team. She's half Egyptian. Her intimate knowledge of Arabic and the local customs will prove invaluable particularly in liaising with the Egyptian authorities."

Halliday shook his head, said emphatically, "This matter is already complicated enough without a third agency becoming involved. The NSA and the DHS have all the tools at their disposal to handle the situation."

"I doubt that—"

"I needn't remind you, Director Hart, that

the press will be all over this incident like flies on shit," Halliday overran her. "We've got to get our people over there, make our findings and take appropriate measures as quickly as possible, otherwise we risk turning this into a worldwide media circus." He turned to the president. "Which is something the administration doesn't need right now. The last thing you want, sir, is to look weak and ineffectual."

"The real problem," the president said, "is that the Egyptian national secret police—what are they called?"

"Al Mokhabarat," Hart said, feeling like she was a contestant on *Jeopardy!*

"Yes, thank you, Veronica." The president made a note on his scratch pad. He'd never forget al Mokhabarat's name again. "The problem," he began again, "is that a contingent of this al Mokhabarat will be accompanying the team."

The secretary of defense groaned. "Sir, if I may say so, the Egyptian secret police are corrupt, vicious, and notorious for their sadistic human rights violations. I submit that we cut them out of the equation entirely."

"Nothing would please me more, believe

me," the president said with some distaste, "but I'm afraid that's the quid pro quo the Egyptian president insisted on in exchange for letting us help in the investigation."

"Our help? What a joke!" Halliday gave a humorless laugh. "The damn Egyptians couldn't find a mummy in a tomb."

"That's as may be, but they're our allies," the president said sternly. "I expect everyone to keep that in mind in the difficult days and weeks ahead."

When he looked around the room the DCI seized her chance. "Sir, may I remind you that Egyptian is Director Moore's native language."

"Precisely why she should be stricken from the list," Halliday said at once. "She's a Muslim, for God's sake."

"Secretary, that's just the kind of ignorant remark we don't need right now. Beside, how many men on that team are fluent in Egyptian Arabic?"

Halliday bristled. "The Egyptians speak damn fine English, thank you very much."

"Not among themselves." As the defense secretary had before her, Hart turned to address the president directly. "Sir, it's important—no, vital—that at this juncture the team has as much information about the Egyptians—especially the members of al Mokhabarat, because Secretary Halliday is correct about them—as is possible. That knowledge may well prove critical."

The president pondered for no more than a moment. Then he nodded. "Director, your proposal makes sense, let's run with it. Get Director Moore up to speed."

Hart smiled. Time to press her advantage. "She may have some people—"

The president nodded at once. "Whatever she needs. This is no time for half measures."

Hart was looking at Halliday, who was directing a poisoned glare in her direction, to which she smiled sweetly as the meeting adjourned.

She exited the West Wing quickly to avoid another vitriolic confrontation with the defense secretary, and took the short ride back to CI headquarters, where she summoned Soraya Moore to her office.

Abdulla Khoury was on his way from the Starnberger See to the headquarters of the Eastern Brotherhood less than ten miles away. Behind him, the snowcapped Alps and the icy blue water of the lake—the fourth largest in Germany—sparkled in the sun. Brightly colored sails rose above sleek boats, and yachts plied the lake. There was no room for such frivolous recreation as sailing in Khoury's life, even before he became head of the Eastern Brotherhood. His life had taken a serious turn when, at the age of seven, he had discovered his calling as Allah's earthly messenger. It was a calling he had kept to himself for a long time, intuiting that no one would believe him, least of all his father, who treated his children even worse than he did his wife.

Khoury was born with the patience of a tortoise. Even when he was a child he had no difficulty waiting for the opportune moment to take advantage of a situation. Not surprisingly, his preternatural serenity was misinterpreted as a form of idiocy by his father, and all of his instructors save one, who saw in the boy the holy spark Allah had placed there at the moment of his conception. From that moment on, Khoury's life changed. He began to frequent this instructor's house after hours for advanced lessons. The man lived alone and welcomed Khoury as his acolyte and protégé.

As a young adult, he had joined the Eastern Brotherhood, patiently moving up in the hierarchy. He did this in his characteristic manner, by winnowing out the wheat from the chaff. In his case the wheat was represented by those in the organization who shared his strict views of Islam. It was he who brought them the notion of fighting for change from within. His was a naturally subversive nature; he was superb at undermining the current order to make way for his own. This he accomplished slowly and carefully, always flying under the twin radars of Semion Icoupov and Asher Sever, because these were not men to be taken lightly or to engage as antagonists without every form of advantage imaginable. He was still amassing his arsenal of such advantages when they were both killed, leaving a vast and intimidating power vacuum.

Not for Abdulla Khoury. Seizing his moment while the Eastern Brotherhood was still in shock, he took control of the organization. Ripping a page from Icoupov's strategic manual, he quickly installed his compatriots in all key positions within the Eastern Brotherhood, thereby ensuring both the short- and the long-term success of his coup.

The motorcade came to a halt at the first of his three stops before he returned to his headquarters. There were lieutenants responsible for two areas of the Middle East and one for Africa whom he needed to brief on the latest developments inside Iran.

As the motorcade took him from one briefing to another, he couldn't help but reflect on the recent interference from Leonid Arkadin. He'd dealt with men like Arkadin before, people who believed that all situations could be settled with the flaming barrel of a gun, weaponized men without faith to guide them, for what use was a weapon if it wasn't in the service of Allah and Islam? He knew something of Leonid Danilovich Arkadin's background: He had come to be a killer of killers through hiring himself out to various Moscow *grupperovka*. It was said he was close with Dimitri Maslov, the head of the Kazanskaya, but not as close as he had been with his mentor, Semion Icoupov, before he'd turned on Icoupov and killed him. Perhaps not surprising, since Arkadin had been born and raised in Nizhny

Tagil, a hell on earth that could only exist in Russia—an industrial slimepit that manufactured tanks for the military, ringed by high-security prisons whose occupants, when they were released, stayed in Nizhny Tagil to prey upon its citizens. It was a minor miracle that Arkadin had been lucky enough to escape.

This sordid, bloody background was why Khoury knew in his heart that Arkadin was nothing more than a man who had lost his soul, condemned to walk among the living, the best part of him already dead and buried.

And it was for the same reason that Khoury had taken extra precautions. He was well protected by two bodyguards in his car, wallowing along beneath the weight of its armor-plated sides and bulletproof glass, as well as sharpshooters with hunting rifles in cars in front and back. He seriously doubted whether the man would be foolish enough to go after him. But since one couldn't read the mind of one's enemy it was prudent to act as if he himself were under attack, rather than the Eastern Brotherhood.

Within fifteen minutes the motorcade pulled into the Eastern Brotherhood's private parking area and the men in the cars surrounding Khoury's leapt out, making a thorough search of the area. Only then did one of them communicate to the bodyguards traveling with Khoury through a wireless network that it was safe to exit.

The elevator took him and four bodyguards directly up to the top floor of the private building owned by the Eastern Brotherhood. Two of the bodyguards stepped off the elevator first, secured the floor, and checked the faces of their boss's personal staff to make sure they were all known. Then they stepped aside and Khoury hurried across the reception area to his office. When his secretary turned toward him, his face pinched and ashen beneath the burnished color of his skin, Khoury realized something was wrong.

"I'm sorry, sir," he said. "There was nothing any of us could do."

Then Khoury looked beyond him to the three strangers, and immediately the primitive part of his brain, the fight-or-flight center, understood. Nevertheless, the civilized part of him was shocked, rooting him to the spot.

"What is this?" he said.

As if sleepwalking, he went across the magnificent jewel-tone carpet, a present from the president of Iran, staring with stupefaction at the three men in tailored suits ranged behind his desk. The men on the left and right stood with their arms hanging loosely at their sides and produced laminated badges identifying them as agents of the US Department of Defense. The one in the middle with hair the color of iron filings and a hard, angular face said, "Good afternoon, Mr. Khoury. My name is Reiniger." A *Bundespolizei* ID card was attached to a black cord around his neck. It said Reiniger was a high-ranking officer in GSG 9, the elite counterterrorism unit. "I'm here to take you into custody."

"Custody?" Khoury was taken aback. "I don't understand. How could you—?"

His voice died in his throat as he looked down at the dossier Reiniger had produced. To his horror he saw photo after photo, green-lit from infrared film, of him with the sixteen-year-old busboy from the See Café, whom he saw three times a week when he went to Lake Starnberg ostensibly for lunch.

Gathering himself with a supreme effort, Khoury pushed the photos across the desk. “I have many enemies with deep resources. This smut is doctored. Anyone can see it isn’t me performing these wicked and disgusting acts.” He looked up into Reiniger’s yellow teeth, wrapped in his fraudulent piety. “How dare you accuse me of such—”

Reiniger made a small gesture with one hand and the man on his right stepped one pace to the left, revealing the sixteen-year-old busboy from the See Café. The boy would not meet Khoury’s dark glare, instead staring fixedly at the tops of his sneakers. In this superheated room, amid the tall, wide-shouldered Americans in their dark suits, he looked younger than his years, slender and fragile as bone china.

“I’d introduce you,” one of the American agents said with an audible snicker, “but that would be redundant.”

Khoury’s brain was on fire. How had this horror been visited on him? Why, if he was the chosen of Allah, had his dark secret, learned at the knee of his childhood instructor, been revealed? He had no thought for who had betrayed him, only that he could not bear to live with the shame, which would strip him of the power and prestige he'd worked for decades to amass.

"This is the end for you, Khoury," the other American said.

Which one was which? They all looked alike to him. They had the evil look of dissolute infidels. He wanted to kill them both.

"The end of you as a public figure," the American went on in his implacable cyborg voice. "But more importantly, it's the end of your influence. Your brand of extremism has been revealed as a sham, a joke, a goddamn hypocritical—"

Khoury growled deep in his throat as he lunged at the boy. He saw the American nearest the boy draw a Taser, but he couldn't stop now. The twin barbed hooks impaled themselves, one in his torso, the other in his thigh, and the pain spasmed him backward. His knees buckled and he fell, flopping and arching, but all was ringing silence, as if he had already passed to another plane. Even as the movement in the room grew frenzied, even when, some minutes later, he was transferred to a gurney, taken down in the elevator, rushed through the ground-floor lobby filled with silent and shocked blobs that must once have been faces, all was silence. All was silence out in the street, even as traffic passed by, even as paramedics and the dark-suited Americans jogged beside the gurney and mouths opened, perhaps to shout warnings for gawping passersby to step aside or move back. Silence. Only silence.

And then he was lifted up as if by the hand of Allah and rolled inside the ambulance. Two paramedics climbed in, along with a third man, and even as the rear doors were closing, the ambulance took off. Its siren must have been wailing, but Khoury couldn't hear a thing. Neither could he feel his body, which seemed to bind him to the gurney like lead weights. All he felt was the fire in his chest, the laboring of his heart, the irregular pulse of blood circulating through him.

He hoped the third man wasn't one of

the Americans; he was afraid of them. The German he knew he could handle once he regained his voice; he had cultivated many friendships in the *Bundespolizei* and as long as he could keep the Americans at a remove for even an hour, he knew he'd be all right.

With a wave of relief, he saw that the third man was Reiniger. He could feel a tingling in his extremities, found that he could move his fingers and toes. He was about to try out his vocal cords when Reiniger bent over him and, with the flourish of a magician on stage, removed a nose and cheeks made out of silicone putty, along with a set of yellowed teeth that he'd worn over his own. Instantly, a premonition overtook Khoury like the flutter of death's black wave.

"Hello, Khoury," Reiniger said slowly.

Khoury tried to speak, bit his tongue instead.

Reiniger grinned as he patted the stricken man on the shoulder. "How you doing? Not well, I see." He shrugged, his grin flowering open. "No matter, because it's a good day to die." He placed the pad of his right thumb against Khoury's Adam's apple and pressed down until something vital popped.

"Good for us, anyway."

4

When Soraya Moore walked into the DCI's office, Veronica Hart got up from behind her desk and beckoned Soraya to sit beside her on a sofa against one wall. In the past year of Hart's tenure as DCI, the two women had become close friends as well as associates. They had been forced by circumstance to trust each other from the moment Hart had come on board following the Old Man's untimely death. The two of them had united against Secretary of Defense Halliday while Willard took down his attack dog, Luther LaValle, and handed Halliday the most humiliating defeat of his political career. That they'd made a mortal enemy in the process was never far from their minds or their discussions. Neither was Jason Bourne, whom Soraya had twice worked with, and whom Hart had come to understand better than anyone else at CI save for Soraya herself.

"So how are you?" Hart said as soon as they were both seated.

"It's been three months and Jason's death still hasn't sunk in." Soraya was a woman who was both strong and beautiful, her deep blue eyes contrasting strikingly with her cinnamon-colored skin and long black hair. A former CI chief of station, she had been thrust unceremoniously into the directorship of Typhon, the organization she helped create, when her mentor, Martin Lindros, had died last year. Since then, she'd struggled with the labyrinthine political maneuvering any director in the intelligence community was forced to master. In the end, however, her struggle with Luther LaValle had taught her many important lessons. "To be honest, I keep thinking I'm seeing him out of the corner of my eye. But when I look—really look, that is—it's always someone else."

"Of course it's someone else," Hart said, not unsympathetically.

"You didn't know him the way I did," Soraya said sadly. "He was able to cheat death so many times it now seems impossible that this last time he failed."

She put her head down, and Hart squeezed her hand briefly.

The night they heard of Bourne's death, she'd taken Soraya out to dinner, then insisted she come back to her apartment, steadfastly ignoring all of Soraya's protestations. The evening was difficult, not the least because Soraya was Muslim; they couldn't go on a good old-fashioned bender. Grieving stone-cold sober was a drag, and Soraya had begged Hart to drink if she wanted to. The DCI refused. That night an unspoken bond had sprung up between them that nothing could now sunder.

Soraya looked up then, gave the DCI a wan smile. "But you didn't call me in to hold my hand again."

"No, I didn't." Hart told Soraya about the downing of the passenger jetliner in Egypt. "Jaime Hernandez and Jon Mueller are putting together a joint NSA-DHS forensics team to fly to Cairo."

"Good luck with that," Soraya said caustically. "Which one of the team is going to interface with the Egyptians, speak to them in their own language, or be able to interpret their thinking by their replies?"

"As a matter of fact, you are." When she saw the look of astonishment on Soraya's face, she added, "I had the same reaction to the task force you did."

"How much of a fight did Halliday put up?"

"He fired off the usual objections, including slurs directed at your heritage," Hart said.

"How he hates all of us," Soraya said. "He can't even make the distinction between Arab and Muslim, let alone Sunni and Shi'a."

"Never mind," Hart said. "I presented my reasons to the president and he agreed."

The DCI handed over a copy of the intel they'd all been reading when news came of the air disaster.

As Soraya looked it over, she said, "This data's from Black River."

"Having worked for Black River, that's precisely my concern. Given the methods they use to gather intel it seems to me that

Halliday is leaning on them a bit too heavily." She tipped her head toward the file. "What do you think of their intel on this pro-Western dissident group in Iran?"

Soraya frowned. "There have been rumors of its existence for years, of course, but I can tell you that no one in the Western intelligence community has met a member or has ever been contacted by the group. Frankly, it always struck me as part of the right-wing neocon fantasy of a democratic Middle East." She continued to page through the file.

"Yet there is a bona fide dissident movement in Iran that has been calling for democratic elections," Hart said.

"Yes, but it's unclear whether its leader, Akbar Ganji, would be pro-Western. My guess is probably not. For one thing, he's been canny enough to reject the administration's periodic offers of money in exchange for an armed insurrection. For another, he knows, even if our own people don't, that throwing American dollars at what we euphemistically call the 'indigenous liberal forces' within Iran is a recipe for disaster. Not only would it endanger the already fragile movement and their aim of a velvet revolution, but it would encourage its leaders to become dependent on America for aid. It would alienate its constituency, as it did in Afghanistan, Iraq, and many other Middle Eastern countries, and turn the so-called freedom fighters into our implacable enemies. Time and again, ignorance of the culture, religion, and real aims of these groups has combined to defeat us."

"Which is why you'll be part of the forensics team," Hart said. "However, as you can see, the Black River intel doesn't concern Ganji or his people. We aren't talking here about a velvet revolution, but one steeped in blood."

"Ganji has said that he doesn't want war, but his policy has been floundering for some time. You know as well as I do that the regime wouldn't allow him to survive, let alone to speak out, if his power was substantial. Ganji's of no use to Halliday, but this new group's aims would suit his purposes to a T."

Hart nodded. "That's just what I was thinking. So while you're in Egypt I want you to nose around. Use Typhon's Egyptian contacts to find out what you can about the legitimacy of this group."

"That won't be easy," Soraya said. "I can guarantee you that the national secret police are going to be all over us—especially me."

"Why especially you?" Hart asked.

"Because the head of al Mokhabarat is Amun Chalthoum. He and I had a heated confrontation."

"How heated?"

Soraya's memory immediately clamped down. "Chalthoum is a complex character, difficult to read—his entire life seems wrapped up in his career in al Mokhabarat, an organization of thugs and assassins to which he's been given a life sentence."

"Lovely," Hart said with no little sarcasm.

"But it would be naive to believe that's all there is to him."

"Do you think you can handle him?"

"I don't see why not. I think he's got a thing for me," Soraya said, not quite understanding why she wasn't telling Veronica the whole truth.

Eight years ago, on a courier mission, she'd been captured by agents of al Mokhabarat who, unbeknownst to her, had infiltrated CI's local network to which she was to deliver a microdot on which was etched the network's new orders. She had no idea what was on the microdot, had no desire to know. She was thrown in a basement cell of al Mokhabarat's offices in downtown Cairo. Three days later, with no sleep and only water and a crust of moldy bread to eat once each day, she was taken upstairs and brought before Amun Chalthoum, who took one look at her and immediately ordered her cleaned up.

She was shown to a shower, where she scrubbed every inch of her body with a soapy washcloth. When she stepped out, a set of new clothes was waiting for her. She assumed her old clothes were being ripped apart and scrutinized by an al Mokhabarat forensics team searching for the intel she was carrying.

Everything fit her perfectly. To her surprise, she was then escorted out of the building. It was night. It occurred to her that she'd had no idea of time passing. In the boiling street a car was waiting at the curb, its headlights illuminating plainclothes guards watching her with studied attention. When she climbed in she had another shock: Amun Chalthoum sat behind the wheel. He was all alone.

He drove very hard and very fast across the city, heading west into the desert. He said nothing, but from time to time when traffic allowed, he watched her with his avid hawk's gaze. She was famished but was determined to keep her hunger to herself.

He took her to Wadi AlRayan. He stopped the car, told her to get out. They stood facing each other in the blue moonlight. Wadi AlRayan was so desolate, they could have been the last two humans on earth.

"Whatever you're looking for," she said, "I don't have it."

"Yes, you do."

"It's already been delivered."

"My sources tell me otherwise."

"You don't pay your sources nearly enough. Besides, you've checked my clothes and everything else."

He didn't laugh, nor would he ever during the time she was with him. "It's in your head. Give it to me." When she didn't respond, he added, "We'll stay out here until you give me the intel."

She recognized his threat, recognized, too, the impetus behind it. In his eyes she was an Egyptian female. As such, she was brought up to unquestioningly obey males;

why should she be any different from any of the other females he knew? Because she was half American? He spit on Americans. Immediately she saw the advantage his mistake gave her. She stood up to him; she kept to her story; she defied him every step of the way; most importantly, she proved she couldn't be intimidated.

In the end, he'd backed down, had taken her back to Cairo, to the airport. At the boarding gate he handed back her passport as a gentleman might. It was a formal and somehow touching gesture. She turned away, certain she'd never see him again.

The DCI nodded. "If you can use his attraction for you to your advantage, do so, because I have an uncomfortable feeling that Halliday is about to propose a major new military initiative based on the premise of an armed insurrection from inside Iran."

Leonid Arkadin was sitting in a café in Campione d'Italia, a picturesque Italian tax haven tucked away in the Swiss Alps. The tiny municipality rose steeply off the glassy ultramarine-blue surface of a clear mountain lake, studded with vessels of all sizes from rowboats to multimillion-dollar yachts, complete with the helipads, the copters, and, on the largest of these, the females to go with them.

In a haze of detached amusement, Arkadin watched two long-stemmed models with the kind of perfectly bronzed skin only the privileged and wealthy know how to acquire. As he sipped a small cup of espresso, which was all but lost in his large, square hand, the two models climbed on top of a bald man with an exceedingly hairy body, stretched out on the sea-blue cushions of the yacht's rear deck.

He lost interest because for him pleasure was such an ephemeral concept, it lacked both form and function. His mind and his body were still bound to the iron-and-fire wheel of Nizhny Tagil, which just went to prove the old saw: You can take the man out of hell but you can't take hell out of the man.

The acrid taste of the toxic Nizhny Tagil sky was still in his mouth when, moments later, a man with skin the color of his espresso approached. Arkadin glanced up with an air close to indifference even as the man slithered into the chair across from him.

"My name is Ismael," the espresso man said. "Ismael Bey."

"Khoury's right hand." Arkadin finished off his cup, set it down on the small round table. "I've heard of you."

Bey, a rather young man, thin and bony as a starving dog, sported a dreadfully haunted look. "It's done, Arkadin. You've won. With the death of Abdulla Khoury, I'm now the head of the Eastern Brotherhood, but I value my life more than my predecessor did. What do you want?"

Arkadin took hold of his empty cup, moved it to the precise center of its saucer, all without taking his eyes from the other man's. When he was ready, he said, "I don't want your position, but I am going to take your power."

His lips formed the ghost of a smile, but there was something in the expression that sent a visible shiver of presentiment down the other's spine. "To everyone in the outside world you have assumed the mantle of your fallen leader. However, everything—every decision, every action you will take from this moment on—originates with me; every dollar the Brotherhood makes flows through me. This is the new order of battle."

His smile turned lupine, and Bey's face took on a green and shiny cast. "First in the order of battle is to choose a contingent of one hundred men from the Black Legion. Within the week I want them at a camp I've set up in the Ural Mountains."

Bey cocked his head. "A camp?"

"They will be trained by me personally."

"Trained for what?"

"For killing."

"Who are they meant to kill?"

Arkadin pushed his empty cup across the table until it was sitting squarely in front of Ismael Bey. The gesture, for Bey, was unmistakable. He had nothing; he would have nothing unless he obeyed Arkadin studiously and completely.

Without another word, Arkadin rose, and left Bey confronting the bleak face of his new future.

Today I woke up thinking of Soraya Moore," Willard said. "I was thinking that she must still be grieving over your death."

It was just after sunrise and, as he did every morning at this time, Bourne was sitting through Dr. Firth's thorough and tedious examination.

Bourne, who had come to know Willard quite well in the three months the two had been together, said, "I haven't tried to contact her."

Willard nodded. "That's good." He was small and dapper, with gray eyes and a face that could assume any expression with an unconscious ease.

"Until I find out who tried to kill me three months ago and I deal with him, I'm determined to keep Soraya out of the loop." It was not that Bourne didn't trust her—on the contrary—but because of her ties to CI and the people with whom she worked, he had decided from the first that the burden of truth would be unfair for her to carry with her to CI every day.

"I went back to Tenganan but I could find no trace of the bullet," Willard said. "I've tried everything else I can think of to discover who shot you, but so far no luck. Whoever he was covered his tracks with commendable ability."

Frederick Willard was a man who had

worn a mask for so long that it had become part of him. Bourne had asked Moira to contact him because Willard was a man for whom secrets were sacred. He had faithfully kept all of Alex Conklin's secrets at Treadstone; Bourne knew with the instinct of an injured animal that Willard would keep the secret that Bourne was still alive.

At the time of Conklin's murder Willard was already in his deep-cover position as chief steward at the NSA's safe house in rural Virginia. It was Willard who had smuggled out the digital photos taken of the rendition and waterboarding cells in the house's basement that had torpedoed Luther LaValle and had necessitated serious damage control from Secretary of Defense Halliday's camp.

"Finished," Benjamin Firth said, getting up off his stool. "Everything is good. Better than good, I might say. The entry and exit wounds are healing at a truly remarkable rate."

"That's because of his training," Willard said confidently.

But privately Bourne wondered whether his recovery was aided by the *kencur*—the resurrection lily—concoction Suparwita had made him drink just before he was shot. He knew he had to speak to the healer again if he was going to discover what had happened to him here.

Bourne rose. "I'm going for a walk."

"As ever, I counsel against it," Willard warned. "Every time you set foot outside this compound you risk compromising your security."

Bourne strapped on a lightweight backpack with two bottles of water. "I need the exercise."

"You can exercise here," Willard pointed out.

"Hiking up these mountains is the only way to build up my stamina."

This was the same argument they'd had every day since Bourne felt fit enough to take extended walks, and it was one bit of Willard's advice that he chose to ignore.

Opening the gate to the doctor's compound, he set off briskly through the steep forested hills and terraced rice paddies of East Bali. It wasn't only that he felt hemmed in within the stucco walls of Firth's compound, or that he deemed it necessary to push himself through increasingly difficult stages of physical exertion, though either was reason enough for his daily treks. He was compelled to return time and again to the countryside where the tantalizing flame of the past, the sense that something important had happened to him here, something he needed to remember, was constantly flickering.

On these hikes down steep ravines to rushing rivers, past animistic shrines to tiger or dragon spirits, across rickety bamboo bridges, through vast rice paddies and coconut plantations, he tried to conjure up the face of the silhouetted figure turning toward him that he saw in his dreams. To no avail.

When he felt fit enough he went in search of Suparwita, but the healer was nowhere to be found. His house was inhabited by a woman who looked as old as the trees around her. She had a wide face, flat nose, and no teeth. Possibly she was deaf as well, because she stared at Bourne indifferently when he asked where Suparwita was in both Balinese and Indonesian.

One morning that was already becoming hot and steamy, he paused above the highest terrace of a rice paddy, crossing the irrigation conduit to sit in the cool shade of a *warung*, a small family-run restaurant that sold snacks and drinks. Sipping green coconut water through a straw, he played with the youngest of the three children, while the eldest, a girl of no more than twelve, watched him with dark, serious eyes as she wove thin-cut palm fronds into an intricate pattern that would become a basket. The child—a boy of not more than two months—lay on the tabletop where Bourne sat. He gurgled while exploring Bourne's fingers with his tiny brown fists. After a while, his mother took him up in her arms to feed him. The feet of Balinese children under the age of three months were not allowed to touch the ground, which meant they were held almost all the time. Maybe that was why they were so happy, Bourne reflected.

The woman brought him a plate of sticky rice wrapped in banana leaf, and he thanked her. While he ate, he chatted with the woman's husband, a wiry little man with large teeth and a cheery smile.

"*Bapak*, you come here every morning," the man said. *Bapak* meant "father." It was the Balinese way of address, at once formal and intimate, another expression of life's underlying duality. "We watch you as you climb. Sometimes you must stop to catch your breath. Once my daughter saw you bend over and vomit. If you are ill, we will help you."

Bourne smiled. "Thank you, but I'm not ill. Just a bit out of shape."

If the man disbelieved him, he didn't show it. His veiny, big-knuckled hands lay on the table like chunks of granite. His daughter, finished with her basket, stared at Bourne while her nimble fingers, as if of their own accord, began work on another. Her mother came over, set her little boy in Bourne's lap. Bourne felt his weight and his heartbeat against his chest, and was reminded of Moira, with whom he'd deliberately had no contact since she'd left the island.

"*Bapak*, in what way can I help you get back in shape?" the boy's father said softly.

Did he suspect something or was he just being helpful? Bourne asked himself. Then he shrugged mentally. What did it matter, after all? Being Balinese, he was being genuine, which, in the end, was all that mattered. This was something Bourne had learned from his interaction with these people. They were the polar opposites of the treacherous men and women who inhabited his own shadow world. Here the only shadows were demons—and, furthermore, there were ways in which you could protect yourself against them. Bourne thought of the double *ikat* cloth that Suparwita had told Moira to buy for him.

"There is a way," Bourne said now. "You can help me find Suparwita."

"Ah, the healer, yes." The Balinese paused, as if listening for a voice only he could hear. "He's not at his home."

"I know. I was there," Bourne said. "I saw an old woman without teeth."

The man grinned, showing his white teeth. "Suparwita's mother, yes. A very old woman. Deaf as a coconut; mute as well."

"She was no help."

The man nodded. "What is inside her head, only Suparwita knows."

"Do you know where he is?" Bourne said. "It's important I find him."

"Suparwita is a healer, yes." The man studied Bourne in a kindly, even courteous, manner. "He has gone to Goa Lowah."

"Then I will go there."

"*Bapak*, it would not be wise to follow him."

"To be honest," Bourne said, "I don't always do the wise thing."

The man laughed. "*Bapak*, you are only human, after all." His grin showed again. "Not to worry. Suparwita forgives foolish men as well as wise ones."

The bat, one of dozens clinging to the damp walls, opened its eyes and stared at Bourne. It blinked, as if it couldn't believe what it was seeing, then returned to its diurnal slumber. Bourne, the lower half of his body wrapped in a traditional sarong, stood in the flowing heart of the Goa Lowah temple complex amid a welter of praying Balinese and Japanese tourists taking time out from their shopping sprees.

Goa Lowah, which was near the town of Klungkung in southeast Bali, was also known locally as the Bat Cave. Many large temple complexes were built around springs because this water, erupting from the core of the island, was deemed sacred, able to spiritually cleanse those who worshipped there and partook of the water by both drinking it and sprinkling it over their heads. The sacred water at Goa Lowah bubbled up from the earth at the rear of a cave. This cave was inhabited by hundreds of bats that by day hung from the seeping calcite walls sleeping and dreaming, and by night flew into the inky sky in search of insects to gorge on. Though the Balinese often ate bats as a matter of course, the bats of Goa Lowah were spared that fate because anything that lived within a sacred space became sacred as well.

Bourne had not found Suparwita. Instead he had come upon a small, wizened priest with splayed feet and teeth like a jackrabbit, performing a cleansing ceremony in front of a small stone shrine in which were set a number of flower offerings. About a dozen Balinese sat in a semicircle. As Bourne watched in silence, the priest took a small, plaited bowl filled with holy water and, using a palm leaf switch that he dunked into the water, sprinkled the heads of those in attendance. No one looked at Bourne or paid him the slightest attention. For them, he was part of another universe. This ability of the Balinese to compartmentalize their lives with utter and absolute authority was the reason their form of Hinduism and unique culture remained uncorrupted by outsiders even after decades of tourist invasions and pressure from the Muslims who ruled every other island in the Indonesian archipelago.

There was something here for him, Bourne knew, something that was second nature to the Balinese, something that would help him to find out who he really was. Both David Webb, the person, and the Jason Bourne identity were incomplete: the one irrevocably shattered by amnesia, the other created for him by Alex Conklin's Treadstone program.

Was Bourne still the conflation of Conklin's research, training, and psychological theories put to the ultimate test? Had he begun life as one person only to evolve into someone else? These were the questions that went to Bourne's very heart. His future—and the impact he had on those he cared about and those he might even love—depended on the answer.

The priest had finished and was putting away the plaited bowl in a niche in the shrine when Bourne felt an urgent need to be cleansed by that holy water.

Kneeling behind the Balinese, he closed his eyes, allowed the priest's words to flow over him until he was dislocated in time. He'd never before felt free of both the Bourne identity given to him by Alex Conklin and the incomplete person he knew as David Webb. Who was Webb, after all? The fact was, he didn't know—or more accurately he couldn't remember. There were pieces of him, to be sure, stitched together by psychologists and Bourne himself, and periodically other pieces, dislodged by some stimulus or other, would breach the surface of his consciousness with the force of a torpedo explosion. Even so, the truth was he was no closer to understanding himself—and ironically, tragically, there were times when he felt he understood Bourne far better than he did Webb. At least, he knew what motivated Bourne, whereas Webb's motivations were still a complete mystery. Having tried and failed to reintegrate himself into Webb's academic life, he'd decided to disengage himself from Webb. With a palpable start he realized that here on Bali he'd also begun to disengage from the Bourne identity with which he'd come to associate so closely.

He thought about the Balinese he'd encountered here, Suparwita, the family that ran the mountain *warung*—even this priest whom he didn't know at all, but whose words seemed to cloak him in an intense white light—and then he contrasted them with the Westerners, Firth and Willard. The Balinese were in touch with the spirits of the land, they saw good and evil and acted accordingly. There was nothing between them and nature itself, whereas Firth and Willard were creatures of civilization with all its layers of deceit, envy, greed. This essential dichotomy had opened his mind as nothing before. Did he want to be like Willard or like Suparwita? Was it a coincidence that the Balinese didn't allow their children's feet to touch the ground for three months—and that he'd been on Bali for precisely the same amount of time?

Now, for the first time in his defective memory, unmoored from everything and everyone he knew, he felt able to look inside himself, and what he saw was someone he didn't recognize—not Webb, not Bourne. It was as if Webb were a dream, or another identity assigned to him just as Bourne had been.

Kneeling outside the Bat Cave with its thousands of denizens stirring restively, with the priest's intonations transforming the intense Southern Hemisphere sunshine into prayer, he contemplated the chimeric landscape of his own soul, a place singularly twilit, like a deserted city an hour before dawn or the desolate seashore an hour after dusk, a place that slipped away from him, shifting like sand. And as he journeyed through this unknown country he asked himself this question:

Who am I?

5

The joint NSA-DHS forensics team arrived in Cairo and, to the consternation of everyone except Soraya, was met at the airport by an elite contingent of al Mokhabarat, the national secret police. Team members and their belongings were poured into military vehicles and driven through the blistering heat, blazing sun, and urban chaos of Cairo. Heading southwest out of the city, they traveled toward the desert in glum and silent single file.

"Our destination is near Wadi AlRayan," Amun Chalthoum, the head of al Mokhabarat, said to Soraya. He had spotted her immediately, culled her out of the team to sit beside him in his vehicle, which was second behind a heavily armored halftrack that Chalthoum was doubtless using to flex his muscles in the face of the Americans.

For Chalthoum time seemed to have stood still. His hair was still thick and dark, his wide copper-colored forehead still unlined. His black crow's eyes deeply set above the hawk-beak of his nose still smoldered with suppressed emotion. He was large and muscular with the narrow hips of a swimmer or a climber. By contrast, he had the long, tapered fingers of a pianist or a surgeon. And yet something important had changed, because there was about him the sense of a fire barely banked. The nearer one got to him, the more one felt the quivering of his leashed rage. Now that she was sitting beside him, now that she felt the once familiar stirrings inside her, she realized why she hadn't told Veronica Hart the whole truth: because she wasn't at all certain that she could handle Amun.

"So quiet. Are you not stirred by being back home?"

"Actually, I was thinking about the last time you took me to Wadi AlRayan."

"That was eight years ago and I was simply trying to get at the truth," he said with a shake of his head. "Admit it, you were in my country passing secrets—"

"I admit nothing."

"—which by right belonged to the state." He tapped his chest. "And I am the state."

"*Le Roi le Veut*," she murmured.

"The king wills it." Chalthoum nodded. "Precisely." And momentarily he took his hands off the wheel and spread his arms wide to encompass the desert into which they were just now driving. "This is the land of absolutism, *Umm al-Dunya,* the Mother of the Universe, but I'm not telling you anything you don't already know. After all, you're Egyptian, like me."

"Half Egyptian." She shrugged. "Anyway, it doesn't matter. I'm here to help my people find out what happened to the airliner."

"Your people." Chalthoum spat out the words as if even the thought of them left a bitter taste in his mouth. "What about your father? What about his people? Has

America so thoroughly destroyed the wild Arabian inside you?"

Soraya put her head back against the seat and closed her eyes. She knew she'd better get her own feelings under control and soon, otherwise the entire mission could spiral out of control. Then she felt Amun's arm brush up against hers and the hair at the back of her neck stirred. *Good God*, she thought, *I can't feel this way about him.* And then she broke out in a cold sweat. *Was this why I withheld the truth from Veronica—because I knew that if I told her everything she'd never have allowed me to come back here?* And all at once she felt herself in jeopardy, not because of Amun but because of herself, her own runaway emotions.

In an effort to regain some form of equilibrium she said, "My father never forgot he was Egyptian."

"So much so he changed his family name from Mohammed to Moore," Chalthoum said bitterly.

"He fell in love with America when he fell in love with my mother. The deep appreciation I have of it comes from him."

Chalthoum shook his head. "Why hide it? It was your mother's doing."

"Like all Americans, my mother took for granted everything her country had to offer. She couldn't have cared less about the Fourth of July; it was my father who took me to the fireworks celebrations on the Mall in Washington, DC, where he spoke to me about freedom and liberty."

Chalthoum bared his teeth. "I have to laugh at his naïveté—and yours. Frankly, I assumed you had a more . . . shall we say pragmatic outlook on America, the country that exports Mickey Mouse, war, and occupying armed forces with equal abandon."

"How convenient of you to forget that we're also the country that keeps you safe from extremists, Amun."

Chalthoum clenched his teeth and was about to respond when the jouncing vehicle rolled through a cordon of his men, armed with submachine guns, keeping the mass of clamoring international press at a safe remove from the crash site, and ground to a halt. Soraya was the first out, settling her sunglasses more firmly on the bridge of her nose and the lightweight hat on her head. Chalthoum had been right about one thing: The airliner had fallen out of the sky not six hundred yards from the southeastern tip of the wadi, a body of water, complete with waterfalls, all the more spectacular because it was surrounded by desert.

"Dear God," Soraya murmured as she began a tour of the crash site, which had already been cordoned off, presumably by Amun's people. The fuselage was in two main chunks, embedded in the sand and rock like grotesque monuments to an unknown god, but other pieces, violently disjointed from the body, were scattered about in a widening circle, along with one wing, bent in half like a green twig.

"Notice the number of fuselage sections," Chalthoum said, as he watched the American task force deploy. He pointed as they moved around the periphery of the site. "See here, and here. It's also clear that the plane broke up in midair, not on impact, which, considering the composition of the ground, caused minimal further damage."

"So the plane looks more or less the way it did directly after the explosion."

Chalthoum nodded. "That's correct."

Say what you wanted about him, when it came to his trade he was a first-rate practitioner. The trouble was that too often his trade included methods of interrogation and torture that would make even those running Abu Ghraib sick to their stomachs.

"The destruction is terrible," he said.

He wasn't kidding. Soraya watched as the forensics team put on plastic suits, slipped shoe coverings on. Kylie, the explosives-sniffing golden Lab, went in first with her handler. Then the task force split in two, the first group heading into the burned-out interior of the plane while the second began its examination of the ripped-open edges in an attempt to determine whether the explosion had been internal or external. Among this latter group was Delia Trane, a friend of Soraya's and an explosives expert from ATF, the Bureau of Alcohol, Tobacco and Firearms. Though Delia was only thirty-four, her abilities were such that she was often on loan to various federal law enforcement agencies desperate for her expertise.

Dogged by Chalthoum, Soraya headed into the circle of death, skirting bits of metal so black and twisted it was impossible to determine what they had once been. Fist-size globs that looked like hail on closer inspection turned out to be plastic parts that had melted down in the fiery conflagration. When she came to a human head, she stopped and crouched down. Almost all the hair and most of the flesh had been scorched to ash, which pocked the partially revealed skull like gooseflesh.

Just beyond, a blackened forearm rose at an angle from the sand, the hand above it like a beckoning flag signifying a land where death ruled absolutely. Soraya was sweating, and not just from the brutal heat. She took a swig of water from a plastic bottle Chalthoum gave her, then proceeded on. Just before the yawning mouth of the fuselage, a team member handed her and Chalthoum plastic suits and shoe coverings that, despite the heat, they put on.

After her eyes adjusted to the gloom, she took off her sunglasses, peered around. The seat rows were canted at a ninety-degree angle; the floor was where the left bulkhead would have been when the jetliner was right-side up and everyone inside had been alive, chatting, laughing, holding hands, or foolishly arguing until the final moment before oblivion. Bodies lay everywhere, some still in their seats, others thrown clear on impact. The explosion had completely disintegrated another section of the aircraft and those in it.

She noticed that wherever a member of the American team went, he or she was shadowed by one of Amun's people. It would have been comical if it weren't so sinister. Her companion was clearly determined that the forensics team would not make a move, including relieving themselves in the dizzying heat and fetid stench of the portable latrines, without him knowing about it immediately.

"The lack of humidity works in your favor, of course," Chalthoum said, "slowing the decomposition of those bodies not incinerated beyond recognition."

"That will be a blessing to their families."

"Naturally so. But really, let's not mince words, you haven't given much thought to either the passengers or their families. You're here to find out what happened to the aircraft: mechanical malfunction or an act of extremist terrorism."

He still had the utterly un-Egyptian knack of cutting directly to the quick. The country was a bureaucratic nightmare; nothing got done, not a single answer was forthcoming until at least fifteen people in seven different divisions were consulted and agreed on it. Soraya debated only a moment as to how to answer. "It would be foolish to pretend otherwise."

Chalthoum nodded. "Yes, because the world wants to know, *needs* to know. But my question to you is this: What then?"

A typically astute query, she thought. "I don't know. What happens then is not up to me."

She spotted Delia, signaled to her. Her friend nodded, picked her way through the debris and hunched-over workers, with their bright task lamps, to where she and Chalthoum stood just inside the roasting gloom.

"Anything to report?" Soraya said.

"We're just beginning the prelim stages." Delia's pale eyes flicked toward the Egyptian and back to her friend.

"It's all right," Soraya assured her. "If you have anything, even if it's speculation, I need to know."

"Okay." Delia's mother was an aristocratic Colombian from Bogotá, and the daughter carried much of her maternal ancestors' fiery blood. Her skin was as deep-toned as Soraya's, but there the similarity ended. She had a plain face and a boyish figure, with blunt-cut hair, strong hands, and a no-nonsense manner that was often interpreted as rudeness. Soraya thought it refreshing; Delia was someone with whom she could let her hair down. "My sense is that it wasn't a bomb. The explosion very clearly didn't emanate from the luggage bay."

"So, what, a mechanical failure?"

"Kylie says no," Delia said. She meant the dog.

There was that hesitation again, and it made Soraya uneasy. She considered pressing her friend, but then thought better of it. She'd have to find a way to talk to her without Amun hanging on their every word. She nodded, and Delia went back to her work.

"She knows more than she's telling," Chalthoum said. "I want to know what's going on." When Soraya said nothing, he continued. "Go talk to her. Alone."

Soraya turned to him. "And then?"

He shrugged. "Report back to me, what else?"

It was very late by the time Moira was ready to leave the office. With a weary hand she switched off CNN, which she'd had on with the volume muted ever since the news of the airliner incident in Egypt broke. The incident unnerved her, as it had many people in the security field. No word on what had really happened—not even from her back-channel, not-for-attribution sources, whose terse responses were so brittle they set her teeth on edge. Meanwhile the press was having a typically monstrous field day—talking heads on TV speculating terrorist attack scenarios. And that didn't even count the more out-and-out fabrications posing as "the truth they don't want you to know" on thousands of Internet sites, including the toxic chestnut trotted out since 9/11 that the American government was behind the incident in order to advance its own *casus belli*, its case for war.

As she took the elevator down to the underground garage, Moira's mind was in two places at once: here with the new organization she was building and in Bali with Bourne. His grave wounds had made it more difficult to separate herself from him. What had seemed so simple when they'd discussed her future in the pool at the resort now seemed nebulous and vaguely anxiety producing. It wasn't that she felt the need to take care of him—God knows she would not have made a decent nurse—but that within the eternity when his life had hung in the balance, she'd been forced to reassess her feelings for him. The possibility that he would be snatched from her filled her with dread. At least, she assumed it was dread, since she'd never before felt anything like it: a suffocating blackness that blotted out the sun at noon, the stars at midnight.

Was this love? she wondered. Could love produce this madness that transcended time and space, that caused her heart to expand beyond its known limits, that turned her bones to jelly? How many times during the night had she been roused out of a shallow and restless sleep, compelled to pad into the bathroom to stare at the reflection in the mirror she did not recognize. It was as if she had been unceremoniously thrust into someone else's life, a life she neither wanted nor understood.

"Who are you?" she said over and over to that strange reflection. "How did you get here? What is it you want?"

Neither she nor her reflection had answers. In the stillness of the night she wept for the loss of who she had been, in despair of the new and incomprehensible future that had invaded her body like a transfusion.

But in the morning she was herself again: pragmatic, focused, ruthless both in her recruiting and in the stringent rules she set out for her operatives. She made each one swear allegiance to Heartland as if it were a sovereign nation—which in many respects Black River, her main rival, already was.

And yet, the moment the sun fell from the sky, twilight and uncertainty crept through her, and her thoughts returned to Bourne with whom she'd had no contact since she had left Bali three months ago with the body of a dead Australian drifter and the paperwork identifying it as Bourne's. It was a recurring disease she'd picked up on the island: The thought of his imminent death was enough to cause her to run, and keep running. Except that wherever she went she ended up at the terrifying place where she'd started, at the moment he'd fallen to the ground, at the moment her heart had stopped beating.

The elevator door opened onto the shadow-drenched concrete expanse of the garage, and she stepped out, her car key in her hand. She hated this late-night walk through the almost deserted garage. The smears of oil and gas, the stench of exhaust, the echoes of her heels ringing against the concrete made her feel sad and achingly lonely, as if there was no place in the world she could call home.

There were very few cars left; the parallel white lines painted on the unsealed concrete stretched away from her, ending where she'd parked her car. She heard the cadence of her own strides, saw the movement of her crooked shadow as it passed across one square pillar after another.

She heard a car engine cough to life and came to a halt, standing still, her senses questing for the source. A dove-gray Audi pulled out from behind a pillar, turned on its headlights, and came toward her, gathering speed.

She drew her custom Lady Hawk 9mm from its thigh holster, moved to an expert sharpshooter's crouch, thumbed off the safety. She was just about to pull the trigger when the passenger's-side window slid down and the Audi screeched to a halt, rocking on its shocks.

"Moira—!"

She bent her knees more to lower her line of vision.

"Moira, it's me, Jay!"

Peering inside the Audi, she saw Jay Weston, an operative she'd poached from Hobart, the largest government ODC—overseas defense contractor—six weeks ago.

At once she put up the Lady Hawk, holstered it. "Jesus, Jay, you could've gotten yourself killed."

"I need to see you."

She squinted. "Well, shit, you could've called."

He shook his head. His face was pinched and tight with unaccustomed tension. "Cell phones are too insecure. I couldn't take the risk, not with this."

"Well," she said, leaning on the window frame, "what's so important?"

"Not here," he said, looking around furtively. "Not anywhere where we can be overheard."

Moira frowned. "Don't you think you're being a bit paranoid?"

"Being paranoid is in my job description, isn't it?"

She nodded; she supposed it was. "All right, how d'you—"

"I need to show you something," he said, patting a pocket of an expensive-looking sapphire-blue suede jacket slung across the passenger's seat, then took off toward the ramp up to the street before she had a chance to climb in or even answer him.

She sprinted to her car, starting it up with the remote as she ran. Hauling open the door, she slid behind the wheel, slammed the door shut behind her, and put the car in gear. Jay's Audi was waiting for her at the top of the ramp. The moment he saw her approach in his rearview mirror, he took off, turning right out of the garage. Moira followed.

Late-night traffic with people returning home from the theater and movies was light, so there was no real reason for Jay to run the lights on P Street, but that's precisely what he continued to do. Moira put on speed to keep up with him; more than once she barely avoided being clipped by the cross-street traffic, tires squealing, horns blaring angrily.

Three blocks from her building they picked up a cop on a motorcycle. She flashed her high beams at Jay, but either he wasn't looking or he chose to ignore her because he kept running the red lights. All at once she saw the cop flash by her, heading toward the Audi in front of her.

"Shit," she muttered, putting on some more speed.

She was thinking of how she was going to explain her operative's repeated infractions when the cop drew up alongside the Audi. An instant later he'd drawn his service revolver, aimed it squarely at the driver's window, and pulled the trigger twice in close succession.

The Audi bucked and swerved. Moira had only seconds to avoid slamming into the car, but she was fighting the immoderate speed of her own vehicle. At the periphery of her vision she saw the motorcycle cop peel off and head north at a cross street. The Audi, in the middle of a series of sickening pendulum-like swings, smashed into her, sending her car spinning.

The collision flipped the Audi over like a beetle on its hard, shiny back. Then, as if a monstrous fingertip had flicked it, it continued to roll over, but Moira lost track of it as her car struck a streetlight and careened into a parked car, staving in the offside front fender and door. A blizzard of shattered glass covered her as she was jerked forward, hit the deployed air bag then dizzyingly was slammed back against her seat.

Everything went black.

Climbing carefully over the rows of seat backs was like wading into a sea frozen solid with reef-struck bodies. It was the small broken bodies of the children that were hardest to pass by without heartbreak. Soraya murmured a prayer for each of the souls deprived of the full flight of life.

By the time she reached Delia's position, she realized that she'd been holding her breath. She let it out now with a small hiss, the acrid odors of burned wiring, synthetic fabrics, and plastics invading her nostrils in full force.

She touched her friend on the shoulder and, mindful of her Egyptian observer, said softly, "Let's take a walk."

The observer made to follow them, but stopped at a subtle hand sign from Chalthoum. Outside, the desert light was blinding, even with sunglasses, but the heat was clean, the arid spice of the desert, the murderous sun a welcome respite from the death pit into which they'd both sunk. Coming home to the desert, Soraya thought, was like returning to a longed-for lover: The sand whispered against your skin in intimate caress. In the desert you could see things coming at you. Which was why people like Amun lied, because the desert told the truth, always, in the history it covered and uncovered, in the bones of civilization from which the eternal sand had scoured away all lies. Too much truth, people like Amun believed, was a terrible thing, because it left you nothing to believe in, nothing to live for. She knew she understood him far better than he understood her. He believed otherwise, of course, but that was a useful delusion for him to hold close.

"Delia, what's really going on?" Soraya asked when they'd plodded some distance away from the al Mokhabarat sentries.

"Nothing I can substantiate at the moment." She looked around to make sure they were alone. Seeing Chalthoum staring after them, she said, "That man is creeping me out."

Soraya moved them farther away from the Egyptian's penetrating gaze. "Don't worry, he can't overhear what we say. What's on your mind?"

"Fucking sun." Squinting behind her sunglasses, Delia used her hands to shadow her face. "My lips are going to peel off before the night is over."

Soraya waited while the sun continued to throb in the sky and Delia's lips continued to burn.

"Fuck it," Delia said at last. "Five to two the crash wasn't caused by something inside the aircraft." She was an inveterate poker player; every situation was a matter of odds. She often transformed nouns into verbs, too. "I instinct a particular explosive."

"So it was no accident." Soraya's blood ran cold. "You ruled out a bomb so, what, an air-to-air missile?"

Delia shrugged. "Could be, but you read the transcript of the flight crew's last conversation with the tower at Cairo International. They saw no sign of a jet coming up on them."

"What about from underneath or behind?"

"Sure, but then the radar would've picked it up. Besides, according to the copilot, he saw something smaller even than a private jet coming up on them."

"But only at the last possible instant. The explosion took place before he had time to describe what it was."

"If you're right, that leads us toward a ground-to-air missile."

Delia nodded. "If we get lucky the black box will be intact, and its recorder might tell us more."

"When?"

"You saw what a mess it is in there. It's going to take a while to ascertain whether it's even retrievable."

Soraya said in the dry, ominous whisper of the hot wind that reshapes the dunes,

"A ground-to-air missile would bring an entire universe of very nasty possibilities into play."

"I know," Delia said. "Such as the involvement, either complicit or implicit, of the Egyptian government."

Soraya couldn't help but turn to look at Chalthoum. "Or al Mokhabarat."

6

Moira awoke to the ticking of her mother's heart. It was as loud as a grandfather clock and it terrified her. For a moment she lay in a fury of darkness, reliving the blur of sound and motion as the paramedics came, took her mother off to the hospital, all seen through a haze of tears. That was the last time she saw her mother alive. She never had a chance to say good-bye; instead, the last words she'd said to her were "I hate your guts. Why don't you stay out of my life!" All of a sudden her mother was dead. Moira was seventeen.

Then the pain set in and she began screaming.

The ticking was real; it was, in fact, the sound of the over-revved engine cooling. Hands were pulling at her, cutting through the web of her seat belt, the flaccid cloud of the air bag. As if in a dream, she felt her body moving, the drag of gravity settling in her shoulder and the pit of her stomach. Her head felt as if it had been split open; she was nauseated with pain. Then, with a crash that reverberated through the cotton in her ears, she was out of her steel cage. She felt the night air soft on her cheek, and there were voices near her, buzzing like angry insects.

Her mother . . . the hospital waiting room, stinking of disinfectant and despair . . . the sight of the wax doll in the open coffin, horrifying in its inhuman lack of animation . . . at the cemetery, the yellow sky reeking of coal gas and sorrow . . . the ground swallowing the coffin whole, like a beast closing its jaws . . . clods of newly turned earth damp with rain and tears . . .

Awareness returned to her slowly, like a fog creeping over a moor, and then, with the suddenness of a floodlight being switched on, full consciousness returned. Awakening from a dream, she knew where she was and what had happened. She felt death close by, knew that it had bypassed her by inches. Each breath felt like fire and ice, but she was alive. She wriggled her fingers and toes. All there; all working.

"Jay," she said into the face of the paramedic bent over her. "Is Jay all right?"

"Who's Jay?" a voice out of her field of vision said.

"There was no one else in your car." The paramedic had a kind face. He looked too young for this kind of work.

"Not my car," she managed. "The one in front."

"Oh, jeez," came the voice at her side.

The kind face above her split in sorrow. "Your friend . . . Jay. He didn't make it."

Tears leaked from the corners of Moira's eyes. "Oh, hell," she said. "Oh, damn."

They began to work on her again, and she said, "I want to sit up."

"That wouldn't be a good idea, ma'am," the kind face said. "You're in shock and—"

"I'm sitting up," Moira said, "with or without your help."

With hands under her arms, he drew her up. She was in the street, next to her car. When she tried to look around, she winced and lights exploded behind her eyes.

"Get me to my feet," she said through gritted teeth. "I need to see him."

"Ma'am—"

"Is anything broken?"

"No, ma'am, but—"

"Then get me to my goddamn feet!"

There were two of them now, the second one improbably looking younger than the first.

"Do you even shave?" she said as they raised her off the tarmac. Her knees nearly buckled and a wave of blackness consumed her so she had to lean on them for a minute.

"Ma'am, you're white as a sheet," the kind face said. "I really think—"

"Please don't call me ma'am. My name is Moira."

"The cops will be here in a minute," the other one said under his breath.

She felt a clutch in the pit of her stomach.

The kind face said to her, "Moira, my

name is Dave and my partner here is Earl. There are policemen who want to ask you what happened."

"It was a policeman who caused all this," Moira said.

"What?" Dave said. "What did you say?"

"I want to see Jay."

"Believe me," Earl said, "you really don't."

Moira reached down, patted her Lady Hawk. "Don't fuck with me, guys."

Without another word they took her down the street. It was littered with car parts and the glitter of blown-out windows and taillights. She saw a fire truck, an EMT ambulance beside the hideous wreck of the Audi. No one could have survived that crash. With each step she gained strength and confidence. She was banged up and bruised, possibly, as they said, in shock, but otherwise unscathed. Luck beyond words. She thought of the pig spirit in Bali, who must still be protecting her.

"Here come the Warm Jets," Earl said.

"He means the cops," Dave translated.

"Guys," she said, "I need some alone time with my friend and the cops won't let me have it."

"Neither should we," Dave said dubiously.

"I'll handle these bozos." Earl peeled off to intercept them.

"Steady on."

Dave gripped her more tightly as she staggered without Earl's countervailing support. She took another couple of deep breaths to clear her mind and steady her body. She knew she had very little time before the cops would brush aside whatever smokescreen Earl managed to concoct.

They passed the all-but-unrecognizable crumple-and-twist of the Audi. She took a deep breath, righted herself, then they were at what remained of Jay Weston. He looked more like a lump of raw meat than a human being.

"How in the world did you get him out?"

"Jaws of Life. In his case, it didn't help." Dave helped her to squat down beside the corpse, held her up as another wave of dizziness threatened to topple her. "It might be my job for this," he said.

"Relax. My friends will keep you safe." Her eyes were roving over every inch of the wasteland that was Jay. "Jesus, nothing could survive this mash-up."

"What are you looking for?"

"I wish I knew, but his jacket . . ."

Dave reached down, drew something out from underneath the wreckage. "You mean this?"

Moira's heart rate accelerated. It was Jay's sapphire-blue suede jacket, miraculously unscathed except for a couple of burned patches on the sleeves. It stank of smoke and toasted cologne.

"Believe it or not, things like this happen all the time," Dave said. He had deliberately positioned himself between Moira and the two cops who now brushed by Earl, having had their fill of his medical gobbledygook. "We find things—wallets, keys, baseball caps, condoms—you wouldn't believe—in virtually mint condition, thrown clear of the most horrendous wrecks."

Moira was listening with only one ear as her nimble fingers rifled through the outer and inner pockets. Rolaids, two rubber bands, a paper clip, a pinch of lint. Inside pockets contained no wallet or ID of any kind, which was standard operating procedure. If he got into trouble or needed clearance he made a call. Money was somewhere on his person, burned to a crisp. But speaking of his cell, she palmed it as Dave rose to intercept the cops.

She was about to give up when she spotted the loose thread at one of the inside seams. Pulling it opened a small hole out of which she dug a two-gigabyte thumb drive. Hearing the sound of heavy footfalls coming up behind her, she made the sign of the cross over Jay's body and, with Dave's strong hand gripping her elbow, stood up to face her wearying interview with the Warm Jets.

Which turned out to be fully as stultifying and dunderheaded as she had foreseen, but at least she had the last laugh because before they got around to asking her the same questions for the third time she pulled out her Federal Securities Act ID, at which point they went silent. It was all Dave and Earl could do not to snicker into their red faces.

"About this traffic cop," Moira said. "I need to know who he was. I've already told you twice even though you clearly didn't believe me, he discharged his weapon through the side window of Mr. Weston's Audi."

"And you say Mr. Weston worked for

you?" The taller of the two cops was a badge named Severin.

When she said yes, he nodded at his partner, who stepped away to use his cell phone.

"What were you doing kneeling over the body?" Severin said. Maybe he was just marking time, because he'd seen what she was doing and he'd already asked her twice.

"Praying for my friend's soul."

Severin frowned, though he nodded, possibly in sympathy. Then he jerked his head at Dave and Earl. "These yahoos shouldn't have let you anywhere near your friend. This is a crime scene."

"So I understand."

His frown deepened, but the nature of his thoughts remained a mystery as his partner returned to the huddle.

"Here's a kick in the groin," he said facetiously. "There's no record of a motorcycle police from traffic or from any other department, for that matter, in this vicinity in the time frame we have."

"Damn it to hell."

Moira palmed open her cell, but before she had a chance to make a call, two men strode up. They wore identical dark suits but had the slope-shouldered military bearing of NSA operatives. She knew she was in trouble the moment they showed their IDs to the detectives.

"We've got it from here, boys," Dark Suit Number One said while his partner gave the cops the thousand-yard stare. As the police backed off, Dark Suit Number One slipped his hand into Moira's pocket with the deftness of a professional pick-pocket. "I'll take that, Ms. Trevor," he said, holding Jay's cell between the tips of his blunt fingers.

Moira lunged for it, but Dark Suit One snatched it out of her reach.

"Hey, that's the property of my company."

"Sorry," Dark Suit One said, "this has been impounded as a matter of national security."

Before Moira could say a word he took her arm. "Now if you'll be kind enough to come with us."

"What?" Moira said. "You have no right to do this."

"I'm afraid we do," Dark Suit One said as his partner positioned himself on her other side. He held aloft Jay's cell. "You were tampering with a crime scene."

As she was taken away, Dave took a step toward her.

"Out of the way!" Dark Suit Number Two barked.

His sharp tone seemed to take the paramedic aback and he stumbled against her, mumbled an apology, then backed away.

Now Moira's view of the scene changed so that she was able to see the man standing behind the NSA agent. It was Noah, staring at her with a feral grin. He took Jay's cell and put it in his inside jacket pocket.

As he walked away, he said, "You can't say you weren't warned."

Astride the motorbike Dr. Firth had rented, Bourne drove up into the East Bali mountains—almost straight up at several points—until he arrived at the foot of Pura Lempuyang, the Dragon Temple complex. He parked under the watchful eye of a diminutive attendant in a canvas chair protected from the fierce sun by the dappled shade of a tree. Buying a bottle of water at one of the line of stands that served both pilgrims and curious tourists, he set off up the stiff incline, wrapped in his traditional sarong and sash.

The priest at the Bat Cave had not seen Suparwita, though he knew of him, but when Bourne had used him as a sounding board to describe his recurring dream, the priest had instantly identified the dragon staircases as those belonging to Pura Lempuyang. Bourne had left him after getting detailed directions to the temple complex high up on Mount Lempuyang.

It did not take him long to reach the first temple, a simple enough affair that seemed more like an anteroom to the steep steps that led up to the second temple. By the time he reached the intricately carved gateway, the ache in his chest had turned into a pain that obliged him to pause. Looking through the arched gate, he saw the three staircases, even steeper than the two he'd just ascended. They were guarded by six enormous stone dragons whose sinuous and scaly bodies undulated up the stairway serving as banisters.

The priest hadn't steered him wrong. This was the place of his dream, this was where he'd been when he'd seen the figure framed in the archway turn toward him.

Turning around, he peered through the archway at the breathtaking view of sacred Mount Agung, rising blue and misty, now wreathed in clouds, its iconic cone shape visible in all its monumental power.

Drawn to the dragon staircases, Bourne continued his ascent. Stopping midway, he turned to look back at the gateway. There was the volcano framed between the soaring teeth that formed the entrance. His heart skipped a beat as a figure was silhouetted against Mount Agung. Involuntarily, he took a step down, then saw the figure was that of a little girl in a red-and-yellow sarong. She turned, moving in that liquid, sinuous way of all Balinese children, and abruptly vanished, leaving only dusty sunlight in her wake.

Resuming his climb, Bourne soon reached the upper plaza of the temple. There were a few people scattered here and there. A man knelt, praying. Bourne wandered aimlessly among the heavily carved structures, feeling somehow that he was floating, as if he had entered his dream, his past, but as a stranger returning to a place of forgotten familiarity.

He wished this place struck a chord, but

it didn't, which bothered him. His experience with his form of amnesia was that a name, a sight, a smell often triggered a return of his lost memory about a place or a person. Why had he been in Bali? Being here in this place he had been dreaming about for months should have released the memories from the well of his mind. But those memories were like a fluke on a sandy sea bottom—that strange creature with two eyes on one side and none on the other—either all there or not at all.

The man at prayer was finished. He rose from his kneeling position and, as he turned around, Bourne recognized Suparwita.

His heart beating fast, he walked over to where Suparwita stood, contemplating him.

"You look well," Suparwita said.

"I survived. Moira thinks it's because of you."

The healer smiled, looked beyond Bourne for a moment, at the temple. "I see you've found part of your past."

Bourne turned, looked as well. "If I have," he said, "I don't know what it is."

"And yet you came."

"I've been dreaming about this place ever since I got here."

"I've been waiting for you, and the powerful entity who guides and protects you brought you."

Bourne turned back. "Shiva? Shiva is the god of destruction."

"And of transformation." Suparwita raised an arm, indicating that they should walk. "Tell me about your dream."

Bourne looked around. "I'm here, looking back at Mount Agung through the entryway. Suddenly, there's a figure silhouetted there. It turns to look at me."

"And then?"

"And then I wake up."

Suparwita nodded slowly, as if he half expected this answer. They had walked the entire circumference of the temple plaza, and now had reached the area just in front of the entryway. The angle of light was just as it was in his dream, and Bourne gave a little shiver.

"You were seeing the person you were here with," Suparwita said. "A woman named Holly Marie Moreau."

The name sounded vaguely familiar, but Bourne couldn't place it. "Where is she now?"

"I'm afraid she's dead." Suparwita pointed to the space between the two heavily carved teeth of the gateway. "She was there, just as you remember in your dream, and then she was gone."

"Gone?"

"She fell." Suparwita turned to him. "Or was pushed."

7

God in heaven, it's hotter than Hades in there, even without these clean suits." Delia wiped the sweat off her face. "Good news. We've recovered the black box."

Soraya, standing with Amun Chalthoum inside one of the tents his people had erected adjacent to the crash site, was grateful for the interruption. Being with Amun in such close quarters had put her nerves on overload. That there were so many layers to their relationship—professional, personal, ethnic—was difficult enough, but they were also frenemies, ostensibly on the same side but underneath fierce competitors for intel, bound to governments with vastly different agendas. So their dance was complex, often dizzyingly so.

"What does it tell you?" Chalthoum said.

Delia gave him one of her Sphinx-like looks. "We've just begun analyzing the instrument data from the aircraft's last moments, but from the cockpit conversation it's perfectly clear the crew didn't see an aircraft of any kind. However, the copilot saw *something* at the very last minute. It was small, coming at them very fast."

"A missile," Soraya said while looking into Amun's face. She wondered whether he already knew this. He would if al Mokhabarat had been complicit in the incident. But Chalthoum's dark face remained impassive.

Delia was nodding. "A ground-to-air missile seems the likeliest scenario at this stage."

"So," Chalthoum said in his native tongue even before Delia had left the tent, "it seems as if the United States isn't protecting us from extremists, after all."

"I think it would better serve both of us to start figuring out who was responsible," she said, "rather than pointing fingers, don't you?"

Chalthoum watched her carefully for a moment, then nodded, and they retreated to opposite sides of the tent to update their superiors. Using the Typhon satellite phone she'd brought with her, Soraya called Veronica Hart.

"This is bad news," Hart said from halfway around the world. "The very worst."

"I can only imagine how Halliday is going to run with it." While Soraya spoke, she assumed Chalthoum was briefing the Egyptian president with the same information Delia had provided. "Why do good things happen to bad people?"

"Because life is chaos, and chaos can't distinguish between good and evil." There was a slight pause before Hart continued. "Any news on the MIG?" She meant the Iranian militant indigenous group.

"Not yet. We've had our hands full with the crash. The scene is horrific and the conditions are next to intolerable. Besides, I haven't had three minutes to myself."

"This can't wait," Hart said firmly. "Finding out about the Iranian indigenous group is your primary mission."

The two of you came to me," Suparwita said. "Holly was extremely agitated, but she wouldn't tell you why."

Bourne stared at the spot where the body must have ended up, where his new beginning lay shattered. Why had he been so foolish to think that his past was dead and buried when, even here in a remote corner of the world, it existed like an egg waiting to hatch? Another piece of his past, another death. Why was he always entwined with loss of life?

He continued to stare down the three steep staircases with the undulating dragon banisters. He tried to remember that day: if he'd rushed to this spot, if the woman was already a bloody heap far away as he flew down the steps. He strained to recall anything about the incident, but his mind was enclosed by a gray fog, thick as the stone dragons, fierce and implacable guardians of the temple. Was the fog protecting him from the terrible event here?

The pain in his chest, his constant companion in the aftermath of the shooting, accelerated, spreading out into his entire torso.

His face must have gone gray because Suparwita said, "This way."

They made their way from the lintel, from the chasm of the past, and walked back onto the temple plaza and into the cool shade of a towering wall into which was carved an army of demons being opposed by the local dragon spirits.

Bourne sat and drank water. The healer stood, hands folded together, waiting patiently. Bourne was reminded of what he liked so much about Moira—no fussing, no coddling, just no-nonsense responses.

At length, Suparwita said, "You came because of Holly. She'd heard about me, I suppose."

As he breathed into the pain, taking long, deep, controlled breaths, he said, "Tell me what happened."

"There was a shadow over her, as if she'd brought something horrible with her." Suparwita's liquid eyes rested gently on Bourne's face. "She'd always been placid, she said. No, that's the wrong word—lacking in affect, that's better. But now she was terrified. She was up at night, she started at loud noises, she bit her nails to the quick. She told me that she never sat near windows. When you went to a restaurant she'd insist on a table in the rear, where she could look out at the rest of the room. Then you said that even in the shadows, you could see that her hands shook. She'd tried to hide it by holding her glass in a death grip, but you would see it when she reached for a fork or pushed her plate away."

The soft thrum of an airplane engine could be heard briefly interrupting the bird chatter. Then all was still again. On an adjacent mountainside, thin streamers of smoke rose from the burn-off fires at the periphery of the rice paddies.

Bourne gathered himself. "Perhaps she had somehow come unhinged."

The healer nodded uncertainly. "Possibly. But I can tell you that her terror came from a real source. I think you knew that, too, because you weren't humoring her, you were trying your best to help her."

"So she could have been running from something or someone. What happened next?"

"I cleansed her," Suparwita said. "She was entangled with demons."

"Yet she died."

"And so did you—almost."

Bourne thought about Moira's insistence that they see the healer; he thought about Suparwita saying, *"All this has happened before, and it will happen again."* Death following on the heels of life. "Are you saying that the two incidents are somehow connected?"

"That wouldn't be credible." Suparwita sat beside him. "But Shiva was here then, and Shiva is here now. We ignore these signs at our peril."

He was the last patient Benjamin Firth was scheduled to see that day. He was a tall, cadaverously thin New Zealander, with yellow skin and feverish eyes. He wasn't from Manggis or any of the surrounding villages—a small enough area—because Firth knew them all. Yet he seemed familiar and when he gave his name as Ian Bowles, Firth recalled him coming in twice or three times over the past several months with massive migraines. Today he complained of stomach and bowel problems, so Firth had him lie down on the examining table.

As he took his vitals, he said, “How’re your migraines?”

“Fine,” Bowles said absently, and then in a more focused tone, “Better.”

After palpating his stomach and abdomen, Firth said, “I can’t find anything wrong with you. I’ll just do a blood workup and in a couple of days—”

“I require information,” Bowles said softly.

Firth stood very still. “I beg your pardon.”

Bowles stared up at the ceiling as if deciphering the shifting patterns of light. “Forget the vampire tactics, I’m right as rain.”

The doctor shook his head. “I don’t understand.”

Bowles sighed. Then sat up so abruptly, he startled Firth. He grabbed Firth’s wrist with a horribly fierce grip. “Who’s the patient you’ve had here for the last three months?”

“What patient?”

Bowles clicked his tongue against the roof of his mouth. “Hey, Doc, I didn’t come here for my health.” He grinned. “You’ve got a patient stashed away here and I want to know about him."

"Why? What do you care?"

The New Zealander jerked even harder on Firth's wrist, pulling the doctor closer to him. "You operate here without interference, but all good things come to an end." His voice lowered significantly. "Now listen up, you idiot. You're wanted for negligent homicide by the Perth police."

"I was drunk," Firth whispered. "I didn't know what I was doing."

"You operated on a patient while under the influence, Doc, and he died. That's it in a nutshell." He shook Firth violently. "Isn't it?"

The doctor closed his eyes and whispered, "Yes."

"So?"

"I have nothing to tell you."

Bowles moved to slide off the table. "Then off we go to the cops, bud. Your life is toast."

Firth, trying to squirm away, said, "I don't know anything."

"Never gave you a name, did he?"

"Adam," Firth said. "Adam Stone."

"That's what he said? Adam Stone."

Firth nodded. "I confirmed it when I saw his passport."

Bowles dug in a pocket, produced a cell phone. "Doc, here's all you have to do in order to stay out of jail for life." He held out the cell. "Get me a picture of this Adam Stone. A good, clear one of his face."

Firth licked his lips. His mouth was so dry he could scarcely speak. "And if I do this you'll leave me alone?"

Bowles winked. "Bank on it, Doc."

Firth took the cell with a hollow feeling in his chest. What else was he to do? He had no expertise with these kinds of people. He tried to comfort himself with the knowledge that at least he hadn't divulged Jason Bourne's real name, but that gesture would become meaningless the moment he gave this man Bourne's photo.

Bowles jumped off the table, but he still hadn't let go of Firth's wrist. "Don't get any stupid ideas, Doc. You tell anyone about our little arrangement and sure as I'm standing here someone will put a bullet in the back of your head, follow?"

Firth nodded mechanically. A numbness had spread through him, rooting him to the spot.

Bowles let him go at last. “Glad you could make room for me, Doc,” he said in a louder voice for anyone who might be around. “Tomorrow, same time. You’ll have the test results by then, isn’t that right?”

8

Nagorno-Karabakh was in the west of Azerbaijan, a hotly contested area of the country ever since Joseph Stalin tried to ethnically cleanse this part of the former Soviet Union of Armenians. The advantage for Arkadin of staging a strike force in Azerbaijan was that it bordered on the northwestern edge of Iran. The advantage of choosing this particular area was threefold: It was rugged terrain, identical to that of Iran; it was sparsely populated; and the people here knew him because he'd made more than a dozen runs for Dimitri Maslov and then Semion Icoupov, trading semi-automatic rifles, grenades, rocket launchers, and so forth to the Armenian tribal leaders who were waging a continuous guerrilla war against the Azerbaijani regime, just as they had against the Soviets until the fall of the Soviet empire. In exchange, Arkadin received packets of brownish morphine bricks of exceedingly high quality, which he transported overland to the port city of Baku, where they were loaded onto a merchant ship that would take them due north across the Caspian Sea to Russia.

All in all, Nagorno-Karabakh was as secure a place as Arkadin could possibly find. He and his men would be left alone, and the tribesmen would protect him with their lives. Without the weapons provided by him and the people he worked for they would have been beaten into the dry red dirt of their homeland, exterminated like vermin. Armenians had settled here, between the Kura and Araxes rivers, during Roman times and had remained here ever since. Arkadin understood their fierce homeland pride, which was why he'd decided that Nagorno-Karabakh was the place to commence trading. It was a politically savvy move as well. Since the weapons sold to the Armenian tribesmen helped destabilize the country and thus gave it a rude shove back toward Moscow's orbit, the Kremlin was all too happy to turn a blind eye to the trades.

Now his strike force was going to train here.

It was hardly a surprise that when he arrived the leaders greeted him like a conquering hero.

Not that this homecoming of sorts was simply pleasant; nothing in Arkadin's life was simple. Possibly he had misremembered the landscape or perhaps something had changed inside him. Either way, the moment he drove into the Nagorno-Karabakh area it was as if he'd been hurled back into Nizhny Tagil.

The camp had been set up precisely to his specifications: Ten tents made of camouflage material ringed a large oval compound. To the east was the landing strip where his plane had touched down. At the other end of it was a short L-shaped extension on which was sitting a Air Afrika Transport cargo plane. The tents had an aspect he hadn't anticipated: They reminded him of the ring of high-security prisons that girdled Nizhny Tagil, the town in which he'd been born and raised, if you could call living with psychotic parents being raised.

But again, memory was not a simple matter. Twenty minutes after arriving, having entered one of the tents that had been set up as his command station, he was inspecting the impressive array of weaponry he'd had transshipped: AK-47 Lancasters, AR15 Bushmasters and LWRC SRT 6.8mm assault rifles, World War II US Marine M2A1-7 flamethrowers, armor-piercing grenades, shoulder-fired FIM-92 Stinger missiles, mobile howitzers, and, the key to his mission, three AH-64 Apache helicopters loaded with AGM-114 Hellfire missiles with specially made dual-charge nose cones of depleted uranium, unconditionally guaranteed by the seller to penetrate even the most heavily armored vehicle.

Dressed in camo fatigues, armed with a metal baton on one hip and an American Colt .45 on the other, Arkadin emerged from the largest of the tents and was met by Dimitri Maslov, the head of the Kazanskaya, the most powerful family of the Moscow mob. Maslov looked like a street fighter who was calculating how to pin you in the least amount of time and with the maximum pain. His hands were large, thick, and broad, and looked like they could wring the neck of anyone and anything. His muscular legs ended in outlandishly dainty feet, as if they'd been grafted on from someone else's body. He'd grown his hair since the last time Arkadin had seen him and, dressed in lightweight camo fatigues, had something of the anarchic air of Che Guevara.

"Leonid Danilovich," Maslov said with false heartiness, "I see you've wasted no time in putting our war matériel to use. Well, good, it cost a fucking fortune."

With Maslov were two no-neck bodyguards, their fatigues sporting immense sweat rings, clearly out of their element in this hot climate.

Looking past the human weapons, Arkadin eyed the *grupperovka* chief with a kind of impersonal distrust. Ever since he'd defected from being the Kazanskaya's main enforcer to working exclusively for Semion Icoupov, he wasn't sure where he stood with the man. That they were doing business now meant nothing; a combination of compelling circumstance and powerful partner thrust them together. Arkadin had the impression that they were two pit bulls deciding how to finish the other off. This was borne out when Maslov said, "I still haven't gotten over the loss of my Mexican pipeline. I can't help feeling that if you'd been available, I wouldn't have lost it."

"Now I believe you're exaggerating, Dimitri Ilyinovich."

"But instead you dropped out of sight," Maslov continued, deliberately ignoring Arkadin. "You were unreachable."

Arkadin thought he'd better pay attention now. Did Maslov suspect that he had taken Gustavo Moreno's laptop, a prize that Arkadin was certain Maslov thought was rightfully his?

Arkadin thought it best to change the subject. "Why are you here?"

"I always like to see my investments firsthand. Besides, Triton, the man coordinating the entire operation, wanted a firsthand report on your progress."

"Triton need only have called me," Arkadin said.

"He's a cautious man, our Triton, or so I've heard. I've never met him myself—frankly, I don't know who he is, only that he's a man with deep pockets and the wherewithal to mount this ambitious project. And don't forget, Arkadin, it was I who recommended you to Triton. 'There's no one better to train these men,' I told him in no uncertain terms."

Arkadin thanked Maslov, even though privately it pained him to do so. On the other side of the ledger, it warmed him to know that Maslov had no idea who Triton was or who he worked for, whereas he himself knew everything. Maslov's amassed millions had made him overconfident and sloppy, which in Arkadin's opinion made him ripe for the slaughter. That would come, he told himself, in time.

When Maslov had phoned him with the proposition laid out by Triton, he'd at first refused. Now that he was the power behind the Eastern Brotherhood he neither needed nor wanted to hire himself out as a freelancer. When Maslov's flattery, describing Arkadin and the Black Legion's crucial part in the plan, had failed to move him, the twenty-million-dollar fee was dangled in front of his face. Still, he hesitated, until he'd learned that the target was Iran, the objective to overthrow the current regime. Then the dazzling prospect of Iran's oil pipeline danced through his head: untold billions, untold power. This prize took his breath away. He was canny enough to know, though Maslov was careful not to mention it, that Triton's aim must be the pipeline, too. His endgame was to double-cross Triton at the last minute, to snatch the pipeline for himself, but to do that he needed to properly assess his enemy's resources. He needed to know who Triton was.

He saw someone emerge from the interior of the jeep that he'd been warned by tribal lookouts had brought Maslov and his thugs here. At first the heat rising from the freshly laid tarmac obscured the man's face. Not that it mattered; Arkadin recognized that easy, loping gait, so deliberately like Clint Eastwood's in *A Fistful of Dollars*.

"What's he doing here?" Arkadin struggled to keep the sharp edge out of his voice.

"Who? Oserov?" Maslov said in all innocence. "Vylacheslav Germanovich is now my second in command." He shook his head ingenuously. "Did I fail to mention that? I would have if I'd been able to get hold of you to protect my Mexican interests." He shrugged. "But, alas . . ."

Oserov was smiling now, in that half-ironic, half-condescending expression that had been tattooed into Arkadin's brain in Nizhny Tagil. Was graduating Oxford a license to act superior to every other *grupperovka* member in Russia? Arkadin didn't think so.

"Arkadin, really?" Oserov said in British English. "Bloody shocking you're still alive."

Arkadin hit him hard on the point of the chin. Oserov, that vile smile still stitched to his face, was already on his knees, his eyes rolling, by the time Maslov's bodyguards stepped in.

Maslov held up one hand to stay them. Nevertheless, his face was dark and congested with anger. "You shouldn't have done that, Leonid Danilovich."

"You shouldn't have brought him."

Unmindful of the weapons drawn on him, Arkadin knelt beside Oserov. "So here you are in the blazing Azerbaijani sun, so far from home. How does it feel?"

Oserov's eyes were bloodshot and a thin trail of pink drool descended like a strand of a spider's web from one corner of his mouth, but he never stopped smiling. All at once, he reached out and grabbed Arkadin by his shirtfront, jerking him closer.

"You'll live to regret this insult, Leonid Danilovich, now that Mischa is no longer alive to protect you."

Arkadin sprang away and rose to his feet. "I told you what I'd do to him if I saw him again."

Maslov's eyes narrowed. His face still had that congested look. "That was a long time ago."

"Not for me," Arkadin said.

Now he had made his stand, made an unequivocal statement that Maslov couldn't ignore. Nothing would be the same between them, which came as a distinct relief to Arkadin, who had the captive's innate horror of inaction. To him, change was life. Dimitri Maslov had always thought of Arkadin as a workman, someone he hired and then forgot about. That perception needed to change. Maslov had to be made aware that the two men were now equals. Arkadin didn't have the luxury of time to finesse his new, elevated status.

As Oserov regained his feet, Maslov threw his head back and laughed, but he sobered quickly enough. "Get back to the car, Vylacheslav Germanovich," he said under his breath to Oserov.

Oserov was about to say something, but changed his mind. With a murderous look at Arkadin, he turned on his heel and stalked away.

"So, you're a big man now," Maslov said in an easy tone that didn't quite mask the undertone of menace in his voice.

Which meant, Arkadin understood, *I knew you when you were nothing but a ragged fugitive from Nizhny Tagil, so if you mean to come after me, don't.*

"There are no big men," Arkadin replied with equanimity, "only big ideas."

The two men stared at each other in total silence. Then, as one, they began to laugh. They laughed so hard, the bodyguards looked at each other questioningly and holstered their handguns. Meanwhile, Arkadin and Maslov punched each other lightly, then embraced as brothers. But for Arkadin, he knew he had to be even more wary of a knife being slipped between his ribs or a bit of cyanide in his toothpaste.

Bourne made his way down the steep hillside from the *warung* at the summit of the rice paddies. Down below, two adolescents were just visible exiting their family compound to go to school in Tenganan village.

He continued to descend the steep, rocky path at an almost breathtaking pace, passing the compound where the two teens had come from. A man—doubtless their father—was chopping wood, and a woman was stirring a wok-like pan over an open flame. Two skinny dogs came out to observe Bourne's passing, but the adults couldn't have cared less.

The path flattened out quickly now, becoming packed dirt, somewhat wider, with the occasional rock and pile of cow manure to circumnavigate. This was the path that he and Moira had been forced to take by the "beater" who had cleverly herded them toward the killing ground in Tenganan.

Passing through the arched gateway, he picked his way past the school and the empty badminton court. Then all at once he was in the sacred open space occupied by the three temples. Unlike the first time he had been here, the temples were empty. High above, curlicue clouds tumbled across the cerulean sky. A small breeze stirred the treetops. His steps, light and virtually silent, caused little or no stir among the herd of cows and their calves lounging against the cool stone walls of the temple at the far end, the one dappled in shade. Save for the animals, the glade was deserted.

As he cut between the central temple and the one on the right he experienced an eerie sense of dislocation. He passed the patch of dirt where he had lain in his own blood while Moira, her face pinched with horror, had knelt over him. Time seemed to stretch into infinity, then, as he moved on, to snap back like a rubber band.

Leaving the rear walls of the temples behind him, he soon found himself back on steeply pitched land. The forest rose like a thick green wall above him, like a many-pagodaed temple complex, reaching toward the sky. This was where the shooter must have been lying in wait for him.

Just inside the lowest fringe of the dense

forest sat a small stone shrine, its flanks wrapped in the traditional black-and-white-checked cloth, the whole protected by a small yellow parasol. The local spirit was in residence, and so was someone else. Seeing a small movement out of the corner of his eye, Bourne lunged into the foliage, wrapped his hand around a thin, brown arm, and drew out of the shadows the eldest daughter of the family that owned the *warung*.

For a long moment, they stood staring silently at each other. Then Bourne knelt down so he was at her eye level.

"What's your name?" he asked her.

"Kasih," she said at once.

He smiled. "What are you doing here, Kasih?"

The girl's eyes were deep as pools, dark as obsidian. She had long hair that came down past her narrow shoulders. She wore a coffee-colored sarong with a pattern of frangipani blossoms just like his double *ikat*. Her skin was silky and unblemished.

"Kasih—?"

"You were hurt three full moons ago in Tenganan."

The smile Bourne kept on his face

turned tissue-thin. "You're mistaken, Kasih. That man died. I went to his funeral in Manggis before his body was flown back to the United States."

The outer corners of her eyes turned up and she gave him a curious smile, as enigmatic as the expression of the Mona Lisa. Then she reached out and her fingers opened his sweat-drenched shirt, revealing the bandaged wound.

"You were shot, *Bapak,*" she said as gravely as an adult. "You didn't die, but it's hard for you to climb our steep hills." She cocked her head. "Why do you do it?"

"So that one day it won't be hard." He rebuttoned his shirt. "This is our secret, Kasih. No one else must find out, otherwise—"

"The man who shot you will come back."

Rocked back on his heels, Bourne felt his heartbeat accelerate. "Kasih, how do you know that?"

"Because demons always return."

"What do you mean?"

Reverently approaching the shrine, she placed a handful of red and violet blossoms in the shrine's small niche, pressing her palms together at forehead height, bowing her head in a brief prayer to protect them against the evil demons that lurked in the forest's restless green shadows.

When she was finished, she stepped back and, kneeling, began to dig at the rear corner of the shrine. A moment later she plucked out of the black, volcanic earth a small package of tied banana leaves. She turned and, with a fearful look in her eyes, presented it to Bourne.

Brushing off the soft clots of dirt, he untied and peeled back the leaves, one by one. Inside, he discovered a human eyeball, made of acrylic or glass.

"It's the demon's eye, *Bapak,*" she said, "the demon who shot you."

Bourne looked at her. "Where did you find this?"

"Over there." She pointed to the base of an immense *pule* or milk wood tree not more than a hundred yards away.

"Show me," he said, following her through the tall fan-like ferns to the tree.

The girl would approach no closer than three paces, but Bourne hunkered down on his hams at the spot she indicated, where the ferns were broken, trampled down as if someone had left in great haste. Cocking his head up, he eyed the network of branches.

As he made to climb up, Kasih gave a little cry. "Oh, please don't! The spirit of Durga, the goddess of death, lives in the *pule*."

He swung one leg up, gaining a foothold on the bark, and smiled reassuringly at the girl. "Don't worry, Kasih, I'm protected by Shiva, my own goddess of death."

Ascending swiftly and surely, he soon came to the thick, almost horizontal branch he had spied from the ground. Arranging himself along it on his belly, he found himself peering out through a narrow gap in the tangle of trees at the precise spot where he'd been shot. He rose up on one elbow, looked around. In a moment he found the small hollow in the place where the branch was thickest as it attached to the trunk. Something glinted dully there. Plucking it out, he saw a shell casing. Pocketing this, he shimmied back down the tree, where he grinned down at the clearly nervous girl.

"You see, safe and sound," he said. "I

think Durga's spirit is in another *pule* tree on the other side of Bali today."

"I didn't know Durga could move around."

"Of course she can," Bourne said. "This isn't the only *pule* on Bali, is it?"

She shook her head.

"That proves my point," Bourne said. "She's not here today. It's perfectly safe."

Kasih still appeared troubled. "Now that you have the demon's eyeball, you'll be able to find him and stop him from coming back, won't you?"

He knelt beside her. "The demon isn't coming back, Kasih, that I promise you." He rolled the eyeball between his fingers. "And, yes, with its help I hope to find the demon who shot me."

Moira was taken by the two NSA agents to Bethesda Naval Hospital, where she was subjected to a medical workup both harrowing and stultifying in its thoroughness. In this way, the night crawled by. When, just after ten the next morning, she was declared physically fit, materially unimpaired by the car crash, the NSA agents told her that she was free to go.

"Wait a minute," she said. "Didn't you say you were taking me in for tampering with a crime scene?"

"We did take you in," one of the agents said in his clipped Midwestern accent. Then the two of them walked out, leaving her confused and not a little alarmed.

Her alarm escalated significantly when she called four different people at the Department of Defense and State, all of whom were either "in a meeting," "out of the building," or, even more ominously, simply "unavailable."

She had just finished putting on her makeup when her cell buzzed with a text message from Steve Stevenson, the undersecretary for acquisition, technology and logistics at the DoD who'd recently hired her.

PERRY 1HR, she read off her screen. Quickly erasing it, she applied lipstick, gathered up her handbag and checked out of the hospital.

It was twenty-three miles from the Bethesda Naval Hospital to the Library of Congress. Google Maps claimed the ride would take thirty-six minutes, but that had to have been at two in the morning. At 11 AM, when Moira took the trip by taxi, it was twenty minutes longer, which meant she got to her destination with almost no time to spare. On the way, she had phoned her office, asked for a car to meet her, giving an address three blocks from her current destination.

"Bring a laptop and a burner," she said before flipping her phone closed.

It was only when she exited the taxi that she felt aches and pains spring up in all parts of her body. She felt a massive post-trauma headache coming on. Digging in her handbag, she took three Advil, swallowing them dry. The day was mild but overcast and dull, no break in the gun-metal sky, no wind to speak of. The pale pink cherry blossoms were already trampled underfoot, tulips were blooming, and there was an unmistakable earthy scent in the air as spring advanced.

Stevenson's text message, PERRY, referred to Roland Hinton Perry who, at the tender age of twenty-seven, had created the Fountain of the Court of Neptune sculpture on the far west side of the entrance to the Library of Congress. It was on the pavement level, rather than at the elevated level of the porte-cochere main entrance. Set into three niches of the stone retaining wall that was flanked by the entryway staircases, the fountain—with its twelve-foot bronze sculpture of the Roman god of the sea as a fearsome centerpiece—emitted a raw and restless energy that contrasted dramatically with the sedate exterior of the building itself. Most visitors to the library never even knew it existed. Moira and Stevenson did, however. It was one of the half a dozen meeting places scattered in and around the district they had agreed upon.

She saw him right away. He was in a navy-blue blazer and gray lightweight wool trousers, his shoulders hunched up around his brick-red ears. He was facing away from her, staring at the rather violent countenance of Neptune, which meant that his head was slightly thrown back, his bald spot coming into prominence.

He didn't move when she came up and stood beside him. They might have been two totally unconnected tourists, not the least because he displayed an open copy of Fodor's guidebook to Washington, DC, the way a pheasant announces its presence by spreading its tail.

"Not a happy day for you, is it?" he said without turning in her direction or even seeming to move his lips.

"What the hell is going on?" Moira asked. "No one in DoD, including you, is taking my calls."

"It seems, my dear, that you've stepped in a great steaming pile of shit." Stevenson flipped a page of the guidebook. He was one of those old-school government functionaries who went to a barber for a shave every day, had a manicure once a week, belonged to all the right clubs, and made sure his opinions were held by the majority before he voiced them. "No one wants to be contaminated with the stink."

"Me? I haven't done a damn thing." *Except piss off my former bosses,* she said to herself.

She thought about the trouble Noah had gone to in order to get Jay's cell phone and to have her detained. Because she worked that part out on the way over here. The only reason for the NSA agents to say they were taking her in for tampering at the accident site and then let her go without charging her was that for some reason Noah needed her out of commission overnight. Why? Maybe she'd find out once she downloaded the files on the thumb drive she'd found sewn into the lining of Jay's jacket, but for now her best strategy was to pretend she knew absolutely nothing.

"No." Stevenson shook his head. "What we have here is something more. I think someone at your company trod on a nerve. The late Jay Weston, perhaps?"

"Do you know what Weston dug up?"

"If I did," Stevenson said slowly and carefully, "I'd be roadkill by now."

"That big?"

He rubbed his immaculate red cheek. "Bigger."

"What the hell is going on between the NSA and Black River?" she said.

"You're a Black River ex-employee, you tell me." He pursed his lips. "No, on second thought, I don't want to know anything, not even speculation. Ever since the news of the jetliner explosion hit the wires, the atmosphere at DoD and the Pentagon has been shrouded in a toxic fog."

"Meaning?"

"Nobody's talking."

"Nobody ever talks up there."

Stevenson nodded. "True enough, but this is different. Everyone's walking around on eggshells. Even the secretaries seem terrified. In my twenty years of government service I've never experienced anything like it. Except—"

Moira felt a ball of ice form in her stomach. "Except what?"

"Except right before we invaded Iraq."

9

Willard watched Ian Bowles as he exited Firth's surgery. He'd marked him the second time he'd showed up at the compound and, as with every other of the doctor's patients, he'd made inquiries. Bowles was the only one about whom nothing was known locally. Willard hadn't spent the last three months simply training Bourne. Like all good agents, he'd immediately begun to acquaint himself with his environment. He'd become friendly with all the key people in the area who, de facto, became his eyes and ears. The advantage of being in Manggis was that neither the village nor the surrounding area was highly populated. Unlike Kuta and Ubud, only a smattering of tourists found their way to the area, so it wasn't difficult to identify the patients who came to see the doctor. By this homespun method, Ian Bowles stood out like a sore thumb. However, Willard wouldn't act until Bowles revealed himself one way or the other.

Ever since he'd been released from his undercover duties at the NSA safe house in rural Virginia, Willard had pondered long and hard how he could be of best use to the clandestine service, which functioned as his mother, father, sister, and brother. Treadstone had been Alexander Conklin's dream. Only Conklin and Willard himself knew Treadstone's ultimate purpose.

He went about this work with extreme caution because he was laboring under a handicap Conklin never had to deal with. In Alex's day the Old Man had signed off on Treadstone. All Conklin had to do was to fly below the CI radar, to make good on the goals he'd promised the Old Man, while working on his own agenda deep in the shadows. Willard did not have the advantage of such support. As far as Veronica

Hart and CI were concerned Treadstone was as dead and buried as Conklin himself. Willard was far too canny to believe Hart would allow him a restart, which meant that he had to work clandestinely within one of the world's largest clandestine organizations. The irony wasn't lost on him.

As he followed Bowles out of the compound and down a deserted lane he reflected on how fortuitous Moira Trevor's phone call had been, since this remote island off the CI grid was the perfect place to begin the resurrection of Treadstone.

Up ahead of him, Bowles had stopped beside a motor scooter, parked beneath the shade of a frangipani tree. Bowles took out his cell phone. As he pressed the SPEED DIAL key, Willard unfurled a thin metal wire with wooden handles on either end. Stepping quickly up behind Bowles, he whipped the wire around the other's throat and pulled so hard on the handles Bowles was lifted onto the tips of his toes.

The New Zealander dropped his cell, reaching around behind him to make a grab at his unseen assailant. Dancing out of the way, Willard maintained the lethal pressure on the wire. Bowles's gestures became more frantic. He tore into the flesh of his own neck in his frenzy to breathe, his eyes bulged in their sockets, red threads mottling the whites. Then there was a sudden foul stench and he collapsed.

Unwinding the wire, Willard scooped up the cell and, as he walked briskly away, checked the number Bowles had been dialing. He recognized the first digits as those of a Russian cell phone. The call had failed, and he walked into Manggis to a spot he knew to be cell-receptive and hit REDIAL. A moment later a familiar male voice answered.

Willard, momentarily stunned, nevertheless gathered himself and said, "Your man Bowles is dead. Don't send another," then hung up before Leonid Danilovich Arkadin could say a word.

When Moira left Stevenson she walked opposite the direction she needed to go. She spent twenty minutes following circuitous routes, checking in car side-mirrors and plate-glass windows, looking for a tail, and when she had assured herself that she wasn't being followed, she walked back to where the car was waiting for her three blocks west of the Fountain of Poseidon.

The driver saw her coming and got out of the car. Not looking at her or acknowledging her in any way, he walked toward her. They passed each other close enough for him to hand off the keys without stopping or even breaking stride.

She went past the parked car, crossed the street, and stood looking around as if unsure which way to go. In fact, she was scrutinizing the environment, breaking it down into vectors, which she inspected for anyone in the least bit suspicious. A boy and a girl, presumably his sister, played with a golden Lab under the watchful eye of their father. A mother wheeled her baby carriage; two sweaty joggers dodged in and out, listening through in-ear plugs to iPods attached to armbands.

Nothing seemed out of place, which was precisely what worried her. NSA agents on the street or even in passing cars she could deal with. It was the people who might be placed behind building windows or on rooftops that concerned her. Well, there was no help for it, she thought. She'd done the best she could, now it was put one foot in front of the other and pray that she'd slipped any surveillance that might have been attached to her once the two NSA agents had left her at Bethesda Naval Hospital.

As an added precaution, she pried the SIM chip out of her phone and ground it beneath the heels of her shoe. She kicked it into a storm drain in the gutter, then chucked her cell in after it. She had the key in her hand as she approached the car from across the street. She crossed in front of it and dropped her handbag. Kneeling down, she dug out her compact, used the mirror inside to check the underside of the car as best she could. She checked under the rear as well. What was she expecting to find? Nothing, hopefully. But there was always a chance that a passing NSA agent had left a bug on the under chassis.

Spotting nothing suspicious, she unlocked the car and slid behind the wheel. It was a late-model silver Chrysler that her own mechanics had customized with a muscular turbocharged engine. Finding the laptop and the burner beneath the seat, she ripped off the burner's pristine plastic wrap. Burners were disposable cell phones loaded with pre-paid minutes. As long as you didn't use them for too long, you were safe talking on them, and no one could use the SIM to triangulate your position as they could with a registered cell.

Fighting an urge to fire up the computer right there, she turned the key in the ignition, put the car in gear, and nosed out into traffic. She was no longer comfortable staying in one place too long; neither did she feel safe going back to the office or even her home.

Heading back across into Virginia, she drove aimlessly for close to an hour, after which time she could no longer control her curiosity. She had to find out what was on the thumb drive she'd lifted off Jay's corpse. Did it hold the key to what was going on between NSA and Black River that, according to Stevenson, held all of the DoD in thrall? Why else would Noah and the NSA come after Jay and now her. She had to assume the DC motorcycle cop was bogus—that he was, in fact, either NSA or Black River. Stevenson had been terrified. The whole scenario chilled her to the marrow.

Passing through Rosslyn, she suddenly

became aware that she was famished. She couldn't remember the last time she'd eaten, apart from whatever they'd given her this morning in the hospital. Who could eat that stuff? More to the point, what kind of chef could concoct such tasteless, overcooked mush?

She turned onto Wilson Boulevard, drove past the Hyatt, and pulled over into a parking space several car-lengths from the entrance to the Shade Grown Café, a place she knew inside and out and thus felt safe in. Taking the laptop and the burner with her, she got out, locked the car, and hurried into the steamy interior. The smells of bacon and toast made her mouth water. Slipping into a well-worn cherry-colored vinyl booth, she gave the plastic-wrapped menu a cursory once-over before ordering three eggs over easy, a double portion of bacon, and wheat toast. When the waitress asked if she wanted coffee, she said, "Please. Cream on the side."

Alone at the Formica table, she opened the notebook so that the screen faced her and the wall behind her. While it was booting up, she bent down and extracted the thumb drive from the underwire section of her bra. The tiny electronic rectangle was warm and seemed to beat like a second heart. Using her thumb on the special reader, she logged in, then answered her three security questions. Finally on, she plugged the thumb drive into one of the USB ports on the left side of the computer. Switching to My Computer, she navigated to the portable drive that had appeared there, then double-clicked on it.

The screen went black, and for a moment she thought the drive had crashed the operating system. But then the screen started scrolling in lines of what looked like gibberish. There were no folders, no files, just this ever-scrolling series of letters, numbers, and symbols. The information was encrypted. That was just like the careful Jay.

At once she hit the ESCAPE key and was back at the My Computer screen. Accessing the C drive, she opened the wireless access connections wizard. Either the coffee shop was Wi-Fi–enabled or someplace close was because the wizard detected an open network. That was both good and bad. It meant she could get on the Web, but there were no network encryption safeguards. Luckily, she'd had all the Heartland laptops fitted with their own mobile encryption package among a host of other security measures, which in this case meant that even if someone hacked her ISP address they wouldn't be able to read the packets of information she sent and received; nor would they be able to locate her.

She pushed the laptop aside when her breakfast arrived. It would take some time for the proprietary Heartland deciphering software to analyze the data on the thumb drive. She uploaded the encrypted data and pressed the ENTER key, which started the program.

By the time she'd mopped up the last of the third egg yolk with a wedge of buttered toast and the last of the bacon, she heard a soft chime. Almost choking on her final bite, she swigged down a mouthful of coffee and stacked her plates at the edge of the table.

Her forefinger hovered over the ENTER key for the tiniest of moments before depressing it. At once words began to flood across her screen, then marched down as the entire contents of the drive were revealed.

PINPRICKBARDEM, she read.

She couldn't believe it. Her eyes traveling over the scrolling lines read PINPRICKBARDEM over and over. The lines came to an end and she checked again. The entire drive had been filled up with these fourteen letters. She broke down the letters into the most obvious words: Pin Prick Bar Dem. Then another: PinP Rick Bar Dem. She wrote down: *Picture in Picture (on a digital TV?), Rick's Bar (?), Democrat.*

Online, she ran a quick Google check. There was a Rick's Bar in Chicago and one in San Francisco, an Andy & Rick's Bar in Truth Or Consequences, New Mexico, but there was no Rick's Bar anywhere in the district or the environs. She scratched out what she had written. What on earth could those letters mean? she wondered. Were they yet another code? She was about to run them through the Heartland software program again when the sudden presence of a shadow at the periphery of her vision caused her to glance up.

Two NSA agents were staring at her

through the window. As she slammed down the laptop's screen one of them opened the door to the coffee shop.

Benjamin Firth was riding his bottle of *arak* with a vengeance when Willard strode into the surgery. Firth was up on the table, head bowed, swigging great mouthfuls of the fermented palm liquor with grim precision.

Willard stood looking at the doctor for a moment, remembering his father who drank himself into dementia and, finally, liver failure. It hadn't been pretty, and along the way there were serious bouts of the kind of lightning Jekyll-and-Hyde personality split that afflicted some alcoholics. After his father had bounced his head off a wall during one of these fits Willard, who was eight at the time, taught himself not to be afraid. He kept his baseball bat under his bed and the next time his father, stinking of booze, lunged at him, he swung the bat in a perfectly level arc and broke two of his ribs. After that, his father never touched him again, neither in anger nor in affection. At the time, Willard thought he'd gotten what he wanted, but later, after the old man died, he began to wonder whether he'd injured himself along with his father.

With a grunt of disgust, he crossed the surgery, ripped the bottle out of Firth's hand, and shoved a small booklet into it. For a moment the doctor looked up at him with red-rimmed eyes as if he was trying to place Willard in his memory.

"Read it, Doc. Go ahead."

Firth glanced down and seemed surprised. "Where's my *arak*?"

"Gone," Willard said. "I brought you something better."

Firth snorted noisily. "Nothing better than *arak*."

"Want to bet?"

Willard opened the booklet for him and the doctor stared down at the passport photo of Ian Bowles, the New Zealander who'd been masquerading as a patient, who was blackmailing him into taking photos of Jason Bourne. This was why he had been getting stone-cold wasted. He couldn't bear to think of what he had to do or what would happen to him if he didn't.

"What . . . ?" He shook his head, confused. "What are you doing with this?"

Willard sat down beside him. "Let's just

say Mr. Bowles will no longer be a problem for you."

Firth sobered as if the other man had thrown a bucket of cold water in his face. "You know?"

Willard took the passport. "I heard it all."

A shiver ran down the doctor's spine. "There was nothing I could do."

"It's a good thing, then, that I was here."

Firth nodded despondently.

"Now I need you to do something for me."

"Anything," Firth said. "I owe you my life."

"Jason Bourne must never know this happened."

"None of it?" Firth looked at him. "Someone suspects he's here, someone is after him."

Willard's face was impassive. "None whatsoever, Doctor." He held out his hand. "Do I have your word?"

Firth gripped the other's hand, which was firm and dry and somehow comforting. "I said anything, didn't I?"

10

As Moira launched herself out of the booth, she pulled the thumb drive out of the USB slot. By this time she'd taken off through the coffee shop, down the narrow, dingy hallway that led to the toilets and the kitchen.

Turning left into the kitchen, she was engulfed by a surge of heat, steam, and raised voices. She was heading for the pantry when the delivery entrance at the rear burst open, and an NSA agent came through the doorway. As he did so, she pressed her thumb into the reader twice in succession even though the computer was still on. Then she threw it at him. He raised his arms reflexively to catch it and she raced into the small pantry cubicle. Kneeling, she pulled the ring on the trapdoor. As she was raising it from its mount flush in the floor, she heard the laptop's incendiary device explode. Shouts and the confusion caused by a fire in a confined space came to her as she slipped down the ladder, closing the trapdoor behind her. The device was a last-ditch security measure she'd had her techs install in all Heartland laptops. Pressing the thumb reader twice while the laptop was on activated the device on a ten-second delay.

At the bottom of the ladder, she found herself in the basement, where bulk deliveries were stored. She felt above her head until she found the cord and pulled it. A bare bulb illuminated her surroundings in chiaroscuro starkness. She saw the metal doors leading to street level and opened them. There was a metal ramp used to slide the cartons of canned goods into the basement. She scrambled up this, bending almost double to hold on to the sides so as not to slip on the smooth surface. To do this, she had to slip the thumb drive, which she'd been clutching for dear life, into her pocket. As she did so, the back of her hand brushed against what felt like a stiff card. Gaining the street, she found herself directly to the right of the entrance to the coffee shop, where people were piling out like boiling water. As she walked away she could hear the klaxon call of fire engines. She walked away from the melee, her hand in her pocket to check that she still had the thumb drive, and she felt again the presence of the card. Drawing it out, she saw that it had the EMS logo on it and Dave's name. Below, he'd handwritten a cell phone number. Then she remembered him brushing by her and knew he'd slipped her the card then. Any port in a storm, she thought. Flipping open the burner, she punched in the number.

Just then, glancing over her shoulder, she saw one of the NSA agents spill out of the entrance and she walked faster. But he'd already spotted her and took off after her.

Rounding the corner, she put her phone to her ear.

"Yes?" She was relieved to hear Dave's familiar voice.

"I'm in trouble." She gave him her approximate location. "I'll be at Fort Myer Drive and Seventeenth Street North in three minutes."

"Wait for us," he said.

"Easy for you to say," she replied and raced around the corner onto North Nash Street.

Watching Maslov and his slope-shouldered Neanderthals climb back into their vehicle and head out, Arkadin suppressed a spasm of murderous rage. It was all he could do to stop himself from grabbing a semiautomatic off one of the stacks and spraying the vehicle with bullets until all four people inside were dead. Luckily, what was left of the rational part of his brain prevented him from making such a foolish move. He might feel better for the moment but in the larger scheme of things he would regret Maslov's premature demise. As long as the head of the Kazanskaya was useful to him he'd allow him to live.

But not a moment longer.

He wouldn't make the same mistake with Maslov he'd made with Stas Kuzin, the mob boss in Nizhny Tagil he'd partnered with, then killed. In those days Arkadin was young and inexperienced; he'd allowed Kuzin to live too long. Long enough to torture and kill the woman Arkadin was sleeping with. Of course, the young Arkadin hadn't considered what would happen in the aftermath of Kuzin's death and the death of a third of his depraved crew.

With the rest of Kuzin's murderers out for his blood he was forced to go to ground. Since they had all the avenues out of the city covered and had turned all the terrified citizens into informers, it was imperative to find a haven as quickly as possible, which unfortunately meant inside Nizhny Tagil, somewhere they'd never find him, where they'd never even think to look. He'd shot Kuzin in the building he and Kuzin owned jointly, where Kuzin had his headquarters, where he kept the young girls Arkadin had swept off the streets for him. Of course, he found the perfect spot, one even Dimitri Maslov wouldn't have been clever enough to think of.

Abruptly Arkadin's mind switched gears to more immediate concerns. The phone call from Willard was very much on his mind as he walked back to where his Black Legion recruits were waiting for him outside the tents erected on the edge of the Azerbaijani plain. He'd relied on that idiot Wayan, who had recommended Ian Bowles. Hiring Bowles clearly had been a mistake.

But now even Bowles was driven out of his mind as he addressed his troops. They were not nearly as well prepared for a coordinated raid as he'd hoped. But then these men had been trained and used in solo missions. Many of them had been waiting for the orders to strap on their C-4 vests, infiltrate a market, a police station, or a school, and press the detonator. Their minds were already halfway to Paradise, and almost immediately Arkadin understood that it was his job as well as his duty as the head of the Eastern Brotherhood, the Black Legion's legitimate umbrella organization, to shape them into a unit, men who could rely on one another—sacrifice for one another if need be—without a second's hesitation.

The group of men—hardy, physically and mentally fit—stood arrayed in front of him, uncomfortable because he'd ordered them to shave their heads and their beards, both of which were against both custom and their Islamic teachings. Not a one of them wasn't wondering how on earth they were going to infiltrate anywhere in the Islamic world looking as they now did.

One man, Farid, chose to voice their concern. He did it forcefully, believing he was speaking for the other ninety-nine recruits, not just himself.

"What was that?" Arkadin's head snapped so hard a vertebra in his neck cracked like a rifle shot. "What did you say, Farid?"

Had he known Arkadin at all, Farid would have kept his mouth shut. But he didn't, and there was no one in the godforsaken land to teach him. So he repeated his question.

"Sir, we're wondering why you ordered us to shave the hair that Allah dictates we must have. We're wondering what your motive could possibly be. We demand an answer because you have shamed us."

Without a word, Arkadin pulled out the baton from his belt, slammed it into the side of Farid's head, driving him down. As he knelt, swaying with pain and dismay,

Arkadin drew his Colt and shot Farid point-blank through his right eye. The man was driven back, his knees cracking, and there he lay in the sandy dirt, mute and inert.

Just around the corner Moira stopped and pressed herself against the wall of the office building. She raised her right elbow and, as the NSA agent came racing around the corner, slammed it into his chest. She'd been aiming for his throat but missed, and though he rocked back against the wall, he immediately came at her, threw a punch that she blocked.

But it was only a feint and he grabbed her left arm from the underside and applied pressure in an attempt to break it at the elbow. Moira, pinioned, trod hard on his instep, but his grip didn't loosen. He applied more pressure until a yelp of pain escaped her throat. Then he came in with the heel of his hand, a blow aimed at the point of her nose.

She let him commit himself completely to the blow, then dodged her head to one side. At the same time, gathering all her strength into her lower belly, she jammed her flexed right knee into his groin. His arms opened wide, his grip on her began to slip, and he went down.

Moira snatched her arm away, but he managed to grasp her wrist, bringing her down to him as he fell to his knees. His eyes were watering and he was clearly struggling not to pant, to deepen his breathing, work through the excruciating pain. But Moira wasn't about to let him. She drove her knuckles into his throat and, as he gagged, she freed herself. Then she struck the left side of his head, slamming it against the building's stonework. His eyes rolled up and he slid to the pavement. Quickly she took his weapon and his ID and took off through the growing crowd of gawking people, drawn to the scuffle like dogs scenting blood, saying, "That man mugged me. Someone call the police!"

On the corner of Fort Myer Drive and 17th Street North she brought herself up short. She was breathing heavily, her pulse rate accelerated. Adrenaline was burning through her like a river of fire, but she managed to slow to a walk, moving against the tide of people who were following the sound of the sirens on the police cruisers, quickening from more than one direction. One was coming directly at her, but, no, it was an EMS ambulance.

Dave had arrived, not a moment too soon. The ambulance slowed and she saw Earl behind the wheel. As the vehicle came abreast of her the back doors banged open and Dave leaned out. As he grabbed her left hand to swing her aboard she gasped. When she'd navigated the metal step Dave, lunging past her, swung the doors shut and said, "Go!"

Earl stepped on the gas. Moira swung around as the ambulance hit a corner at speed. Dave put his arms around her to steady her, led her to one of the benches.

"You okay?" he asked.

She nodded, but winced as she bent her left arm.

"Let me see that," Dave said, pushed back the sleeve of her blouse. "Nice," he said and started to work on the bruised and puffy joint.

At that point, Moira knew she was nearing the end of her rope. One of her operatives had stumbled on a secret so important that either Black River, the NSA, or both working in concert had killed him. Now they were after her. Her fledgling company had just over a hundred operatives, more than half of them recruited from Black River. Any one of them could be a traitor, because of one thing she was absolutely certain: Someone inside Heartland had tracked her ISP address to the Wi-Fi network at the Shade Grown Café and had given it to the NSA. That was the only explanation for them showing up so quickly.

Now she was out of options. She had no one to trust. Except, she thought bleakly, one person. The person she'd vowed never to see or speak to again, not after what had happened between them, which was unforgivable.

Moira closed her eyes, swaying slightly with the motion of the speeding ambulance. While now was not the time for forgiveness, maybe it was time for a truce. Who else could she call? Who else could she trust? She gave a little gasp of despair. If it weren't so sad it would be funny, really, turning for help to the last person she'd ever accept anything from. *But that was then,* she told herself grimly, *and this is now.*

With a silent curse, she used her burner

to dial a local number. When the male voice answered, she took a deep breath and said, "Veronica Hart, please."

"Who shall I say is calling?"

Oh, the hell with it, she thought. "Moira."

"Moira? Ma'am, she'll need your last name."

"No, she won't," Moira said. "Just tell her Moira, and be damn quick about it!"

The moon is out." Amun Chalthoum checked his watch. "It's time we talked."

Soraya had been on her satellite phone with her local Typhon agents in place. They were all running down leads on the new Iranian MIG, but so far none of them had made any progress. It was as if the group was so far underground their contacts had come up empty. Whether this was because their contacts knew nothing or were too afraid to divulge the group's existence was anyone's guess. If it was the latter, she had to admire the level of their security.

She decided to agree to Amun's suggestion, but not in the way he wanted. As he held the tent flap back for her, she said, "Leave your firearm here."

"Is this really necessary?" he said. When

she didn't reply he narrowed his eyes for a moment to show his displeasure then, sighing, took his pistol from its polished leather holster and set it down on a field desk.

"Satisfied?"

She passed out of the relative warmth of the interior into the chill night. Some distance away the American task force was busy sifting through the wreckage for clues, but as yet Delia hadn't given her another update, although—as Veronica had said—the downed plane wasn't her primary mission. She shivered in the ascetic chill of the desert air. The moon was immense, lent a kind of grandeur by the eternal and seemingly endless sea of sand.

They began heading for the bare perimeter, where Chalthoum's guards should have been posted, but she saw no one, and she stopped. Though he was a pace ahead of her, he sensed something amiss, and turned back.

"What is it?" he said.

"I won't go another step in that direction," she said. "I want to be in shouting distance." She indicated the constellation of lights on the other side of the site, safely beyond the perimeter dictated by Chalthoum, the glowing encampment of the international news media, somehow alien in the ominous night, as if it were a ship that had come to ruin on the teeth of the reef of the downed plane.

"They?" he scoffed. "They can't protect you. My people won't let them past the perimeter."

She gestured. "But where are your people, Amun? I don't see them."

"I made certain of that." He lifted an arm. "Come, we have very little time."

She was going to refuse but something in his voice caused her to relent. She thought again about the tension she'd first sensed in him, the leashed rage. What, really, was going on here? Now he'd piqued her curiosity. Had he done that deliberately? Was he leading her into a trap? But to what end? Unconsciously, her hand patted her back pocket where the ceramic switchblade rested, waiting to protect her.

They walked on in silence. The desert seemed to whisper around them, restlessly shifting, filtering between clothes and skin. The sheen of civilization ground down until only a hard nub was left, rough and primitive. Chalthoum reveled in his element. He was larger than life, which was of course why he'd taken her out here years ago, why they were here now. The farther they moved away from the others the more he seemed to grow both in stature and in power, until he towered over her. Turning, his eyes glittered, reflecting the blue-white moonlight.

"I need your help," he said with his usual bluntness.

She almost laughed. "You need *my* help?"

He looked away for a moment. "You're about the last person I'd think of asking for help."

And with that one statement she understood how dire his circumstances must be. "What if I refuse?"

He pointed to the satellite phone in her hand. "Do you think I don't know who you were calling with that?" The whites of his eyes looked eerily blue in the monochrome light. "Do you think I don't know why you're really here? It isn't about this air disaster; it's about this new Iranian MIG."

11

Willard, standing in the center of Dr. Firth's compound, waited anxiously for Bourne to return. He had thought briefly of going out after him, but rejected the idea. As often happened when he thought of Bourne, his thoughts turned to his own son Oren. He hadn't seen or heard from Oren in fifteen years, and as for his wife, she was dead and buried. He'd often assumed that his breach with Oren had come at the funeral, when he'd stood dry-eyed and mute as the casket containing the mortal remains of his wife was lowered into the ground.

"Don't you feel anything?" Oren had

confronted him with an anger that had apparently been building for years. "Anything at all?"

"I'm relieved that it's over," Willard had said.

It was only much later that he realized telling his son the truth had been a grievous mistake. That was a time, however brief, when he'd grown tired of lies. He never made that error again. Human beings, it became clear to him, thrived on lies; they needed them in order to survive, to be happy, even. Because the truth was often unpleasant, and people didn't care for that. Furthermore, it didn't suit many of them. They'd much rather lie to themselves, have those around them lie to them to preserve the illusion of beauty. Reality wasn't pretty, *that* was the truth.

But now, here in Bali, he wondered whether he was like all the others, weaving a prison of lies around himself to blot out the truth. For years, he'd tunneled his way into NSA like a mole, arriving at last at the safe house in Virginia, where all the lies were housed. For years, he'd told himself it was his duty. Other people, even his own son, seemed like ghosts to him, part of someone else's life. What else did he have? he asked himself over and over as he toiled away as an NSA steward. It was duty, only duty he could connect with.

The NSA mission had been fulfilled. By necessity his cover had been blown with them, and he was free. No one inside CI had yet figured out what to do with him. In fact, so far as the new DCI was concerned, he was on a long-overdue vacation.

Now, free of the servile persona of Willard, the NSA steward, he'd come to realize that being a steward was only a role he'd been playing; a role that wasn't him at all. When Alex Conklin had begun to train him, Willard had had visions of perilous derring-do in far-off corners of the world. He'd read all the James Bond novels countless times; he itched for the adrenaline rush of covert battles. As he became more and more accomplished, as he excelled at his teacher's increasingly difficult exercises, Conklin had begun to confide in him. Then the fatal mistake: As he began to learn Treadstone's secrets, he'd allowed himself the fantasy of becoming Conklin's successor: the master manipulator. But reality had sent him crashing to earth. The Old Man had called, wanting Willard for the role in which he'd already cast him. Willard was sent underground, into NSA, into prison with, it seemed, no chance for a reprieve.

He'd done whatever had been asked of him, had done it well, masterfully, even. That's what everyone had told him. But what had he gotten out of it? Truth, the truth: nothing, not a damn thing.

Now, at last, he had the freedom to fulfill his dream of becoming a master manipulator, of outdoing his old teacher. Because, in the end, Conklin had failed. He'd allowed Leonid Arkadin to slip away, and then, instead of going after Arkadin and bringing him back, he'd forgotten about the Russian and had tried to better him with Jason Bourne. But you can't turn your back on a creation like Arkadin. Willard knew every decision Conklin had taken with Treadstone, he was aware of every misstep. He wouldn't repeat the last one, which was to allow Leonid Arkadin to escape. He'd do better, much better. He'd fulfill Treadstone's final goal. He'd succeed in creating the ultimate fighting machine.

He turned as the gate to Firth's compound opened and Jason Bourne stepped inside. It was twilight, the western sky streaked with sherbet colors, overhead pure cobalt. As he approached, Bourne was holding a small object between the thumb and forefinger of his right hand.

"A .30 M118 shell," Bourne said.

Willard held out his hand and took a close look at it. "Military-grade, specifically made for a sniper rifle." He gave a short, warbly whistle. "No wonder the bullet went clear through you."

"Ever since the 2005 bombings in Kuta and Jimbaran, the government has been fanatic about weaponry. No matter how good this sniper is there's no way he could have smuggled in the gun and ammo." Bourne smiled grimly. "Now, how many places on Bali do you think would carry full-metal-jacket .30-caliber M118 ammo and the rifle that could fire it?"

Arkadin said: "Anyone else have a question?"

Still holding both his weapons, he looked hard into the eyes of each of the ninety-nine remaining Black Legion recruits, and saw in equal measure abject fear and unquestioning obedience. Whatever might happen next, wherever he might lead them, they were his.

It was at this moment that his satellite phone buzzed. He turned on his heel and walked away from the men, who stood silent, rigid as if made of stone. They wouldn't move a muscle, he knew, until he gave the order, which wouldn't be for a while.

Wiping sweat off his ear, he put the phone up to it, said, "What now?"

"How was your visit from Maslov?" Triton's voice reverberated through the ether. As always, it was absolutely accentless English.

"Thrilling," Arkadin said, "as usual." As he spoke, he turned in a complete circle, trying to figure out the location of Triton's men.

"You won't find them, Leonid," Triton said. "You don't want to find them."

Fair enough, Arkadin thought. Triton was the power putting this mission together, or at any rate he worked for the power that was footing the bill, including his own extremely generous pay package. He could see no advantage in antagonizing him.

Arkadin sighed, for the moment putting his rage aside. "What can I do for you?"

"Today, it's what I can do for you," Triton replied. "Our timetable has been moved up."

"Moved up?" Arkadin glanced at the men, well conditioned but untrained for this mission. "I told you at the outset that I needed three weeks, and you assured me—"

"That was then, this is now," Triton said. "The theoretical stage has passed; we're now in real time, and the clock that's ticking belongs neither to you nor to me."

Arkadin felt his muscles contract as they did just before a physical confrontation. "What's happened?"

"The cat is about to come out of the bag."

Arkadin frowned. "What the fuck does that mean?"

"It means," Triton said, "that evidence is quickly coming to light. Incontrovertible evidence that will set everything in motion. There's no turning back now."

"I knew that from the beginning," Arkadin snapped. "So did Maslov."

"You have until Saturday to carry out your mission."

Arkadin nearly jumped. "What?"

"There is no other recourse."

Triton disconnected with a finality that rang like gunfire in Arkadin's ear.

Willard wanted to go with him, but Bourne refused. Willard was smart enough to understand it; he simply wanted his desire on the record. During the time Bourne was recovering, Willard had amassed a list of a baker's dozen individuals on the island either known or suspected of trading in contraband weapons, but only one who reputedly dealt in the highly specialized sniper's rifles and full-metal ammo that had been used to shoot Bourne. On an island as small as Bali it would have been a breach of the security net he'd thrown around Bourne to canvass all of the purported dealers—it would have drawn too much attention to himself.

Firth rented Bourne a car, and he drove into the chaos of the capital city of Denpasar. It wasn't difficult to locate the Badung Market, but finding a place to park was another matter. Finally, he found an area presided over by an old man with a split-melon smile.

Bourne wove through the spice and vegetable areas to the rear, where the butchers and the meat vendors had their stalls. Willard had said that the man he wanted looked like a frog, and he wasn't far off the mark.

The vendor was selling a brace of suckling pigs, live, still trussed to bamboo poles, to a young woman who by her dress and attitude must work for someone with money and status. People were queued up at the next stall to buy loins and breasts, and cleavers came down on sinew and bone, blood flying like the blooming of flowers.

As soon as the young woman had paid for her pigs and signaled for two waiting men to take them away, Bourne stepped up and addressed the squat man. His name was Wayan, which meant "first." All Balinese were given their names based on the order of their birth, first through fourth; the fifth child, if there was one, became Wayan again.

"Wayan, I need to speak with you."

The vendor regarded Bourne with indifference. "If you wish to buy a pig—?"

Bourne shook his head.

"They're the best on the island, ask anyone."

"Another matter," Bourne said. "In private."

Wayan smiled blandly, spread his hands. "As you can plainly see there is no privacy here. If you don't wish to make a purchase—"

"I didn't say that."

Wayan's eyes narrowed. "I don't know what you're talking about."

He was about to turn away when Bourne produced five hundred-dollar bills. Wayan glanced down at the money and something flickered behind his eyes. Bourne was willing to bet it was greed.

Wayan licked his thick lips. "Unfortunately, I don't have that many pigs."

"I only want one."

As if by magic, the .30-caliber M118 casing Bourne had found in Tenganan appeared between his fingers. He dropped it into the center of Wayan's palm.

"One of yours, I believe."

The pig merchant, recalcitrant still, merely shrugged.

Bourne flourished another five hundred in a tight roll. "I don't have time to bargain," he said.

Wayan gave Bourne a sharp look, then, gathering up the thousand, jerked his head for Bourne to follow him.

Contrary to what he had said, there was an enclosed space at the rear of the stall. On a rickety bamboo bench sat several paring and boning knives. As Bourne followed Wayan inside a burly man rushed him from the left. At the same time, a tall man stepped toward him from the right.

Bourne slammed the burly man in the face, breaking his nose, ducked under the grasp of the tall one, and, rolling himself into a ball, launched himself across the small space. He crashed into the bamboo poles, sending the pigs and knives down around him. Grabbing a paring knife, he cut the bonds of three of the piglets. Squealing in their newfound freedom, they ran across the floor, forcing both Wayan and the tall man to dance out of the way.

Bourne threw the paring knife into the meat of the tall man's left thigh. His squeal was indistinguishable from those of the piglets, which continued to run wildly. Ignoring them, Bourne grabbed Wayan by his shirtfront, but just then the thickset man grabbed a boning knife off the floor and launched himself at Bourne, who swung Wayan between them. The moment the attacker checked his knife thrust, Bourne kicked the weapon out of his hand, took him down, and slammed the back of his head against the floor. His eyes rolled up in their sockets.

Bourne rose, grabbed Wayan to keep him from fleeing, and whipped him around. Slapping him hard across the face, he said, "I told you I didn't have time to bargain. Now you'll tell me who bought that cartridge from you."

"I don't know his name."

Bourne slapped him again, harder this time. "I don't believe you."

"It's true." Wayan's indifference had been ripped away; he was truly frightened. "He was referred to me, but he never told me his name and I never asked. In my business the less I know the better."

That, at least, was true. "What did he look like?"

"I don't remember."

Bourne grabbed him by the throat. "You don't want to lie to me."

"Clearly not." Wayan's eyes rolled wildly in their sockets. His skin had taken on a greenish hue, as if at any moment he was going to be sick. "Okay, looked Russian. He wasn't big, wasn't small. Well muscled, though."

"What else?"

"I don't—" He gave a little yelp as Bourne slapped him again. "He had black hair and his eyes . . . they were light. I don't remember . . ." He held up his hands. "Wait, wait . . . they were gray."

"And?"

"That's it. That's all."

"No, it isn't," Bourne said. "Who recommended him?"

"A client . . ."

"His name." Bourne shook the pig man like a rag doll. "I need his name."

"He'll kill me."

Bourne bent, withdrew the knife from the downed man, and placed the blade against Wayan's throat. "Or I can kill you now." He moved the blade just enough so a trickle of blood ran down Wayan's chest, staining his shirt. "Your choice."

"Don . . ." The pig man gulped. "Don Fernando Hererra . . . He lives in Spain, in the heart of the city of Seville." Without further urging he provided Bourne with his client's address.

"How does Don Hererra make his living?"

"International banking."

Bourne could not keep a smile from curling his lips. "Now, of what use would your services be to an international banker?"

Wayan shrugged. "As I told you, the less I know about my clients the healthier it is for me."

"In the future, you should be more careful." Bourne let go of him, pushed him roughly against the legs of one of the men, who was beginning to stir. "Some clients are just plain toxic."

The moon had been called into the underworld by the ghosts of Anubis and Thoth, leaving only a forsaken starlight in its wake.

"Once again, I was wrong about you," Chalthoum said, but without bitterness. "Your primary mission is this Iranian indigenous group."

When she said nothing, he went on. "I need you to help me."

"You are the state," she said. "How could I possibly help you?"

He looked around, possibly to make sure none of his sentries had returned. Soraya watched him closely. If he was concerned with being overheard by one of his own men, what did that tell her? Had he finally broken away from al Mokhabarat? Had he turned rogue? But no, there was another explanation.

"There's a mole in my division," he said, "someone very high up."

"Amun, you're the head of al Mokhabarat, who—"

"I suspect that it's someone higher up than me." He puffed out his cheeks, let the stale air out of his lungs. "Your contacts, your Typhon people, I think they could find out who the mole is."

"Isn't it your job to ferret out spies and traitors?"

"Don't you think I tried? Here's what I got for my efforts: four agents killed in the line of duty and a severe reprimand about the growing incompetence of my agency." The rage behind his eyes returned full force. "Believe me when I tell you that the threat to me was thinly veiled."

Soraya considered this. Why should she care or help him when his organization might have shot down the plane? She said, "Give me one good reason why I should help you."

"I know your people haven't gotten anywhere with confirming the identity of the Iranian indigenous group—and they won't, I promise you that. But I can."

At that moment a beam of light caused a swath of stars to vanish. Soraya moved several paces to her left in order to get a look at who was coming.

Delia approached over a low rise, the beam of her flashlight playing over them for a moment. Her face was turned into a Halloween mask by the illumination from below.

"I know the origin of the missile that hit the plane."

Chalthoum, with a quick warning glance at Soraya, crossed his arms over his chest. "So?"

"So." Delia took a deep breath, let it all out before she continued. "The missile was a ground-to-air Kowsar 3."

"Iranian." Soraya felt a chill run through her. "Delia, are you certain?"

"I found fragments of the electronic guidance system," her friend said. "They're Chinese, similar to those on the C-701, which is an air-to-surface missile. While the EGS is similar to that of the Sky Dragon, this one had a millimeter-wave radar seeker."

"Which is how it locked on so effectively to the aircraft," Soraya said.

Delia nodded. "That particular EGS is unique to the Kowsar." She shot Soraya a significant look. "This baby's got a speed of just below Mach One; the aircraft had no chance, none at all."

Soraya felt sick to her stomach.

Chalthoum's voice vibrated in genuine fury. "*Yakhrab byuthium!*" May their houses be destroyed! "The Iranians shot down the plane."

And with those words the world moved a giant step closer to war. Not one of the recent crop of regional wars like Vietnam, Afghanistan, and Iraq, which were terrible and bloody enough, but a full-blown world war. A war to end all wars.

Book Two

12

I just got off the phone with the Iranian president," the president said. "He categorically denies any knowledge of the incident."

"Which precisely echoes the official response from their foreign minister," Jaime Hernandez responded. The door opened and the intelligence czar received a stack of printouts from a slim man with dark hair, graying on the sides. He had the bland face of an accountant, but there was something hard and withholding in his eyes that belied that surface assessment.

After checking over the papers, Hernandez nodded and introduced the slim man as Errol Danziger, the NSA's deputy director of signals intelligence. "As you can see," Hernandez said while he handed out the printouts, "we're leaving nothing to chance. This material is strictly senior staff, Eyes Only."

With that, Danziger nodded to them and departed as silently as he'd entered.

Five people ranged around the table in one of the Pentagon's vast electronic war rooms, three levels below the basement. Each had before him identical printouts, which comprised the latest findings from the joint forensics team sent to Cairo as well as up-to-the-minute intelligence assessments of the rapidly morphing situation. Paper shredders stood guard beside each of the leather-backed chairs.

As if Hernandez's pause was a cue, Secretary of Defense Halliday said, "Of course they categorically deny their involvement, but the provocation is serious and they're behind it."

"They can't refute the evidence we delivered to them," said Jon Mueller, the head of the Department of Homeland Security.

"And yet they have." The president sighed deeply. "That very issue occupied a good part of my contentious phone conversation. Their claim is that our forensics team rigged the 'so-called evidence'—their president's exact phrase."

"Why would he give the order to shoot down one of our planes?" Veronica Hart asked.

At which Halliday shot her a withering look. "He's tired of taking heat for their nuclear program. We've been pushing them, now they're pushing back."

"The way I see it, this provocation actually serves two purposes," Hernandez offered. "As Bud accurately points out, it redirects the international spotlight away from their nuclear program while at the same time serving as a warning to us—and the rest of the world, for that matter—to back off."

"Let me get this straight." Hart leaned forward. "You're saying they've decided to go beyond their long-standing threats to close off the Straits of Hormuz to oil traffic."

Mueller nodded. "That's right."

"But surely they must know that's suicidal."

Halliday watched this exchange much

as a hawk follows two rabbits racing across a field. Now he pounced. "We've all suspected that the Iranian president is mentally unbalanced."

"A mad hatter," Hernandez affirmed.

Halliday agreed. "But far more dangerous." He looked around the room, his face eerily lit by reflections from the large flat-panel computer monitors ranged along the walls. "Now we have incontrovertible proof."

Hernandez gathered up the printouts, aligning their corners. "I think we should take our findings public. Share them with the media, not just our allies."

Halliday looked to the president. "I concur, sir. And then we convene a special session of the UN Security Council that you address personally. We need to formally give attribution to this cowardly act of terrorism."

"We need to charge and condemn Iran," Mueller added. "They've committed nothing short of an act of war."

"Right." Hernandez hunched his shoulders like a prizefighter in the ring. "Bottom line, we've got to move against them militarily."

"Now, that *would* be suicidal," Hart said emphatically.

"I agree with the DCI," Halliday said.

This response was so unexpected that Hart goggled at him for a moment. Then he continued and everything was made clear to her.

"Going to war with Iran would be a mistake. Just as we're on the verge of winning the war in Iraq, we're obliged to redeploy our troops back to Afghanistan. No, a frontal assault on Iran would, in my estimation, be a grave misstep. Not only would it stretch our already overtaxed military personnel, but the consequences for other countries in the region, especially Israel, could be catastrophic. However, if we could destroy the current Iranian regime from within—now, that would be a worthy goal."

"To do that we would need a proxy," Hernandez said, as if on cue. "A destabilizing influence."

Halliday nodded. "Which, by dint of hard work, we now have in the form of this new indigenous revolutionary group inside Iran. I say we hit Iran on two fronts: diplomatically through the United Nations and militarily by backing this MIG in every way possible: money, arms, strategic advisers, the works."

"I agree," Mueller said. "However, to implement the MIG initiative we'll need a black budget."

"And we'll have to have it yesterday," Hernandez added, "which means keeping Congress in the dark."

Halliday laughed, but there was an altogether serious look on his face. "So what else is new? The only thing those people are interested in is getting reelected. As for what's good for the country, they haven't got a clue."

The president placed his elbows on the polished table, his fists against his mouth in a pose of deep meditation that was emblematic of him. As he processed the decisions, their implications, and their possible consequences, his eyes flicked from one of his advisers to the next. At length, his gaze returned to the DCI. "Veronica, we haven't heard from you. What's your opinion of this scenario?"

Hart considered for a moment; her response was too important to rush it. She was aware of Halliday's eyes on her, glittering and avid. "There's no question that the missile that killed our citizens was an Iranian Kowsar 3 so I agree with the diplomatic response, and the sooner the better because gathering a worldwide consensus is crucial."

"You can forget about China and Russia," Halliday said. "They're too tightly allied with Iran economically to take our side no matter the evidence, which is why we need the third column to foment revolution from the inside out."

Now we come to the crux of it, Hart thought. "My problem with the military part is that we've tried the third-column option many times in many places, including Afghanistan, and what did it get us? The rise to power of the Taliban, an indigenous revolutionary group, and Osama bin Laden, among other very nasty extremist groups turned terrorists."

"This time it's different," Halliday insisted. "We have assurances from the leaders of this group. Its philosophy is moderate, democratic, in short, Western-oriented."

The president tapped his fingers on the table. "It's settled then. We go forward with this two-pronged attack. I'll set the diplomatic wheels in motion. In the meantime,

Bud, draw up a preliminary budget for your MIG. The sooner you have it, the sooner we can get rolling, but I don't want it anywhere near my desk or the White House, for that matter. In fact, I was never at this meeting." He looked at his advisers as he rose. "Let's make this work, people. We owe it to the hundred and eighty-one innocent Americans who lost their lives in this missile attack."

Veronica Hart watched Moira Trevor walk into her office, as cool, as elegant as always. And yet she recognized something dark and squirmy behind her former colleague's eyes that sent a shiver down her spine.

"Take a seat," Veronica said from behind her desk, still not believing this was happening. When she had left Black River she'd been certain she'd never have to see, let alone deal with, Moira Trevor again. And yet here the woman was, skirt rustling drily as she sat facing her, one knee crossed over the other, back as straight as any military officer.

"I imagine you're as surprised as I am," Moira said.

Hart said nothing; instead she continued to stare into Moira's brown eyes, trying to read the reason for her visit. But after a moment, she abandoned the effort. It was useless to try to peer behind that stony facade, she knew that all too well.

She processed what she could get, though: Moira's swollen and bandaged left arm, the minor cuts and scrapes on her face and the backs of her hands. She could not help saying: "What the hell happened to you?"

"That's what I came here to tell you," Moira said.

"No, you came here for help." Hart leaned forward, elbows on the desk. "It's damn difficult being on the outside, isn't it?"

"Jesus, Ronnie."

"What? The past is lying in wait for both of us like a serpent in the grass."

Moira nodded. "I suppose it is."

"You suppose?" Hart cocked her head. "Pardon me if I don't wax sentimental. You were the one who made the threat. What were your actual words?" She pursed her lips. "Oh, yes, 'Ronnie, I will fuck you up for this, I'll rain down a shitstorm on you like no other.'" Hart sat back. "Did I leave out anything?" She felt her pulse accelerating. "And now here you are."

Moira stared at her in stony silence.

Hart turned to a sideboard, poured out a tall glass of ice water, pushed it across the desk. For a moment, Moira did nothing. Perhaps, Hart thought, she didn't know whether taking it would be a sign of trust or of capitulation.

Moira reached out then, very deliberately swung the back of her hand against the glass, pitching it hard against the wall, where it smashed, water and tiny glass shards sparkling in the air like a burst from a cannon. By this time Moira was on her feet, her arms rigid, her fists on the desktop.

Immediately two men entered the office, their guns drawn.

"Back off, Moira." Hart's voice was at once low and steely.

Moira, refusing to sit back down, turned her back on Hart and stalked across the carpet to the other side of the office.

The DCI waved at the two men, who holstered their sidearms and backed out. When the door had shut behind them, she steepled her fingers and waited for Moira to cool off. After a time, she said, "Now why don't you tell me what the hell is going on?"

When Moira turned around, she had, indeed, gathered herself. "You've got it all wrong, Ronnie. I'm the one who's going to help you."

While his men were burying Farid, Arkadin sat on a rock outcropping in the sapphire Azerbaijani twilight. Even without the rhythmic sound of pickaxes and the sight of the corpse sprawled in the dirt, the atmosphere would have been suffused with melancholy. The wind blew fitfully, like the panting of a dog; the tribesmen of the region had turned their faces to Mecca, on their knees in prayer, their submachine guns beside them. Beyond the dun-colored hills lay Iran, and all at once Arkadin was homesick for Moscow. He missed the cobblestone streets, the onion domes, the late-night clubs where he reigned supreme. Most of all, he missed the endless array of tall, blond, blue-eyed *dyevs* in whose perfumed flesh he could lose himself, blotting out the memory of Devra. Though he had loved her, he hated her now, because she wasn't really dead. Like a specter, she haunted him night and day, driving him to revenge himself on Jason Bourne, the last link to her life—and her murder. To make matters even worse, it was also Bourne who'd killed Mischa, Arkadin's mentor and best friend. If it hadn't been for Mischa Tarkanian, Arkadin doubted he'd ever have survived his ordeal in Nizhny Tagil.

Mischa and Devra, the two most important people in his life, both dead because of Jason Bourne. Bourne had a lot to pay for, Christ, did he ever.

The men were almost finished with the grave. A pair of vultures, black shadows against the dimly glimmering sky, turned in lazing circles. *I'm like those vultures*, he thought. *Patiently waiting for my moment to strike.*

Perched on his rock, knees drawn up, he turned his satellite phone over and over in the palm of his hand. Amazingly, several good things had happened because of Willard's call. Willard was a mole, not a field man, and he'd made a fatal mistake: His ego had gotten the better of him. He should have quietly taken Ian Bowles apart, buried the pieces, and gone on with his business. Of course he'd wanted to know who'd sent Bowles, but his mistake was in announcing himself to Arkadin—worse, in warning him—because he'd as much as told Arkadin that Bourne was still alive. Why else would he be at Dr. Firth's compound? Why else would he have killed Bowles? Now Arkadin had proof that Bourne was still alive, though how Bourne managed to survive a shot to the heart was something that nagged at him. Whatever else he might be, Bourne was no superman. Why hadn't he been killed?

With a sharp shake of his head, Arkadin set the imponderable aside for the moment. He dialed a number on his phone. Bowles had been nothing more than a temporary stopgap, someone to make a survey and report back. He'd failed; now it was time to bring in the big guns.

The men unceremoniously threw Farid into the grave. Sweaty and ill tempered, they had long ago lost patience with their normally solemn task. Farid had violated the laws of the group; he was no longer one of their own. Good, Arkadin thought, lesson learned.

The line was ringing.

"Are you set up with the job?" Arkadin said as soon as the familiar voice answered. "Good. Because I've decided to play it your way, and now the clock is ticking. I'll be sending you the last-minute details within the hour."

Two men began to shovel dirt over the body; the others spat into the grave.

The DCI shook her head. "Moira, I'm afraid I'm just not feeling it."

The cords of Moira's neck stood out. How long had she waited for this confrontation? "Did you feel it when you gave me up in Safed Koh?" Safed Koh was the local name for the White Mountains in eastern Afghanistan, where the notorious Tora Bora caves tunneled their way across the border into terrorist-controlled western Pakistan.

Hart spread her hands. "I never gave you up."

"Really?" Moira advanced on her. "Then please tell me how I was taken prisoner in the dead of night and held hostage for six days on Mount Sikaram with nothing to eat and only polluted water to drink."

"I have no idea."

"Whatever bacteria was in that water put me out of commission for three weeks after that"—Moira kept coming closer to the front edge of Hart's desk—"during which time you led my mission—"

"It was a Black River mission."

"—that I'd planned for, trained for. A mission I'd wanted more than anything."

Hart tried for a smile, missed. "That mission was a success, Moira."

"Meaning it wouldn't have been a success if I'd been in charge?"

"You said it, I didn't."

"You thought I was a hothead."

"That's right," Hart acknowledged, "I do."

The deliberate present tense brought Moira up short. "So you still think—"

The DCI spread her hands. "Look at yourself. What would *you* think if you were me?"

"I'd be wanting to know how Moira Trevor could help me take down my one true nemesis."

"And who would that be?"

She said it blandly, but Moira discerned the quickening of interest behind her eyes. "The man who's had it in for you from the moment the president floated your name to take over the DCI position. Bud Halliday."

For a moment Moira was certain she felt the brief crackle of heat lightning in the room. Then Veronica Hart pushed her chair back and stood up.

"What precisely do you want from me?"

"I want an admission of your guilt."

"A signed confession? You must be joking."

"No," Moira said. "Just between us chickens."

Hart shook her head. "Why would I do that?"

"So that we can have something other than the past, so that we can go on, so that there isn't this poison between us."

The telephone rang several times, but the DCI ignored it. Finally, it stopped, and only the small sounds remained: the humming of the air vents, the soft intakes of their breathing, the beating of their hearts.

Hart sighed then, a long exhalation of breath. "You don't want to hear this."

At last! Moira thought. "Try me."

"What I did," Hart said slowly, "I did for the good of the company."

"Bullshit, you did it for yourself!"

"You were never in any real danger," Hart persevered, "I made sure of that."

Instead of feeling better Moira was feeling more and more wronged. "How *could* you have made sure of it?"

"Moira, can't we leave it at that?"

Moira was back in her attack position, leaning over the desk, resting on her white knuckles. "End it," she said. "End it now."

"All right." The DCI raked her fingers through her hair. "I was sure you'd be okay because Noah said he'd take care of you."

"Oh." Moira felt the floor open up beneath her. Dizziness forced her back to the chair, where she sat heavily, staring at nothing. "Noah." Then it hit her and she felt sick. "It was all Noah's idea, wasn't it?"

Hart nodded. "I was his runner. I did his dirty work for him. I was required to be the one you hated when you came back so he could keep using you when he saw fit."

"Jesus God." Moira stared down at her hands. "He didn't trust me."

"Not for that mission." Hart said it so softly that Moira had to lean forward to hear her. "But for others, as you know perfectly well, he preferred you."

"No matter." Moira felt numb from the inside out. "What a shitty thing to do."

"Yes, it was." Hart sat back down. "In fact, it was the reason I left Black River."

Moira looked up, her eyes focusing on the woman who had been her archenemy for so long. She felt as if her mind had been stuffed with steel wool. "I don't understand."

"I'd done a lot of awful things while at Black River; you're the last person I have to explain that to. But this—what Noah had me do—" She shook her head. "Afterward I was so ashamed of myself I couldn't bear to face you, so after the mission was completed I went to see you. I wanted to apologize—"

"I wouldn't let you; I cursed you instead."

"I couldn't blame you. I wasn't angry at the hurtful things you said, who was more entitled? And yet it was a lie. I wanted to disobey orders, to tell you the truth. Instead, I quit. It was a cowardly act, really, because then I was certain I'd never have to face you."

"And now here we are." Moira felt drained, sick at heart. She'd known Noah was amoral, she knew he was devious; he wouldn't have risen to his position at Black River otherwise. But she'd never have thought him capable of fucking her over so thoroughly, of using her like a piece of meat.

"Here we are," Hart agreed.

Moira felt a shudder run through her. "Noah is the reason I'm in this situation, the reason I'm here without a place to go."

The DCI frowned. "What do you mean? You have your own organization."

"It's been compromised, either by Noah or by the NSA."

"There's a big difference between Black River and the NSA."

Moira looked at Hart and realized she no longer knew how she felt about anyone or anything. How did one recover from a betrayal like this? All at once she was suffused with a terrible fury. If Noah had been in the room she would have grabbed the lamp off Veronica Hart's desk and swung it into the side of his face. But no, better he wasn't. She recalled a line from *Les Liaisons Dangereuses,* her favorite novel because it involved drawing room spies: *Revenge is a dish best served cold.* And in this case, she thought, in a perfectly clean kitchen. She took a deep breath and let it out slowly and completely.

"Not in this case," she said. "Jay Weston, my operative, was killed and I barely escaped being gunned down because Black River and the NSA are feathering the same nest, and whatever they've hatched is so big they're willing to kill anyone who comes sniffing around."

Into the ensuing shocked silence, Hart said, "I do hope you have proof of that allegation."

In response, Moira handed over the thumb drive she'd gotten from Jay Weston's corpse. Ten minutes later the DCI looked up from her computer and said, "Moira, so far as I can make out all you have is a motorcycle cop no one can find, and a thumb drive full of nonsense."

"Jay Weston didn't die in an automobile accident," Moira said hotly, "he was shot to death. And Steve Stevenson, the undersecretary for acquisition, technology and logistics at the DoD, confirmed that Jay was killed because he was on to something. He told me that ever since the news of the jetliner explosion hit the wires the atmosphere at DoD and the Pentagon has been shrouded in a toxic fog. Those were his words exactly."

Still staring at Moira, Hart picked up the phone and asked her assistant to connect her to Undersecretary Stevenson at the Department of Defense.

"Don't," Moira said. "He was scared shitless. I had to beg him to even meet with me, and he's a client."

"I'm sorry," the DCI said, "but it's the only way." She waited a moment, drumming her fingers on the desktop. Then her expression shifted. "Yes, Undersecretary Stevenson, this is— Oh, I see. When is he expected back?" Her gaze returned to Moira. "Surely you have to know when— Yes, I see. Never mind, I'll try again later. Thank you."

She replaced the receiver and her finger drumming began again.

"What happened?" Moira asked. "Where's Stevenson?"

"Apparently, no one knows. He left the office at eleven thirty-five this morning."

"That was to meet me."

"And as yet hasn't returned."

Moira dug out her phone, called Stevenson's cell, which went right to voice mail.

"He's not answering." She put her phone away.

Hart stared hard at the screen of her computer terminal and mouthed the word *Pinprickbardem,* then returned her gaze to Moira. "I think we'd better find out what the hell has happened to the undersecretary."

Wayan, well pleased with his sales for the day, was in the enclosed rear of his stall, preparing the one or two pigs left unsold to take back to his farm, when the man appeared. He didn't hear him for all the shouted cacophony as the huge market began to close for the night.

"You're the pig man named Wayan."

"Closed," Wayan said without looking up. "Please come back tomorrow." When he discerned no movement he began to turn, saying, "And in any event, you cannot come back—"

The powerful blow caught him square on the jaw, sending him reeling into the piglets, which squealed in alarm. So did Wayan. He barely had time to see the man's rough-edged face when he was hauled upright.

The second punch buried itself in his stomach, sending him breathless, to his knees.

He peered up through watering eyes, gasping and retching pitifully, at the impossibly tall man. He wore a black suit so shiny and ill fitting it was hideous. There was stubble on his face, blue as the shadows of evening, and coal-black eyes that regarded Wayan without either pity or conscience. One side of his neck was imprinted with a rather delicate scar, like a pink ribbon on a child's birthday present, that ran up into his jaw where the muscle had been severed and was now puckered. The other side of his neck was tattooed with a clutch of three skulls: one looking straight out, the other two in profile, looking forward and behind him.

"What did you tell Bourne?"

The man spoke English with a guttural accent that Wayan, in his addled state, couldn't place. A European, but not British or French. Perhaps a Romanian or a Serb.

"What did you tell Bourne?" he repeated.

"W-who?"

The man shook Wayan until his teeth rattled. "The man who came to see you. The American. What did you tell him?"

"I don't know what y—"

Wayan's attempt at a denial turned into a grunt of pain as the man took his right forefinger and bent it back until it snapped. The rush of blood from Wayan's head almost made him lose consciousness, but the man slapped him twice so that his eyes focused on his tormentor.

The man leaned in so that Wayan could smell his sour odor, knew that he must have just flown in without having showered or changed his clothes.

"Do not fuck with me, you little prick." He already had a grip on the middle finger of Wayan's right hand. "You have five seconds."

"Please, you're wrong about this!"

He gave a little yelp as the man snapped his middle finger. All the blood seemed to have left his head. As before, the man slapped his jowls several times.

"Two down, eight to go," the man said, trapping Wayan's right thumb.

Wayan's mouth opened wide, like a fish

gasping for air. “All right, all right. I told him where to find Don Fernando Hererra.”

The man sat back on his haunches and let out a short breath. “You are so fucking unreliable.” Then he turned, picked up a length of bamboo pole, and without the slightest expression drove it through Wayan’s right eye.

13

For the next eighteen hours Arkadin did nothing but train his recruits. He did not allow them to eat, to sleep, or to do more than take breaks to urinate. Thirty seconds, that's all they had to empty their bladders into the red Azerbaijani dust. The first man who took longer received a solid whack from Arkadin's baton behind his knee; the first man became the only man to disobey that or any other order, for that matter.

As Triton had warned him, he had five days to turn these killers into a platoon of shock troops. Easier said than done, true, but Arkadin had plenty of experience to draw from, because something similar had been done to him when he was a young man in Nizhny Tagil and on the run from having killed Stas Kuzin and a third of his gang.

Nizhny Tagil was more or less founded on iron ore so rich that an enormous quarry was immediately dug. This was in 1698. By 1722 the first copper-smelting plant was established and a town began to stretch its bones, groaning around the plant and the quarry, a vice- and crime-ridden machine to service and house exhausted workers. A hundred thirteen years later the first Russian steam locomotive was constructed there. Like most frontier towns ruled by industry and its money-hungry barons, there was a raw and lawless nature about the place that the semi-civilizing influence of the modern-day city never was able to tame, let alone eradicate. Possibly that was why the federal government had ringed the toxic site with high-security penitentiaries, blinding spotlights bleaching the night.

There were only lonely sounds in Nizhny Tagil, or else frightening, like the faraway hoot of the train whistle echoing off the Ural Mountains or the sudden shriek of one of the prison sirens; like the wail of a child lost in the filthy streets or the wet snap of bones breaking during a drunken brawl.

As Arkadin sought to evade the armada of gang members fanning out through the streets and slums of the city, he learned to follow the yellow curs slinking through shadowed alleyways, their tails curled between their legs. Then quite suddenly he ran across two men canvassing the very same network of exhausted backwaters that a moment before had seemed safe enough. Turning, he let them believe they were running him down. As he turned a corner, he snatched up a piece of splintered wood, part of a discarded bed set, and, crouching down, slammed it across the lead man's legs. The man shouted, toppling forward. Arkadin was prepared, grabbing hold of him, pitching him down so that his face slammed into the filthy concrete. The second man was on him, but Arkadin drove a cocked elbow into his Adam's apple. As the man began to choke, Arkadin wrested the pistol from his hand and shot him point-blank. Then he turned the gun on the first man and put a bullet through the back of his head.

From that moment on he knew the streets were too dangerous for him; he needed to find a sanctuary. He thought of getting himself arrested and thrown into one of the nearby prisons as a way of protecting himself, but quickly discarded the notion. What might have worked in another part of the country was out of the question in Nizhny Tagil, where the cops were so corrupt it was often impossible to distinguish them from the city's criminals. Not that he was out of ideas; far from it. His experiences thus far had made clever thinking a way of life.

Continuing onward, he considered and rejected any number of possibilities, all of which were too public, too riddled with potential snitches who'd be on the lookout for him in exchange for the promise of a bottle of real liquor or a night of free rutting with underage girls. Finally, he hit upon what he was certain was the perfect solution: He'd hole up in the basement of his own building, where the gang and its maniacal new boss, Lev Antonin, were still headquartered. Lev Antonin's avowed goal was to find and destroy the murderer of the man he'd succeeded. He wouldn't rest, wouldn't let his men rest until Arkadin's severed head was brought to him.

Because Arkadin was the one who had bought it during the acquisition phase of his real estate business, he was intimately familiar with every square inch of the building. He knew, for instance, that an updated sewage system had been planned for the building, started, but never completed. Through a long-vacant municipal lot overgrown with weeds and refuse, he entered this dank and disused symbol of his birth city, a repellent underground conduit that stank of decomposition and death, emerging at length into the cavernous bowels of the building. He would have laughed at how easily this was accomplished had he not been acutely aware of his plight. He was a prisoner of the one place he wanted most desperately to leave.

The plane lurched sickeningly and Bourne woke with a start. Rain drummed hard against the Perspex window. He'd dozed off, dreaming of the conversation he'd had with

Tracy Atherton, the young woman seated beside him. In his dream, they were talking about Holly Marie Moreau instead of Francisco Goya.

He had slept deeply and without dreaming during the twenty-three-plus–hour trip from Bali, first to Bangkok, then Madrid on Thai Air. This flight, from Madrid to Seville on Iberia, was the shortest one, but now it had turned miserable. Sudden air pockets within a lashing storm caused the plane to lurch and dip. Tracy Atherton went quiet and still, staring straight ahead while her complexion turned ashen. Bourne held her head while she vomited twice into the airsick bag he pulled from the seat back.

She was a whisper-thin blonde with large blue eyes and a smile that seemed to wrap around her face. Her teeth were white and even, her nails cut straight across, her only bits of jewelry a gold wedding band and diamond stud earrings, large enough to be expensive but small enough to be discreet. She wore a flame-colored blouse under a lightweight silver silk suit with a pencil skirt and tapered jacket.

"I work at the Prado in Madrid," she'd

said. “A private collector hired me to authenticate a recently unearthed Goya that I think is a fake.”

“Why do you say that?” he’d asked.

“Because it’s purported to be one of Goya’s Black Paintings, done later in life when he was already deaf and going mad with encephalitis. There are fourteen in the series. This collector believes he owns the fifteenth.” She shook her head. “Frankly, history isn’t on his side.”

As the weather calmed, she thanked Bourne and went off to the toilet to clean up.

He waited several seconds, then reached down, unzipped her slim attaché case, and rifled through the contents. To her, he was Adam Stone, the name on the passport Willard had given him before he’d left Dr. Firth’s compound. According to the legend Willard had devised, he was a venture capitalist on his way to see a potential client in Seville. Ever mindful of the unknown assailant who’d tried to kill him, he was wary of anyone sitting next to him, anyone striking up a conversation with him, anyone wanting to know where he’d been and where he was going.

Inside the attaché case were photos—some quite detailed—of the Goya painting, a horrific study of a man being drawn and quartered by four rearing, snorting stallions while army officers lounged around, smoking, laughing, and playfully poking the victim with their bayonets.

Along with these photos was a set of X-rays, also of the painting, accompanied by a letter authenticating the painting as a genuine Goya, signed by a Professor Alonzo Pecunia Zuñiga, a Goya specialist at the Museo del Prado in Madrid. With nothing else of interest, Bourne returned the sheets to the attaché case and rezipped it. Why had the woman lied to him about not knowing if the painting was a genuine Goya? Why had she lied about working for the Prado when, in his letter, Zuñiga addressed her as an outsider, not as an esteemed colleague of the museum? He'd find out soon enough.

He stared out the window at the infinity of gray-white, turned his mind to his quarry. He'd used Firth's computer to gather information on Don Fernando Hererra. For one thing, Hererra was Colombian, not Spanish. Born in Bogotá in 1946, the youngest child of four, he was shipped off to England for university studies, where he took a First in economics at Oxford. Then, inexplicably, for a time his life took another path entirely. He worked as a *petrolero* for the Tropical Oil Company, working his way up to *cuñero*—a pipe capper—and beyond, moving from camp to camp, each time raising the output of barrels per day. Ever restless, he pushed on, buying a camp dirt-cheap because Tropical Oil's experts were certain it was in decline. Sure enough, he turned it around and, within three years, sold it back to Tropical Oil for a tenfold profit.

That's when he got into venture capital, using his outsize profits to move into the more stable banking sector. He bought a small regional bank in Bogotá, which had been on the verge of failing, changed its name, and spent the decade of the 1990s building it into a national powerhouse. He expanded into Brazil, Argentina, and, more recently, Spain. Two years ago he'd vigorously resisted a buyout by Banco Santander, preferring to remain his own master. Now his Aguardiente Bancorp, named after the fiery local licorice-flavored liquor of his native country, had more than twenty branches, the last one opening five months before in London where, increasingly, all the international action was.

He had been married twice, had two daughters, both of whom lived in Colombia, and a son, Jaime, whom Don Fernando had installed as the managing director of Aguardiente's London branch. He seemed to be clever, sober, and serious; Bourne could find not the remotest hint of anything sinister about either him or AB, as it was known inside international banking circles.

He felt Tracy's return before her scent of fern and citrus reached him. With a whisper of silk, she slid into the seat beside him.

"Feeling better?"

She nodded.

"How long have you been working at the Prado?" he said.

"About seven months."

But she'd hesitated a moment too long and he knew she was lying. Again, why? What did she have to hide?

"If I remember correctly," Bourne said, "didn't some of Goya's later works come under a cloud of suspicion?"

"In 2003," Tracy said, nodding. "But since then the fourteen Black Paintings have been authenticated."

"But not the one you're going to see."

She pursed her lips. "No one has seen it yet, except for the collector."

"And who is he?"

She looked away, abruptly uncomfortable. "I'm not at liberty to say."

"Surely—"

"Why are you doing this?" Turning back to him, she was abruptly angry. "Do you think me a fool?" Color rose up her neck into her cheeks. "I know why you're on this flight."

"I doubt you do."

"Please! You're on your way to see Don Fernando Hererra, just like I am."

"Don Hererra is your collector?"

"You see?" The light of triumph was in her eyes. "I knew it!" She shook her head. "I'll tell you one thing: You're not going to get the Goya. It's mine; I don't care how much I have to pay."

"That doesn't sound like you work at the

Prado," Bourne said, "or any museum for that matter. And why do you have an unlimited budget to buy a fake?"

She crossed her arms over her breasts and bit her lip, determined to keep her own counsel.

"The Goya isn't a fake, is it?"

Still she said nothing.

Bourne laughed. "Tracy, I promise I'm not after the Goya. In fact, until you mentioned it, I had no idea it existed."

She shot him a look of fear. "I don't believe you."

He took a packet out of his breast pocket, handed it over. "Go on, read it," he said. "I don't mind." Willard really did extraordinary work, he thought, as Tracy opened the document and scanned it.

After a moment, she glanced up at him. "This is a prospectus for a start-up e-commerce company."

"I need backing and I need it quickly, before our rivals get a jump on the market," Bourne lied. "I was told Don Fernando Hererra was the man to cut through the red tape and get the balance of the seed money my group requires yesterday." He couldn't tell her the real reason he needed to see Hererra, and the sooner he convinced her he was an ally the faster she'd take him where he needed to go. "I don't know him at all. If you get me in to see him I'd be grateful."

She handed back the document, which he put away, but her expression remained wary.

"How do I know I can trust you?"

He shrugged. "How do you know anything?"

She thought about this for a moment, then nodded. "You're right. Sorry, I can't help you."

"But I can help you."

She raised an eyebrow skeptically. "Really?"

"I'll get you the Goya for a song."

She laughed. "How could you possibly do that?"

"Give me an hour when we get to Seville and I'll show you."

All leaves have been canceled, all personnel have been recalled from vacations," Amun Chalthoum said. "I've put my entire force to work on finding how the Iranians crossed my border with a ground-to-air missile."

This situation was bad for him, Soraya knew, even if he hadn't already been on shaky ground with some of his superiors. This breach of security had *personal disaster* written all over it. Or did it? What if everything he'd told her was disinformation meant to distract her from the truth: that with the knowledge either of the Egyptian government or of certain ministers too afraid of raising their own voice against Iran, al Mokhabarat had chosen to use the United States as a bellicose proxy?

They'd left Delia, left the crash site, driven through the phalanx of media vultures circling the perimeter, and were now racing along the road at top speed in Amun's four-wheel-drive vehicle. The sun was just above the horizon, filling the bowl of the sky with a pellucid light. Pale clouds lay across the western horizon as if exhausted from swimming through the darkness of the night. A wind blew the last of the morning's coolness against their faces. Soon enough, Amun would have to crank up the windows and put the air on.

After sifting through all the pieces of the blast site in the belly of the plane, the forensics team had put together a 3-D computer rendering of the last fifteen seconds of the flight. As Amun and Soraya huddled around a laptop inside a tent, the head of the team had begun the playback.

"The modeling is still somewhat crude," he'd cautioned, "because of how fast we needed to put this together." When the streaking missile came into the frame, he pointed. "Also, we can't be one hundred percent certain of the missile's actual trajectory. We could be off by a degree or two."

The missile struck the airliner, breaking it in two and sending it earthward in several fiery spirals. Despite what the leader had said the effect was realistic, and chilling.

"What we do know is the Kowsar's maximum range." He pressed a key on the laptop, and the imaging changed to a satellite topographic map of the area. He pointed to a red X. "This is the crash site." Pressing another key caused a blue ring to be superimposed on the area around the site. "The circle shows the missile's maximum range."

"Meaning the weapon had to be fired within that space," Chalthoum said.

Soraya could see that he was impressed.

"That's right." The leader nodded. He was a beefy man, balding, with a typical American beer gut and too-small glasses he kept pushing back up the bridge of his nose. "But we can narrow it down for you even more." His forefinger pressed still another key and a yellow cone appeared on the screen. "The point at the top is where the missile impacted the plane. The bottom is wider because we factored in an error of three percent for our trajectory site."

Once again his finger depressed a key and the scene zoomed in on a square of nearby desert. "As well as we can determine, the missile was launched from somewhere within this area."

Chalthoum took a closer look. "That's, what, a square kilometer?"

"Just under," the leader had said with a small smile of triumph.

This relatively small section of the desert was where they were headed now, hoping to find some sign of the terrorists and their identities. They were part of a convoy, in fact, of five jeeps filled with al Mokhabarat personnel. Soraya found it strange and vaguely disquieting that she was getting used to having them around. She had a map unfolded on her lap. The area they'd seen on the laptop was marked off, and another zoomed image had grid lines through it. A navigator in each of the other jeeps had similar material. Chalthoum's plan was to send a jeep to each corner of the section and work inward, while he and Soraya drove straight to the center and started their part of the search there.

As they rattled along at a breathtaking pace she looked over at Amun, whose face was grim and tight as a fist. But what was he leading her to? Surely if al Mokhabarat was involved, he wouldn't allow her even the faintest glimmering of the truth. Were they on a wild goose chase?

"We'll find them, Amun," she said, more to alleviate the tension than because of any strong conviction.

His laugh was as unpleasant as a jackal's bark. "Of course we will." His tone was dark, sardonic. "But even if by some miracle we do, it's already too late for me. My enemies will use this breach of security against me, they'll say I've brought disgrace not only on al Mokhabarat, but on all of Egypt."

His uncharacteristic tone of self-pity rattled her, made her harden her own voice. "Then why are you bothering with the investigation? Why not simply turn tail and run?"

His dark face turned even darker with the sudden rush of blood to his cheeks. She felt him gathering himself, his muscles tensing, and for a moment she wondered if he was going to strike her. But then, just as quickly as it came, the storm of emotion passed, and now his laugh, when it presented itself, was bright and deep.

"Yes, I should have you at my side always, *azizti*."

Once again she was rattled, this time by his use of the intimate endearment, and she felt a sudden rush of latent affection for him. She could not help wondering whether he was this good an actor, and with this thought came the flush of instant shame because she wanted him to be innocent of involvement in this heinous act. She wanted something from him she felt she couldn't have, certainly never would have if he was guilty. Her heart said he was innocent, but her mind remained dappled in the shadows of suspicion.

He turned to her for a moment, his dark eyes alighting on her. "We *will* find these sons of camel turds, and I will bring them in front of my superiors shackled and on their knees, this I swear on the memory of my father."

Within fifteen minutes they had arrived at a patch of desert that looked not a bit different from the bleak countryside through which they had been traveling. The other four jeeps had peeled off some time ago, their drivers in constant radio contact with Amun and one another. They gave running commentaries as they began their respective searches.

Soraya took up a pair of binoculars and began to scan for any anomalous object, but she wasn't optimistic. The desert itself was their worst enemy because the winds would have shifted the sand, most likely burying anything the terrorists might have inadvertently left behind.

"Anything?" Chalthoum said twenty minutes later.

"No—wait!" She took her eyes from the binocular cups and pointed off to their right. "There, at two o'clock—about a hundred yards."

Chalthoum turned in that direction and put on some speed. "What do you see?"

"I don't know—it looks like a smudge," she said as she trained the binoculars on the spot.

She jumped out of the jeep even as it reached the location. Staggering for two steps from the momentum and the softness of the sand, she pushed on. She was squatting down in front of the dark patch by the time Chalthoum reached her.

"It's nothing," he said with obvious disgust, "just a blackened branch."

"Maybe not."

Reaching out, she used her cupped hands to excavate away from the branch, which was almost fully buried. As the hole widened, Chalthoum helped keep the sand from running back into the hole. About eighteen inches down, her fingertips found something cool and hard.

"The stick is caught on something!" she said excitedly.

But what she unearthed was an empty can of soda, the end of the stick lodged into its opened pop-top. When she pulled the stick out the can fell over, causing a shower of gray ash to scatter from the opening.

"Someone made a fire here," she said. "But there's no way to tell how long the ashes have been here."

"Maybe there is a way."

Chalthoum was staring intently at the spill of ashes, which was more or less the shape of the cone of yellow on the laptop's screen representing the margin of error for the missile launch site.

"Did your father teach you about Nowruz?"

"The Persian pre-revolutionary festival of the new year?" Soraya nodded. "Yes, but we never celebrated it."

"It's had a resurgence in Iran over the past couple of years." Chalthoum upended the can, shook out the contents, and nodded. "There is more ash here than one could reasonably expect for a cooking fire. Besides, a terrorist cell would have pre-

prepared food that wouldn't require heating."

Soraya was racking her brains for the rituals of Nowruz, but in the end she needed Chalthoum to give her a refresher course.

"A bonfire is lit and each member of the family jumps over it while asking for the pale complexion winter breeds to be replaced by healthy red cheeks. Then a feast is consumed during which stories are told for the benefit of the children. As the festival passes from day into night, the fire dies out, then the ashes, which represent winter's bad luck, are buried off in the fields."

"I can hardly believe that Nowruz was observed here by Iranian terrorists," Soraya said.

Chalthoum used the stick to poke around in the ashes. "That looks like a bit of eggshell and here is a piece of burned orange rind. Both an egg and an orange are used at the end of the festival."

Soraya shook her head. "They'd never risk someone seeing the fire."

"True enough," Chalthoum said, "but this would be a perfect place to bury the bad luck of winter." He looked at her. "Do you know when Nowruz began?"

She thought a moment, then her pulse began to race. "Three days ago."

Chalthoum nodded. "And at the moment of Sa'at-I tahvil, when the old year ends and the new one begins, what happens?"

Her heart flipped over. "Cannons are fired."

"Or," Chalthoum said, "a Kowsar 3 missile."

14

Bourne and Tracy Atherton entered Seville late on the third afternoon of the Feria de Abril, the weeklong festival that grips the entire city at Eastertime like a fever. Only weeks before, during the Semana Santa, masses of hooded penitents followed behind magnificently adorned floats, tiered and filigreed like baroque wedding cakes, filled with ranks of white candles and sprays of white flowers, at the center of which sat images of Christ or the Virgin Mary. Bands of colorfully dressed musicians accompanied the floats, playing music both melancholy and martial.

Now as then avenues were blocked off to vehicular traffic, and even on foot many streets were all but impassable because, it seemed, all of Seville was out taking part in or observing the eye-popping pageant.

In the packed Avenida de Miraflores, they pushed their way into an Internet café. It was dark and narrow, the manager behind a cramped desk in back. The entire left-hand wall was taken up with computer stations hooked up to the Internet. Bourne paid for an hour, then waited along the wall for one of the stations to free up. The place was dim with smoke; everyone had a cigarette except the two of them.

"What are we doing here?" Tracy said in a hushed voice.

"I need to find a photo of one of the Prado's Goya experts," Bourne said. "If I can convince Hererra I'm this man, he'll know he's got a very clever fake rather than a real lost Goya."

Tracy's face lit up and she laughed. "You really are a piece of work, Adam." All at once a frown overtook her. "But if you present yourself as this Goya expert, how on earth are you going to get any money out of Don Fernando for your consortium?"

"Simple enough," Bourne said. "The expert leaves and I return as Adam Stone."

A seat opened up and Tracy began to move toward it when Bourne stopped her with a taut shake of his head. When she looked at him questioningly, he spoke to her very softly.

"The man who just walked in—no, don't look at him. I saw him on our flight."

"So what?"

"He was on my Thai Air flight as well," Bourne said. "He's traveled with me all the way from Bali."

She turned her back to him, using a mirror to glance at him briefly. "Who is he?" Her eyes narrowed. "What does he want?"

"I don't know," Bourne said. "But you noticed the scar on the side of his neck that runs up into his jaw?"

She risked another glance in the mirror, then nodded.

"Whoever sent him wants me to know he's there."

"Your rivals?"

"Yes. They're thugs," he improvised. "It's a typical intimidation tactic."

A look of alarm crossed Tracy's face

and she shrank away from him. "What kind of dirty business are you in?"

"It's precisely what I told you," Bourne said. "But the venture capital business is riddled with industrial espionage because being first to market with a new product or idea can often mean the difference between Google or Microsoft buying you out for half a billion dollars or going bust."

This explanation appeared to calm her slightly, but she was clearly still on edge. "What are you going to do?"

"For the moment, nothing."

Bourne crossed the floor and sat down, and Tracy followed him. As he brought up the Museo del Prado on Google, she bent low over his shoulder and said, "Don't bother. The man you want is Professor Alonzo Pecunia Zuñiga."

This was the Prado's Goya expert who'd authenticated Hererra's Goya. Bourne recalled seeing his letter in her attaché case.

Without a word, he typed in the name. He had to scroll through several news items before he came upon a photo of the professor, who was accepting an award from one of the many Spanish foundations concerned with promoting Goya's history and work worldwide.

Alonzo Pecunia Zuñiga was a slim man who appeared to be in his midfifties. He had a dapper spade-shaped beard and thick eyebrows that shaded his eyes like a visor. Bourne checked the date of the photo to be certain it was current. Zooming in on the photo, he printed it out, which cost him an extra couple of euros. Using Google Local, he looked up the addresses of a number of shops.

"Our first stop," he said to Tracy, "is just off Paseo de Cristóbal Colón, around the corner from the Teatro Maestranza."

"What about the man with the scar?" she whispered.

Bourne closed out the screen, then went into the browser cache and deleted both the site history and the cookies from the sites he'd visited. "I'm counting on him following us," he said.

"God." Tracy gave a brief shudder. "I'm not."

The broad paseo ran beside the eastern branch of the Guadalquivir River in the El

Arenal *barrio* of the city. It was the historical district called home by many of the Semana Santa brotherhoods. From the beautiful Maestranza bullring, next door to the massive theater, they could see the thirteenth-century Torre del Oro, the great tower, once clad in gold, part of the fortifications to protect Seville from its ancient enemies, the Muslims of North Africa, the fundamentalist Almohads, Berbers from Morocco who were driven out of Seville and all of Andalusia in 1230 by the armies of the Christian kingdoms of Castile and Aragón.

"Have you ever been to a *corrida*?" Bourne asked.

"No. I hate the idea of bullfighting."

"Here's your chance to see for yourself." Taking her by the hand, he went to the ticket office by the main gate and bought two *sol barreras*, the only front seats left, which were in the sun.

Tracy hung back. "I don't think I want to do this."

"You either come with me," Bourne said, "or I leave you here to be questioned by Scarface."

She stiffened. "He's followed us here?"

Bourne nodded. "Come on." As he

handed his tickets over and pushed her through the entrance, he added, "Don't worry, I'll take care of everything. Trust me."

A ferocious roaring signaled that the *corrida* had already begun. The place was filled with tiers of seats, above which rose a continuous line of decorative arches. As they made their way down the aisle, the first bull was in the process of being tenderized via the *suerte de picar*. The *picadores*, mounted on horses, padded and blindfolded for the animals' protection, drove their short lances into the bull's neck while he expended energy attempting to toss their mounts. The horses had oil-soaked cloths in their ears to keep them from shying at the roaring of the crowd. Their vocal cords had been cut to render them mute so as not to distract the bull.

"Okay," Bourne said, handing her a ticket. "I want you to go get a beer from the stand over there. Drink it in back with plenty of people around you, then make your way to our seats."

"And where will you be?"

"Never mind," he said, "just do as I've told you and wait for me in the seat."

He'd caught sight of the man with the pink scar, who'd entered the *corrida* high up to give himself a better vantage point. Bourne watched Tracy picking her way back to the refreshment stalls, then he took out his cell phone and pretended to talk to a contact he wanted Scarface to believe he was meeting here. With an emphatic nod, he put the cell away and made his way around the ring. He had to find a place in shadow, private enough for a meet, where he could handle Scarface without interference.

Out of the corner of his eye, he saw Scarface glance briefly at Tracy before moving down one of the aisles that intersected with the lowest tier where Bourne was heading.

Bourne had been here before and knew the basic layout. He was looking for the *toril*, the enclosure where the bulls were kept, because he knew a corridor near it led to the toilets on this side of Maestranza. A couple of young *toreros* were leaning on the bull gate. Beside them the matador, having exchanged his pink-and-gold cape for the red one, stood still as death, waiting for the moment of *suerte de matar*, when he would enter the ring with nothing but his sword, his cape, and his athletic skill to bring down the snorting, panting beast. At least, that's how these *corrida* fans saw it. Others, like the Asociación para la defensa del anima, saw quite another picture.

As he neared the *toril*, there came a jolt against the door that sent the young *toreros* scattering in fright. The matador briefly turned his attention to the animal in the pen.

"Good, you are eager to come out," he said in Spanish, "into the smell of blood."

Then he returned his attention to the *corrida* proper where, as the bull tired, his moment was upon him.

"*Fuera!*" came the fevered cries from the aficionados. "*Fuera!*" Get out! they called to the *picadores*, for fear their lances were weakening the bull too much, that the final confrontation would not be the blood match they craved.

Now, as the *picadores* backed their mounts away from the beast, the matador was on the move, entering the *corrida* as his underlings exited it. The tumult from the crowd was almost ear shattering. No one paid the slightest attention to Bourne as he reached the area near the *toril*, save for Scarface who, Bourne could see now, had the tattoo of three skulls on the opposite side of his neck. They were crude, ugly, without doubt prison tattoos, most likely received inside a Russian penitentiary. And this man was more than an intimidator. A skull meant that he was a professional killer: three skulls, three kills.

Bourne was at the very end of this section of the stands—beyond was a decorative archway that led back to the area under the stands. Just below him was the wall that divided the pit where the *toreros* crouched to evade the charges of the bull. At the end of that, to Bourne's right, was the *toril*.

Scarface was rapidly approaching, moving down the aisle and across the tiers like a ghost or a wraith. Bourne turned and passed through the archway and down an incline into the shadowed interior. Immediately he was hit by a miasma of human urine and strong animal musk. To his left was the concrete corridor that led to the toilets. There was a door along the wall to his right, outside of which was a uniformed guard.

As he walked toward this tall, slim man a figure blotted out the daylight: Scarface. Bourne approached the guard, who told him, rather brusquely, he had no business being in an area so close to the bulls. Smiling, Bourne placed himself between the guard and Scarface, then reached out and, talking amiably to the guard, pressed the artery at the side of his neck. Even as the guard reached for his weapon, Bourne blocked him with his other hand. The man tried to fight, but Bourne, moving swiftly, used an elbow to temporarily paralyze the guard's right shoulder. He was rapidly losing consciousness from loss of blood to his brain and, as he fell forward, Bourne held him up, continued talking to him because he wanted Scarface to think that this was the man he'd spoken to on his cell, a colleague of the man Bourne had come here to see. It was essential that he keep the fiction going now that Scarface was closing in.

Taking the key from the chain at the guard's hip, he unlocked the door and pushed the guard into the darkened interior. As he followed him in, he shut the door behind him, but not before he'd caught a glimpse of Scarface hurrying down the ramp. Now that he'd ascertained the place of Bourne's meet, he was prepared to close in on his quarry.

Bourne found himself in a small anteroom filled with wooden bins containing food for the bulls and an enormous soapstone sink with outsize zinc spout and taps, beneath which sat buckets, cloths, mops, and plastic bottles of cleaning fluids. The floor was covered with straw, which absorbed only a minuscule part of the stench. The bull, hidden behind a concrete barrier that rose to Bourne's chest, snorted and bellowed, scenting his presence. The frenzied shouts of the crowd broke like waves over the *toril*, above which sunlight, multicolored from the reflections spinning off the costume of the matador and the outfits of the patrons, splashed across the upper walls of the pen like an artist's broad and reckless brushstrokes.

Bourne drew a cloth from one of the buckets and was halfway across the anteroom when the door behind him opened so slowly one needed to be looking straight at it to be aware of the movement. Putting his back to the barrier, he moved to his left, toward the part of the room where the opening door would block Scarface's view of him.

The bull, frightened, angered, or both by the sudden new human scents, struck the concrete barrier with its hooves, the force so powerful it sent bits of stucco flying on Bourne's side. Scarface seemed to hesitate, no doubt trying to identify the noise. Bourne was almost certain that he had no idea that the next bull was waiting here for its turn to die a bellowing death in the *corrida*. It was a creature of pure muscle and instinct, easily provoked, easily bewildered, fast and deadly unless brought low by exhaustion and a hundred wounds out of which its life dribbled into the dust of the *corrida*.

Bourne crept behind the door as it slowly opened, as Scarface's left hand appeared holding a knife with a long, slender blade shaped like that of the matador's sword. The wicked tip was tilted slightly up, a position from which he could thrust it, slash it, or throw it with equal ease.

Bourne wrapped the cloth around the knuckles of his left hand, providing sufficient padding. He let Scarface take one tentative step into the anteroom and then rushed him from the side. The killer's instinct caused the blade to come up and out in a semicircular sweep as he turned toward the blur of motion he detected at the extreme corner of his field of vision.

Deflecting the blade with wrapped knuckles caused Scarface's defense to open up, and Bourne stepped in, planting his feet, turning from his hips, and drove his right fist into Scarface's solar plexus. The killer gasped almost inaudibly and his eyes opened in a moment of shock, but an instant later he'd wrapped his right arm around Bourne's, locking the back of his hand against the inside of Bourne's elbow. Instantly he applied both pressure and leverage in an attempt to break the bones in Bourne's forearm.

Pain shot up Jason's arm, and he faltered. Scarface took the opening and brought the knife blade down, inside Bourne's wrapped left hand so that the point was directed at Bourne's rib cage. He couldn't concentrate on both motions at once, so he let up fractionally on Bourne's forearm long enough to drive the blade inward toward Bourne's heart.

Bourne stepped into the lunge, surprising him. Bourne was suddenly too close and the blade passed along his side, allowing him to trap Scarface's hand between his side and his left arm. At the same time, he kept his forward momentum going, driving Scarface across the room at an angle, backing him up against the stucco barrier.

Scarface, enraged, redoubled his efforts to break Bourne's arm. A moment more and the bones would snap. On the other side of the barrier, the bull scented the blood in the air, which further maddened it. Once again, its great hooves struck the barrier. The shock reverberated down Scarface's spine and jolted him from his position of superior leverage.

For a moment Bourne broke free, but Scarface had maneuvered the knife in his trapped hand so that the blade raked down Bourne's back, drawing blood. Bourne swiveled, but the knife blade followed him, jabbing ever closer until he vaulted over the barrier.

Scarface followed without hesitation, and now both of them were in unknown territory, facing not only each other but the enraged bull as well.

Bourne had the immediate advantage of knowing it was there, but even he was surprised by its size. Like the *corrida*, the pen was divided by sunlight and shadow. Dust motes hung in the light in the upper half of the pen, but below was the darkness of the Minotaur's cave. He saw the bull in the shadows, red eyes glittering, black lips flecked with foam. It was staring at him, pawing the ground with massive hooves. Its tail switched back and forth, its massive shoulders were bunched with muscle and sinew. Its head lowered ominously.

And then Scarface was on him. The man, solely intent on Bourne, was as yet unaware of the creature with which they shared the pen. The three skulls, each peering in a different direction, filled Bourne's vision. He brought an elbow up, aiming for the throat, slammed it into Scarface's chin instead as the killer partially deflected the blow. At almost the same time Scarface smashed his fist into the side of Bourne's head, bringing him down to the packed-dirt floor. Rolling over, he grabbed Bourne's ears, pulled Bourne's head off the ground, then slammed it back down.

Bourne was rapidly losing consciousness. Scarface was astride him, his bulk painfully pressed down on Bourne's rib cage. There was a moment when Scarface grinned. He slammed Bourne's head down again and again, taking increasing pleasure.

Bourne thought, *Where's his knife?*

He felt around on the floor with both hands, but there were flashes behind his eyes, the light and dark of the room were spinning, merging into a pinwheel of silver sparks. He felt his breath laboring, his heart hammering in his chest, but as his head was once again slammed into the dirt even these vital sensations began to slip away, replaced by a numbing warmth that flooded inward from his extremities. This warmth was soothing, taking away all pain, all effort, all will. He saw himself floating on a river of white light, moving away from his world of shadows and darkness.

And then something cold intruded and for a moment he was certain it was the breath of Shiva, the destroyer, whose face he sensed hovering over him. Then he knew the blade of cold for what it was. Taking hold of the knife's hilt brought him back from the brink, and he plunged the blade into Scarface's side, piercing the flesh between his ribs, skewering his heart.

Scarface reared up, his shoulders trembling, but perhaps, Bourne thought, they weren't trembling at all, because his head was still spinning from the pounding it had taken. He had trouble focusing. How else to explain Scarface's head being replaced by that of a bull? This wasn't Crete, he wasn't in the Minotaur's cave. He was in Seville, at the Maestranza *corrida*.

Then full consciousness returned and, with it, the knowledge of precisely where in the *corrida* he was.

The pen!

And as he looked up from his prone position he saw the bull, huge and menacing, its head lowered, its razor-tipped horns angled to disembowel him.

Undersecretary Stevenson did not look at all well when Moira and Veronica Hart found him, but then no one looks particularly good stretched out on a slab in the cold room of the DC morgue. The two women had been searching the area surrounding the Fountain of the Court of Neptune sculpture near the entrance to the Library of Congress. As fieldwork protocol dictated, they began at the point of origin—in this case, the fountain—and began moving outward in a spiral, hoping to spot some clue that Stevenson might have left as to what had happened to him.

Moira had already called Stevenson's wife and married daughter, neither of whom had seen or heard from him. She had just looked up the number of Humphry Bamber, Stevenson's friend and old college roommate, when Hart got the call that a corpse fitting the undersecretary's description had just been brought into the morgue. The Metro police wanted a positive ID. The DCI had turned to Moira, who said she'd give the prelim. If it was Stevenson, the cops could call his wife to make the formal ID.

"He looks like shit," Hart said now as they stood over the cadaver of the late Steve Stevenson. "What happened to him?" she asked the associate ME.

"Hit-and-run. C1 to C4 of his spine

crushed, as well as most of his pelvis, so the vehicle must've been something big: an SUV or a truck." The AME was a small, compact woman with an enormous coppery halo of wild curls. "He never felt a thing, if that's any consolation."

"I doubt it will be to his family," Moira said.

The AME went on unperturbed; she'd seen and heard it all before. It wasn't that she was callous, just that her job demanded dispassion. "The cops are investigating now but I doubt they'll find anything." She shrugged. "In these cases they rarely do."

Moira stirred. "Did you find anything out of the ordinary?"

"Not in the prelim, anyway. His alcohol level was almost two, more than double the legal limit, so it's all too likely he became disoriented and walked off the curb when he should have stayed put," the AME said. "We're waiting on the formal ID to begin the full autopsy."

As the two women turned away, Hart said, "What I find curious is they found no wallet on him, no keys, nothing to indicate who he was."

"If he was deliberately hit," Moira said, "his killers wouldn't necessarily want him identified right away."

"Your conspiracy theory again." Hart shook her head. "Okay, let's play this game for a minute. If he was murdered, why have him found at all? They could have snatched him, killed him, and buried him where he wouldn't be dug up for ages, if at all."

"Two reasons," Moira said. "First, he's an undersecretary at DoD. Can you imagine the scope of the manhunt the moment he was reported missing, the amount of time his name would be in the forefront of the news? No, these people wanted him dead, wanted it over and done with, which defines an accident."

Hart cocked her head. "What's the second reason?"

"They want to scare me away from whatever Weston found, whatever Stevenson was afraid of."

"Pinprickbardem."

"Precisely."

"You've become as bad as Bourne was with these conspiracy theories."

"All of Jason's conspiracy theories proved correct," Moira said hotly.

The DCI appeared unconvinced. "Let's not get ahead of ourselves, shall we?"

They reached the door and Moira turned back to take one last look at Stevenson. Then she opened the door. When they'd entered the corridor she said, "Would we be getting ahead of ourselves if I told you that Stevenson was a reformed alcoholic?"

"Could be his fear made him slip off the wagon."

"You didn't know him," Moira said. "He'd converted his disease into a religion. Staying sober was his watchword, the reason he stayed alive. He hadn't had a drink in the last twenty years. Nothing could have induced him to do it."

The bull was coming, nothing could stop it. Bourne grabbed the knife, pulled it out of Scarface's side, and rolled to one side. The bull, scenting fresh blood, flicked its horns, goring Scarface in the groin. The animal twisted its massive head, lifting Scarface's bulk off the ground as if it were made of papier-mâché and tossing it against the barrier.

Snorting and stomping its front hooves, the bull then charged the corpse, impaling it on both horns, shaking it back and forth. The beast would surely tear it to shreds within moments. Bourne rose slowly, moving toward the bull with measured steps. When he was close enough, he slapped it smartly on its glistening, black snout with the flat of the blade.

The bull pulled up short, confused, and backed up, allowing the blood-soaked body to crumple to the ground. There it stood its ground, with forelegs spread wide, and shook its head from side to side as if it couldn't decide where the blow came from or what it meant. Blood spiraled down the horns, dripping onto the dirt. Staring at Bourne, uncertain how to deal with this second interloper in its territory, it made a sound deep in its throat. The moment it took a step toward him, Bourne smacked it once again with the blade and it halted, blinking, snorting, shaking its head as if to rid itself of the stinging pain.

Bourne turned, knelt beside the ragged corpse. Quickly he went through Scarface's pockets. He needed to find out who had sent this man. According to Wayan's description of a man with gray eyes, Scarface wasn't the one who'd tried to kill him in Bali.

Had he been sent by the same man who'd hired the marksman? He needed to find some answers because Scarface was unfamiliar to him. Had Bourne known him in the past he couldn't remember? As always when there was the possibility of someone resurfacing, these questions were maddening, required immediate solving, otherwise he'd never rest.

Save for a roll of blood-soaked euros, Scarface's pockets were predictably empty. He must have stashed his false passport and other equally fake papers at a safe house or perhaps a locker at the airport or rail station—but if that was the case, where was the key?

Then Bourne turned the body slightly, looking for it when the bull came out of its temporary stupor and made a run at him. His arm was directly in the path of the horns. At the last instant he snatched it away, but the bull twisted its head violently and the length of the horn rode up his arm, flaying off the skin in a thin ribbon.

Grabbing on to the horn, Bourne used it as a fulcrum to swing himself onto the bull's back. For an instant the beast did not know what happened. Then, as the weight on its back shifted, it stomped forward, charging the barrier again. But this time the bull slammed into it sideways, and if Bourne hadn't lifted his right leg it would have been smashed between the muscle of the beast and the stucco. As it was, he was jarred halfway off the bull. Had he fallen, it would have been the end of him, the creature mindlessly stomping him to death within seconds.

Now he had to hang on as the bull made another run at the barrier in an attempt to shake him off. Bourne still had Scarface's knife; there was a chance the blade was long enough to deliver the coup de grâce and bring the bull to its knees if he chose precisely the right spot and the correct angle. But he knew he wouldn't do it. To kill this beast from behind when it was terrified of him seemed cowardly, craven. He thought of the wooden pig overlooking the pool in Bali, its painted face carved with the eternal smile of the mystical sage. This bull had its own life to live; Bourne had no right to take it.

At that moment he was almost thrown

off as the beast slammed into the barrier at an angle, twisting its head down and to the left in a more desperate attempt to dislodge the shifting weight on its back. Bourne, bounced painfully around, was clinging to the bull's horns. His arm ached where Scarface had tried to break it, his back was still bleeding from the knife wound, and worst of all his head felt as if it were splitting into a thousand pieces. He knew he couldn't last much longer, but rolling off the bull meant almost certain death.

And then, as the massed shouts from the *corrida* came to an ear-shattering crescendo, the bull folded its front legs, its back canted steeply down, and Bourne was shaken loose at last, tumbling head over heels, fetching up against the barrier, which now was spiderwebbed with cracks from the force of the bull's charges.

He lay in a heap, half dazed. He could feel the beast's hot breath on him; the horns were no more than a handbreadth from his face. He tried to move, but couldn't. His breath labored in and out of his lungs and he was gripped by a terrible dizziness.

The red eyes fixed him in their glare, the

muscles beneath the glistening hide were bunching for the final lunge at him, and he knew that in the next moment he would be nothing more than a rag doll skewered like Scarface on the points of those bloody horns.

15

The bull lurched forward, covering Bourne's face with a spray of hot mist. The beast's eyes rolled up and its massive head hit the floor at Bourne's feet with a heavy thud. Bourne, struggling with clearing his fuzzy brain, wiped his eyes with his forearm, put his head back against the barrier, and saw the guard he had taken out and dragged into the anteroom.

He stood in the classic marksman's pose, legs spread, feet planted firmly, one hand cupping the butt of the pistol with which he'd shot the bull twice and which, now that it was dead, was aimed squarely at Bourne.

"*¡Levántese!*" he ordered. "Stand up and show me your hands."

"All right," Bourne said. "One moment." Using one hand on top of the barrier to brace himself, he struggled to his feet. Placing Scarface's knife carefully on top of the barrier, he raised his hands, palms outward.

"What are you doing here?" The guard was livid with rage. "Son of a bitch, look what you made me do. Have you any idea what that bull cost?"

Bourne pointed to the ripped-apart body of Scarface. "I'm nothing. It was this man, a professional assassin, I was trying to get away from."

The guard frowned deeply. "Who? Who do you mean?" He took several tentative steps toward Bourne, then he saw what was left of Scarface. "*Madre de Dios!*" he cried.

Bourne leapt across the barrier into the bull pen and the guard toppled backward. For a moment, the two men grappled for the gun, then Bourne chopped down on the side of the guard's neck and his body went limp.

Before rolling off him, he checked the guard to make sure his pulse was steady, then climbed back over the barrier and put his head under the tap over the soapstone sink, using the cold water to sluice away the remainder of the bull's blood as well as to revive himself. Using the cleanest of the rags under the sink, he wiped himself dry, then—still slightly dizzy—retraced his steps up the ramp into the colored dazzle of the *corrida*, where the triumphant matador was slowly and majestically parading around the perimeter of the ring with the bull's ears held high to the screaming throng.

The bull itself lay near the center of the *corrida*, mutilated, forgotten, flies buzzing around its immobile head.

Soraya felt Amun beside her as if he were a small nuclear plant. How many lies had he told her, she wondered. Did he have powerful enemies high up in the Egyptian government, or were these the same people who had given him the order to barter a Kowsar 3 missile and bring down the American jet?

"What is particularly troubling," he said,

breaking the short silence, "is that the Iranians had to have help getting here. It would be easy enough to pass through the chaos in Iraq, but after that what choice did they have? They wouldn't have taken the northern route, crossing into Jordan and the Sinai, because it's too risky. The Jordanians would have shot them dead and the Sinai is too open, too heavily patrolled." He shook his head. "No, they had to have come here via Saudi and the Red Sea, which means the most logical landfall was Al Ghardaqah."

Soraya was aware of this tourist city on the Red Sea, a relaxed, sun-drenched mecca for the overly stressed not unlike Miami Beach. Amun was right: Its laid-back, carnival atmosphere would make it an ideal landing place for a small terrorist group, passing as tourists or better yet Egyptian fishermen, to arrive and depart unrecognized.

Amun floored the gas pedal, streaking past cars and trucks alike. "I've arranged for a small plane to take us to Al Ghardaqah as soon as we arrive at the airfield. Breakfast will be served on board. We can strategize while we eat."

Soraya called Veronica Hart, who answered immediately.

When she had been updated, Hart said, "The president is addressing the UN Security Council tomorrow morning. He'll be asking for a formal condemnation of Iran."

"Without definitive proof?"

"Halliday and his NSA people have convinced the president that their written report is all the proof we need."

"I take it you don't agree," Soraya said drily.

"I most certainly don't. If we go out on a limb like we did with the WMDs in Iraq and are subsequently proven wrong it will be an unmitigated disaster, both politically and militarily, because we'll have enmeshed the world in a wider war than anyone can currently handle, and that includes us, no matter what Halliday says. You've got to find me definitive proof of Iranian involvement."

"That's just what Chalthoum and I are working on, but the situation has become more complicated."

"What do you mean?"

"Chalthoum theorizes that the Iranians must have had help in transshipping the missile, and I agree." She repeated the logistics that Amun had given her. "Many of the people who took part in the nine-eleven disaster were Saudis. If the same group is now involved with an Iranian terrorist network or, far more ominously, the Iranian government itself, the implications are far reaching because the Iranians are Shi'a and the overwhelming majority of Saudis are Wahhib, a branch of the Sunni sect. As you know, Shi'a and Sunni are blood enemies. This raises the possibility that they have somehow entered into either a temporary truce or an alliance of shared purpose."

Hart sucked in her breath. "God in heaven, we're talking about a nightmare scenario that's frankly terrified us and the European intelligence community for years."

"With good reason," Soraya said, "because it means that a united Islam is girding itself for an all-out war with the West."

Bourne felt the wound near his heart throbbing so badly, he feared it might have reopened. Exiting the pen, he headed for the toilets where he could at least get the remainder of the blood off his clothes, but halfway there he saw two police rounding the corridor, heading toward the pens. Had someone in the *corrida* seen something and raised the alarm? Or perhaps the guard had regained consciousness. There was no time for speculation as he reversed course and headed, somewhat unsteadily, up the ramp into the spangled Seville twilight. Behind him, he heard someone calling. Was it to him? Without a backward glance, he turned to look for Tracy, but as if intuiting the increasing danger of the situation, she was already out of her seat, searching for him. The moment they saw each other, she headed not toward him but toward the nearest exit, leading him there by example.

The clamor around the *corrida* was of a more general nature as the crowd stood, stretched, milled, and talked among themselves or headed for the refreshment stands and the toilets. In the ring men dragged the fallen bull's carcass away, raked over the dirt to cover the fresh blood, and generally prepared for the next bull.

Bourne felt the pain in his chest detonate like a bomb. He staggered and fell against two women, who turned back to glare at him as he righted himself. But even in his debilitated state he was conscious of a proliferation of police entering the stadium. There was no doubt now that the alarm had been sounded.

One of the police officers he'd seen coming toward him in the bowels of the *corrida* had emerged, looking around for him. He eeled his way through the crowd, thankful that virtually everyone was on the move, making it easier for him to lose himself as he made his way toward the exit where Tracy was waiting for him.

But the police officer must have caught a glimpse of him, because he was hurrying after Bourne, expertly threading his way through the people. Bourne tried to judge the distance to the exit and wondered whether he was going to make it, because the officer was closing fast. A moment later he saw Tracy appear out of the throng. Without a glance at him, she rushed past him, heading in the opposite direction. What was she doing?

Still picking his way forward, he risked a glance over his shoulder and saw her confront the police officer. In snatches he heard her voice, raised and plaintive, complaining of having her cell phone snatched from her handbag. The officer was understandably impatient with her, but when he tried to brush her off Tracy's voice rose to such a pitch that everyone around her turned to stare and the officer was forced to deal with her.

Through his growing pain Bourne managed a small smile. Three strides later he came to the exit, but as soon as he turned into it, he felt a deeper stab of pain in his chest and fell against the rough concrete wall, gasping for breath as people pushed past him, coming and going.

"Come on," Tracy urged in his ear as she slid her arm through his and drew him into the flow of the crowd, down the ramp, and into the enormous vestibule, where a mass of people were smoking and chattering away about the merits of the matador. Beyond the crowd, the glass doors to the street were directly ahead.

Somehow she'd disentangled herself from the officer to find him. It took all his concentration to breathe deeply, to breathe through the pain.

"Christ, what happened to you in there?" she said. "How badly are you hurt?"

"Not badly."

"Really? You look like you're already dead."

At that moment, three police came crashing through the *corrida*'s front doors.

Moira and Veronica Hart decided to take the sedan Moira had rented, since the white Buick was as anonymous a car as possible. They found Humphry Bamber, the late Undersecretary Stevenson's closest friend, at his health club. He had just finished his workout, and one of the attendants had fetched him from the sauna. He padded out in sky-blue flip-flops, a towel wrapped around his waist and another, smaller one around his neck, which he used to wipe sweat off his face.

Really, Moira thought, he had no reason to wear anything more. His body was rock-hard, as well formed as a professional athlete's. In fact, he looked as if he spent the majority of his time in the gym maintaining his washboard abs and hillock biceps.

He greeted them with a quizzical smile. He had thick blond hair that fell over his forehead, making him seem boyish. His wide-apart, clear eyes took them in with a cool precision that seemed oddly neutral to Moira.

"Ladies," he said, "what can I do for

you? Marty said it was urgent." He meant the attendant.

"It is urgent," Hart said. "Is there somewhere private we can talk?"

Bamber's expression sobered. "Are you cops?"

"What if we are?"

He shrugged. "I'd be more curious than I am now."

Hart flashed her credentials, which sent his eyebrows up.

"Do you suspect me of passing secrets to the enemy?"

"Which enemy?" Moira said.

He laughed. "I like you," he said. "What's your name?"

"Moira Trevor."

"Uh-oh." At once, Bamber's expression grew dark. "I was warned about you."

"Warned?" Moira said. "By whom?" But she thought she already knew.

"A man named Noah Petersen."

Moira recalled Noah taking Jay Weston's cell phone from her at the scene of the killing. It was a sure bet that's how he found Bamber.

"He said—"

"His real name's Perlis," Moira interrupted.

"Noah Perlis. You shouldn't trust anything he told you."

"He said you'd say that."

Moira laughed bitterly. Hart said, "A private place, Mr. Bamber. Please."

He nodded and walked them to an unused office. They went in and he closed the door. When they were all seated, Hart said, "I'm afraid we have some bad news. Steve Stevenson is dead."

Bamber looked stricken. "What?"

Hart continued: "Did Mr. Peter—Perlis tell you that?"

Bamber shook his head. He put the smaller towel around his shoulders as if he'd suddenly grown cold. Moira couldn't blame him.

"My God." He shook his head in disbelief, then he looked at them in a kind of pleading way. "It must be a mistake of some kind, one of those idiotic bureaucratic snafus Steve was always complaining about."

"I'm afraid not," Hart said.

"Noah—one of Mr. Perlis's people—killed your friend, making it look like an accident," Moira said in a rush of emotion. Ignoring Hart's warning glare, she continued: "Mr.

Perlis is a dangerous man working for a dangerous organization."

"I—" Bamber ran a hand distractedly through his hair. "Shit, I don't know what to believe." He looked from one of them to the other. "Can I see Steve's body?"

Hart nodded. "That can be arranged, as soon as we're through here."

"Ah." Bamber gave her a rueful smile. "Like a reward, is that it?"

Hart said nothing.

He nodded in capitulation. "Okay, how can I help you?"

"I don't know if you can," Hart said with a significant glance at Moira. "Because if you could, Mr. Perlis wouldn't have left you alive."

For the first time Bamber looked truly alarmed. "What the hell is this?" he said with understandable indignation. "Steve and I have been close friends since college, that's it."

Ever since Bamber had appeared Moira had been wondering about this aging jock's decades-long friendship with Steve Stevenson, a man who didn't know a softball from a football and, furthermore, didn't care. Now something Bamber just said caused a number of small anomalies to click into place.

"I think there's another reason Noah felt confident in leaving you with a warning, Mr. Bamber," she said, "am I right?"

Bamber frowned. "I don't know what you're talking about."

"What would frighten you so much that Noah could be assured that you wouldn't talk?"

He stood up abruptly. "I've had just about enough of this badgering."

"Sit back down, Mr. Bamber," Hart said.

"You and Undersecretary Stevenson were more than roommates at college," Moira pressed on. "Just as you were more than good friends. Isn't that right?"

Bamber sat down as if all the strength had gone out of his legs. "I want protection from Noah and his people."

"You have it," Hart said.

He looked at her steadily. "I'm not kidding."

Pulling out her cell, she punched in a number. "Tommy," she said into the phone, "I need a security detail in double-quick time." She gave her assistant the address of the health club. "And Tommy, not a word of this to anyone outside the detail, is that clear? Good."

She tucked away her phone, said to Bamber, "Neither am I."

"Good." He sighed in relief. Then, turning to Moira, he smiled bleakly. "You're not wrong about Steve and me, and Noah knew neither of us could survive if the true nature of our relationship was made public."

Moira felt the breath rush out of her. "You called him Noah. Do you mean to tell us you know him?"

"In a way, I work for him. That's the other, more important, reason he couldn't touch me. You see, I created a custom software program for him. It's still got some minor bugs and I'm the only one who can work them out."

"Funny," Hart said, "you don't look like a tech geek."

"Yeah, well, Steve used to say that was one of my charms. I never looked anything like what I really am."

"What does this software program do?" Moira said.

"It's a highly sophisticated statistical analysis program that can take into account millions of factors. What he's doing with it I don't know. He made sure I was locked out of that side of it, that was part of our agreement, the reason I asked for and got a higher fee."

"But you said you're working on fixes."

"That's right," Bamber said, nodding, "but it's necessary that I work on a clean copy of the program. When I'm finished I electronically transfer it to Noah's laptop. What happens after that is anyone's guess."

"Let's hear your guess," Moira said.

He sighed again. "Okay, here's my best shot. The level of complexity of the program makes it almost a sure bet that he's using it on a real-world basis."

"Translation, please."

"There are lab scenarios and real-world scenarios," Bamber said. "As you can imagine, anything that tries to figure out what would happen during certain real-life situations has to be incredibly complex because of all the factors involved."

"Millions of factors."

He nodded. "Which my program provides."

A possibility hit Moira between the eyes and for a moment she sat back, dazzled.

Then she said, "Have you given this program a name?"

"In fact, I did." Bamber seemed a bit embarrassed. "It's a private joke between Steve and me." His use of the present tense brought the news of his friend and lover's death back to him, and he stopped, put his head down, moaning low in his throat, "Jesus, Jesus, Steve."

Moira waited a moment, then cleared her throat. "Mr. Bamber, we're truly sorry for your loss. I knew Undersecretary Stevenson, I did business with him. He always helped me, even if it meant going out on a limb."

Bamber's head came up, his eyes red-rimmed. "Yeah, that was Steve, all right."

"The name you gave the program you created for Noah Perlis?"

"Oh, that. It's nothing, as I said, a joke because Steve and I both like—liked—Javier—"

"Bardem," Moira said.

Bamber looked surprised. "Yes, how did you know?"

And Moira thought, *Pinprickbardem*.

16

The Museo Taurino was located inside the Maestranza *corrida,* and this was where Bourne told Tracy to take him. They had just enough time to change direction within the crowd before the officers entered the throng in the vestibule. Two of them headed directly for the bullring itself. From their positions on either side of the glass doors, the remaining pair began to scan the crowd for their suspect.

The museum was closed today, the interior door shuttered. Bourne, leaning against the door, used a paper clip Tracy found at the bottom of her handbag to pick the lock, and they slipped inside, closing the door behind them. The stuffed heads of all the great bulls killed in this *corrida* stared down at them with glass eyes. They passed glass cases containing the splendid costumes worn by the famous matadors going back to the seventeenth century, when Maestranza was built. The entire history of the *corrida* was on display in these musty rooms.

Bourne was uninterested in any of the flamboyant displays; he was looking for the utility closet. It was in the rear of the museum, beside a little-used room. Inside, he had Tracy dig out cleaning fluid, which he had her apply to the wound down his back. The searing pain took his breath away and, with it, a full sense of consciousness.

He awoke to Tracy's grip on his shoulder. She was shaking him, which made his head hurt even more.

"Wake up!" she said urgently. "You're in worse shape than you let on. I've got to get you out of here."

He nodded; the words were hazy, but the gist hit home. Together they staggered back through the museum to the separate entrance that led out onto the street around the circle from the bullring's main entrance. Tracy unlocked the door and poked her head outside. When she nodded, he emerged into the semi-darkness.

She must have used her cell to call for a taxi because the next thing he knew she was maneuvering him into a backseat, leaning forward as she slid in beside him to give an address to the driver.

As they took off, she turned and peered out the rear window. "The police are crawling all over the Maestranza," she said. "Whatever you did has sent them into a frenzy."

But Bourne didn't hear her; he was already passed out.

Soraya and Amun Chalthoum arrived in Al Ghardaqah just before noon. Not that many years before, it had been nothing more than a modest fishing village, but a combination of Egyptian initiative and foreign investment had turned it into the leading Red Sea resort. The hub of the town was El Dahar, the oldest of the three sections, home to the traditional villas and bazaar. As was the case with most Egyptian coastal towns, Al Ghardaqah did not venture far inland, but rather clung to the shore of the Red Sea as if for dear life. The Sekalla district was more modern, made ugly by the proliferation of cheap hotels. El Korra Road was prettier, filled with upscale hotels, lush plantings, lavish fountains, and walled private compounds owned by Russian moguls with nothing better to do with their easy money.

They hit the fishermen first, what was left of them, anyway—time and the tourist business had decimated their ranks. They were old men now, skin wrinkled and brown as well-worn leather, their eyes paled by the sun, their work-hardened hands like boards, gnarly with outsize knuckles from decades in seawater. Their sons had abandoned them to work in air-conditioned offices or in jets that flew high above, leaving their homeland far behind. They were the last of their line and so an insular lot, their suspicions heightened by sweet-talking Egyptians taking their launching sites away from them to accommodate more and more Jet Skis and Sea-Doos. Their innate fear of Chalthoum and his al Mokhabarat manifested itself in cold hostility. After all, they must have reasoned, having lost everything, what more did they have to lose?

On the other hand, they were charmed by Soraya. They adored the soft way she spoke to them even while they admired her beautiful face and shapely figure. For her they would answer questions, although they insisted that it would be impossible for anyone outside their close-knit circle to pose as a native fisherman without their knowledge. They knew by sight every boat and ship that plied the local waters, and they assured her that nothing out of the ordinary had occurred in their recent collective memory.

"But there are the dive companies," one grizzled seaman told them. His hands, as they mended his nets, were as big as his head. He spat to one side to show his displeasure. "Who knows who their clients are? And as for their staffs, well, they seem to change from week to week, so no one can keep track of them, let alone note their comings and goings."

Soraya and Chalthoum divided up the list of twenty-five dive firms the fishermen gave them, setting out for different ends of the city, agreeing to meet at a carpet shop in the El Dahar bazaar whose owner was a good friend of Amun's.

Soraya went down to the sea, visiting eight of the dive companies, one by one, crossing them off her list as she went. With each she boarded their boats, interviewed the skippers and crew, looked at the customer logbooks for the past three weeks. Sometimes, she had to wait for the boats to return. Other times, the owner was kind enough to ferry her out to the dive sites. After four hours of frustrating work asking the same questions and getting the same answers, she was faced with the reality: This was an impossible task. It was like looking for a needle in an endless line of haystacks. Even if the terrorists had used this method to enter Egypt, there was no assurance that the dive operators would know. And how in the world would they have explained a crate large enough to house the Kowsar 3? Once again, she was plagued with doubts about Amun's story, with a dread that he had been involved in the downing of the airliner.

What am I doing here? she thought. *What if Amun and al Mokhabarat are the real culprits?*

Despairing, she decided to can the entire enterprise after she was through interviewing the personnel at the ninth dive shop. She was ferried out to its boat by a grizzled Egyptian who constantly spat over the side. It was exceptionally hot, the sun beating down on her head; the only breath of wind came from the movement of the boat through the listless air. Even through her sunglasses, everything appeared washed out in the glare. The brine of the sea filled her nostrils, heady and mineral. The repetition had sapped her of keen interest, otherwise she would have marked the young man with the tousled dirty-blond hair edging away from her as she was introduced by the dive shop owner. She began her interviews, asking the same questions: Have you noticed any out-of-place faces in the last three weeks? Any group of seeming Egyptians who came from another boat and who went ashore the same day? Any unusually large packages? No, no, and no, what else did she expect?

She didn't see the young man with the tousled hair gather up equipment as he backed away, and it was only when he jumped overboard that she awoke from her bored lethargy. Running down the length of the boat, she stripped off her handbag, kicked off her shoes, and dived into the sea after him. He had pulled on a mask and an air tank before going over the side, and she saw him below her. Even though he lacked fins, he was diving deep where he must have suspected that she—not being similarly equipped—would not follow.

He was wrong about both her ability and her resolve. Her father had thrown her into a pool on her first birthday, much to her mother's horror, and had taught her endurance, stamina, and speed, all of which had served her well throughout high school and college, when she'd won every award imaginable. She could have made the Olympic team, but by that time the intelligence system had engaged her and she had more important things on her agenda.

Now she powered down, slicing her way through the water, but as she neared him, he turned, startled that she had drawn so close, so quickly, and raised his spear gun. He was cocking the mechanism that drew back the barbed bolt when she struck him.

He tenaciously maintained his grip on the weapon, successfully readying it to fire even as she twisted his body backward. He brought the butt of the spear gun down against her temple and as her hands came off him, he lowered the barb until it was aimed at her chest.

She scissored her legs in a powerful kick just before he pulled the trigger, and the bolt shot by her. Then she made a grab for him. Now she was uninterested in the weapon or in his hands and feet. Her sole imperative was to pull off his mask, to even the playing field between them, because her lungs were beginning to burn and she knew she couldn't stay under for much longer.

Her pounding heart beat off the seconds, one, two, three, as they struggled, until at last she managed to rip off his mask. Water flooded against his face and, though he twisted to the left and right, she pulled the mouthpiece out and inserted it into her mouth, taking a couple of breaths before she kicked upward, holding him in an armlock. She spat out the mouthpiece as they bobbed to the surface.

The captain had raised the anchor while

they'd been underwater, and now the boat maneuvered close enough for hands to reach down and pull them both aboard.

"Get my handbag," Soraya said breathlessly as she sat on the young man's back, pinning him to the deck. She took deep, even breaths, smoothed her hair back from her face, and felt the water already warmed by the sun trickling over her shoulders.

"Is this the one you're looking for?" the owner asked anxiously as he handed over the bag. "He's been here for three days, no more."

Shaking her hands to dry them, Soraya rummaged for her phone. She opened it, slowed her breathing even more, and punched in Chalthoum's number. When he answered, she told him where she was.

"Good work. I'll meet you on the dock in ten minutes," he said.

Putting her cell away, she glanced down at the young man beneath her.

"Get off me," he panted. "I can't breathe."

Sitting on his diaphragm wasn't helping, she knew, but she could summon up no sympathy.

"Sonny," she said, "you are in a world of hurt."

Bourne awoke into a web of shadows. The soft, intermittent hiss of traffic drew his eyes to a shaded window. Outside, streetlights shone through the darkness. He was lying on his side on what felt like a bed. Moving his head, he looked around the bedroom, which was small and comfortably furnished but didn't feel well lived in. Beyond an open doorway a slice of living room was visible. He stirred, sensing he was alone. Where was he? Where was Tracy?

In answer to his second question, he heard the front door open in the living room and recognized Tracy's sharp, quick gait as she came across a wooden floor. When she entered the bedroom, he tried to sit up.

"Please don't, you'll only aggravate your wound," she said. She put down some packages and sat beside him on the bed.

"My back was barely scratched."

She shook her head. "A bit deeper, but I'm talking about the wound in your chest. It's started seeping." She unpacked items she had obviously bought at the local pharmacy: alcohol, antibiotic cream, sterile pads, and the like. "Now hold still."

As she went to work stripping the old bandage and cleaning the wound, she said, "My mother warned me about men like you."

"What about me?"

"Always getting into trouble." Her fingers worked quickly, nimbly, surely. "The difference is that you know how to get yourself out of whatever mess blows up around you."

He grimaced at the pain but didn't flinch. "I have no choice."

"Oh, I don't think that's true." She bunched up a wad of soiled sterile pads, then took up another, soaking it in alcohol and applying it to the reddened flesh. "I think you go looking for trouble, I think that's who you are, I think you'd be unhappy—and, worse for you, bored—if you didn't."

Bourne laughed softly, but he didn't think she was far off the mark.

She examined the newly cleaned wound. "Not so bad, I doubt you'll need a fresh round of antibiotics."

"Are you a doctor?"

She smiled. "On occasion, when I have to be."

"That answer requires an explanation."

She palpated the flesh around his wound. "What the hell happened to you?"

"I got shot, don't change the subject."

She nodded. "Okay, as a young woman—a *very* young woman—I spent two years in West Africa. There was unrest, fighting, horrible atrocities perpetrated. I was assigned to a field hospital where I learned triage, how to dress a wound. One day we were so overloaded with wounded and dying, the doctor put an instrument in my hand and said, 'There's an entry wound but no exit wound. If you don't get the bullet out right away your patient will die.' Then he went off to work on two other patients at once."

"Did your patient die?"

"Yes, but not because of his wound. He'd been terminal before he'd been shot."

"That must have helped some."

"No," she said, "it didn't." Throwing the last of the used pads into a wastebasket, she applied the antibiotic cream and began the bandaging process. "You must promise not to abuse this again. The next time the bleeding will be worse." She sat back inspecting her work. "Ideally, you should be in hospital, or at least see a doctor."

"This isn't an ideal world," he said.

"So I've noticed."

She helped him to sit up. "Where are we?" he asked.

"An apartment of mine. We're on the other side of town from Maestranza."

He transferred to a chair, sat back gingerly. His chest felt as if it were made of lead. It beat with a dull ache as if from pain remembered from long ago. "Don't you have an appointment with Don Fernando Hererra?"

"I postponed it." She looked at him inquiringly. "I couldn't possibly go without you, Professor Alonzo Pecunia Zuñiga." She was speaking of the Goya expert from the Prado he was going to impersonate. Then, abruptly, she smiled. "I like money too much to spend it when I don't have to."

She stood, moving him back to the bed. "But now you must rest."

He was going to answer her but his eyelids had already slid down. With the darkness came a deep and peaceful sleep.

Arkadin pushed his recruits through the desolate landscape of Nagorno-Karabakh, working them twenty-one hours a day. When they began to doze on their feet, he slammed them with his baton. He never had to hit any of them twice. For three hours they slept wherever they happened to be, sprawled on the ground, all except Arkadin himself for whom sleep had been completely banished months ago. Instead, his mind was filled with scenes from the past, from the end of his days in Nizhny Tagil, when Stas's men were closing in on him and it seemed as if his only choice was to kill as many of them as he could before they shot him to death.

He wasn't afraid to die, that was clear to him from the outset of his forced incarceration in the basement, venturing out only at night for quick forays for food and fresh water. Above him was a hive of activity as the remaining members of Stas's gang feverishly coordinated the ever-intensifying search for him. As the days turned into weeks, and the weeks into months, he might have had reason to think that the gang would move on to other matters, but no, they nursed their grudge like a colicky baby, inhaling its poison until to a man they were gripped by an unshakable obsession. They wouldn't rest until they dragged his corpse through the streets as an object lesson for anyone else who might think of interfering with their business.

Even the cops, who were, in any event, on the gang's payroll, had been co-opted into the citywide dragnet by the random storms of violence visited on Nizhny Tagil night after night. They were used to turning a blind eye, even at times laughed about it, but not now—the attacks had escalated to a level that made them a laughingstock in the eyes of the state police. It was typical of their thinking that rather than clamping down on Stas's gang, they took the easy way and capitulated to its demands. So almost everyone was on the lookout for Arkadin, there was no surcease, there could only be a nasty end.

That was when Mikhail Tarkanian, whom Arkadin would eventually call Mischa, arrived in Nizhny Tagil from Moscow. He had been sent by his boss, Dimitri Ilyinovich Maslov, head of Kazanskaya, the most powerful family of the Moscow *grupperovka*, the Russian mafia, involved in drugs and black-market cars. Through his many eyes and ears Maslov had heard of Arkadin, had heard of the bloodbath he'd single-handedly caused and its stalemate aftermath. He wanted Arkadin brought to him. "The problem," Maslov told his men, "is that Stas's men want to tear him limb from limb." He handed them a file. Inside were a sheaf of grainy black-and-white surveillance shots, a gallery of Stas's remaining crew, each with his name carefully written on the reverse. Maslov's eyes and ears had been busy, indeed, and it occurred to Tarkanian, even if it didn't to the scowling Oserov, that Maslov must want Arkadin very badly to go to so much trouble to extract him from what seemed like an intractable situation.

Maslov could have sent his chief enforcer, Vylacheslav Germanovich Oserov, at the head of a raiding party to take Arkadin by force, but Maslov was a canny dispenser of his power. Far better to make Stas's gang part of his empire than to start a blood feud with whoever was left after his own people got through with them.

So instead he sent Tarkanian, his chief political negotiator. He ordered Oserov along to protect Tarkanian, an assignment Oserov openly despised, adamant that if Maslov had listened to him he, Oserov, could easily have taken Arkadin from the hick baboons of Nizhny Tagil, as he called them. "I'd have this Arkadin back in Moscow within forty-eight hours, guaranteed," he told Tarkanian several times during their tedious journey into the foothills of the Ural Mountains.

By the time they arrived in Nizhny Tagil, Tarkanian was sick to death of Oserov who, as he later told Arkadin, "felt like a woodpecker attached to my head."

In any event, even before Maslov's emissaries left Moscow, Tarkanian had formed the outline of the plan to extract Arkadin from his predicament. He was a man with a natural Machiavellian mind. The deals he made for Maslov were legendary in both their bewildering complexity and their unerring effectiveness.

"The mission is misdirection," Tarkanian

told Oserov as they approached their destination. "To that end we need to create a straw man for Stas's gang to go after."

"What do you mean *we*?" Oserov said with typical surliness.

"I mean you're the perfect man to establish the straw man for me."

"Oserov looked at me with that dark look of his," Tarkanian told Arkadin much later, "but he was powerless to do more than yelp like a kicked dog. He knew my importance to Dimitri, and this kept him in line. Barely."

"You're right about one thing, we're dealing with baboons," he told Oserov, throwing him a bone. "And baboons are motivated by only two things: the carrot and the stick. I'm going to provide the carrot."

"Why should they want anything to do with you?" Oserov said.

"Because the moment you hit town you're going to do what you do best: make life a living hell for them."

This answer drew a rare smile from Oserov's face.

"And do you know what he said to me then?" Tarkanian whispered to Arkadin much later. "He said, 'The more blood, the better.'"

And he meant it. Forty-three minutes from the moment he entered Nizhny Tagil, Oserov found his first victim, one of Stas's oldest, most loyal soldiers. He put a bullet through one ear at close range, then went to work butchering him. The head he left intact, looking out from the chest cavity in a gruesome parody of a cheap horror film.

Needless to say, the rest of Stas's men were incensed. Business ground to a halt. Three death squads with three men each were sent out, searching for this new killer. They knew it wasn't Arkadin because the killing wasn't his typical method.

They weren't frightened yet, but that would come. If there was anything Oserov knew how to engender in others, it was fear. Choosing another victim at random among the photos in the dossier Maslov had given them, Oserov stalked the gang member. Finding him on the doorstep of his house, with the door open and his children peeping out, Oserov shot him, shattering the bone in his right thigh. With his victim's children screaming and his wife running to the front door from the kitchen, Oserov sprinted across the pavement, leapt up the concrete steps, and put three bullets in the man's abdomen in precisely the places where he'd bleed most heavily.

That was day two. Oserov was just warming up, there was far worse to come.

Pinprick," Humphry Bamber said. "What do you mean, *Pinprick*?"

Veronica Hart shot Moira a nervous look. "I was hoping you could tell us," she said.

Hart's cell buzzed and she walked out of earshot to take it. When she returned, she said, "The backup I ordered is waiting outside."

Moira nodded, leaned forward, toward Bamber, forearms resting on her crossed knee. "The word *pinprick* was paired with the name of your software program."

He looked from her to the DCI. "I don't understand."

Moira felt the air go out of her. "I met with Steve just before . . . before he disappeared. He was terrified of what was going on at the DoD and the Pentagon. He intimated that the fog of war had already started to permeate the atmosphere at both places."

"And, what, you think Bardem has something to do with that fog of war?"

"Yes," Moira said firmly. "I do."

Bamber had begun to sweat. "Christ," he said, "if I had any idea the real-world situation Noah was going to use the program for included war—"

"Excuse me," Moira said hotly, "but Noah Perlis is a high-ranking member of Black River. How could you not know—or at least suspect?"

"Back off, Moira," Hart said.

"I will not back off. This—idiot savant—has given Noah the keys to the castle. Because of Bamber's stupidity Noah and the NSA are planning something."

"Something what?" Bamber's voice was almost pleading. He seemed desperate to know what he was complicit in.

Moira shook her head. "That's just it, we don't know what, but I'll tell you one thing: Unless we find out and stop them I'm afraid that we'll all live to regret it."

Bamber, clearly shaken, rose. “Whatever I can do, however I can help, just tell me.”

“Go get dressed,” Hart said. “Then we’d like to take a look at Bardem. My hope is that we’ll get a better idea from the program itself what Noah and the NSA have in mind.”

“It won’t take me a minute,” he said. He ducked out of the office.

For a time, the two women sat in silence. Then Hart said, “Why do I get the feeling that I’m being outmaneuvered?”

“You mean Halliday?”

Hart nodded. “The secretary of defense has decided to reach out to the private sector for whatever he has in mind—and make no mistake, no matter how clever Noah Perlis is, he’s taking his orders from Bud Halliday.”

“Taking his money, too,” Moira said. “I wonder what Black River’s bill for this little escapade is going to be.”

“Moira, whatever differences we’ve had in the past, we agree on one thing—that our former employer is without scruples. Black River will do anything if the price is right.”

"Halliday has a virtually unlimited source, the US Mint. You and I both saw the flats of hundred-dollar bills Black River trans-shipped from here to Iraq during the first four years of the war."

Hart nodded. "One hundred million in each flat, and where did the money go? To fight the insurgents? To pay off the army of indigenous informers Black River claimed to get their intel from? No, you and I know, because we saw it, that ninety percent of it went into blind bank accounts in Liechtenstein and the Caymans of dummy corporations owned by Black River."

"Now they don't have to steal it," Moira said with a cynical laugh, "because Halliday is giving it to them."

A moment later they rose and went out of the office as Humphry Bamber emerged from the men's locker room. He was dressed in neatly pressed jeans, polished loafers, a blue-and-black–checked shirt, and a gray suede car coat.

"Is there another exit?" Moira asked him.

He pointed. "There's an employee and delivery entrance behind the administrative offices."

"I'll get my car," Moira said.

"Hold on." Hart opened her phone. "It's better for me to do it; my people are outside and I need to instruct them to deploy outside the front entrance to make it look as if we're taking Bamber out that way." She held out her hand and Moira gave her the keys. "Then I'll go get your car and pick you two up around back. Moira?"

Moira drew her custom Lady Hawk from its thigh holster while Bamber goggled with his mouth half open.

"What the hell is going on?" he said.

"You're getting the protection you wanted," Hart said.

As she disappeared down the corridor, Moira motioned to Bamber, allowing him to lead her back toward the admin offices. She used her DoD-issue ID on the few managers who questioned their presence in the health club's back office.

When they approached the rear door, she pulled out her phone and dialed Hart's private number. Once the DCI answered, she said, "We're in position."

"Count to twenty," Hart's reply came in her ear, "then bring him out."

Moira snapped shut her phone and put it away. "Ready?"

Bamber nodded even though it wasn't really a question.

She counted off the rest of the time, then wrenched the door open with her free hand and, with her gun at the ready, moved out, presenting only her profile. Hart had stopped the white Buick directly in front of the entrance. She'd opened the near-side rear door.

Moira took a look around. They were in a remote section of the parking lot. The blacktop was surrounded by a twelve-foot Cyclone fence topped with razor wire. To the left was a row of huge lidded bins to hold the health club's trash and recyclables between garbage pickups. To the right was the turnaround to exit the lot. Beyond rose blocks of anonymous-looking apartment and mixed-use buildings. No other vehicles were in this section of the lot, and a view of the street was blocked off by screening on the outside of the fence.

Glancing back over her shoulder, Moira made eye contact with Bamber. "Okay," she said, "keep your head low and get into the backseat as quickly as you can."

Crouching down, he scuttled across the

short distance from the doorway to the Buick, Moira covering him the whole way. Within the safety of the car, he scrambled across the seat to the far side.

"Get your head down!" Hart ordered as she swiveled her torso around the front bucket seat. "And keep it down no matter what."

Then she called to Moira. "Come on, come on! What are you waiting for? Let's get the hell out of Dodge!"

Moira went around the back of the Buick and took one last surveillance look at the garbage bins up against the Cyclone fence. Had there been some movement there or was it just a shadow? She took several steps toward the bins, but Veronica Hart stuck her head out the window.

"Dammit, Moira, would you get into the car!"

Moira turned back. Ducking her head, she came around the back of the Buick and stopped dead in her tracks. Kneeling down, she peered into the tailpipe. There was something there, something with a tiny red eye, an LED that now began to blink rapidly . . .

Jesus, she thought. *Oh, God!*

Tearing around to the open door, she yelled, "Out! Get out now!"

She bent, pulling Bamber across the leather seat, hauling him out of the car. "Ronnie," she called, "get out! Get out of the fucking car!"

She saw Hart turn, momentarily bewildered, then move to unbuckle her seat belt. In a moment it became clear that something was wrong because she couldn't get free; something was in the way or the locking mechanism was malfunctioning.

"Ronnie, do you have a knife?"

Hart had a penknife out and was sawing through the material that held her fast.

"Ronnie!" Moira screamed. "For God's sake—!"

"Get him away!" Hart yelled at her, and then, as Moira took a step toward her, "Get the fuck away!"

In the next instant the Buick went up like a Roman candle, the shock wave slamming Moira and Bamber to the blacktop, showering them with smoldering patches of plastic and spirals of hot metal that stung like bees flushed from their hive.

17

A hymn of deep-throated cathedral bells woke Bourne. Sunlight filtered through the jalousied bedroom window, fingers of pale gold striping the polished floorboards.

"Good morning, Adam. The police are after you."

Tracy had come into the doorway, stood leaning against one side of the frame. The robust scent of fresh-brewed coffee entered with her and swirled enticingly about him like a flamenco dancer.

"I heard it on the TV earlier." She had her arms crossed over her breasts. Her hair was still wet from the shower, slicked off her face, tied with a black velvet ribbon into a ponytail. Her face was bright, freshly scrubbed. She wore umber slacks, a cream man-tailored shirt, and shoes without heels. She looked ready for Don Fernando Herrera or whatever else the day might hold. "Not to worry, though, they don't have your name, and the single witness, a guard at the Maestranza, didn't—or couldn't—give an accurate description of you."

"He saw me in very low light." Bourne sat up and moved across the bed. "Sometimes in no light at all."

"All the better for you."

Was the smile she gave him sardonic? In his present state he couldn't tell.

"I got breakfast, and we have an appointment to see Don Fernando Hererra at three this afternoon."

His head still throbbed and his mouth was as dry as a desert, distinguished only by an acrid taste that was faintly nauseating.

"What time is it?" he asked.

"Just after nine."

The arm Scarface had tried to break felt better when he flexed it and the flesh wound down his back scarcely burned at all, but the pain in his chest made him wince as he wrapped the top sheet around his waist and rose out of bed.

"Perfect," Tracy said. "A Roman senator."

"Let's hope by this afternoon I look more Castilian than Roman," he said as he padded toward the bathroom, "because it will be Professor Alonzo Pecunia Zuñiga who'll be accompanying you to Don Hererra's this afternoon."

She gave him a curious look, then turned and went back into the living room. He closed the bathroom door behind him and ran the shower. Over the sink was a mirror surrounded by small incandescent lightbulbs: a woman's bathroom, he thought, made for putting on makeup.

Returning to the bedroom after his shower, he found a thick Turkish terry-cloth robe, which he wrapped around himself. She had covered his chest wound with a waterproof plastic layer, which he hadn't noticed until he stepped into the stream of hot water.

When he came into the living room, Tracy was pouring coffee into an enormous cup. The small kitchen was merely a niche at one end of the single open room, which was spacious but, like the bedroom, as sparsely and anonymously furnished as a hotel room. On the wooden trestle table was the typical Andalusian workingman's breakfast: a mug of hot chocolate and a plate of *churros*, slender twists of fried dough, dipped in sugar crystals.

Bourne pulled up a chair and he and Tracy ate their breakfast, and she let him have all the *churros*, he was still hungry when he finished. He went to the refrigerator.

"There's nothing much in there, I'm afraid," she said. "I haven't been here in some time."

Still, he found some bacon in the freezer. As he fried up the strips, she said, "Write down your size and I'll get you some fresh clothes."

He nodded. "While you're at it, I need you to run an errand for me." Finding a pencil and scratch pad on the kitchen counter, he tore off a sheet and wrote out a list of items, along with his clothes size.

When he handed the slip of paper to

her, Tracy glanced over it and said, "Professor Zuñiga, I presume?"

He nodded, tending the browning strips. "I gave you the addresses of the theatrical stores I found yesterday. We were on our way there when Scarface picked up our scent."

She got up, grabbed her handbag, and went to the door. "This should take me about an hour," she said. "In the meantime, enjoy the rest of your breakfast."

After she left, Bourne took the skillet off the burner, laid the bacon on a sheet of paper towel. Then he returned to the scratch pad. The sheet he'd torn off was from the middle because he wanted to keep the top one intact. With the pencil at an extreme angle, he ran the lead lightly over the sheet. Letters began to form, the imprint of the writing left over from the last note someone—presumably Tracy—had made.

Don Hererra's name and address came up, along with the time, 3 PM, just as she'd told him. He ripped off the sheet and put it in his pocket. That was when he noticed indentations on what was now the top sheet of the pad. He tore that off as well. Running the side of the pencil over this sheet brought up a line of numbers and letters all run together.

He ate the bacon standing beside the front window, staring out at the shimmering morning. It was still too early for people to be out at the *feria*, but the Moorish scrollwork balcony on the building across the street was garlanded in flowers and gaily colored fabric. His eyes scanned both sides of the street for anyone and anything even remotely suspicious, but nothing presented itself. He watched a young woman herd three children across the street. An old woman in black, small and bent, carried a mesh bag filled with fruit and vegetables.

Popping the last of the bacon into his mouth, he wiped his hands down on a kitchen cloth, then crossed to Tracy's laptop, which was set up on the far end of the trestle table. It was on and he saw that she had a Wi-Fi connection to the Internet.

Sitting down in front of it, he Googled the string of numbers and letters only to get this result:

Your search—**779elgamhuriaave**—did not match any documents.
Suggestions:
* Make sure all words are spelled correctly.
* Try different keywords.
* Try more general keywords.

Then he saw his error, and placed spaces in the appropriate places: 779 El Gamhuria Avenue. An address, but where?

Returning to Google, he typed in "El Gamhuria Avenue" and up popped Khartoum, Sudan. Now, that was interesting. What was Tracy doing with a North African address?

He typed in the full address, including the number, which, as it turned out, belonged to Air Afrika Corporation. He sat back. Why did that name sound so familiar? There were a number of entries for Air Afrika, some of them from very odd sites, others from blogs of dubious nature, but the information he wanted came from an entry on the second page from Interpol, where speculation was cited from numerous sources that Air Afrika was owned and operated by Nikolai Yevsen, the legendary arms dealer. Ever since Viktor Anatoliyevich

Bout had been arrested, Yevsen had taken his place as the largest and most powerful illegal arms dealer in the world.

Bourne rose from the chair, walked back to the window, on reflex checking the street again. Tracy was an art expert buying a Goya unknown until just recently. The price must be astronomical; maybe a handful of people in the world could afford it. So who was her client?

With church bells pealing the hour, his gaze snapped back into focus as Tracy walked into his field of vision. She was carrying a mesh shopping sack. He watched the confident rat-a-tat of her stride, the heels of her shoes rhythmically striking the pavement. A young man appeared behind her and Bourne felt his muscles tense. Halfway down the block, the young man lifted an arm, waving, and ran across the street where a young woman waited for him. They embraced as Tracy entered the building. A moment later she came through the door, put the mesh sack down on the table.

"If you're still hungry, I bought some Serrano ham and Garrotxa cheese." She placed the food, wrapped in white paper, on the table. "The rest is everything you asked for."

After he'd dressed in the light, comfortable clothes she'd chosen for him, he pored over the contents of the mesh sack, lining the items up, opening the lids, smelling the contents, and nodding to himself.

She regarded him solemnly. "Adam," she ventured, "I don't know what you're involved in . . ."

"I already told you," he said mildly.

"Yes, but now I see how badly you're injured, and that man who was following us was evil looking."

"He was evil," Bourne acknowledged. Then he looked up at her and smiled. "It's part of the industry I'm in, Tracy. There isn't the capital floating around there was in 2000, so more start-ups are chasing less money. That makes for cutthroat competition." He shrugged. "It can't be avoided."

"But from the looks of you, this kind of work could send you to the hospital."

"I've just got to be more careful from now on."

She frowned. "Now you're making fun of me." She came and sat next to him.

"But there's nothing amusing about that wound in your chest."

He produced the photo he'd printed out at the Internet café, set it out between them. "To become Professor Alonzo Pecunia Zuñiga I'm going to need your help."

She held quite still, her liquid eyes studying his face for a moment. Then she nodded.

Day three of Oserov's reign of terror brought a downpour such as no one in Nizhny Tagil could remember, and this was a city where grudges were nursed, meaning memories were as long and vibrant as the winter chill. Day three also brought other deaths, ones so brutal, so horrific that there now came to the remnants of Stas Kuzin's people a black fear. One that crept into their bones, lodging there like a grain of polonium, eroding their confidence the way the radioactive material eats away flesh.

It began in the early hours of the morning, just past two o'clock, as Oserov boasted to Arkadin afterward.

"With great stealth I broke into their head enforcer's house, tied him up, and forced him to watch what I did to his family," Oserov told Arkadin later.

When he was finished, he dragged his victim into the kitchen, where he went to work on him using the fire-reddened tip of a carving knife he slid from a wooden rack. The pain of what Oserov did to him hammered the enforcer out of his state of shock and he began screaming until Oserov cut out his tongue.

An hour later, Oserov was finished. He left him in a pool of his own blood and vomit, alive, but just barely. When the enforcer's associates came for him as they did each morning to begin their daily patrol, they found the front door flung open, which led them to the abattoir inside. It was then, and only then, that Mikhail Tarkanian entered Nizhny Tagil. By then, the criminals were in such a frenzy that they'd all but forgotten about Arkadin.

"Lev Antonin, I think I can provide the solution to your problem," Tarkanian said to the new head of Stas's gang when he met with him in his office. There were seven heavily armed men standing guard. "I'll find this killer for you and take care of him."

"Who are you, stranger? Why would you do this?" Lev Antonin squinted at him suspiciously. He had a gray face with long ears and stubble on his chin and cheeks. He looked like he hadn't slept in a week.

"Who I am is of no importance, except to say that I'm intimately familiar with men such as your murderer," Tarkanian replied without hesitation. "And as to why I'm here the answer is simple: I want Leonid Danilovich Arkadin."

At once Antonin's expression changed from suspicious to enraged. "And why would you want that fucking whoremonger, that shit-faced miscreant?"

"That's my business," Tarkanian said mildly. "Your business is keeping your people alive."

This was true. Antonin was a pragmatic man, with none of the mad fire that had burned within his predecessor. Tarkanian could read him like a comic book: Clearly, he was all too aware that the current of fear lapping at the knees of his men was undermining both their effectiveness and his authority. He also knew that once fear made its presence felt, it spread like wildfire. On the other hand, he wasn't about to give away the farm. Arkadin's head on a platter was what they'd all dreamed of since Arkadin had killed Kuzin and set their world ablaze with bullets and death. Letting go of that dream wouldn't endear him to his rank and file.

He scrubbed his face with his hands and said, "Fine, but you'll bring me the killer's head so all my men can see for themselves the end of this filth. And then if you can find that bastard Arkadin you can have him."

Naturally enough, Tarkanian did not believe this Neanderthal. He recognized the greed in his yellow eyes and intuited that it was not enough for him to be given the head of the murderer; he wanted Arkadin as well. The two bloody heads would cement his power over his people for all time.

"What Lev Antonin wanted was irrelevant," Tarkanian told Arkadin afterward. "I had planned for such a treacherous eventuality."

It would have amused Oserov no end to "find the murderer" for the baboon named Lev Antonin and bring him the freshly cut head, but no, he was to be denied this pleasure. He scowled when Tarkanian told him that Tarkanian himself would find and deliver the "murderer" to Antonin.

"To take the fury out of your heart, I have another assignment for you," Tarkanian told him. "A much more important job that only you can do."

"I strongly suspect he doubted that very much," Tarkanian told Arkadin later, "but when he heard what I wanted him to do a smirk spread across his face. Poor bastard, he couldn't help it."

Tarkanian needed someone to bring to Lev Antonin. But not just anyone—he had to look like a murderer. Moving through the twilit streets of Nizhny Tagil, Tarkanian scoured the bars for a likely victim. Now and again he was forced to sidestep puddles as big as small ponds, caused by the deluge that had only recently been reduced to a light mist. As it had been since dawn the claustrophobically low sky was a dull gray, but now it was marred here and there by bruises of yellow and lavender, as if the storm had brutalized the day.

Tarkanian parked himself outside the most raucous of bars and lit a harsh Turkish cigarette, pulling the smoke deep into his lungs and exhaling it in a gray cloud as thick as those above his head. Night gathered around him like an acolyte as the drunken laughter spilled out to him, along with the shattering of glass and the chunky exhalations of a fistfight. A moment later a big man, bleeding from the nose and several cuts on his face, staggered out onto the sidewalk.

As he bent over, hands on knees, wheezing and retching, Tarkanian ground out his cigarette under his boot heel, walked over, and delivered a vicious chop to the exposed back of the man's neck. The drunk pitched forward, hitting his forehead on the pavement with a satisfying smack.

Tarkanian grabbed him under the arms and pulled him into the alley. If any passersby noticed what he was up to none of them gave the slightest indication. All of them hurried on about their business without even a glance in his direction. Life in Nizhny Tagil had trained them to ignore anything that wasn't their business. It was the only way to keep healthy in this city.

In the deepening shadows of the stinking alley, Tarkanian checked his watch.

There was no way to contact Oserov; he'd just have to hope he'd accomplished his part of the plan.

Fifteen minutes later he walked into a bakery and bought the largest layer cake in the glass case. Back in the alley, he dumped the cake and, lifting the man's severed head by his beer- and blood-damp hair, placed it carefully in the cake box. The glassy eyes stared blankly back at him until he lowered the lid.

Across town he was admitted to Lev Antonin's office, where the boss was still guarded by his seven heavily armed goons.

"Lev Antonin, as promised I brought you a present," he said as he placed the box on Antonin's desk. On the way over, it had grown surprisingly heavy.

Antonin looked from him to the box, evincing little enthusiasm. Signaling to one of his bodyguards, he had him open the box. Then he stood up and peered inside.

"Who the fuck is this?" he asked.

"The murderer."

"What's his name?"

"Mikhail Gorbachev," Tarkanian said sardonically, "how the hell should I know?"

Antonin's face was particularly ugly when he smirked. "If you don't know his name, how d'you know he's the one?"

"I caught him in the act," Tarkanian said. "He had broken into your house, he was about to kill your wife and children."

Antonin's face darkened and, snatching up the phone, he dialed a number. His face relaxed somewhat when he heard his wife's voice.

"Are you all right? Is everyone safe?" He frowned. "What do you mean? What—? Who the fuck is this? Where's my wife?" His face had grown dark again and he looked at Tarkanian. "What the fuck is going on?"

Tarkanian kept his voice calm and even. "Your family is safe, Lev Antonin, and they'll remain safe as long as I have free passage to take Arkadin. If you interfere in any way—"

"I'll surround the house, my men will break in—"

"And your wife and three children will die."

Antonin whipped out a Stechkin handgun and aimed it at Tarkanian. "I'll shoot you right here where you stand, and I promise your death won't be quick."

"In that event, your wife and children will die." Tarkanian's voice had an edge now. "Whatever you do to me will be done to them."

Antonin glared at Tarkanian, then dropped the Stechkin on the desktop next to the cake box. He looked ready to tear his hair out.

"The idea with Neanderthals," Tarkanian said to Arkadin later, "is to lead them by the hand through all their possible responses, showing them the futility of each one."

He said, "Listen to me, Lev Antonin, you have what we bargained for. If you still want everything, try to remember that pigs get slaughtered."

Then Tarkanian left the office to find Leonid Danilovich Arkadin.

Tracy Atherton and Alonzo Pecunia Zuñiga presented themselves on the front steps of Don Fernando Hererra's house at precisely three o'clock in the afternoon, bathed in brilliant sunshine amplified by a virtually cloudless sky.

Bourne, with his spade beard and new hairstyle, had shopped for clothes suitable for a distinguished professor from Madrid. Their last stop was an optician's, where he purchased a pair of contact lenses the color of the professor's eyes.

Hererra lived in the Santa Cruz *barrio* of Seville, in a beautiful three-story stucco house painted white and yellow, whose upper-story windows were guarded by magnificent wrought-iron balconies. Its facade formed one side of a small plaza in the center of which was an old well that had been turned into an octagonal fountain. Small haberdashery and crockery shops lined the other three sides, their quaint fronts shaded by palm and orange trees.

The door opened at their knock, and when Tracy gave him their names a well-dressed young man escorted them into the high-ceilinged wood-and-marble entryway. There were fresh white and yellow flowers in a tall porcelain vase on a polished fruitwood table in the center, while on a marquetry sideboard an engraved silver bowl was filled to overflowing with fragrant oranges.

A piano melody, soft and sinuous, came to them. They could see an Old World drawing room with a wall of ebony bookshelves illuminated by raking light from a line of French doors that led out onto an inner courtyard. There was an elegant escritoire, a matching pair of sofas of cinnamon-colored leather, a sideboard on which were arranged five delicate orchids, like girls at a beauty pageant. But the drawing room was dominated by an antique spinet piano behind which sat a large man with an enormous shock of luxuriant white hair brushed straight back off his wide, intelligent forehead. His body was bent in an attitude of exacting concentration, and there was a pencil gripped between his teeth so that he looked like he was in pain. In fact, he was composing a song with a rather florid melody that owed a debt to any number of Iberian virtuosos, as well as to certain flamenco folk tunes.

As they entered, he looked up. Don Herrera had startling blue, slightly exophthalmic eyes, making him look something like a praying mantis as he rose, unfolding from the piano bench in stages. He had dark, leathery skin, wind-burned and sun-wrinkled, marking him as an inveterate outdoorsman. His body was lean and flat, as if he had been constructed in two dimensions instead of three. He appeared to wear the years he'd spent in the Colombian oil fields as a second skin.

Taking the pencil from between his teeth, he smiled warmly. "Ah, my distinguished guests, what a pleasure." He kissed the back of Tracy's hand and shook Bourne's. "Dear lady. And Professor, it's an honor to welcome you both to my house." He gestured toward one of the leather sofas. "Please make yourselves comfortable." He was dressed in an open-neck white shirt under an immaculate cream-colored suit of lightweight silk that looked soft as a baby's cheek. "Would you care for sherry, or something stronger, perhaps?"

"Sherry and some Garrotxa, perhaps, if you have it," Bourne said, playing his part to the hilt.

"An excellent idea," Hererra proclaimed, calling in the young man for the order. He wagged a long, tapered forefinger at Bourne. "I like the way your palate works, Professor."

Bourne looked fatuously pleased, while Tracy carefully hid her amusement from the older man.

The young man arrived carrying a chased silver salver on which was set a cut-crystal decanter of sherry, three glasses of the same cut crystal, along with a platter of the sheep cheese, crackers, and a wedge of deep orange quince jelly. He set the salver down on a low table and departed as silently as he had come.

Their host poured the sherry and handed out the glasses. Hererra raised his glass, and they followed suit.

"To the unsullied pursuit of scholarly inquiry." Don Hererra sipped his sherry, and Bourne and Tracy tasted theirs. As they ate the cheese and quince jelly, he said, "So tell me your opinion. Is the world, in fact, going to war against Iran?"

"I don't have enough information to make a judgment," Tracy said, "but in my opinion Iran has been flaunting their nuclear program in our faces for too long."

Don Hererra nodded sagely. "I think finally the United States has gotten it right. This time, Iran has provoked us too far. But to contemplate another world war, well, to sum up, war is bad for business for most, but uncommonly good for a few." He swung around. "And Professor, what is your learned opinion?"

"When it comes to politics," Bourne said, "I maintain a strictly neutral posture."

"But surely, sir, on such a grave issue that affects us all, you must come down on one side or the other."

"I assure you, Don Hererra, I'm far more interested in the Goya than I am in Iran."

The Colombian gave him a disappointed look, but then wasted no more time in getting down to business. "Señorita Atherton, I have given you full access to my unearthed treasure, and now you have brought with you the Prado's—and by extension all of Spain's—leading expert on Goya. So." He spread his hands. "What is the verdict?"

Tracy, smiling noncommittally, said, "Professor Zuñiga, why don't you provide the answer?"

"Don Hererra," Bourne said, taking his cue, "the painting in your possession, attributed to Francisco José de Goya y Lucientes, is in fact not painted by him at all."

Hererra frowned and for a moment his

lips pursed. "Do you mean to tell me, Professor Zuñiga, that I have been harboring a fake?"

"That depends on your definition of a fake," Bourne said.

"With all due respect, Professor, either it is a fake or it isn't."

"You may look at it that way, Professor, but there are others. Let me explain by saying that the painting, though by no means commanding the price you have set on it, is far from worthless. You see, tests I've made confirm that it was produced in Goya's studio. It may even have been sketched out by the master himself before he died. In any event, there can be little doubt that the design is his. The actual painting, however, lacks the particular slightly mad attack of his brushstrokes, though it mimics these quite convincingly even to the trained eye."

Don Hererra drained the last of his sherry then sat back, his large hands folded over his lower belly. "So," he said at length, "my painting is worth something, just not the price I've quoted to Señorita Atherton."

"That's right," Bourne affirmed.

Hererra made a sound deep in his throat. "This turn of events will take some getting used to." He turned to Tracy. "Señorita, given the circumstances I fully understand your desire to withdraw from our arrangement."

"On the contrary," Tracy said. "I'm still interested in the painting, though an adjustment markedly downward in price would be necessary."

"I see," Hererra said. "Well, naturally." His gaze turned inward for some time. Then he roused himself. "Before proceeding further, I'd like to make a call."

"By all means," Tracy said.

Don Hererra nodded, rose, and went to a desk with delicate cabriole legs. He punched in a number on his cell phone, waited a moment, then said, "This is Don Fernando Hererra. He's expecting my call."

He smiled at them while he waited. Then he said into the phone, "*Por favor, momentito.*"

Quite unexpectedly he handed the cell to Bourne. Bourne looked up at him expectantly, but Don Hererra's face bore no hint of what was happening.

"Hello," Bourne said, continuing in perfect Spanish.

"Yes," the voice on the other end of the line said, "Professor Alonzo Pecunia Zuñiga here, to whom am I speaking?"

18

Nothing," Amun Chalthoum said with evident disgust.

He was staring down at the young man Soraya had fished out of the Red Sea after he'd jumped overboard to escape her questioning. They were in one of the shipboard cabins provided for them by the owner of the dive shop, a narrow, foul-smelling place whose exaggerated rocking made the sunlight an inconstant companion.

Chalthoum's expression was a combination of frustration and fear. "He's nothing but a runner—an advance man for drug smugglers."

That didn't seem like nothing to Soraya, but she could see that Amun wasn't in the mood for thinking about anything other than the terrorist cadre. It was at this moment, when his distress was most evident, that she abandoned the notion that he might be misleading her. She was sure he wouldn't be so emotional about this situation if he was covering up al Mokhabarat's involvement. The wave of relief that ran through her was so powerful, she rocked on her feet. When she recovered, she turned her full concentration on the origin of the terrorist cell.

"All right, so they didn't come through here," she said, "but there must be other places along the coast—"

"My men have checked," Amun said darkly. "Which means the route I proposed is wrong. They didn't come overland through Iraq, after all."

"Then how did they get into Egypt?" Soraya asked.

"I don't know." Chalthoum seemed to chew over this notion for some time. "They wouldn't be stupid enough to try transshipping the Kowsar missile from Iran by plane.

It would have been picked up by our radar—or one of your satellites."

That was true enough, she thought. Then how did the Iranian terrorists get the missile into Egypt? This enigma brought her full circle, back to her first suspicion that Egyptians—but not al Mokhabarat—had been involved, but it wasn't until they were back on deck, the runner was in custody, and the boat was heading back to land that she proposed it aloud to Chalthoum.

They were standing by the starboard rail, the wind whipping at their hair, sunlight turning the skin of the water to a white dazzle. He had his forearms on the rail, his hands clasped loosely, staring down into the water.

"Amun," she said softly, "is it possible that someone in your government—one of your enemies, one of our enemies—created the opportunity for the Iranian terrorists?"

Even though she'd been careful to phrase the question in the most benign way, she felt him stiffen. A muscle in his cheek began to spasm, but he surprised her when he answered.

"I've already thought of that, *azizti*, and much to my chagrin I made several discreet inquiries this afternoon while I was alone in my search of the dive clubs. It cost me in political capital, but I did it, and it came to nothing." He turned to her, his dark eyes more sorrowful than she'd ever seen them. "Truly, *azizti*, it would have been the end of me if what you asked had been the truth."

And it was at this precise moment that she knew. He'd been fully cognizant of her suspicions, had accepted them uncomfortably until the possibility became too much for him to bear. He'd been humiliated making his calls, because just asking the question was traitorous in nature, and now she realized what he meant by "political capital," because it was likely—probable, even—that some of the people he'd called would not forgive him his doubts. This, too, was part of the modern-day Egypt, something he'd have to live with for the rest of his life. Unless . . .

"Amun," she said so softly he had to lean into the wind to hear her, "after this is over, why don't you come back with me?"

"To America?" He said it as if she were speaking about Mars, or someplace even more distant and alien, but when he continued there was a kindness in his voice she'd never heard before. "Yes, *azizti*, that would solve many problems. On the other hand, it would raise an army of different ones. What would I do, for instance?"

"You're an intelligence officer, you could—"

"I am an Egyptian. Worse, I am the head of al Mokhabarat."

"Think of the intel you could provide."

He smiled sadly. "Think of how I would be reviled, both here and in your America. To them, I am the enemy. No matter what intel I provided I would always be the enemy, always distrusted, always watched, never accepted."

"Not if we were married." It came out practically before she thought it.

There was a shocked silence between them. The boat, nearing the dock, had slowed, and the wind had died. The sweat, popping out, dried against their skin.

Amun took her hand, his thumb rubbing the splay of small bones in its back. "*Azizti*," he said, "marrying me would be the end of you as well—the end of your career in intelligence."

"So what?" Her eyes were fierce. Now that she had said what was in her heart she felt a kind of wild freedom she'd never experienced before.

He smiled. "You don't mean that, please don't pretend you do."

She turned fully to him. "I don't want to pretend with you, Amun. All the secrets I carry have made me sick at heart, and I keep saying to myself that there must be an end to it somewhere, with someone."

He slipped one arm around her narrow waist and, as the crew around them snapped to, tying off the ropes on the gleaming metal cleats on the side of the slip, he nodded. "At least on this one thing we can agree."

And she tilted her face up into the sunlight. "This is the one thing that matters, *azizti*."

Ms. Trevor, have you any idea who could have . . . ?"

Though the man heading the investigation into DCI Veronica Hart's death—what was his name? Simon Something—Simon

Herren, yes, that was it—kept asking her questions, Moira had ceased to listen. His voice was barely a drone in ears that were filled with the white noise of the explosion's aftermath. She and Humphry Bamber were lying side by side in the ER, having been examined and treated for fistfuls of cuts and abrasions. They were lucky, the ER doctor had said, and Moira believed him. They had been transported via ambulance, made to stay lying down while they were given oxygen, and given superficial exams for concussions, broken bones, and the like.

"Who do you work for?" Moira said to Simon Herren.

He smiled indulgently. He had short brown hair, small rodent eyes, and bad teeth. The collar of his shirt was stiff with starch, and his rep tie was strictly government issue. He wasn't going to answer her and they both knew it. Anyway, what did it matter what part of the intelligence alphabet soup he belonged to? In the end, weren't they all the same? Well, Veronica Hart wasn't.

All at once, the hammer blow hit her and tears leaked out of the corners of her eyes.

"What is it?" Simon Herren looked around for a nurse. "Are you in pain?"

Moira managed to laugh through her tears. *What an idiot,* she thought. To stop herself from telling him so, she asked how her companion was.

"Mr. Bamber is understandably shaken up," Herren said without a hint of sympathy. "Not surprising, since he's a civilian."

"Go to hell." Moira turned her head away from him.

"I was told you could be difficult."

That got her attention, and she turned back, catching his eyes with hers. "Who told you I could be difficult?"

Herren gave her his most enigmatic smile.

"Ah, yes," she said, "Noah Perlis."

"Who?"

He shouldn't have said that, she thought. If he'd kept his mouth shut he might have stopped the flicker of response in his eyes before it gave him away. So Noah was still just a step away from her. Why? He didn't want anything from her, which meant that he'd become afraid of her. That was good to know; that would help her through the bleak days and weeks ahead when, alone and at risk, she would blame herself for Ronnie's death, because hadn't the bomb been meant for her? It had been slipped into the tailpipe of her rental car. No one—not even Noah—could have foreseen that Ronnie would be driving it. But even the small satisfaction that he had failed paled against the collateral damage.

She'd been near death before, she'd had colleagues or targets die in the field, that was part of wet work. She'd been prepared for it, as much as any human being could be prepared for the death of someone known to you. But the field was far away, across one ocean or another; the field was at a certain remove from civilization, from her personal life, from home.

Ronnie's death was something altogether different. It was caused by a series of events and her reaction to those events. All at once a tide of ifs engulfed her. If she hadn't started her own firm, if Jason weren't "dead," if she hadn't gone to Ronnie, if Bamber weren't working for Noah, if, if, if . . .

But they'd all happened, and like a daisy chain she could look back and see how all these events interlocked, how one led inexorably to another, and how the end result was always the same: the death of Ronnie Hart. She thought then of the Balinese healer Suparwita, who had looked into her eyes with an expression she hadn't been able to decipher until now. It had been the sure knowledge of loss, as if even then, back in Bali, he'd known what was in store for her.

The insistent buzzing of Simon Herren's voice drew her away from the blackness of her own thoughts. Her eyes refocused.

"What? What did you say?"

"Mr. Bamber is being released into my custody."

Herren stood between her bed and Bamber's, as if daring her to defy him. Bamber was already dressed and ready to go, but he seemed frightened, indecisive, shell-shocked.

"The doctor tells me you need to stay here for more tests."

"The hell I will." She sat up, swung her legs over the side, and stood up.

"I think you'd best lie down," he said in that vaguely mocking tone of his. "Doctor's orders."

"Fuck you." She started putting on her clothes, not caring if he saw flashes of her body or not. "Fuck you and the broom you flew in on."

He could not keep the contempt off his face. "Not a very professional response, is—"

In the next instant he doubled over as she buried her fist in his solar plexus. Her knee came up to meet his descending chin, and as he crumpled, she dragged him up, splaying him out on the bed. Then she turned to Bamber and said, "You have only one shot at this. Come with me now or Noah will own you forever."

Still Bamber didn't move. He was staring at Simon Herren as if in a daze, but when she extended her hand, he took it. He needed someone to guide him now, someone who might tell him the truth. Stevenson was gone, Veronica Hart had been blown apart in front of him, and now there was only Moira, the person who had dragged him out of the doomed Buick, the woman who had saved his life.

Moira led him out of the emergency room as swiftly and efficiently as possible. Fortunately, the ER was a madhouse, EMTs and cops trotting this way and that alongside their patients, giving reports on the fly to the residents, who in turn barked orders to the nurses. Everyone was overworked and overstressed; no one stopped them or even noticed their departure.

A contingent of Amun's men met them on the dock, where he held the young drug trafficker by the scruff of his neck. The poor kid was scared shitless. He wasn't one of the tough Egyptian youths who knew very well what they were getting into. He looked like what he was: an indigent tourist who'd been hoping to score some quick money to continue his world odyssey. It was probably why he'd been chosen by the drug runners in the first place. He looked innocent.

Chalthoum could have let him go with a warning, but he was in no mood to be magnanimous. He'd cuffed his hands behind his back, then leapt back when the young boy had heaved up his last meal.

"Amun, have some pity," Soraya said now.

"Drug trafficking cannot be dismissed."

This was the Amun she knew, rock-hard and gimlet-eyed. An involuntary shiver ran through her. "He's nothing, you said so yourself. If you put him away, they'll just find another fool to take his place."

"Then we'll find him, too," Chalthoum said. "Lock him up, and throw away the key."

At this, the young man began to wail. "Please help me. I never signed on for this."

Chalthoum looked at him so darkly that the young man recoiled. "You should have thought of that before you took the criminals' money." He slung him roughly into the arms of his men. "You know what to do with him," he said.

"Wait, wait!" The young man tried to dig in his heels as Chalthoum's men turned to take him away. "What if I have information? Would you help me then?"

"What information could you have?" Chalthoum said dismissively. "I know how these drug networks are structured. Your only contact was with the people on the rung right above you, and since you're on the lowest rung . . ." He shrugged and signed to his men to take the prisoner away.

"I don't mean those people." The young man's voice had risen in fear. "There's something I overheard. Other divers talking."

"What divers? Talking about what?"

"They're gone now," the young man said. "They were here ten days ago, maybe a little more."

Chalthoum shook his head. "Too long ago. Whoever they were, whatever they said is of no interest to me."

Soraya stepped toward the young man. "What's your name?"

"Stephen."

She nodded. "My name is Soraya, Stephen. Tell me, were these divers Iranian?"

"Look at him," Chalthoum interrupted. "He wouldn't know an Iranian from an Indian."

"The divers weren't Arab," Stephen said.

Chalthoum snorted. "You see what I mean? Sonny, Iranians are Persians, descended from the Scythian-Sarmatian nomads of Central Asia. They're Shi'a Muslims, not Arabs."

"What I mean . . ." Stephen swallowed hard. "What I meant to say was that they were white like me. Caucasians."

"Could you tell what nationality they were?" Soraya asked.

"They were Americans," Stephen said.

"So what?" Chalthoum was losing patience.

Soraya ventured closer still. "Stephen,

what did you overhear? What were these divers talking about?"

With a fearful glance at Chalthoum, Stephen said, "There were four of them. They were coming off a vacation, that was clear. Only they called it leave."

Soraya made eye contact with Chalthoum. "Military men."

"So he says," he rumbled. "Continue."

"They'd just come up from the second dive of the day and they were kind of giddy. I was helping them off with their tanks, but they acted as if I wasn't there. Anyway, they were grumbling about having their leave cut short. There was some kind of emergency—an assignment for them that came out of the air—that was what they said. It appeared out of thin air."

"This is nonsense," Chalthoum said. "It's clear he's making this up to spare himself life imprisonment."

"Oh, God." At the pronouncement of his mortal sentence, Stephen's knees gave way and Chalthoum's men were obliged to hold him tightly in order to keep him on his feet.

"Stephen." Soraya reached out, turned the young man's face toward her. He was as pale as death, and she could see the whites all around his eyes. "Tell us the rest of what you overheard. Did the divers say what their assignment was?"

He shook his head. "I got the impression they didn't yet know."

"Enough!" Chalthoum cried. "Dispose of this rancid piece of meat!"

Stephen was openly weeping now. "But they knew their destination."

Soraya held up her hand for Chalthoum's men to stop dragging him away. "Where was it, Stephen? Where were the men headed?"

"They were flying to Khartoum," the young man said through his tears, " 'wherever that godforsaken place is.' "

19

The president was met by Secretary of Defense Halliday as he was exiting the United Nations. Having sent the General Assembly into a frenzy by presenting the evidence against Iran in the bombing of the American airliner and the loss of 181 lives, the president had stopped for an impromptu press conference with the media, clustered around him like hens at feeding time. He obligingly gave them half a dozen choice sound bites to air or to carry back to their editors before his press secretary whispered in his ear that Secretary Halliday was waiting with urgent news.

The president was on a high. It had been a long time since an American president could address that august body of the United Nations armed with evidence so damning it had shocked the representatives from Russia and China into silence. The world was changing, tilting against Iran in a way never before seen. The president, whose presence here was in no small part due to Bud Halliday, thought it fitting that the first person he speak with regarding his unqualified success was the defense secretary.

"Break out the champagne!" the president called as he signaled to Halliday, and the two men entered the long bullet- and bombproof limousine.

The vehicle took off the moment the pair were seated. Across from them was the press secretary, his cheeks as flushed with victory as the president's, a bottle of chilled American sparkling wine in his hand.

"Sir, if you don't mind, let's hold the celebration," Bud Halliday said.

"Mind?" the president said. "Of course I mind! Solly, open the damn champagne!"

"Sir," Halliday said, "there's been an incident."

The president froze in mid-gesture, then slowly turned to his defense secretary. “What kind of an incident, Bud?”

“Veronica Hart, the director of Central Intelligence, is dead.”

At once the color drained from the president’s flushed cheeks. “Good Christ, what happened, Bud?”

“A car bomb—we think. There’s an ongoing investigation, but that’s the most recent theory.”

“But who—?”

“Homeland Security, ATF, and the FBI are all coordinating their efforts under the NSA umbrella.”

“Good.” The president, all business now, nodded curtly. “The sooner we clear up this car bomb mess, the better.”

“As usual, we’re on the same page, sir.” Halliday glanced Solly’s way. “Speaking of which, we’re going to need a comprehensive press release, and spin control. After the plane incident, the last thing we need is speculation about terrorists and another bombing.”

“Solly, get our talking heads on it right away,” the president said, “then get into overdrive on an official release. Coordinate it with Secretary Halliday's office, would you?"

"Right away, sir." Solly slipped the sweating bottle back into its bucket of ice and started calling contacts on his cell phone.

Halliday waited until the press secretary was engaged in his first conversation. "Sir, we've got to think about a replacement for DCI Hart." And before the president could jump in, he continued: "It seems fair to say that the experiment with hiring from the private sector has run its course. In any event, we need to move quickly to fill the gap."

"Get me a list of the qualified senior people at CI."

"I will certainly do that." Halliday texted a message to his office as they spoke. He looked up. "The list will be on your desk inside an hour." But his face was still deeply troubled.

"What is it, Bud?"

"It's nothing, sir."

"Oh, come on, Bud. We've known each other a long time, haven't we? There's something on your mind, now's not the time to hold back."

"Okay." Halliday exhaled deeply. "This is

the perfect time to merge all the intelligence organizations into one organic whole that shares raw intel, makes coordinated decisions, and cuts through the bloated red tape that frustrates all of us."

"I've heard all this before, Bud."

With some effort Halliday stitched a grin on his face. "No one knows that better than I do, sir, and I understand. In the past you agreed with the DCI, whoever it was."

The president worried his lower lip. "There's history to be observed, Bud. CI is the oldest, most venerable institution in the constellation of the intelligence communities. In many ways it's the crown jewel. I can understand why you'd want to get your hands on it."

Rather than waste time in denial of the truth, Halliday decided to take another tack altogether. "The current crisis is another case in point. We're having difficulty coordinating with CI—especially Typhon, which might very well have the intel we need to ensure that our retaliation against Iran doesn't hit a snag."

The president stared out the smoked window at the monumental public buildings at the district's heart. "You've received the money for—you know—for the—what have you named the operation?"

The secretary of defense gave up trying to follow the train of the president's thoughts. "Pinprick, sir."

"Who thinks of these names?"

Halliday sensed his boss didn't want an answer.

The president turned back to him. "Who d'you have in mind?"

With his choice in the forefront of his mind, Halliday was ready for that one. "Danziger, sir."

"Really? I thought you were going to propose your intelligence czar."

"Jaime Hernandez is a career office man. We need someone with a more—robust—background."

"Quite right," the president agreed. "Who the hell is this Danziger?"

"M. Errol Danziger. The NSA's current deputy director of signals intelligence for analysis and production."

The president returned to his contemplation of the passing streetscape. "Have I met him?"

"Yes, sir. Twice, the last time when you were at the Pentagon just last—"

"Remind me, please."

"He brought in the printouts Hernandez distributed."

"I don't recall the man."

"Hardly surprising, sir. There's nothing remarkable about him." Halliday chuckled. "That's what made him so valuable during his stint in the field. He worked Southeast Asia before moving into the Operations Directorate."

"Wet work?"

Halliday was startled by the question. Nevertheless, he saw no point in lying. "Indeed, sir."

"And returned home to tell the tale."

"Yes, sir."

The president made an unintelligible sound deep in his throat. "Bring him to the Oval Office at—" He snapped his fingers for the press secretary's attention. "Solly? Opening, today."

Solly put his call on hold, scrolled through a second PDA. "Five twenty-five, sir. But you only have ten minutes before the formal press conference. We need to make the six o'clock news."

"Of course we do." The president lifted a hand, smiling. "Five twenty-five, Bud.

Ten minutes is more than enough time for a yea or nay."

Then, abruptly, he turned to other matters, a crisis agenda packed with daunting security issues, at the end of which was not a hot bath and a good meal, but a phone conference with his director of protocol, deciding on who to invite to the state funeral for DCI Hart.

Seconds after Bourne took the phone, Hererra's young man had stolen into the room. Now he pressed the muzzle of a Beretta Px4 9mm pistol to Tracy's left temple. She was wide-eyed, sitting painfully erect at the edge of the sofa.

"My dear fellow," Don Fernando Hererra said as he took the cell from Bourne, "I may not know who you are, but I know this much: My threatening you will avail me nothing." His smile was sweet, almost soft. "Whereas if I tell you that I will have Fausto blow her brains out—pardon the crudeness of my words, Señorita Atherton—unless you tell me who you are, I feel certain that you will be more inclined to tell me the truth."

"I admit that I've underestimated you, Don Hererra," Bourne said.

"Adam, please tell him the truth." Tracy was clearly terrified for her life.

"I know that you're a confidence man, just as I know you've come to swindle me out of my Goya, which, by the way, Professor Alonzo Pecunia Zuñiga—the *real* Don Alonzo—has confirmed to me is authentic." He pointed. "He has also confirmed that Señorita Atherton is genuine. How you seduced her into going along with your scheme is between the two of you." But his expression conveyed his dismay and disappointment at Tracy's fall from grace. "My concern is who you are and which of my enemies hired you to con me."

Tracy shivered. "Adam, for God's sake—"

Hererra cocked his head. "Come, come, Señor Con Man, you have forfeited your right to scare the young lady."

It was time for him to act, Bourne knew that. He also knew that the situation was on a razor's edge. Hererra was the wild card. On the surface it seemed unlikely that such a polished gentleman of Seville would actually direct the young man to pull the trigger. However, Hererra's black-hands work in the oil fields of Colombia belied his current gentlemanly identity. At heart, he might still be that rough-and-tumble man who fought, finessed, and bullied his way to a fortune in the oil industry. A man didn't successfully do business with the Tropical Oil Company without a heart as hard as mahogany, and without spilling some blood. In any event, it was not for Bourne to gamble with Tracy's life.

"You're right, Don Hererra. My apologies," Bourne said. "Now to the truth: I was hired by one of your enemies, but not to take the Goya from you."

Tracy's eyes opened even wider.

"I came up with this ruse to get in to see you."

Hererra's eyes glittered as he drew up a chair to sit in front of Bourne. "Continue."

"My name is Adam Stone."

"Forgive me if I'm skeptical." He snapped his fingers. "Passport. And use your left hand. You don't want to alarm Fausto, believe me."

Bourne did. With the tips of the fingers on his left hand, he produced his passport, which Hererra scrutinized as if he were a special agent from immigration.

As he handed back the document, he

said, "All right, Señor Stone, what are you?"

"I'm a freelance specialist in let us say hardware of a special nature."

Hererra shook his head. "Now you've lost me."

"Don Hererra, you know a Balinese merchant by the name of Wayan."

"I do not."

Bourne made a show of ignoring the lie. "I work for the people who supply Wayan."

"Adam, what is this?" Tracy said. "You told me you were interested in seed money for an e-commerce start-up."

At this, Hererra sat back, contemplating Bourne in, it seemed, an entirely new light. "It seems, Señorita Atherton, that Adam Stone lied to you as easily as he did to me."

Bourne knew he'd made a desperate gamble. He'd calculated that the only way to take control of the situation was to astonish the Colombian. In this, it appeared, he'd been successful.

"The question is why?"

Bourne saw his chance to tip the scales in his favor. "The people who hired me—the people who supply Wayan—"

"I told you I don't know anyone named Wayan."

Bourne shrugged. "The people I work for know better. They don't like the way you're doing business. In fact, they want you out of it completely."

Don Hererra laughed. "Fausto, do you hear this, do you hear this man?" He hunched forward so his face was close to Bourne's. "Are you threatening me, Stone? Because the air in my house is vibrating in such a way."

Now there was a stiletto in his hand. The hilt was inlaid with jade, the long blade as tapered as Hererra's own fingers. He tipped the blade forward until the point touched the skin above Bourne's Adam's apple.

"You should know I don't take kindly to threats."

"What happens to me is irrelevant," Bourne said.

"The señorita's blood will be on your hands."

"Surely you know how powerful my employers are. Whatever is going to happen is going to happen."

"Unless I change my business practices."

Bourne felt the shift in Hererra's thinking even before he said it. He was no longer denying his business in arms shipping. "That's correct."

Don Hererra sighed and made a sign to Fausto, who removed the muzzle and holstered the Beretta at the small of his back. Then he threw the stiletto onto the sofa cushion and, slapping his thighs, said, "I think, Señor Stone, we both could do with a walk in the garden."

Fausto unlocked the French doors, and the two men stepped out onto the flagstone path. The garden was an octagon embraced by the sturdy arms of the house. There was a small grove of lemon trees and, in the center, a tiled fountain in the Moorish style shaded by a palm tree. Here and there stone benches were scattered, both in sunlight and in dappled shade. The air was perfumed by the lemon trees, whose new leaves were emerging like butterflies from their winter cocoons.

Because it was cool out, Don Hererra indicated a bench in full sun. When they were seated side by side, he said, "I must admit Yevsen surprises me; he sends a man who is not only not a thug, but possesses uncommon wisdom." His head inclined a fraction, as if he were tipping his hat to Bourne. "How much is that Russian sonovabitch paying you?"

"Not enough."

"Yes, Yevsen is one cheap bastard."

Bourne laughed. His great gamble had paid off: He had his answer. Wayan was being supplied by Nikolai Yevsen. Scarface had been sent by Yevsen, following Bourne all the way from Bali where he'd first tried to kill him. He still didn't know why Yevsen wanted him dead, but he knew he'd just moved a giant step closer to finding out. He had a line on who Don Fernando Hererra really was: Nikolai Yevsen's competitor. And if he convinced Hererra Bourne could be turned, Hererra would give up everything he knew about Yevsen, which just might include what Bourne needed to know.

"Certainly not enough for having a stiletto held to my throat."

"No one regrets that necessity more than I do."

The fissures in Hererra's face were set in high relief as they were struck by the slanting rays of the sun. There was a fierce pride in that face he'd held in abeyance while he was playing the part of the gentleman, a granite toughness Bourne could appreciate.

"I know about your history in Colombia," he said. "I know how you took on the Tropical Oil Company."

"Ah, yes, well, that was a long time ago."

"Initiative never fades away."

"Listen to you." The Colombian gave him a shrewd sideways look. "Tell me, should I sell my Goya to Señorita Atherton?"

"She has nothing to do with me," Bourne said.

"A chivalrous thing to say, but not quite true." Hererra held up an admonishing finger. "She was all too ready to take the Goya at an unfair price."

"That just makes her a good businessman."

Hererra laughed. "Indeed, it does." He delivered another sidelong glance. "I suppose you won't tell me your real name."

"You saw my passport."

"Now is not the time to insult me."

"What I meant is that one name is as good as another," Bourne said, "especially in our line of work."

Hererra shivered. "Christ, it's getting cold."

He stood up. The shadows had grown long during their talk. Only one sliver of sunlight remained on the top of the west-facing wall, while day turned into fugitive night.

"Let's rejoin the lady businessman, shall we, and find out how badly she wants my Goya."

M. Errol Danziger, the NSA's current deputy director of signals intelligence for analysis and production, was watching three monitors at once, reading real-time progress reports from Iran, Egypt, and Sudan, and taking notes. He was also periodically speaking into the microphone of an electronic headpiece, using terse signals-speak he himself had devised, even though he was speaking on an NSA-approved encrypted line.

His Signals Sit Room was where Secretary of Defense Bud Halliday found Danziger analyzing and coordinating intel, and directing the far-flung elements of this blackest of black-ops missions. To those who worked most closely with him, he was known, ironically, as the Arab, because of the unceasing missions he'd successfully run against Muslim extremists of all sects.

No one else was in the room, just the two men. Danziger glanced up briefly, gave his boss a deferential nod before returning to his work. Halliday sat down. He didn't mind the curt treatment that in anyone else would warrant a severe dressing-down. Danziger was special, deserving of special treatment. In fact, this manifestation of intense concentration was a sign that all was well.

"Give me your nibble, Triton," Danziger said into the mike. *Nibble* was signals-speak for "timetable."

"High and tight. Bardem is on the money."

Triton was Noah Perlis's ops designation, the secretary knew. The software program Bardem, which analyzed the changing field situation in real time, was his responsibility.

"Let's get started on the Final Four," the Arab said. *Final Four:* the mission's last phase.

Halliday's heart skipped a beat. They were close to the finish line now, nearing the biggest power coup any American official had ever managed. Damping down his excitement, he said, "I trust you'll be finished with this session soon."

"That all depends," Danziger replied.

Halliday moved closer. "Make it happen. We're going to see the president in just under three hours."

Danziger's attention shifted from his screens and he said, "Triton, five," into the mike before he flipped a switch, temporarily muting the connection. "You met with the president?"

Halliday nodded. "I brought your name up and he's interested."

"Interested enough to meet with me, but it's not yet a done deal."

The defense secretary smiled. "Not to worry. He's not going to choose either of the candidates from inside CI."

The Arab nodded; he knew better than to question his boss's legendary influence. "We have a bit of a situation developing in Egypt."

Halliday hunched forward. "How so?"

"Soraya Moore, whom we both know, and Amun Chalthoum, the head of the

Egyptian intelligence service, have been snooping around the farm."

The farm was signals-speak for a current mission's theater of operations. "What have they found?"

"The original team was on vacation when their orders were transmitted. Apparently they were pissed off enough about their leave being cut short that their destination was overheard."

Halliday scowled. "Are you saying that Moore and Chalthoum are aware that the team was headed for Khartoum?"

Danziger nodded. "This problem has to be nipped in the bud; there's only one solution."

Halliday was taken aback. "What? Our own men?"

"They violated security protocol."

The secretary shook his head. "But still—"

"Containment, Bud. Containment while it's still possible." The Arab leaned forward and patted his boss on the knee. "Just think of it as another regrettable case of friendly fire."

Halliday sat back, scrubbed his face

with the heels of his hands. “It’s a good thing humans have an infinite capacity for rationalization.”

About to swivel back to his screens, Danziger said, “Bud, this is my mission. I devised Pinprick, I designed it down to the last detail. But you approved it. Now, I know for a fact you’re not about to let four disgruntled sons-of-bitches put our heads in the crosshairs, are you?”

20

Don Fernando Hererra paused at the French doors, lifted a finger, and his eyes engaged Bourne's. "Before we go inside, I must make one thing clear. In Colombia, I have taken part in the wars between the military and the indigenous guerrillas, the struggle between fascism and socialism. Both are weak and flawed because they seek only control over others."

The blue shadows of Seville lent him a keen and hungry look. He was like a wolf that has sighted the face of his prey.

"I and others like me were trained to kill

a victim who has been stripped of his defenses, who lacks any capacity for response. This act is known as the perfect crime. Do you understand me?"

He continued to peer into Bourne's face as if he were connected to an X-ray machine. "I know you weren't hired by Nikolai Yevsen or by Dimitri Maslov, his silent partner. How do I know this? Though I know almost nothing about you—including your real name, which is the least important thing about you—I know that you are not a man to hire himself out to anyone. Instinct tells me this, instinct steeped in the blood of my enemies, whose eyes I have looked into many times as I spilled their guts, men who measure their intelligence solely by their zeal for torture."

Bourne felt galvanized. So Yevsen and Maslov were partners. Bourne had met Maslov several months ago in Moscow, when the *grupperovka* boss was in the midst of a war with a rival mob family. If he was now in partnership with Yevsen it could only mean that he'd won the war and was consolidating his power. Was it Maslov, not Yevsen, who was behind the attack on him?

"I understand," Bourne said. "You're not afraid of Yevsen or Maslov."

"Nor am I interested in them," Hererra said. "But I am interested in you. Why have you come to see me? It's not my Goya, and it's not the señorita inside, beautiful and desirable though she may be. What, then, do you want?"

"I was followed here by a Russian hitman with a scar on one side of his neck and a tattoo of three skulls on the other."

"Ah, yes, Bogdan Machin, better known as the Torturer." Hererra tapped the tip of his forefinger against his lower lip. "So it was you who killed that bastard at the Maestranza yesterday." He gave Bourne an appraising look. "I'm impressed. Machin had left a litter of the dead and maimed behind him like a train wreck."

Bourne was similarly impressed. Hererra's intel was swift and excellent. Bourne unbuttoned his shirt, revealing his chest wound. "He tried to shoot me dead in Bali. He bought a Parker Hale Model Eighty-five and a Schmidt and Bender Marksman Two scope from Wayan. It was Wayan who gave me your name. He said you recommended Machin to him."

Hererra's eyebrows lifted in surprise. "You must believe me, I never knew."

Bourne grabbed the Colombian by the shirtfront and slammed him against the French doors. "Why should I believe you," he said into Hererra's face, "when the man who bought the Parker Hale couldn't be Machin because he had gray eyes?"

At that moment Fausto appeared from a doorway on the other side of the garden, his gun aimed at Bourne, who pressed his thumb into Hererra's Adam's apple and said, "I have no desire to hurt you, but I will know who tried to kill me on Bali."

"Fausto, we're all civilized individuals here," Hererra said as he stared into Bourne's eyes, "put away your weapon."

When the young man had obeyed, Bourne released the Colombian. At that moment the French door opened and Tracy appeared. She looked at each of the three men in turn, and said, "What the hell is going on?"

"Don Hererra is about to tell me what I need to know," Bourne said.

Her gaze returned to the Colombian. "And the Goya?"

"It's yours at the full asking price," Herrera said.

"I'm prepared to—"

"Señorita, don't try my patience. I will have my full asking price, and with what you tried to pull you're lucky at that."

She pulled out her cell. "I'll have to make a call."

"By all means." Hererra raised a hand. "Fausto, show the señorita to a place where she can have privacy."

"I'd rather be outdoors," Tracy said.

"As you wish." The Colombian led the way back inside. When Fausto had shut the door and disappeared down the hallway, he turned to Bourne and very softly and very seriously said, "Do you trust her?"

Harvey Korman had just bitten down into an indifferent roast beef and Havarti on rye when, to his astonishment, Moira Trevor and Humphry Bamber exited GWU Hospital's ER entrance without his partner, Simon Herren, anywhere in sight. Korman threw down a twenty, got up, tossed on his padded jacket, and swung out the coffee shop door, which was almost directly across the street from the hospital entrance.

It was a quirk of luck that Korman was small and slightly pudgy, with round cheeks and almost no hair, more Tim Conway than his namesake. Still, with his physique and unprepossessing manner no one would take him for a private intelligence operative, let alone a member of Black River.

What the fuck? he thought as he carefully tailed the pair down the street. *Where the hell is Simon?* Noah Perlis had told him that the Trevor woman was dangerous but, of course, he'd taken the warning with a couple of grains of salt. Not that he or Simon had ever met Trevor, which was why Perlis had chosen them for this assignment, but everyone in Black River knew Perlis had a thing for Moira Trevor, tinting his judgment of her. He never should have been her handler while she was working for Black River. In Korman's judgment, Perlis had made some key mistakes, including using Veronica Hart as a stalking horse, so Trevor wouldn't think ill of him when he'd abruptly taken her off mission.

That was all in the past, however. Korman needed to concentrate on the present.

He turned the corner and looked around, bewildered. Bamber and Trevor had been half a block ahead of him. Where the hell had they gone?

This way! Hurry!" Moira guided Bamber into the corner lingerie shop. It had two doors, one on New Hampshire Avenue, NW, the other on I Street, NW. She spoke on her cell as she led him through the shop and out the opposite door, back onto New Hampshire Avenue, where they lost themselves in the crowd. Five minutes later and four blocks away the Blue Top taxi Moira had called pulled up to the curb and they quickly climbed in. As it accelerated away, she pushed Bamber down in the seat. Just before she herself slid down she caught a glimpse of the man who had been following them, a man who looked comically like Tim Conway. There was nothing comical, however, about his grim expression as he spoke into his cell, no doubt apprising Noah of the situation.

"Where to?" the taxi driver said over his shoulder.

Moira realized she had no idea where to go to ground.

"I know a place," Bamber said hesitantly, "somewhere they won't find us."

"You don't know Noah like I do," Moira said. "By now he knows you better than your own mother does."

"He doesn't know about this place," Bamber insisted. "Not even Steve knew."

Why should I trust anyone?" Bourne said.

"Because, my friend, in this life you must learn to trust someone. Otherwise you will be consumed by paranoia and a longing for death." Hererra poured three fingers of Asombroso Anejo tequila into two glasses, handed one to Bourne. He sipped his, then said, "Me, I don't trust women, period. For one thing they talk too much, especially among themselves." He walked over to the wall of books and ran his fingertips over the bound spines. "Down through history there were uncountable times when men from bishops to princes were undone by a bit of discreet pillow talk." He turned. "While we fight and kill for power, that's how women amass theirs."

Bourne shrugged. "Surely you don't blame them."

"Of course I blame them." Hererra finished off his tequila. "The bitches are the root of all evil."

"Which leaves you for me to trust." Bourne put aside his drink untouched. "The problem, Don Hererra, is that you've already proved yourself untrustworthy. You've lied to me once."

"And how many times have you lied to me since you walked through my door?" The Colombian crossed the room, took up Bourne's tequila, and drank it down in one long shot. Smacking his lips, he wiped his mouth with the back of a hand and said, "The man Wayan described, the man who tried to kill you, was hired by one of your own people."

"The killer's name."

"Boris Illyich Karpov."

Bourne froze, unable for a moment to believe what he'd just heard. "There must be some mistake."

Hererra cocked his head. "You know this man?"

"Why would a colonel in FSB-2 hire himself out to an American?"

"Not just an American," the Colombian said. "Secretary of Defense Ervin Reynolds Halliday, who as we both know is among the most powerful men on the planet. And he wasn't hiring himself out."

But it couldn't be Boris, Bourne told himself. Boris was a friend, he'd helped Bourne in Reykjavik and then in Moscow, where he'd surprised Bourne by showing up at a meeting with Dimitri Maslov, with whom he was clearly friendly. Were they more than friends? Was Boris a partner of Yevsen, along with Maslov? Bourne felt cold sweat break out on his back. The spider's web he'd stepped into was growing exponentially with each interconnecting strand he discovered.

"But here . . ." Hererra had turned away for a moment, rummaging through the drawer of the escritoire. When he turned back, he had a manila folder in one hand and a micro-recorder in the other. "Take a look at these."

Bourne opened the folder when the Colombian handed it to him and saw what were clearly surveillance photos, black and white, grainy, but clear enough to see two men talking in earnest conversation. Though the faces were in close-up the low light rendered everything slightly fuzzy.

"They met in a Munich beer hall," Herrera said helpfully.

Bourne recognized the shape and features of Boris's face. The other man, older, taller, was probably American. It was, indeed, the secretary of defense, Bud Halliday. Then he saw the electronic datestamp, which was several days before he was shot.

"Photoshopped," he said, handing back the photos.

"In these times, all too possible, I admit." Hererra presented him with the microrecorder as if it were a prize. "Perhaps this will convince you the photos are undoctored."

When Bourne pressed the PLAY button, this is what he heard above the reduced background clamor:

"Terminate Jason Bourne and I will use the full might of the American government to put Abdulla Khoury where he belongs."

"Not good enough, Mr. Smith. An eye for an eye, this is the true meaning of quid pro quo, yes?"

"We don't assassinate people, Colonel Karpov."

"Of course not. No matter, Secretary Halliday. *I have no such compunctions."*

After a slight pause, Halliday said: "*Yes, of course, in the heat of the moment I forgot our protocols, Mr. Jones. Send me the entire contents of the hard drive and it will be done. Agreed?*"

"**Agreed.**"

Bourne pressed STOP and looked at Hererra. "What hard drive are they talking about?"

"I have no idea, but as you can imagine I'm trying to find out."

"How did you come into possession of this material?"

A slow smile reemerged on the Colombian's face as he put a forefinger across his lips.

"Why would Boris want to kill me?"

"Colonel Karpov didn't inform me when he asked for the favor." Hererra shrugged. "But as a matter of routine I ran a check on the phone he was calling from. It was a satellite phone and it was located in Khartoum."

"In Khartoum," Bourne said. "Perhaps at Seven Seventy-nine El Gamhuria Avenue, Nikolai Yevsen's headquarters."

Hererra's eyes opened wide. "Now, truly, I am impressed."

Bourne lapsed into a meditative silence. Could there be a connection between Boris and Nikolai Yevsen? Could they be collaborators instead of adversaries? What grand scheme could bring these two disparate men together, could cause Boris to try to kill him and, once discovering that he was still alive, hire the Torturer to finish the job?

Something didn't make sense, but there was no time now to figure out what because Tracy was opening the French door to enter the room, and Hererra, smiling at her, said, "Has your principal made a decision?"

"He wants the Goya."

"Excellent!" Don Hererra rubbed his hands together. He was grinning like a cat that has caught a particularly rare and tasty morsel. "The world has no idea who Noah Petersen is, but I have a suspicion our friend here does." He lifted his eyebrows as he gazed at Bourne.

"Not talking?" He shrugged. "No matter. Mr. Petersen is Señorita Atherton's principal."

Tracy stared at Bourne. "You know Noah? How is that possible?"

"His real name is Noah Perlis." Bourne, thunderstruck, looked at both of them in turn. The spider's web had presented an entirely new dimension. "He works for a private American military contracting company by the name of Black River. I've had some dealings with him in the past."

"What do you know?" Hererra said. "The world is filled with chameleons and, not surprisingly, they all know one another." He turned from Bourne and gave Tracy a mock bow. "Señorita Atherton, why don't you tell the gentleman where you're to deliver the Goya?" When she hesitated, he laughed good-naturedly. "Go on, you've nothing to lose. We all trust one another here, don't we?"

"I'm to deliver the Goya by hand to Khartoum," Tracy said.

Bourne could hardly catch his breath. What in the world was going on? "Please don't tell me you're to deliver it to Seven Seventy-nine El Gamhuria Avenue."

Tracy's mouth opened wide in an O of astonishment.

"How did he know?" Hererra shook his head. "That's a question we'd all like answered."

Book Three

21

Americans!" Soraya said. "God in heaven, what madness is this?"

She half expected Amun to make an acerbic comment, but he remained mute, watching her with his large scarab eyes.

"A cadre of American military men who just happen to be on leave here in Al Ghardaqah are given a mission that begins in Khartoum two weeks or so before an Iranian Kowsar 3 missile brings down an American passenger jet in Egyptian airspace. It's unthinkable." She raked a hand through her thick black hair. "For God's sake, Amun, say something."

They were sitting at a seaside restaurant, eating because they knew they had to. Soraya had no appetite and, she saw, Amun apparently didn't have much more. Three of his men were sitting nearby, guarding Stephen, who was scarfing down a meal as if it was going to be his last. The sun was a ruddy, flattened disk near the horizon. The cloudless sky arched above them, vast and somehow desolate.

Chalthoum pushed his food around his plate. "I still think he's lying to save his skin," he said sourly.

"What if he's not? The dive shop owner corroborated his story. There were four Americans diving off the boat approximately two weeks ago. They dived for three days, paid cash, and left abruptly, without talking to anyone."

"Sounds like anyone and everyone." Amun shot a poisonous glance over at the prisoner. "It does make a compelling story, doesn't it?"

"Amun, I don't think we can afford to take the chance he's lying. I think we should go to Khartoum."

"And abandon the probability that Iranian terrorists were here in Egypt?" He shook his head. "Not a chance."

Soraya was already on her phone, punching in Veronica Hart's number. If she was going to go to Khartoum—with or without Amun—she had to confirm her decision with the DCI. Heading into Sudan was serious business.

She frowned as the phone continued to ring and no voice mail intervened. At length, a male voice answered.

"Who is this?"

"Soraya Moore. Who the hell are you?"

"It's Peter, Soraya. Peter Marks." Marks was the chief of CI operations, smart and reliable.

"What are you doing answering the DCI's private cell?"

"Soraya, DCI Hart is dead."

"What?" The blood drained from Soraya's face and all at once she felt the breath rush out of her. "Dead? How could—?" Her voice sounded thin, attenuated, faraway. Dimly, she realized she was in shock. "What happened?"

"There was an explosion—a car bomb, we think."

"Oh, my God!"

"There were two individuals with her: Moira Trevor and someone by the name of Humphry Bamber, a software designer with his own boutique firm."

"Are they alive or dead?"

"Alive, presumably," Marks said, "though that's pure speculation. We have no idea where they are. For all we know, they were responsible for the DCI's death."

"Or they fled for their lives."

"Another possibility," Marks conceded. "At the very least, they need to be brought in and questioned as the only witnesses to the incident." He paused for a moment. "The thing is, the Trevor woman was involved with Jason Bourne."

Events were moving faster than Soraya could follow in her current state. "How is that relevant?" she said curtly.

"I don't know if it is, but she was also involved with Martin Lindros. Some months ago, DCI Hart was investigating the connection."

"I was part of that investigation," Soraya said. "There was nothing to it. Moira Trevor and Martin were friends, period."

"And yet, both Lindros and Bourne are

now dead." Marks cleared his throat. "Did you know Ms. Trevor was with Bourne when he was killed?"

A tremor of premonition chilled her. "I didn't, no."

"I've done some digging. It turns out that Ms. Trevor used to work at Black River."

Soraya's mind was reeling. "So did DCI Hart."

"Interesting, no? There's more: Ms. Trevor and Bamber were admitted to the ER at George Washington University Hospital less than twenty minutes after the blast. No one saw them leave, but—and here's the really good part—a man who flashed a government ID asked for them by name less than five minutes after they began treatment."

"Someone followed them."

"I would say so," Marks said.

"What was the man's name and what department of the government is he with?"

"The billion-dollar question. No one could remember, the place was a madhouse. So I checked myself. Either no one is owning up to this agent or he wasn't government. On the other hand, it wouldn't surprise me to learn that the DoD has secretly authorized some Black River ops to carry government IDs."

Soraya took several deep breaths both to calm herself and to allow her mind to start making connections. "Peter, the DCI sent me to Egypt to try to find out about the indigenous Iranian freedom fighters Black River made contact with, but in my most recent conversation with her she agreed to let me explore a theory that the Iranian terrorists who shot down our jet had help transshipping the missile, possibly from the Saudis."

"Jesus, and . . . ?"

"The reason I was calling her now is that there's a possibility that the Iranians weren't involved at all."

"What?" Marks exploded. "You've got to be kidding."

"I wish I were. Two weeks ago, four American military men on leave were suddenly sent on a mission that began in Khartoum."

"So?"

"Amun Chalthoum and I have been operating under the supposition that the Saudis helped the Iranian terrorists transport the Kowsar 3 missile through Iraq and across the Red Sea, to someplace along the east coast of Egypt. His people have been swarming the coast all day with nothing to show for it, so we've been searching for alternatives. The only other access into Egypt is from the south."

She heard Marks's sharp intake of breath. "That would be Sudan."

"And Khartoum would be the logical staging area, the place where the Kowsar 3 could be flown in under everyone's radar."

"I don't understand. What's the connection between our military and Iranian terrorists?"

"That's just the point, there isn't any," Soraya said. "We're looking at a scenario that doesn't involve either Iranians or Saudis."

Marks laughed uneasily. "What are you implying, that we shot down our own jet?"

"The government wouldn't," she said perfectly serious. "But Black River might."

"That theory is almost as crazy," he said.

"What if the terrible incidents back home are connected to what's happened over here?"

"That's something of a stretch, even for you."

"Listen to me carefully, Peter. DCI Hart was concerned about the current relationship between the NSA—specifically Secretary Halliday—and Black River. Now she's the victim of a car bomb." She allowed that pronouncement to hang in the air for a moment before continuing. "The only way to get to the bottom of the mystery is eyes on the ground. I need to go to Khartoum."

"Soraya, Sudan is far too dangerous for a director to—"

"Typhon has an agent in place in Khartoum."

"Good, let him investigate."

"This is too big, Peter, the ramifications too grave. Besides, after all that's happened, I don't trust anyone."

"What about this Chalthoum character? He's the head of al Mokhabarat, for chrissakes."

"Believe me, he has as much to lose from this situation as we do."

"It's incumbent on me to point out that your agent in Khartoum can't guarantee your safety."

By his tone, she knew he'd acquiesced. "No one can, Peter. Keep DCI Hart's phone with you. I'll keep you apprised."

"Okay, but—"

As Soraya severed the connection, she looked at Amun. "The director of Central Intelligence was just killed in Washington by a car bomb. This situation stinks, Amun. We're not up against Iranian terrorists, I know it. Will you come with me to Khartoum?"

Amun rolled his eyes, then threw his hands into the air. "*Azizti,* what choice have you left me?"

After Moira and Humphry Bamber exited the taxi in Foggy Bottom, he led her west across the bridge and into Georgetown. He was nervous, walking so quickly that several times she had to take him by the arm to slow him down because he was too terrified to listen to her. Along the way she checked plate-glass windows and cars' side-mirrors for any signs of a tail, both vehicular and pedestrian. At least twice she had them walk around the block or enter a shop as a double blind, to make certain they were absolutely clean. Only then would she allow Bamber to take her to their destination.

This turned out to be on R Street: a redbrick Federal-style town house with a copper mansard roof and four dormer windows where fat-breasted pigeons sat, cooing drowsily. They climbed the slate steps, and Bamber used the brass knocker on the polished wooden door. In a moment it swung inward to reveal a slender man with longish brown hair, green eyes, and angular cheekbones.

"H, you look— What happened to you?"

"Chrissie, this is Moira Trevor. Moira, meet Christian Lamontierre."

"The dancer?"

Bamber was already on the threshold. "Moira saved my life. Can we come in?"

"Saved your . . . ? Of course." Lamontierre stepped back into the small, jewel-like entryway. He did so with a grace and power no untrained human being could muster. "Where are my manners?" His face was clouded by worry. "Are you two all right? I can call my doctor."

"No doctor," Moira said.

As their host closed the heavy door, Bamber double-locked it.

Seeing this, Lamontierre said, "I think we could use a drink." He gestured, leading the way into a beautifully appointed living room in dove gray and cream. It was a world of calm and elegance. Books on ballet and modern dance were scattered about the coffee table; on shelves were photos of Lamontierre on stage and in informal poses with Martha Graham, Mark Morris, Bill T. Jones, and Twyla Tharp, among others.

They sat on gray-and-silver–striped sofas while Lamontierre crossed to a sideboard, then abruptly turned.

"You two look like you need a rest and some food. Why don't I toddle on off to the kitchen and make us all something to eat?"

Without waiting for a reply, he left them alone, for which Moira was grateful, since she had a number of questions she wanted to ask Bamber without causing him embarrassment.

Bamber was one step ahead of her. Sighing as he leaned back against the sofa, he said, "When I hit my thirties, it began to dawn on me that men weren't designed to be monogamous, either physically or emotionally. We were designed to propagate, to continue the species at all costs. Being gay doesn't change that biological imperative."

Moira recalled him telling her that he was taking her somewhere even Stevenson hadn't known about. "So you've been having an affair with Lamontierre."

"It would've killed Steve to talk about it."

"You mean he knew?"

"Steve wasn't stupid. And he was intuitive, if not about himself, then about those around him. He might have suspected, or not. I don't know. But his self-image wasn't the best; he was always concerned that I would leave him." He rose, poured some water for both of them, brought the glasses back, and handed one to her.

"I wouldn't have left him, not ever," he said as he sat down.

"I'm not going to judge you," Moira said.

"No? Then you'd be the first."

Moira took a long drink of water; she was parched. "Tell me about you and Noah Perlis."

"That fucker." Bamber pulled a face. "A tidy little war, that's what Noah wanted from me, something he could tie up in a bow and present as a gift to his client."

"You got paid well enough."

"Don't remind me." Bamber drained his glass. "That blood money's going straight to AIDS research."

"Back to Noah," Moira said gently.

"Right."

"Please explain the phrase, 'a tidy little war.'"

At that moment, Lamontierre called to them and they rose wearily, Bamber leading the way down a hall, past a bathroom, and into the kitchen at the rear of the town house. Moira was eager to hear Bamber's reply, but her stomach was growling, and in order to regain her strength she knew she needed to get some food in her.

When she'd been house hunting, Moira had been inside homes like this one. Lamontierre had had a skylight installed, so instead of the dark and gloomy space it must once have been, the kitchen was now bright and cheery. It was painted a rich egg-yolk yellow, with backsplashes behind the umber granite countertops of glass tiles in a complex Byzantine pattern of golds, greens, and blues.

They sat at an antique parquet wood table. Lamontierre had made scrambled eggs with turkey bacon and whole-grain toast. As they ate, he kept stealing worried glances at Bamber because when he asked what had happened Bamber said: "I don't want to talk about it." And then because Lamontierre looked hurt, added: "It's for your own good, Chrissie, trust me."

"I don't know what to say here," Lamontierre said. "Steve's death—"

"The less said about that the better," Bamber cut in.

"I'm sorry. That's all I was going to say. I'm sorry."

Bamber finally looked up from his plate and tried for a bleak smile. "Thank you, Chrissie. I appreciate it. I apologize for being such a godawful shit."

"He's been through a lot today," Moira said.

"We both have." Bamber's gaze returned to his plate.

Lamontierre looked from one to the other. "Okay, then, I have to practice." He stood up. "If you need me, I'll be in the studio downstairs."

"Thanks, Chrissie." Bamber gave him a tender smile. "I'll be down in a while."

"Take your time." Lamontierre turned to Moira. "Ms. Trevor."

Then he left the kitchen. They saw he hadn't touched his food.

"That went well," Moira said, trying, and failing, to lighten the mood.

Bamber put his head in his hands. "I acted like a total jerk. What's happening to me?"

"Stress," Moira offered. "And a whole lot of delayed shock. It's what happens when you try to stuff two pounds of shit in a one-pound bag."

Bamber laughed briefly, but when he brought his head up, his eyes were enlarged with tears. "What about you? Are car bombs part of your daily routine?"

"Frankly, they used to be. Car bombs and so much more."

He stared wide-eyed at her for a moment. "Jesus, what did Noah get me involved in?"

"That's what I need you to tell me."

"He said he had a client who—he wanted to run real-life scenarios, as close to real-world simulations as possible. I told him there wasn't anything on the market that would fit his criteria, but that I could build him a program that could."

"For a fee."

"Of course, for a fee," Bamber said shortly. "I'm not running a not-for-profit."

Moira wondered why she was being so harsh on him. Fleetingly, she realized that her ill temper had nothing at all to do with Bamber. She had called Dr. Firth in Bali, anxious to talk to Willard for an update on Jason's recovery, only to be told that Willard had returned to DC. Firth didn't know where Bourne was—or claimed not to, anyway. She'd tried Bourne's cell several times since then, but the call went straight to his voice mail. This made her terribly uneasy, though she tried to calm herself with the thought that if Jason was with Willard he was safe and in good hands.

"Go on," she said now, abruptly ashamed and vowing to be kinder to Bamber.

Bamber rose, collected their plates, and took them to the double sink, where he scraped what was left of the food into the Disposall, then placed plates and silverware into the dishwasher. When he was finished clearing the table, he stood behind his chair, hands wrapped around the top slat of the back, his knuckles standing out starkly. His renewed fear created a circuit of nervous energy he was barely able to contain.

"To be honest, I thought his client wanted

to test out a new hedge fund formula. I mean Noah offered so much money, so I thought, what the hell, I'll have my fuck-you money in a month or two and then no matter what happens in my business I'll have this substantial stash. It's tough working freelance, the minute a downturn hits, the business dries up like you wouldn't believe."

Moira sat back for a moment. "Didn't you know that Noah worked for Black River?"

"He presented himself as Noah Petersen. That's all I knew."

"You mean you don't run ID checks on your clients?"

"Not when they deposit two and a half million dollars in my bank account." He shrugged. "Besides, I'm not the FBI."

Moira could see his point. In any case, she knew firsthand how persuasive Noah could be, how good he was at being someone else. He loved playing roles as much as a Hollywood actor. That way he never had to be himself.

"At any time during the creation of Bardem did you get a hint that the program wasn't meant for a hedge fund?"

A certain sadness came into Bamber's face, and he nodded. "But not until near the end. Not even when Noah gave me instructions from his client for the second revision. He told me I needed to expand the parameters of the real-life data to include government responses to terrorist attacks, military incursions, and the like."

"And that didn't set off alarm bells?"

Bamber sighed. "Why should it? These factors are important to hedge funds since they would significantly impact the financial markets, and it's my understanding that some hedge funds are set up to take advantage of short-term market dislocations."

"But at some point you came to a different conclusion."

Bamber paced around the kitchen, rearranging items that didn't need rearranging. "The anomalies kept piling up with each revision, I can see that quite clearly now." He stopped talking abruptly.

"But at the time?" she prompted.

"I kept telling myself everything was okay," he said with a good degree of anguish. "I put my head deeper into the increasingly complex algorithms of Bardem. At night, when doubts began to plague me, I focused on the two and a half mil I'd put to work in Treasury bills, my fuck-you money." He leaned over the sink, his head down. "Then a couple of days ago I hit a tipping point and I knew I couldn't let things go on the way they had been. I didn't know what to do."

"So you told Steve about Bardem, and Steve did the search on Noah you'd failed to perform and discovered that he worked for Black River."

"And Steve being Steve, he couldn't sit on the information. He was too frightened to go to his superiors, so he passed a thumb drive on to the man he'd gone to when his internal search at the DoD turned up nothing on Noah."

"Jay Weston," Moira said. "Of course! I poached Jay from Hobart, another private contractor to the military. He'd have ID'd Noah right away."

"And now Steve is dead," Bamber moaned, "because of my stupidity and my greed."

Flushed with rage, Moira got up and crossed the kitchen. "Dammit, Bamber, get a grip on yourself. The last thing I need from you is self-pity."

He turned on her. "What's the matter with you, don't you have even an ounce of humanity? My partner was just murdered."

"I don't have time for sentiment or—"

"And if I remember right a friend of yours was blown six ways from Sunday right in front of you. Don't you have any remorse, any pity? Is there anything inside you except exacting your revenge on Noah?"

"What?"

"I mean that's it, isn't it? That's what this is all about—you and Noah at each other's throats and never mind the collateral damage. Well, fuck him and fuck you!"

As he stalked out of the kitchen Moira grabbed on to the sink in order to keep her feet. All at once the kitchen began to tumble over, she seemed to lose her bearings, to have become unmoored so that she could no longer distinguish the floor from the ceiling.

My God, she thought, *what's happening to me?* And immediately an image of Ronnie Hart came to her, those lambent eyes watching her from inside the white Buick, Ronnie knowing the end had come and helpless to stop it. The explosion bloomed again in her mind, blotting out sight, sound, and thought.

Why didn't I save her? Because there wasn't time. *Why didn't I try, anyway?* Again, there was no time and Bamber had grabbed her. *Why didn't I break free?* Because the wall of percussion had already hit her, hurling her backward, and if she had been any closer she would have been caught up in the conflagration, she'd be dead now or, worse, lying in a burn unit, her skin ripped and charred, covered in third-degree burns that would kill her slowly and painfully.

Still. Ronnie was dead. She had survived. Where was the justice in that? The rational part of her brain told the grieving, irrational part that the world was chaos, it didn't care about justice, which was, in any case, a human concept and, therefore, subject to its own form of irrationality. None of this interior debate could stem the tears that stung her eyes, ran down her cheeks, and set her to shivering as if she were ill.

Bamber's words came back to haunt her. Was this what it was all about, a blood feud between her and Noah? All at once she was back in Munich with Bourne, climbing the rolling stairs to the airplane bound to take them to Long Beach, California. Then Noah had appeared in the doorway and she recalled the poisonous look in his eye. Had it been jealousy? She'd been far too distracted then, far too intent on her immediate goal of getting to Long Beach. But now that curdled expression on his face recurred to her like the acrid taste of spoiled food. How could she be certain she wasn't misinterpreting this remembered moment between them? Because, now she thought of it, his reaction to her leaving Black River was personal, as if he were her spurned lover. And so moving on from there, could her decision to start a rival company by poaching a select few of the best people from Black River have been in retaliation for Noah not making a play for her when he could have? All at once, she recalled the conversation she'd had with Jason that night in Bali when they'd been alone in the pool together. When she'd told him of her idea to start a rival company to Black River, he'd warned her that she would make an enemy of Noah, and he was right. Had he known then how Noah felt about her? And what had she felt about Noah? *"I gave up trying to please him six months before I quit Black River. It was a fool's game,"* she'd told Jason that night. What precisely had she meant by that? Hearing it now reverberate in her mind, mixing with all the other subtle revelations, it sounded like something a hurt lover would say.

God almighty, the collateral damage she and Noah had wrought!

Slowly, like a punctured tire, the unreasoning anger went out of her, her grip loosened, and she slid to the floor. If her back hadn't been braced against the wooden cabinets, she would have pitched over.

It seemed a long time later—but surely it couldn't have been—when she became aware that somebody was in the kitchen with her. In fact, two somebodies. They were crouched down beside her.

"What happened?" Bamber asked. "Are you all right?"

"I slipped and fell, that's all." Moira's eyes were perfectly dry now.

"I'll fetch you a brandy." Lamontierre, in a white unitard and ballet slippers, a towel draped around his neck, headed back into the living room.

Moira, shrugging off Bamber's proffered hand, levered herself to her feet. Lamontierre returned with a snifter half filled with an amber liquid, some of which she drank immediately. The fire worked its way down her throat and flooded her body, bringing her fully back to herself.

"Mr. Lamontierre," she said, "thank you for your hospitality, but to be honest I need to talk to Mr. Bamber in private."

"Of course. If you're all right . . ."

"I am."

"Excellent, then I'll go shower. H, if you want to stay here for the time being . . ." He regarded Moira for a moment. "Actually, both of you are welcome here for as long as you need."

"That's extremely generous of you," Moira said.

"It's nothing." He waved away her words. "I'm afraid I don't have any fresh clothes for you."

Moira laughed. "I can take care of that easily enough."

"Well, then." Lamontierre gave Bamber a brief hug, and left them alone.

"He's a good man," Moira said.

"Yes, he is," Bamber acknowledged.

By unspoken mutual consent, they returned to the living room, where they collapsed, exhausted, on the sofas.

"What happens now?" Bamber said.

"You help me find out exactly what Noah Perlis is using Bardem for."

"Really?" His entire body stiffened. "And how do you propose I do that?"

"How about hacking into his computer?"

"How easy for both of us that would be!" He shifted his position, perching himself on the edge of the cushion. "Unfortunately, it's impossible. Noah uses a laptop. I know this because he has me send the updated versions of Bardem directly to it."

"Ugh!" Though Wi-Fi networks were notoriously porous, Black River's was not. It had established its own worldwide network that was, as far as she knew, impenetrable. Of course, in theory no network was 100 percent secure, but it might take a platoon of hackers years to get through. Unless . . .

"Wait a minute," she said, suddenly excited. "If you had a laptop loaded with the Black River Wi-Fi encryption, would that help?"

Bamber shrugged. "Probably, but how on earth are you going to get your hands on one?"

"I used to work for Black River," she said. "I cloned the hard drive from my laptop before I sent it back." She considered the remaining obstacle to this possible solution. "The only problem is every time a Black River agent leaves the company the encryption is updated."

"Doesn't matter. If they're using the same root algorithm, which I'm sure they are, I should be able to crack it." He shook his head. "Not that it matters." His voice had soured. "We can't go back to our respective apartments, remember? Noah's people are sure to be waiting for us in both places."

Moira stood, looked around for her coat. "Nevertheless," she said, "I've got to try."

22

On the one-hour flight from Seville to Madrid, Bourne realized that Tracy was no longer wearing her wedding band. When he asked her about it, she plucked it out of her handbag.

"I usually wear it when I'm traveling to discourage unwanted conversations," she said, "but there's no reason to wear it now."

From Madrid they were booked on an Egyptair flight to Cairo. Once there, they were set to be taken to a military airfield just outside the Cairo International Airport, where a charter flight was waiting to fly them to Khartoum. She had already had her visas, and Don Hererra was kind enough to expedite Bourne's—still under the name of Adam Stone, of course. He'd also provided Bourne with a satellite phone, because his cell would have only spotty coverage in Africa.

As Tracy put the ring away, she brought her briefcase onto her lap. "I'm sorry about that call to Professor Zuñiga."

"Why? It wasn't your fault."

She sighed. "I'm afraid it was." With a sheepish look, she opened the briefcase. "I'm afraid I have a rather awful confession to make." She took out the sheets Bourne had already seen: the X-rays of the Goya and the letter from the professor.

As she handed them over, she said, "You see, I'd already met him. Those are the X-rays he took, that's his letter authenticating the Goya. He was really very excited by the find—so much so, in fact, that he actually wept when I took it away from him."

Bourne turned his laser gaze on her. "Why didn't you tell me this in the first place?"

"I thought you were a rival. I was under strict orders to avoid a bidding war at all costs. So you can see why I didn't want to reveal anything that would drive up the price."

"And later?"

She sighed again, taking the sheets back and stowing them carefully away. "Later, it was already too late. I didn't want to admit that I'd lied to you, especially after you'd saved us both at the *corrida*."

"That was my fault," he said. "I should never have involved you in my dealings."

"It makes no difference now. As it turns out, I am involved."

That was hard to argue with. Still, he didn't like her traveling with him to Khartoum, to the heart of Nikolai Yevsen's arms empire, into what must certainly be the center of the web he'd been thrust into by the bullet that almost killed him. Khartoum was where Yevsen's headquarters lay, at 779 El Gamhuria Avenue. According to Tracy, that was where Noah Perlis was going to accept the Goya. From what Don Hererra said it was also likely that Boris Karpov was there; last month, he'd told Bourne he'd just come back from Timbuktu, in Mali, and now Bourne had seen the photos, had heard the tape of Boris bartering a deal with Bud Halliday. Bourne still hadn't figured out how he would handle a situation where a trusted friend was the man who was trying to kill him. The question of the Torturer still nagged at him. Why would Boris hire someone else when he could go after Bourne himself?

"But speaking of lying," Tracy said now, "why did you lie to me about why you really wanted to see Don Hererra?"

"Would you have taken me to see him if I'd told you the truth?"

"Probably not." She smiled. "So now that we've admitted our mistakes, why don't we start fresh?"

"If you wish."

She gave him a pensive look. "Would you rather not?"

He laughed. "All I meant was that lying comes easily to both of us."

It took a moment but color rose to her cheeks. "My line of work—and clearly yours—is infested with unscrupulous people, con men, swindlers, even violent criminals. Hardly surprising since, these days especially, artwork commands such astronomical prices. I've had to learn methods of protection against these dangers, one of which is becoming a convincing liar."

"I couldn't have said it better myself," Bourne said.

They broke off the conversation as a flight attendant approached to ask them what they'd like to drink.

When she'd brought what they'd ordered, Bourne said, "I have to wonder why you're working for Noah Perlis."

She shrugged and sipped at her champagne. "He's a paying client like any other."

"I wonder whether that's the truth or a lie?"

"It's the truth. At this stage, I have nothing to gain by lying to you."

"Noah Perlis is a very dangerous individual who works for an ethically unsound company."

"Perhaps, but his money is as good as the next person's. What Noah does is none of my business."

"It is if it brings you into the line of fire."

Tracy's frown deepened. "But why should it? This is a straightforward job, pure and simple. I think you're reacting to shadows that aren't there."

When it came to Noah Perlis, no job was straightforward. Bourne had learned that from Moira. But he felt nothing would be served in continuing this topic with Tracy. If Noah was playing her, he'd find out soon enough. He was disturbed by the insertion of Noah Perlis's name in the mix. Nikolai Yevsen was a top arms dealer, Dimitri Maslov, the head of the Kazanskaya mob; he could explain away even Boris's tangential involvement. But what was Noah Perlis, a high-level operative of Black River, doing with these unsavory Russian criminals?

"What is it, Adam, you look perplexed?"

"I had no idea," Bourne said, "that Noah Perlis was an art collector."

Tracy frowned. "Do you think I'm lying?"

"Not necessarily," he said. "But I'm willing to bet someone is."

Arkadin received the call from Triton right on schedule. The pestilential Noah might be arrogant, patronizing, disrespectful, possessive of his power and his influence, but at least he was punctual. A sad victory, really, because it was so minuscule to everyone but himself. He was a man for whom mystery was important enough that it had taken on mythic proportions. In the way Arkadin was a physical chameleon, having learned to remake his face, his gait, his very mien, depending on the role he was playing, so Noah was a vocal chameleon. He could be social and hearty, convincing and ingratiating, anything and everything in between, depending on the role he was playing. It took an actor, Arkadin thought, to mark another actor.

"The president's UN address had the desired effect," Noah told Arkadin. Rather than listening, he was always telling Arkadin something. "Not only are the American allies on board, but most of the neutrals and even a couple of the normally antagonistic nations. You have eight hours to finalize the squad's training. By then the plane will be on the landing strip, ready to take you to your drop point in the red zone. Are we clear?"

"Never clearer," Arkadin said automatically.

He was no longer interested in the drivel Noah was spouting. He had his own plans to go over for the ten thousandth time, the crucial alteration to the joint American-Russian foray into Iran. He knew he'd only have one shot at victory, only one brief window while the chaos was at its height to implement his plan. Failure never entered his mind, because it would spell certain death for him and for every one of his men.

He was fully prepared, unlike Mischa and Oserov when, on the fly, they'd created their straw man in an attempt to spring him from his basement prison in Nizhny Tagil.

Word of the increasingly grisly and bizarre murders of Stas's men had raced around Nizhny Tagil with such unstoppable virulence that it even filtered down to Arkadin, securely hidden like a rat in the basement of the gang's headquarters. The news was disturbing to him, so much so, in fact, that it was the one thing that pried him from his dank and dreary haven. Who could be poaching on his territory? It was his job to make life for Stas's gang a living hell; no one else had the right.

So up he went into the thickly hellish atmosphere of Nizhny Tagil. Night shrouded him, along with a noxious ashy drizzle that did little to obscure the skyline's fiery beacons: smokestacks belching ferrous sulfur into the air. Like church bells in some other, more salubrious town, the blinding searchlight beams emanating atop the walls of the high-security prisons that ringed the benighted city marked off time at regular, soul-destroying intervals.

Arkadin still thought of it as the late Stas Kuzin's gang, even though a moron named Lev Antonin had taken over by dint of brute force. Three men had died violently in his ascent to power—needlessly, as Arkadin well knew, because if you had a brain that worked it wasn't difficult to figure out how to finesse your way to being Stas's successor. Lev Antonin wasn't one of those men, so in some sense he was the right man to lead Kuzin's band of cutthroats, sadists, and homicidal dimwits.

It was the death of the gang's head enforcer, along with his family, that galvanized Arkadin: You didn't need to be a rocket scientist to figure out that Lev Antonin was going to be the unknown killer's next target. Whoever he was, he was going about his business in methodical fashion. With each victim he was moving up the ladder of the gang's hierarchy, the surest way to instill fear even in those who considered themselves inured to fear.

In the dead of night Arkadin approached Lev Antonin's house, a large, unspeakably ugly two-story affair that equated brutal modern architecture with style. He spent a good forty minutes reconnoitering the block, checking out the house from all angles, calculating the risk factors involved in every vector of approach. All the security lights had been switched on; the stucco looked flat and two-dimensional in the blue-white glare.

As it happened, there was a half-dead cherry tree on one side of the house. It was an elderly, twisted specimen, as if it were a proud but exhausted veteran of many wars. Halfway up its height, its intertwined branches made a Gordian knot sturdy enough to support several men. They were thick enough that the night caught in its web, repulsing in its sphere even the man-made glare.

As a boy, whenever he managed to escape the prison-like confines of his parents' home, Arkadin would climb trees, rocks, hills, and mountains, the steeper the better. The more death defying the more he loved it and the higher he was prodded to climb. If he died in the attempt at least he'd die on his own terms, doing what he loved, not beaten to death by his mother.

Without hesitation, he mounted the nether side of the tree, where its thick trunk afforded him deep shadow. Climbing hand over hand, he felt once again the old exhilaration he'd experienced when he was nine and ten, before his mother, discovering him slipping out of the house yet again, had broken his leg.

Once inside the Gordian knot, he paused to survey the scene. He was more or less at the level of the second-story windows, which were, of course, all shut tight against both intruders and the city's toxic ash. Not that a closed window was much of a problem for Arkadin; what mattered far more was choosing one that fronted an empty room.

He moved closer, looking through the glass from one darkened room to another. There were four windows, two and two, in line with the second story—which he guessed meant two rooms, doubtless bedrooms. Lights out didn't necessarily guarantee an empty room. Peeling off a bit of bark from the branch nearest his right shoulder, he tossed it against the glass of the second window of the first pair. When nothing happened, he peeled off another piece, larger this time, and threw it harder. It hit the pane with a clearly discernible smack. He waited. Nothing.

Now he made his way through the front half of the Gordian knot until he was almost up against the window pane. Here the knotty branches had been sawed or clipped back, presenting their sheared side to the house. There was a gap of perhaps eighteen inches between the lopped-off stumps and the light-mottled wall of the house into which the windows were set like the dull eyes of a cuboid doll.

As Arkadin set himself in a convenient crotch, he saw his reflection staring back at him as if from out of some mythic, sentient forest. The paleness of his face startled him. It was as if he were looking at a future version of himself who was already dead, a version from whom the fire of life had been suddenly and cruelly drained, not by time but by circumstance. In that face he recognized not himself, but some stranger who had stepped into his life and, like a puppet master, had directed his hands and feet onto a ruinous path. A moment later the image or illusion vanished and, leaning across the gap, he jimmied open the window, slid it up, and clambered silently inside.

He found himself in a very ordinary bedroom with a bedstead, a pair of lamps on nightstands, a dresser, all on a circular hooked rug. Nevertheless, at that moment it looked to him like a room in a sultan's palace. He sat on the corner of the bed for a moment, luxuriating in the give of the mattress, inhaling the homey swirl of perfume and body powder, which made him salivate like a beast scenting blood. Oh, for a hot bath, or even a shower!

A narrow floor-length mirror announced the door to a closet, which he opened. He had, quite naturally, a marked aversion to closets, a confined space into which his mother locked him as punishment. But here he steeled himself, reaching in to run his open hand along the downy backs of the hanging clothes: dresses, slips, nightgowns, pale and shimmering as his face had been in reflection. What he breathed in, however, along with traces of perfume and powder was the odor of solitude so familiar to someone like him. In his crummy basement lair this scent was altogether familiar, almost a given, but here in a family home it seemed strange and ineffably sad.

He was just about to turn away and go about his business when he sensed something in the well of darkness below. Tensed and ready for anything, he crouched down and, pushing aside a handful of hideous tweed skirts, perceived a pale oval face rising out of the gloom. It belonged to a small child. They stared at each other for a moment, transfixed. He recalled that Lev Antonin had four children—three girls and a rather sickly boy who, had his father been anyone else, would have had his life made miserable by his peers. It was this very boy whom he now faced, crouched in a closet as he himself had once been.

A sense of loathing for his past overcame even his hatred of Lev Antonin.

"Why are you hiding in here?" he whispered.

"Shhh, me and my sisters're playing a game."

"They haven't found you?"

He shook his head, then he grinned fiercely. "And I've been up here a long time."

It was a sound rising up the stairwell from the first floor that refroze them both, a noise so unexpected it intruded upon this momentary and unaccustomed conversation. It was a moan, a female voice caught not in the midst of sex, but in abject terror.

"Stay here," Arkadin said. "Whatever you do, don't come downstairs until I come get you, okay?"

The boy, clearly frightened now, nodded.

Quitting the bedroom, Arkadin stole along the hall. The lights might have been extinguished all through the second story, but downstairs they blazed like a house on fire. As he approached the wooden balustrade he heard the moan again, more distinctly this time, and now he began to wonder what Lev Antonin could be doing to his wife to cause her such excruciating terror. Where were the other children while Lev Antonin was punishing his wife? No wonder they hadn't come upstairs looking for their brother.

Light rose up the stairs in decreasing amounts as Arkadin crept down bent almost double so he wouldn't be seen. He was not more than a third of the way down when he was greeted by a strange tableau. A man was standing with his back to Arkadin. In front of him was Joškar, Lev Antonin's wife, hog-tied to a ladder-backed kitchen chair. The gag that had been over her mouth was halfway off, hence the moans emanating from her mouth. One eye was swollen and there were cuts on her face out of which drooled smears of blood. Huddled around her, like chicks around a hen, were three of her four children, all of whose ankles were tied together. Thus hobbled, they couldn't move and, given the menacing stance of the man looming over them, surely wouldn't. Where was Lev Antonin?

The man took a lazy swing at Joškar Antonin's head. "Stop your whining," he said. "Your fate is sealed. No matter what your husband decides, you and these brats—" He kicked out, the sharp toe of his shoe making contact with a hip bone here, a rib there. The children, already crying, began to sob in earnest, and their mother moaned again. "You and these brats are finished. Dead, six feet under, get me?"

As Arkadin listened to the man's manifesto, something important occurred to him. The man, whoever he was, must be an outsider; otherwise he'd know that one of Lev Antonin's children was still free. Could he be the one who had been killing the gang members? At that moment it seemed to Arkadin to be a good bet, one he ought to put his money on.

Retracing his steps, he returned to the bedroom closet, where he instructed Lev Antonin's son to come with him, but to stay quiet no matter what happened. Keeping the cringing boy behind him, he went silently down the steps until he was perhaps halfway down. Nothing much had changed in the scene below, except the gag was back in place and there was more blood on Joškar's face.

When Lev Antonin's son tried to peep out from behind him, Arkadin pushed him back out of sight behind his legs.

Crouching down, he whispered, "Don't move until I tell you it's okay."

He recognized the look of abject fear in

the boy's eyes and something tugged at him, an emotion perhaps, buried beneath the silt of his past. Ruffling the boy's hair, he stood and drew the Glock he'd tucked into the waistband of his pants at the small of his back.

Rising to his full height, he said, "Why don't you take a step away from those people."

The man whirled around, his face twisted into an ugly mask for a split second before the soon-to-be-familiar smile full of condescension replaced it. Arkadin recognized that expression and what it revealed about the man behind it. Here was a man who lived for subjugation; the blunt instrument he used to gain it: fear.

"Who the fuck're you, and how did you get here?" Despite being surprised, despite staring down the barrel of a Glock, there wasn't an iota of concern either on his face or in his voice.

"My name is Arkadin, and what the fuck're you doing here?"

"Arkadin, is it? Well, well . . ."

His smile turned smugly ironic. It was the kind of smile, Arkadin thought, that begged to be expunged, preferably with a balled fist.

"My name's Oserov. Vylacheslav Germanovich Oserov, and I'm here to get you the fuck out of this shithole."

"What?"

"That's right, jerk-off, my boss, Dimitri Ilyinovich Maslov, wants you back in Moscow."

"Who the hell is Dimitri Ilyinovich Maslov?" Arkadin said. "And why should I give a fuck?"

At this, Oserov's mouth opened and a sound not unlike fingernails drawn down a blackboard emanated from it. With a start, Arkadin realized the other man was laughing.

"You really are a hick. Maybe we should leave you here with all the other cretins." Oserov shook with mirth. "For your information Dimitri Ilyinovich Maslov is the head of the Kazanskaya." He cocked his head. "Ever hear of the Kazanskaya, sonny?"

"Moscow *grupperovka*." Arkadin spoke on autopilot. He was in shock. The head of one of the capital's premier mob families had heard of him? He had sent

Oserov—and presumably someone else, since Oserov had said "we"—here to fetch him? Either idea seemed improbable, but taken together the scenario seemed absurd.

"Who else is with you?" Arkadin said, trying desperately to recover his wits.

"Mischa Tarkanian. He's with Lev Antonin negotiating your safe passage out, not that you seem worth the effort, now that you've made an appearance."

There was no particular reason for Arkadin to believe that Mischa Tarkanian wasn't somewhere on the ground floor—in the toilet, perhaps. "Here's what's confusing about your story, *gospadin* Oserov. I'm wondering why this Maslov sent an incompetent to do a man's job?"

Before the Muscovite could form a reply, Arkadin reached around behind him, grabbed the boy by the back of his shirt, and brought him into the light. He needed to regain control, and the boy was his ace in the hole.

"Lev Antonin has four children, not three. How could you make such a basic mistake?"

Oserov's left hand, which had been at

his side, out of Arkadin's sight, gave a flick and the knife with which he had been cutting Joškar's face whirred through the air. Arkadin jerked the boy away, but it was too late, the blade buried itself to the hilt, and the child was torn from his grasp.

With a feral shout, Arkadin discharged his Glock, then leapt after it as if he could ride the bullet straight into Oserov's black soul. The bullet missed, but he didn't. He landed atop the Muscovite and both of them went flying across the floorboards. They fetched up against sofa legs as thick and sturdy as a *babushka*'s ankles.

Arkadin allowed Oserov to go on the offensive the better to get a sense of his style, strength, and coordination. Oserov proved to be a street fighter, vicious but undisciplined, someone who obviously relied on power and animal cunning rather than his wits to win battles. Arkadin took a few on the chin and the ribs, deflecting at the last instant a rabbit punch aimed squarely at his kidneys. Then he went to work on Oserov.

He was motivated not only by rage and a need for revenge, but by a sense of shame and humiliation for quite deliberately putting the boy in harm's way, relying on the twin elements of surprise and firepower to maintain control of the situation. Plus, he had to admit that he had been completely blindsided by the Muscovite killing a child in cold blood. Terrifying him, yes, roughing him up a little, maybe, but throwing a knife through his heart? Never.

His knuckles were split and bloodied but he scarcely noticed. As he systematically pummeled the man beneath him he was overcome with images of his childhood, of the young ashen-faced boy he'd once been, who'd been terrorized by his mother, locked in her closet for hours, sometimes for days with scurrying, avid rats that had finally eaten three toes off his left foot. Lev Antonin's boy had put his faith in Arkadin and now he was dead. This outcome was unconscionable, and the only possible redemption was Oserov's death.

And he would have killed Oserov, too, without remorse or consideration of the consequences of beating to death someone owned body and soul by Dimitri Maslov, head of the Kazanskaya. In a murderous rage, Arkadin cared nothing for Maslov, the Kazanskaya, Moscow, or anything else. All he could see was that face in the closet upstairs. Whether it was the boy's or his own he could no longer tell.

Then something hard and heavy hit him in the side of the head and everything went black.

23

Moira lived in a Georgetown town house of red-brown brick on Cambridge Place, NW, near Dumbarton Oaks. More than a home, it was her sanctuary, a place where she could curl up on the chenille sofa, a snifter of amber brandy in her hand, and lose herself in a good novel. Traveling almost constantly, such nights had become rarer and rarer, making them, when they did come, all the more precious.

Now, as twilight gave way to a glittering evening, she was haunted by the thought that someone was watching her house. Which was why she circled the block twice in a new rental car, because if the house really was under surveillance a second drive-by would surely arouse suspicion. As she went by the second time, she heard a car start up and, checking the rearview mirror, she saw a black Lincoln Town Car pull out of its parking spot almost directly across from her house and take up position several car-lengths behind her. She smiled to herself as she wove her way through Georgetown, whose maze-like streets she knew intimately.

She'd left Bamber at Lamontierre's house. He'd offered to come along even though he was clearly scared to death. "I appreciate the offer," she had said in all seriousness, "but you can help me most by staying safe and sound. I have no intention of allowing Noah's people anywhere near you."

Now as she took the Town Car through a series of evasive maneuvers she was doubly glad she'd made him stay away, even though this plan would have been far easier to execute with someone else driving the car. They could have left her off and driven on, leading the Town Car away while she doubled back to her house to fetch her Black River laptop. But nothing came easy in life, at least not in her life and not in anyone else's she knew, so why bother complaining about it. Take the hand you're dealt and then finesse it, that was what she'd always done, that was what she'd do now.

Night closed in as she drove down streets that became narrower and narrower as they approached the canal. Finally, she wheeled around a corner, made another left, braked to a halt, and, with the headlights still blazing, got out of the car in time for the driver of the Lincoln, its headlights off, to catch a glimpse of her as it nosed around the corner.

It came to an abrupt halt just as she ducked into a doorway, and two men in dark suits got out and jogged down the cobbles toward the spot where she'd disappeared. They discovered a metal door deep in the shadows, and drew their snub-nosed sidearms. The one with a shaved head pressed his back against the building's brickwork while the other one tried the knob. Shaking his head, he raised his right leg and kicked the door open so hard it slammed back against the inside wall. Weapon at the ready, he stepped aggressively into the stygian blackness. As he did so, the door swung hard into his face, breaking his nose. His jaws clamped shut, his teeth snapping off the tip of his tongue.

His howl of pain was short-lived. Moira drove a knee into his groin and, as he reflexively bent double, brought her joined fists down onto the back of his neck.

The bald man heard a muffled metallic clang, and without further hesitation, he stepped into the open doorway and fired three shots point-blank into the blackness to center, right, and left. He heard nothing, saw nothing, and, in a tense crouch, made his run into the interior.

Moira slammed the spade-shaped end of the shovel she'd stumbled over into the back of the bald man's head. He pitched headfirst onto the bare concrete floor. As she picked her way through the darkness and out into the gathering night, she heard the sound of police sirens. Doubtless, someone had heard the shots and called 911.

She walked back to her car at a brisk pace, an absorbed look on her face, as if she were late for a dinner rendezvous. It was crucial now to appear normal, to blend into the heavy traffic on M Street, until she lost herself amid the cobbled streets, shining in the light of old-fashioned street lamps.

Another ten minutes brought her back to her block, which she circled warily, on the lookout for another car with the lights off, someone in it, a sudden movement inside so he wouldn't be seen. But all appeared normal and serene.

She parked and took another look around before mounting the steps to her front door. Turning the lock, she opened the door and, drawing her Lady Hawk from its thigh holster, stepped inside. Closing the door softly behind her, she double-locked it, then stood for some time with her back against it, listening to the house breathe. One by one she identified the homey sounds of the hot-water circulator, the refrigerator condenser, the heating fan. Then she sniffed the air to see if there was the trace of an odor that didn't belong to her or her things.

Satisfied at last, she flipped the switch and the entryway and hallway were flooded with a warm, yellowish light. She let out the long breath she'd been unconsciously holding in. Moving silently through the house, she checked every room, every closet on the ground floor; she made sure the door to the basement was securely locked. Then she ascended the stairs. Halfway up, she heard a noise and froze in midstep, her heart hammering in her breast. It came again, and she identified it as a branch scratching at the rear wall, where a narrow alley ran behind the row of town houses.

Resuming her climb, she took the staircase step by step, counting down from the top to make certain she bypassed the one tread that creaked. At the top of the stairs, something happened. The hot-water circulator cycled off, and the resulting silence seemed to her eerie and ominous. Then, like an old friend, it returned, reassuring her.

As she had on the ground floor, she moved from room to room, turning on lights, checking behind furniture, even, she thought, idiotically, under her bed. There was nothing and no one. The window to the left of her bed was unlatched, and she slid the semicircular tab home.

Her Black River laptop was on the back shelf of her closet, under a line of shoe boxes. Picking her way across the room, she turned the doorknob, pulled the door open, and stepped in, leading with her weapon. She swept one hand across her hanging clothes, dresses, suits, skirts, and jackets all familiar to her, but which had now taken on a sinister aspect as curtains behind which someone could hide.

No one jumped out at her, causing her to expel a small laugh of relief. Her gaze moved upward to the line of shoe boxes on the back shelf above her hanging clothes, and there was the laptop just as she'd left it. She was reaching up to grab it when she heard the sharp crackle of breaking window glass and the dull thud as someone landed on the carpet. She whirled, stepped forward, only to have the closet door slam shut in her face.

Her hand went to the doorknob and pushed, but something was keeping the door shut, even when she put her shoulder to it. Stepping back, she fired off four shots at the knob. The sharp scent of cordite tickled her nose, and her ears rang with noise. She pushed the door again. It was still firmly shut, but now she had other things to think about. The light filtering in from the tiny gap between door and frame was systematically vanishing. Someone was taping up the gap.

And then, down at floor level, the slightly wider gap began to go dark, except for a space that was soon filled by the open end of the crevice attachment of her vacuum cleaner. A moment later a portable generator coughed to life and, with a mounting horror, Moira sensed the oxygen in the closet being sucked out. Carbon monoxide was being pumped in through her own vacuum cleaner attachment.

When Peter Marks found the Metro police report on Moira Trevor he was dumbfounded. He'd just returned from the White House, where he'd had a ten-minute evening interview with the president regarding the vacancy at the top of CI. He knew he wasn't the only candidate, but no one else at CI was talking. Still, he assumed the other six heads of the CI directorates were in line for similar interviews, if they hadn't already answered the president's summons. Of them all, he figured Dick

Symes, the chief of the Intelligence Directorate, who was the interim DCI, would get the post. Symes was older, with more experience than Peter himself, who had only recently risen to the hallowed level of chief of operations under Veronica Hart's tragically short tenure as DCI. She hadn't even had time to vet candidates for deputy director, and now she never would. On the other hand, unlike Symes, he'd been handpicked and trained by the Old Man himself, and he knew the reverence in which the president held the longtime DCI.

Peter was not certain he wanted the Big Chair, anyway, simply because it would take him another giant step away from the field, which was his first love. *"No matter how high you climb,"* the Old Man had told him, *"you never outgrow your first love. You simply learn to live without it."*

On the other hand, maybe having doubts about occupying the Big Chair was a way of insulating himself from disappointment in the event he wasn't chosen to succeed Hart. Doubtless that was why he buried himself in the Moira Trevor files the moment he sat down at his desk. The Metro police report, almost perfunctorily brief, wasn't part of the stack of printouts and electronic data his staff had amassed for him; he'd had to go looking for it himself. Not that he was looking for a police report per se, but having exhausted the so-called leads overflowing his in-box, he had decided to go on a fishing expedition, just as he'd learned to do when he was a rookie field agent. *"Never rely on intel other people feed you unless you absolutely can't get it yourself,"* the Old Man had lectured when he'd first brought Marks into the fold. *"And never, ever rely on other people's intel when your life is on the line."* Excellent advice, which Marks had never forgotten. And now, behold, the Metro police report from yesterday describing a two-car crash in which a man named Jay Weston, a former employee of Hobart Industries and current employee of Heartland Risk Management, was killed and Moira Trevor, founder and president of Heartland, was injured. Two oddities: First, Weston hadn't died from injuries sustained in the crash; he'd been shot to death. Second, Ms. Trevor had claimed—"loudly and repeatedly," as the first-on-the-scene officer wrote—that a uniformed motorcycle cop had fired the shot through the driver's-side front window into Mr. Weston's head. Basic forensic evidence at the scene confirmed Ms. Trevor's story, at least as far as the shot was concerned. As for the motorcycle cop, the report went on to say that no such department individual was even in the vicinity anywhere near the time of the shooting.

When Marks came to the end of the report, there was an even more baffling oddity. There had been no follow-up, no reinterview of Ms. Trevor, no investigation into Mr. Weston's recent whereabouts that day or into his background in general. Apart from this brief report, it was as if the incident had never occurred.

Marks picked up the phone and called the appropriate Metro precinct, but when he asked for the author of the report, he was told the officer, as well as his partner, had been "reassigned." No further information was available. He asked for Lieutenant McConnell, their immediate superior, but McConnell refused to tell Marks where they had gone or what had happened to them, either, and no amount of threats could open him up.

"My orders come straight from the commissioner himself," McConnell said with no rancor, only weariness in his voice. "That's all I know, pal. I only work here. You got a beef, it's with him."

For a minute everything went black, then powerful hands gripped Arkadin beneath the armpits and hauled him roughly off the Muscovite. When he blindly rushed back toward his antagonist he received a kick to his rib cage that caused him to fall short, to wind up on his back gasping for air.

"What in the name of Saint Stephen is going on here?" a voice roared.

He looked up to see another man, feet spread, hands closed into fists, looming over him. He wasn't Lev Antonin so Arkadin figured he must be Mischa Tarkanian.

"My name is Leonid Danilovich Arkadin," he said, through gasps. "Your poorly trained animal, Oserov, just put a knife into that boy's heart." As Tarkanian glanced over at the small crumpled form on the stairs, Arkadin continued: "That's Lev Antonin's son, in case you have any interest."

Tarkanian jerked as if struck by an electrical current. "Oserov, for the love of—"

"If you don't finish off what I started," Arkadin said, "I will."

"The fuck you will," Tarkanian roared. "You'll lie there and keep still until I tell you otherwise." Then he knelt beside Oserov. There was a lot of blood, and his right collarbone was sticking through the skin. "You're lucky he's still breathing."

Arkadin wondered whether Tarkanian was talking to him or to himself. He wondered if it mattered, then realized that it certainly didn't to him.

"Oserov, Oserov." Tarkanian was shaking his compatriot. "Shit, his face looks like a piece of ground meat."

"I do good work," Arkadin said.

While Tarkanian shot him a violent look, he got to his feet.

Tarkanian raised a warning forefinger. "I told you—"

"Relax, I'm not going near him," Arkadin said with a wince of pain, and went over to Joškar Antonin. Kneeling down, he untied her, then unwound her gag.

At once, her wail of grief and despair filled the room. She rushed past the men, mounting the stairs to take her dead son in her arms. And there she sat, sobbing uncontrollably, rocking her child against her breast, insensible to anything else.

The other three children were crouched at Arkadin's feet, weeping and sniffling. He turned his attention from mother and son to free the three girls, who immediately rushed to their mother's side, brushing their hands over their brother's hair, briefly holding his legs before resting their heads against their mother's thigh.

"How did this happen?" Tarkanian said.

Again, Arkadin couldn't tell whether he was talking to him or to himself. Nevertheless, he spoke up, recounting everything that had happened as he'd seen and experienced it. He was quite detailed, he left nothing out, and he was absolutely truthful, intuiting that this was the best—indeed, the only—course to take.

When he was finished, Tarkanian sat back on his hamstrings. "Dammit to hell, I knew Oserov was going to present a problem. My error was in underestimating its size and scope." He looked around at the homey surroundings, made bleak now by the bloodstains, the female keening, and the stench of death. "Essentially, we're screwed. Once Lev Antonin gets wind of what Oserov did to his family, our safe passage out of this shithole of a town will evaporate faster than you can say *Not with My Wife, You Don't!*"

Arkadin said, "Tony Curtis, Virna Lisi, George C. Scott."

Tarkanian raised his eyebrows. "Norman Panama."

"I love American comedies," Arkadin said.

"So do I."

As if acknowledging the inappropriateness of this conversation, Tarkanian hastily added, "All we'll have are those memories, and then not even those once Lev Antonin and his crew get ahold of us."

Arkadin's mind was in full gear. He was in the middle of yet another life-or-death crisis, but unlike the two Muscovites he was in his own territory. He could abandon them, of course, and go on the run. But then what, back to his hole in the basement? He shuddered, knowing he couldn't spend another minute in enforced confinement. No, like it or not, his fate was now bound to these people because they were his ticket out of here, because they would take him all the way to Moscow.

"On the way in I saw Joškar's car in the driveway," he said. "Is it still here?"

Tarkanian nodded.

"I'll gather her and the children. Find her purse, the car keys ought to be in there."

"You do realize that I'm not leaving without Oserov."

Arkadin shrugged. "That piece of shit is strictly your business. You want him along, you can carry him, because if I get near him again I swear to you I'll finish the job I started."

"That won't sit well with Maslov, I promise you."

Arkadin had just about enough of these interlopers. He got up into Tarkanian's face. "Fuck Maslov, your worry should be Lev Antonin."

"That cretin!"

"Here's a news flash: A cretin can kill you just as efficiently as a genius—and usually a whole lot quicker, because a cretin has no conscience." He pointed to Oserov. "Just like your boy over there. An attack dog has more sense than he does."

Tarkanian gave Arkadin a penetrating look, as if he were seeing him for the first time. "You intrigue me, Leonid Danilovich."

"Only my friends call me Leonid Danilovich," Arkadin said.

"So far as I can see, you don't have any friends." Tarkanian went searching for Joškar's handbag and found it on the floor just past the end of the sofa where it had apparently been knocked off the end table. Opening it, he dug around, a moment later lifting out the car keys in triumph. "Maybe, if we all get lucky, that will change."

Asphyxiated in her own home was not a fate Moira had ever contemplated. Her eyes were watering and she was slightly dizzy from holding her breath for so long. Holstering her Lady Hawk, she hauled out a low stepstool leaning against the rear wall, shook it open in the center of the small space, and climbed up until she could reach the ceiling—which, like the rest of the closet, was lined with cedar. A buzzing in her ears had already begun, product of a lack of oxygen, as she felt for the outline of the square in the cedar planking that was invisible from below. Tracing a line to the center of the square, she used both fists to pop the hatch she'd built in the closet. Pulling out the laptop, she hauled herself up into the crawl space in which she stored her bulky winter items in the summer months. Crawling across the bare plywood floor, she jammed the hatch back into place, collapsed onto her side, and gasped air into her burning lungs.

She gave a little moan, knowing she couldn't afford to stay there long: The carbon monoxide would seep into the crawl space soon enough. The small storage area gave out onto a jungle gym of beams and raised roof joists, across which she now crawled with great care.

Because she had built the storage space herself, she was familiar with every square inch of it. On either end, as the building code specified, there were venting triangles. She didn't know whether they'd be large enough for her to squeeze through, but she knew she had to try.

The distance wasn't great, but, sweating, her heart pounding, it seemed to take her forever to traverse the treacherous expanse of crisscrossing beams to the far end, where a glimmer of streetlight announced the venting triangle. That light drew her like a moth, growing in size as she approached it. Still, when she arrived her heart sank, because it didn't look nearly large enough to accommodate her body. She hooked her nails around the nether side of the metal band that described the triangle, and pulled it off. A freshet of cool night air brushed her face like a lover's caress, and for a moment she lay still, simply breathing.

Setting the triangle carefully aside, she slid headfirst through the opening. Now she could see that she was at the rear of her house, overhanging the narrow alley where she and her neighbors put out their garbage for the sanitation truck that weekly rumbled down the cobbles, disturbing the residents' sleep every Thursday at daybreak.

The glow of her neighbors' security lights streamed harshly into the interior, illuminating the laptop as she placed it on the lip of the opening. It was then that she saw to her consternation and alarm that the laptop's hot-swappable hard drive was missing. She checked and checked again as one will when a wallet is lost, because the enormity of the loss is such a shock.

Then with a grunt of disgust, she shoved

the laptop away. All this effort, putting herself in harm's way—and for nothing!

With her hands against the brickwork of the facade, she began to lever herself out, rounding her shoulders to get them through the triangle at its widest point, no mean trick—she had barely enough room to squeeze them through. Then she grasped one of the decorative stone outcroppings to increase her leverage. Now she had to contend with her hips, which didn't look as if they'd make it.

She was struggling with this problem of solid geometry when she heard a sound directly below her. Twisting her neck painfully, she saw that her rear door was opening. Someone was coming out—a figure in black. Though he looked severely foreshortened because of her awkward view from above, she could see him clearly enough. He stood motionless on the back step, peering around.

Now she turned back to her task, desperate to free herself. Resettling her grip on the ornamental stone lip, she redoubled her effort to haul her lower body through the opening. Unfortunately, this resulted in her hips getting stuck in the triangle. Belatedly, she saw how she should have twisted to have the best shot at getting through. She tried to push herself back, to free herself, but she was stuck. Down below, the man in black had lit a cigarette. By the way he was glancing up and down the alley, she figured that he must be waiting for the Lincoln Town Car to pick him up. As she continued to struggle, she saw him pull out his cell phone. Any moment now he would punch in his confederates' number and, finding they didn't answer, would take off on his own. With him would go her hard drive and any chance of hacking into Noah's Wi-Fi network.

The man in black put his phone to his ear, and she willed herself to relax, to exhale, so her body would soften. There! She was free! Now she twisted her hips and hauled herself through. Hanging precariously from the stone ornamentation, she heard the man's soft voice spiral up to her, along with the smoke from his cigarette. Knowing she was out of time, she let go and, plunging downward, landed on him.

As he fell to the cobbles, his cell phone flew through the air, shattering some feet away. His head hit the street with a sickening smack.

Jolted, aching, and slightly disoriented, she crawled over the corpse of the man in black, and in so doing found his cell phone. She stared at it curiously for a moment. If she was holding his cell, what had flown through the air?

Staggering to her feet, she zigzagged her way to where the splintered plastic and metal shards lay shining on the cobbles. On one of the small rectangular pieces was a thick red lightning bolt from upper right corner to lower left, symbol of all of Black River's specially designed hardware.

"Oh, God," she moaned. "No."

Sinking to her knees, she scooped up the disks, remnants of her hard drive, which was split open, unusable, unsalvageable, utterly ruined.

24

While Bourne and Tracy waited in the first-class lounge in Madrid for their Egyptair flight, Bourne excused himself and walked toward the men's room. He passed the shiny ranked shelves displaying newspapers from all over the world, in a great many languages, but all with more or less the same screaming headlines: "Negotiations Break Down," or "On The Brink," or "Last Diplomatic Hope Gone," but which invariably included the words "Iran" and "War."

When he was out of Tracy's sight, he extracted his cell and called Boris's number. There was no answer, no ring even, which meant that Boris had his phone off. He thought a moment and, walking to the windows so that he was away from everyone, he scrolled through his phone's address book until he brought up another Moscow number.

"What the hell?" a crusty old voice shouted down the line.

"Ivan, Ivan Volkin," he said. "It's Jason Bourne, Boris's friend."

"I know whose friend you are. I'm old, not senile. Besides, you caused enough mayhem when you were here three months ago to remain indelible in the mind of an Alzheimer's patient."

"I'm trying to get in touch with Boris."

"What else is new?" Volkin said tartly. "Why don't you try calling him instead of bothering me?"

"I wouldn't be calling you if he answered his cell."

"Ah, then you don't have his satellite phone number."

Which meant, Bourne thought, that Boris had returned to Africa. "You mean he's back in Timbuktu?"

"Timbuktu?" Volkin said. "Where did you get the idea Boris had been in Timbuktu?"

"From Boris himself."

"Hah! No, no, no. Not Timbuktu. Khartoum."

Bourne leaned against the glass chilled by the fierce air-conditioning of the lounge. He felt as if the ground were sliding out from under his feet. Why did all strands of the spider's web lead to Khartoum?

"What's Boris doing in Khartoum?"

"Something he doesn't want you, his good friend, to know about." Volkin laughed throatily. "Obviously."

Bourne took a stab in the dark. "But you know."

"Me? My dear Bourne, I'm retired from the world of the *grupperovka*. Who's got the bad memory, me or you?"

There was something very wrong with this conversation, and a moment later Bourne knew what it was. Surely, with all his contacts, Volkin must have heard of Bourne's "death." And yet there was no surprise in his voice when Bourne announced himself, no awkward questions being asked. Which meant he already knew Bourne had survived the attack on Bali. That meant Boris knew.

He tried another tack. "Do you know a man named Bogdan Machin?"

"The Torturer. Of course I know him."

"He's dead," Bourne said.

"No one's going to mourn, believe me."

"He was sent to Seville," Bourne said, "to kill me."

"Aren't you already dead?" Volkin said with an ironic twist.

"You knew I wasn't."

"Me, I still have a couple of brain cells left, which is more than could be said for the late, unlamented Bogdan Machin."

"Who told you? Boris?"

"Boris? My dear fellow, Boris went on a weeklong drunk when he heard—through me, I might add—that you'd been killed. Now, of course, he knows better."

"So Boris wasn't the one who shot me."

The explosion of laughter obliged Bourne to hold the phone away from his ear for a moment.

When Volkin had calmed down, he said, "What an absurd notion! You Americans! Where on earth did you come up with that bit of insanity?"

"Someone in Seville showed me surveillance photos of Boris in a Munich beer hall with the American secretary of defense."

"Really? On what planet would that happen?"

"I know it sounds crazy but I heard a tape of them talking. Secretary Halliday ordered my death and Boris agreed to it."

"Boris is your friend." Volkin's tone had turned deadly serious. "He's Russian; friendships don't come easily to us, and they're never betrayed."

"It was a barter," Bourne persisted. "Boris said he wanted Abdulla Khoury, the head of the Eastern Brotherhood, killed in return."

"It's true Abdulla Khoury was killed recently, but I assure you that Boris would have no reason to want him dead."

"Are you certain?"

"Boris has been working on anti-narcotics, yes? You know this or, at least, must have surmised as much. You're a clever one, hah! The Eastern Brotherhood was funding its Black Legion terrorists through a drug pipeline that ran from Colombia to Mexico to Munich. Boris had someone inside the cartel who provided him with the other end of the pipeline, namely Gustavo Moreno, a Colombian drug lord living in a vast hacienda outside Mexico City. Boris attacked the hacienda with his elite team of FSB-2 men and shut Moreno down. But the really big prize—Moreno's laptop with the details of every inch of the pipeline—eluded him. What happened to it? Boris spent two days searching every inch of the compound, to no avail, because before he died Moreno insisted it was in the hacienda. It wasn't, but Boris being Boris caught a whiff of a strange scent."

"Which eventually brought him to Khartoum."

Volkin deliberately ignored the comment. Perhaps he thought the answer was self-evident. Instead, he said: "Do you have the date this alleged meeting between Boris and the American secretary took place?"

"It was stamped on the photos," Bourne said. When he told Volkin, the Russian said emphatically, "Boris was here with me for three days, including that date. I don't know who was sitting down with the American secretary of defense, Bourne, but as sure as Russia is corrupt it wasn't our mutual friend Boris Karpov."

"Who was it then?"

"A chameleon, certainly. Do you know any, Bourne?"

"Besides myself, I do. But, unlike me, he's dead."

"You seem certain of that."

"I saw him fall from a great height into the water off the Port of Los Angeles."

"That is not the same as death. By God, you, of all people, should know," Volkin said.

A cold chill swept down Bourne's spine.

"How many lives have you had, Bourne? Boris tells me many. I think it must be the same with Leonid Danilovich Arkadin."

"Are you telling me that Arkadin didn't drown? That he survived?"

"A black cat like Arkadin has nine lives, my friend, possibly even more."

So it was Arkadin who'd tried to kill him on Bali. Though the picture had suddenly become clearer, there was still something wrong, something missing.

"Are you sure of all this, Volkin?"

"Arkadin is now the new head of the Eastern Brotherhood, how's that for being sure?"

"All right, but why would he hire the Torturer when he seems to want so desperately to kill me himself?"

"He wouldn't," Volkin said. "The Torturer is much too unreliable, especially against a foe like you."

"Then who hired him?"

"That, Bourne, is a question even I cannot answer."

Having decided to take to the field himself in an effort to find the missing Metro police officers, Peter Marks was waiting in front of the bank of elevators to take him to the ground floor when an elevator door slid open. The only person inside was the enigmatic Frederick Willard, up until three months ago the Old Man's mole inside the NSA's Virginia safe house. The older man was, as usual, dapper, urbane, utterly self-contained. He wore an impeccable gunmetal-gray, chalk-striped three-piece suit over a crisp white shirt and a conservative tie.

"Hello, Willard," Marks said as he stepped into the elevator. "I thought you were on leave."

"I got back several days ago."

From Marks's point of view, Willard was

remarkably well suited to play the role of steward in the safe house, evincing an old-school professorial air, musty and rather boring. It wasn't difficult to see how he melted into the woodwork. Being invisible made it so much easier to eavesdrop on intimate conversations.

The door slid shut and they descended.

"I imagine it's been difficult getting back into the swing of things," Marks said, more to be polite to the older man than anything else.

"Frankly, it was like I was never gone." Willard glanced over at Marks with a grimace, as if he'd just come from the surgeon's office and his agony was of such magnitude that he could not hide it. "How did your interview with the president go?"

Surprised that Willard knew about it, Marks said, "Well enough, I suppose."

"Not that it matters, you're not getting the post."

"It figures. Dick Symes was the logical front-runner."

"Symes is out, too."

Marks's acceptance turned to consternation. "How do you know that?"

"Because I know who did get the post

and, fuck us all, it isn't anyone from inside CI."

"But that makes no sense."

"On the contrary, it makes perfect sense," Willard said, "if your name happens to be Bud Halliday."

Marks turned toward the older man. "What's happened, Willard? Come on, man, out with it!"

"Halliday has used Veronica Hart's sudden death to his advantage. He's proposed his own man, M. Errol Danziger, and after meeting with Danziger the president's agreed."

"Danziger, the NSA's current deputy director of signals intelligence for analysis and production?"

"That's the one."

"But he knows nothing about CI!" Marks cried.

"I believe," Willard said with some asperity, "that's precisely the point."

The doors opened and the two men stepped out into the marble-and-glass reception area, as chilly as it was vast.

"Under the circumstances, I think we need to talk," Willard said. "But not here."

"Certainly not." Marks was about to propose a meeting for later, but then changed his mind. Who better than this mysterious veteran with a thousand and one sources, who knew all of Alex Conklin's back-channel intelligence secrets, to help him find the missing cops? "I'm off on an investigation in the field. Care to join me?"

A smile creased Willard's face. "Ah, me, it'll be just like I've dreamed!"

When Arkadin approached Joškar, she spat at him, then turned her face away. All her four children—the three girls and the dead son—were clustered around her like foam surrounding a basalt outcropping rising from the sea. They, the living, little ones, rose up as he approached as if to protect her from an assault or an unwanted intrusion.

Tearing off one shirtsleeve, Arkadin leaned in and dabbed the blood off her face. It was when he touched the point of her chin to turn her face back toward him that he saw the deep bruises on her face, the welts on her neck. Rage at Oserov flared anew inside him, but then he noticed that the welts and bruises weren't recent—he was certain they hadn't been made in the last several days. If Oserov hadn't caused them then, in all likelihood, her husband, Lev Antonin, had.

Her eyes met his for a moment, and in them he saw a bleak reflection of the bedroom upstairs, filled with both her intimate scent and her abject solitude.

"Joškar," he said, "do you know who I am?"

"My son," she said, hugging him to her breast. "My son."

"We're going to get you out of here, Joškar, you and your children. You don't have to be afraid of Lev Antonin anymore."

She stared at him, as dumbfounded as if he'd told her she was getting her lost youth back. The crying of her youngest girl brought her around. She looked at Tarkanian who, with her car keys in one hand, had slung Oserov over his shoulder.

"He's coming with us? The man who killed my Yasha?"

Arkadin said nothing, because the answer was clear.

When she turned back to him, a light had gone out in her eyes. "Then my Yasha comes, too."

Tarkanian, bent over like a coal miner, was already carrying his heavy load to the front door. "Leonid Danilovich, come on. The dead have no place among the living."

But when Arkadin took Joškar's arm, she snatched it away.

"What about that piece of filth? The moment he killed my Yasha he died, too."

With a grunt, Tarkanian opened the door. "We don't have time for negotiation," he said brusquely.

"I agree." Arkadin took Yasha into his arms. "The boy comes with us."

He said it in such a tone that Tarkanian gave him another of his penetrating looks. Then the Muscovite shrugged. "She's your responsibility, my friend. All of them are your responsibility now."

They trooped out to the car, Joškar herding her three confused and shivering daughters. Tarkanian placed Oserov in the trunk and tied the lid to the bumper with a length of twine he'd found in a kitchen drawer so that his compatriot would have fresh air. Then he opened the two doors on the near side, and went around to slide behind the wheel.

"I want to hold my son," Joškar said as

she urged her daughters into the backseat.

"Better that I take him up front," Arkadin said. "The three girls need your undivided attention." When she hesitated, pushed the hair back from her son's forehead, he said, "I'll take good care of him, Joškar. Don't worry. Yasha will be right here with me."

He got into the front passenger's seat and, with the boy cradled in one arm, closed the door. He noted that they had almost a full tank of gas. Tarkanian fired the ignition, let out the clutch, and put the car in gear. They took off.

"Get that thing off me," Tarkanian said as they took a corner at speed and Yasha's head brushed against his arm.

"Show some fucking respect," Arkadin snapped. "The boy can't hurt you."

"You're as loony as a *tyolka* in heat," Tarkanian retorted.

"Who's got a friend locked in the trunk?"

Tarkanian honked the horn mightily at a truck lumbering in front of him. Maneuvering around, he braved oncoming traffic to pass the huge vehicle, ignoring the angry blare of horns and the near misses as cars coming the other way scrambled to get out of his way.

When they were back on their side of the road, Tarkanian glanced over at Arkadin. "You've got a soft spot for this kid, huh."

Arkadin did not respond. Though he was staring straight ahead, his gaze had turned inward. He was acutely aware of Yasha's weight, even more his presence, which had opened a door into his own childhood. When he looked down at Yasha's face it was as if he were looking at himself, carrying his own death with him like a familiar companion. He wasn't frightened of this boy, as Tarkanian clearly was. On the contrary, it seemed important for him to hold Yasha, as if he could keep safe whatever remained of a human being, especially such a young and innocent one, after death. Why did he feel that way? And then a murmuring from the backseat compelled him to lean over to peer at the reflections in the rearview mirror. He saw Joškar with her three young daughters gathered around her, her arms encompassing them, sheltering them from further harm, fear, and indignities. She was telling them a story filled with bright fairies, talking foxes, and clever elves. The love and devotion in her voice was like an alien communication from a distant, unexplored galaxy.

All of a sudden a profound wave of sorrow swept through him, so that he bent his head over Yasha's thin blue eyelids, as if in prayer. In that moment, the boy's death and the part of his childhood his mother had torn from his breast merged, became one, indistinguishable both in his febrile mind and his damaged soul.

Humphry Bamber was waiting anxiously for Moira when she returned to Lamontierre's brownstone.

"So, how did it go?" he said, as he ushered her into the living room. "Where's the laptop?"

When she handed him the wrecked disk, he turned it over and over. "You've got to be kidding."

"I wish I was," Moira said wearily.

She sat heavily on the sofa while he

went to fetch her a drink. When he returned, he sat opposite her. His face looked haggard and drawn, the first signs of constant anxiety.

"These disks are utterly useless," he said, "you realize that?"

She nodded and sipped at her drink. "Just like the cell I got off the guy who pulled the hard drive from my laptop. It was a burner."

"A what?"

"A disposable cell phone you can buy in practically any drug- or convenience store. It has a set number of pre-paid minutes. Criminals use them and discard them daily; that way their conversations can't be tapped and their whereabouts can't be traced."

She waved her own words away. "Not that it matters now. Where tapping into Noah's computer is concerned, we're essentially screwed."

"Not necessarily." Bamber hunched forward. "At first, when you left I thought I'd go out of my mind. I kept replaying you pulling me out of the Buick, seeing Hart behind the wheel, and then the whole thing exploded to hell." His eyes slid away. "My stomach rebelled. Maybe that wasn't such a bad thing because while I was splashing cold water on my face I got the idea."

Moira put her empty glass down beside the wreck of the hard drive disks. "What idea?"

"Okay, it occurred to me that each time I deliver a new iteration of Bardem, Noah insists that I download it directly to his laptop."

"Security reasons, I'm sure. So?"

"Well, in order for the program to install correctly, he's got to shut down all other programs."

Moira shook her head. "I'm still not following."

Bamber drummed his fingers for a moment as he thought of a suitable example to illustrate his point. "Okay, you know how when you install some programs, the install shield asks you to shut down all programs including your virus protection?" When she nodded, he went on. "That's to ensure they load properly. It's the same with Bardem, only to the nth degree. It's so complex and so sensitive that it needs a completely clear field, as it were, to install properly. So here's my thought. I could contact Noah and tell him I found a bug in his current version of Bardem, that I need to send him an update. Usually, the new version overwrites the previous one, but with a bit of work I think I can upload his version while I download the new one."

Moira, suddenly galvanized, sat up straight. "Then we'll have everything that's in his program, including the scenarios he's been running. We'll know precisely what he's planning, and where!"

She jumped up and kissed Bamber on the cheek. "That's brilliant!"

"Plus, I could embed a tracer in the new version that would let us track what he's inputting in real time."

She knew just how clever—and paranoid—Noah was. "Could he find out about the tracer?"

"Anything's possible," Bamber said, "but it's highly unlikely."

"Then let's not get too cute."

He gave her a slightly embarrassed nod. "Anyway, it's all pie in the sky," he said. "I've got to get to my office and find a way to reassure Noah that everything's okay with me."

Moira's mind was already spinning out possible scenarios. "Don't worry about that. You concentrate on the nuts and bolts of the two-way transfer. I'll take care of Noah."

After reading everything he could about the rapidly escalating Iran situation in the *International Herald Tribune* he'd picked up in the lounge in Madrid, Bourne sat brooding all during the flight to Khartoum. Once or twice, he became aware that Tracy was trying to engage him in conversation, but he didn't care to answer. He was wondering why the possibility of Arkadin surviving his trial at sea hadn't occurred to him; after all, the precise same thing had happened to him off Marseilles, when he'd been pulled half dead out of the water by the crew of a fishing boat. He'd been nursed back to health by a local doctor, as inveterate a drunk as Dr. Firth, only to discover that the trauma he'd suffered had caused amnesia. His memories of his life had been wiped out. Once in a while something familiar would trigger a shard of memory, but when it did surface, it most often arrived in incomplete fits and starts.

Since then he'd struggled to find out who he was, and though many years had passed he seemed no closer to the truth—the identities of Jason Bourne and, to a limited extent, David Webb were all he could remember. It had seemed to him that the path that would lead him to himself lay through his memories on Bali.

But first, there was the matter of Leonid Arkadin to consider. That Arkadin wanted him dead was beyond doubt, but he also intuited that more was going on here than a simple case of revenge. Though he'd learned that nothing with Arkadin was simple, there was an overarching plan to this particular web in which he found himself that transcended even Arkadin, who seemed to be one strand among many that was leading Bourne to Khartoum.

Whether or not Don Fernando Hererra was in league with Arkadin—and it seemed a sure bet that Arkadin had sent him the photos and audio "incriminating" Boris—was for the moment beside the point. Now that he knew Arkadin was behind the attempt on his life, he had to assume that a trap was being laid for him at 779 El Gamhuria Avenue. Whether that trap was Arkadin's alone, or whether it included Nikolai Yevsen, the arms dealer, and Noah Perlis, he didn't yet know. But it was interesting to speculate on what business Noah had with Yevsen. Was it personal or on behalf of Black River? Either way, the two constituted a sinister team, one that he needed to know more about.

And what was Tracy's role in all this? She had taken possession of the fantastic Goya only after she had electronically transferred the required sum to Don Hererra's bank account and he had ordered his banker to deposit the funds into a second account, the number of which was unknown to her. That way, Hererra had said with a sly smile, he was assured that the money had actually been delivered and would remain his. His years in the oil fields had turned the Colombian into a sly old fox who considered every angle and planned for every contingency. Bourne thought it ironic that he held a peculiar affection for Hererra even though clearly the Colombian and Arkadin were in some sense allies. He hoped he'd run into Hererra again one day, but in the meantime he needed to deal with Arkadin and Noah Perlis.

The dying sun, red as a fireball, was moving ponderously downward to the earth when Soraya and Amun Chalthoum reached Chysis Military Airdrome. Chalthoum showed his credentials and was directed to a small parking lot. After passing through another security check, they were striding across the tarmac toward the plane Chalthoum had ordered to be fueled and ready to take off when Soraya saw two people walking on a tangent course toward a waiting Air Afrika jet. The woman was thin, blond, and quite striking. She was closer to Soraya so, for a moment, her male companion was blocked from her view. Then the vectors changed as they neared one another. Soraya caught a glimpse of the man's face and, stricken, felt her knees grow momentarily weak.

Chalthoum, at once noticing her faltering stride, turned back to her.

"What is it, *azizti*?" he said. "You've no blood in your face."

"It's nothing." Soraya breathed deeply and slowly in an attempt to calm herself.

But since the new DCI had called and summarily ordered her back to DC without giving her a chance to explain the situation, nothing could calm her now. And then she saw Jason Bourne walking along the tarmac at a military airport outside Cairo. At first she thought, *It can't be him. It must be someone else.* But as he neared her and his features became more detailed, she realized there could be no doubt.

My God, my God, she thought. *What's happening? How could Jason be alive?*

She had to restrain herself from calling out his name, from rushing up to him and embracing him. He hadn't contacted her, so there must be a reason—a damn good one, she suspected—he didn't want her to know that he was alive. He was talking intently with his companion and so hadn't yet seen her—or if he had, he was pretending that he hadn't.

On the other hand, she had to find a way to get him the number of her satellite phone. But how to do it without either Amun or Jason's companion knowing?

Your silence is painful," Tracy said.

"It's that bad?" Bourne didn't look at her,

but rather stared straight ahead at the red-and-white fuselage of the Air Afrika jet, waiting like a large and dangerous cat just off the head of the main runway of the military airstrip. He'd spotted Soraya the moment she and the tall, lanky Egyptian had passed through security and come onto the tarmac, and he was trying to ignore her because the last thing he wanted now was for someone from CI—even Soraya—to see him.

"You haven't said a word for hours." Tracy sounded genuinely hurt. "It's as if there's a glass wall around you."

"I've been trying to figure out the best way of protecting you once we arrive in Khartoum."

"Protect me from what?"

"Not what. Who," Bourne said. "Don Herrera lied about the photos and the audio, so who knows what else he's lied about?"

"Whatever you have going doesn't have anything to do with me," Tracy said. "I'm going to stay as far away from your business as I can because, quite frankly, it scares the hell out of me."

Bourne nodded. "I understand."

She had the carefully packed Goya

safely tucked under her arm. "The difficult part of my job is finished. All that's left to do now is to deliver the Goya, collect the remainder of my fee from Noah, and fly home."

It was at that precise moment that Tracy looked up and said, "That exotic-looking woman keeps staring at you. Do you know her?"

25

There was no help for it, Bourne thought, now that Tracy had noticed. Soraya and the Egyptian were only paces away, so Bourne strode up to Soraya.

"Hello, sis," he said, kissing her warmly on both cheeks. Then, before she had time to respond, he turned to her companion and held out his hand. "Adam Stone. I'm Soraya's half brother."

The Egyptian shook his hand briefly. "Amun Chalthoum." But his eyebrows shot up. "I didn't know Soraya had a brother."

Bourne's laugh was easy. "I'm the black

sheep, I'm afraid. No one in the family likes to talk about me."

By this time Tracy had come up beside him, and he introduced everyone.

Taking him up on his cue, Soraya said to him, "There's a problem with Mom's health I think you ought to know about."

"Excuse us a moment, would you?" Bourne said to Tracy and Chalthoum.

When the two of them were far enough away to afford them adequate privacy, Soraya said, "Jason, what the hell?" She was still looking at him as if she couldn't quite believe what her eyes were telling her.

"It's a long story," he said, "and we don't have the time now." He led Soraya a few more paces away from the other two. "Arkadin is still alive. He almost succeeded in killing me on Bali."

"No wonder you don't want anyone to know you're still alive."

Bourne glanced at Chalthoum. "What are you doing here with that Egyptian?"

"Amun's with Egyptian intelligence. We're trying to find out who actually shot down the American jet."

"I thought the Iranians—"

"Our forensics team determined that it was an Iranian Kowsar 3 missile that brought down the plane," Soraya said, "but now, inexplicably, it looks as if a cadre of four American military men might have brought it into Egypt through Sudan. That's why we're on our way to Khartoum."

Bourne could feel the strands of the spiderweb coming into sudden focus, and he bent toward Soraya as he said softly and urgently, "Listen carefully. Whatever Arkadin is up to involves both Nikolai Yevsen and Black River. I've been wondering what would bring these three together. It could be that the cadre you're looking for aren't military per se, but are Black River personnel." He directed her attention to the red-and-white jet where he and Tracy had been headed. "Air Afrika is rumored to be owned by Yevsen, which would make sense—he needs a way to transship the illegal arms consignments to his clients."

While Soraya studied the plane, he continued: "If you're right about the American cadre, then where do you think they could possibly obtain an Iranian Kowsar 3 missile—from the Iranians themselves?"

He shook his head. "Yevsen is probably the only arms dealer in the world with enough contacts and power to get one."

"But why would Black River—?"

"Black River's only there to do the heavy lifting," Bourne said. "It's whoever hired them that's guiding everything. You've read the headlines. I think someone high up in the US government wants to go to war with Iran. You'll know better than me who it might be."

"Bud Halliday," Soraya said. "The secretary of defense."

"Halliday's the one who ordered my death."

She goggled at him for a moment. "Right now this is all speculation, so it's nothing I can use. I need proof of these connections, so we'll need to stay in touch. I'm reachable on a sat phone," she said at length, and rattled off a string of numbers for him to memorize. He nodded, giving her the number of his own sat phone, and was about to break away when she said, "There's something else. DCI Hart has been killed by a car bomb. A man named M. Errol Danziger is the new DCI and he's already recalled me from the field."

"An order you're clearly refusing to obey. Good for you."

Soraya grimaced. "Who knows what kind of trouble it's going to get me into." She took his arm. "Jason, listen, this is the hardest part. For some reason Moira was with DCI Hart when the car bomb detonated. I know Moira survived the blast, because she checked herself into and out of an ER right afterward. But now she's gone completely off the grid." She squeezed his arm. "I thought you'd want to know."

She kissed him as he had kissed her moments before. As she walked back to the Egyptian, who had clearly become impatient at the delay, Bourne felt as if he had vacated his body. He seemed to be looking down on the three people on the tarmac as if from a great height. He saw Soraya say something to Chalthoum, saw the Egyptian nod, saw them both head toward a small military jet. He saw Tracy staring after them, an expression of both curiosity and consternation on her face; he saw himself standing apart, as still as if he had been suspended in amber. He observed all these things without a trace of emotion or awareness of consequence, flooded as he was by images of Moira in Bali with the sun in her eyes, turning them luminous, lambent, phosphorescent, unforgettable. It was as if in his memory he needed to protect her, or at least keep her safe from the dangers of the outside world. It was an absurd impulse, but, he told himself, a wholly human one. Where was she? How badly was she injured? And over all, the terrifying question loomed: Was the car bomb that killed Veronica Hart meant for Moira? Adding to his concern, when he'd called, her number was out of service, which meant she'd changed phones.

So deep had he sunk into himself that it was several moments before he realized that Tracy was talking to him. She stood facing him, her face a mask of concern.

"Adam, what's going on? Did your sister give you bad news?"

"What?" He was still slightly distracted by the swirl of emotions that had been loosed from his tight control. "Yes, she told me that yesterday our mother passed away unexpectedly."

"Oh, I'm so sorry. Is there anything I can do to help?"

His mouth smiled, though he remained

far away. "That's very kind, but no. There's nothing anyone can do now."

M. Errol Danziger had a soul like an angry fist. From adolescence onward, he had made it his business to know everything there was to know about Muslims. He had studied the histories of Persia and the Arabian Peninsula; he spoke both Arabic and Farsi fluently, could recite entire sections of the Qur'an by heart, as well as a multitude of Muslim prayers. He had absorbed the essential differences between Sunni and Shi'a, and despised them both with equal fervor. For years now he had used his knowledge of the Middle East in the service of a destructive force against those who wished his country harm.

His intense—some believed obsessive—antipathy toward Muslims of all stripes might very well have stemmed from his high school years in the South, when a rumor that he harbored Syrian blood raced around the schoolyard, causing him to be the butt of endless jokes and taunting. Finally, inevitably, systematically, he was isolated, then ostracized, from social life. That the rumor was based on the truth—

Danziger's paternal grandfather was of Syrian descent—made his misery complete.

He buried his curdled heart at precisely 8 AM when he took formal control of CI. He had still to appear on Capitol Hill, to be asked absurd and irrelevant questions by preening legislators looking to impress their constituents with probing questions fed them by their assistants. But that dog-and-pony show, Halliday had assured him, was a mere formality. The secretary of defense had amassed more than enough votes to push through his confirmation without a struggle or even much debate.

At precisely 8:05 AM he convened a meeting of the senior staff in the largest of the conference rooms at CI headquarters, an elongated oval without windows because glass was an excellent carrier of sound waves and an expert with field glasses trained on the room could read lips. Danziger was quite clear as to the attendees: the heads of the seven directorates, their immediate subordinates, and the chiefs of all the departments attached to the various directorates.

The spacious room was illuminated by

indirect lights hidden by massive soffits built into the circumference of the ceiling. Specially designed and manufactured carpeting was so dense it absorbed nearly all sound, so that all those present were forced to focus their entire attention on whoever was speaking.

On this particular morning that was M. Errol Danziger, also known as the Arab, who, as he looked around the oval table, saw nothing but pale and anxious faces whose owners were still trying to digest the shocking news of his being anointed by the president as the next DCI. To a man—and of this he was quite certain—they had been expecting one of the seven, most likely Dick Symes, chief of intelligence and the most senior of the heads of the seven directorates, to be convening this meeting.

Which was why his gaze fixed on Symes last, why, as he commenced his inaugural address to the troops, he kept his eyes firmly fixed on Symes. After studying the CI organizational chart, he had made up his mind to reach out to Symes, to make of him an ally, because he would need allies, would need to gather to his side a cadre of the CI faithful whom he could bend to his will, whom he could slowly indoctrinate in the new ways, and who, as disciples of the new religion he meant to bring to CI, would spread the gospel as chosen ones should. They would do his work for him, work that would be too difficult, if not impossible, for him to accomplish on his own. Because his mission was not to replace CI personnel, but to convert from within, until a new CI emerged along the lines of the blueprint Bud Halliday had drawn up for him.

To this end, he had already decided to promote Symes to DDCI, after a suitable time. In this way, through flattery and then recruitment, he meant to cement his power at CI.

"Good morning, gentlemen. I suspect you have heard rumors—and here I hope I'm wrong, but in the event I'm not, my aim this morning is to set the record straight. There will be no firings, no transfers, no forced reassignments, although in the natural course of events, there will inevitably be, as we move forward, reassignments, as, I understand, there have always been here, and, indeed, in any organically evolving organization. In preparation for this moment, I've studied the hallowed history of CI, and I can confidently state that no one understands the legacy of this great organization better than I do. Let me assure you—and my door is always open for discussion on this and any other topic that may be of concern to you—that nothing will change, that the legacy of the Old Man, who, I might add, I venerated from the time I was a young man fresh out of college, remains paramount in my mind, which leads me to say in all honesty and humility that it is a privilege and an honor to be among you, to become a part of you, to lead this great organization into the future."

The men ranged around the table sat in complete silence, trying to parse this long-winded preamble while, at the same time, trying to register it on their individual bullshit meters. It was a curious fact that Danziger had absorbed the involuted rhythm of Arabic so thoroughly that it had infected his English, especially when he was addressing a group. Where a word would do, a sentence would present itself; where a sentence would do, a paragraph appeared.

As a palpable feeling of relief washed over the conference room, he sat down, opened the file in front of him, and paged through the first half of it. All at once, he looked up. "Soraya Moore, the director of Typhon, isn't present because she is currently on assignment. You should know that I've canceled that assignment and ordered her to return at once for a thorough debriefing."

He watched some heads turning in consternation, but there was no murmuring at all. Taking one last glance down at his notes, he said, "Mr. Doll, why isn't your boss, Mr. Marks, in attendance this morning?"

Rory Doll coughed into his fist. "I believe he's in the field, sir."

As the Arab looked at Doll, a fair-haired wisp of a man with electric blue eyes, he smiled winningly. "You *believe* he's in the field or you *know* he's in the field?"

"I know it, sir. He told me himself."

"All right, then." Danziger's smile hadn't budged. "*Where* in the field?"

"He didn't specify, sir."

"And I assume you didn't ask him."

"Sir, with all due respect, if Chief Marks wanted me to know, he would've told me."

Without taking his eyes off Marks's second, the Arab closed the file in front of him. It seemed as if the entire room were holding its collective breath. "Quite right. I approve of sound security procedure," the new DCI said. "Please ensure Marks comes to see me the moment he returns."

His gaze broke away from Doll at last and roved around the table, engaging in turn each of the senior officers. "All right, shall we proceed? From this moment on all the resources of CI will be bent toward the undermining and destruction of the current regime in Iran."

A frisson of excitement raced like wildfire from officer to officer.

"In a few moments I'll outline to you the overarching operation to exploit a new pro-American indigenous Iranian underground, ready and able, with our support, to topple the regime from inside Iran."

When it comes to the police commissioner in this town," Willard said, "throwing your weight around is worse than useless. I say that because the PC is used to getting his own way, even with the mayor. He isn't intimidated by feds, and he's not shy about saying so."

Willard and Peter Marks were mounting the stone steps of a brownstone far enough off Dupont Circle not to be snooty, but close enough to be a recipient of the area's innate urbanity. This was wholly Willard's doing. Having ascertained that Lester Burrows, the police commissioner, was gone for the day, Willard had directed them to this block, to this specific brownstone.

"That being the case, the only smart way to play him is with psychology. Honey is a powerful incentive inside the Beltway, never more so than with the Metro police."

"You know Commissioner Burrows?"

"Know him?" Willard said. "He and I trod the boards in college; we played *Othello* together. He was a helluva Moor, let me tell you, scary-good—I knew his rage was genuine because I knew where he came from." He nodded, as if to himself. "Lester Burrows is one African American who has transcended the utter poverty of his childhood in every sense of the word. That's not to say he's forgotten it, not by a long shot, but, unlike his predecessor, who never met a bribe he didn't take, Lester Burrows is a good man underneath the mean streak he's cultivated to protect himself, his office, and his men."

"So he'll listen to you," Marks said.

"I don't know about that"—Willard's eyes twinkled—"but he sure as hell won't turn me away."

There was a brass knocker in the shape of an elephant that Willard used to announce their presence.

"What is this place?" Marks asked.

"You'll see soon enough. Just follow my lead and you'll be okay."

The door opened, revealing a young African American woman dressed in a fashionable business suit. She blinked once and said, "Freddy, is that really you?"

Willard chuckled. "It's been a while, Reese, hasn't it?"

"Years and years," the young woman said, a smile creasing her face. "Well, don't just stand there, come on in. He's going to be tickled beige to see you."

"To fleece me, you mean."

Now it was the young woman's turn to

chuckle, a warm, rich sound that seemed to caress the listener's ear.

"Reese, this is a friend of mine, Peter Marks."

The young woman stuck out her hand in a no-nonsense fashion. She had a rather square face with an aggressive chin and worldly eyes the color of bourbon. "Any friend of Freddy's . . ." Her smile deepened. "Reese Williams."

"The commissioner's strong right hand," Willard supplied.

"Oh, yes." She laughed. "What *would* he do without me?"

She led them down a softly lit, wood-paneled hallway, decorated with photos and watercolors of African wildlife, most predominantly elephants, with a smattering of rhinos, zebras, and giraffes thrown in.

They arrived soon after at double pocket doors, which Reese threw open to a blue cloud of aromatic cigar smoke, the discreet clink of glassware, and the fast-paced dealing of cards on a green baize table in the center of the library. Six men—including Commissioner Burrows—and one woman sat around the table, playing poker. All of them were high up in various departments of the district's political infrastructure. The ones Marks didn't know on sight, Willard identified for him.

As they stood on the threshold, Reese went ahead of them, crossing to the table, where Burrows sat, patiently playing his hand. She waited just behind his right shoulder until he'd raked in the considerable pot, then leaned over and whispered in his ear.

At once the commissioner glanced up and a wide smile spread over his face. "Goddammit!" he exclaimed, pushing his chair back and rising. "Well, wash my socks and call me Andy, if it isn't Freddy Fucking Willard!" He strode over and engulfed Willard in a bear hug. He was a massive man with a bowling-ball head, who looked like an overstuffed sausage. His freckle-dappled cheeks belied the master manipulator's eyes and the pensive mouth of a seasoned politician.

Willard introduced Marks and the commissioner pumped his hand with that sinister warmth peculiar to people in public life, which flicks on and off with the quickness of a lightning strike.

"If you've come to play," Burrows said, "you've come to the right joint."

"Actually, we've come to ask you about Detectives Sampson and Montgomery," Marks said impulsively.

The commissioner's brow pulled down, darkening into a furry mass. "Who are Sampson and Montgomery?"

"With all due respect, sir, you know who they are."

"Son, are you some sort of psychic?" Burrows turned on Willard. "Freddy, who the hell is he to tell me what I know?"

"Ignore him, Lester." Willard inserted himself between Marks and the commissioner. "Peter's been a little on edge since he went off his medication."

"Well, get the man back on it, stat," Burrows said. "That mouth is a fucking menace."

"I will certainly do that," Willard said as he grabbed Marks to keep him out of the line of fire. "In the meantime, do you have room for one more at the table?"

Noah Perlis, sitting in the lime-scented shade of the lavish rooftop garden at 779 El Gamhuria Avenue, could see all of

Khartoum, smoky and indolent, laid out before him to his right, while to his left were the Blue and White Nile rivers that divided the city into thirds. In central Khartoum the hideous Chinese-built Friendship Hall, and the weird futuristic Al-Fateh building, so like the nose cone of an immense rocket, mixed uneasily with the traditional mosques and ancient pyramids of the city, but the unsettling juxtaposition was a sign of the times—hidebound Muslim religion seeking its way in the alien modern world.

Perlis had his laptop open, the latest iteration of the Bardem program running the last of the scenarios: the incursion by Arkadin and his twenty-man cadre into that section of Iran where, like Palestine, the milk and honey flowed, in the form of oil.

Perlis never did one thing when he could do two or, preferably, three at once. He was a man whose mind was so quick and restless that it needed a kind of internal web of goals, puzzles, and conjectures to keep from imploding into chaos. So while he studied the probabilities of Pinprick's end phase the program was spitting out he thought about the devil's deal he'd been forced to make with Dimitri Maslov and, by extension, Leonid Arkadin. First and foremost, it galled him to partner with Russians, whose corruption and dissolute lifestyle he both loathed and envied. How could a bunch of scummy pigs like that be so awash in money? While it was true that life was never fair, he mused, sometimes it could be downright malevolent. But what could he do? He'd tried many other routes but, in the end, Maslov had been the only way to get to Nikolai Yevsen, who felt about Americans the way he, Perlis, felt about Russians. Accordingly, he'd been forced to make a deal with too many partners—too many partners for whom double dealing and backstabbing had been ingrained in their nature virtually from birth. Contingencies had to be made against the threat of such treachery, and that meant triple the planning and man-hours. Of course, it also meant he'd been able to triple the fee he was charging Bud Halliday, not that the price meant anything to the secretary, the way the US Mint was printing up dollars as if they were confetti. In fact, at the last Black River board meeting, members of the steering committee were so concerned with the threat of hyperinflation that they had voted unanimously to convert their dollars into gold bullion for the next six months while they put their clients on notice that starting September 1, the company would accept fees only in gold or diamonds. What bothered him about that meeting was that Oliver Liss, one of the three founding members and the man he reported to, was absent.

Simultaneously, he was thinking of Moira. Like a cinder in his eye, she had become an irritant. She was firmly lodged in a corner of his mind ever since she had abruptly quit Black River and, after a short hiatus, had started her own company in direct competition with him. Because, make no mistake, Perlis had taken her defection and subsequent treachery personally. It hadn't been the first time, but he vowed to himself that it would be the last. The first time . . . well, there were good reasons not to think about the first time. He hadn't for years and he wasn't about to start now.

Besides, how else should he take actions that directly drained him of his best personnel? Like a jilted lover, he seethed for revenge, his long-withheld affection for her curdled into outright hatred—not only of her, but of himself. While she was under his control, he'd played his cards too close to the vest—had, he had to admit bitterly, misplayed them altogether. And now she was gone, out of his control and in complete opposition to him. He took whatever solace he could salvage from the fact that her lover, Jason Bourne, was dead. He wished her only ill now, he wanted to see her not simply defeated but humiliated beyond redemption; nothing less would appease his appetite for vengeance.

When his satellite phone rang, he assumed it was Bud Halliday, giving him the signal to launch the final phase of Pinprick, but instead he discovered Humphry Bamber on the line.

"Bamber," he shouted, "where the hell are you?"

"Back at my office, thank God." Bamber's voice sounded thin and metallic. "I finally managed to escape because the woman Moira Something was too badly hurt in the explosion to hold on to me for long."

"I heard about the explosion," Noah said

truthfully, though of course he didn't add that he'd ordered it to keep Veronica Hart and Moira from finding out about Bardem from Bamber. "Are you all right?"

"Nothing a few days' rest won't cure," Bamber said, "but listen, Noah, there's a glitch in the version of Bardem you're running."

Noah stared out at the rivers, the beginning and the end of life in North Africa. "What kind of a glitch? If the program needs another security patch, forget it, I'm almost finished using it."

"No, nothing like that. There's a calculation error; the program isn't producing accurate data."

Now Noah was alarmed. "How the hell did that happen, Bamber? I paid through the nose for this software and now you tell me that—"

"Calm down, Noah, I've already solved the internal error and corrected it. All I need to do now is to upload it to you, but you'll have to shut down all your programs."

"I know, I know, and Jesus, I ought to know the protocol by now considering how many versions of Bardem we've been through."

"Noah, you have no idea how complex this program is—I mean, come on, literally millions of factors had to be incorporated into the software's architecture, and per your orders at the speed of light, too."

"Can it, Bamber. The last thing I need now is a lecture from you. Just get the fucking thing done." Perlis's fingers were running over his laptop's keyboard, shutting down programs. "Now, you're sure the latest parameters I've loaded into the program will be there when I bring up the new version?"

"Absolutely, Noah. That's why Bardem has one monster-size cache."

"Nothing better be missing," Noah said, and silently he added, *Not at this late date. We're almost at the finish line.*

"Just let me know when you're ready," Bamber prompted.

All the programs were closed, but it took several minutes of going through one deliberately convoluted protocol after another until he exited the proprietary Black River security software. While this was happening, he muted his line with Bamber and dialed a number on a second satellite phone.

"Someone needs to be put to sleep," he said. "Yes, right away. Hold on and I'll transfer the particulars in a minute."

He unmuted the line with Bamber. "All set," he said.

"Then here we go!"

26

Khartoum had about it the air of a disreputable mortuary. The sweet rot of death was everywhere, mingled with the sharp odor of gun barrels. Baleful shadows hid men smoking as they observed the night-lit street with the inscrutable look of a hunter searching for prey. Bourne and Tracy, in a jangling three-wheeled *raksha,* going at a hellish speed against traffic, rushed down avenues filled with donkey-pulled carts, wheezing minibuses, men in both traditional and Western dress, and vehicles belching blue smoke.

They were both tired and on edge—Bourne had had no luck contacting either Moira or Boris, and, despite what she'd claimed, Tracy's experience in Seville seemed to have made her anxious about meeting Noah.

"I don't want to be caught napping when I walk in the door," she'd said as they checked into a hotel in the main section of the city. "That's why I told Noah I wasn't coming over until tomorrow morning. Tonight I need a good night's sleep more than I need his money."

"What did he say?"

They rode up in the mirrored elevator, heading for the top floor, which Tracy had requested.

"He wasn't happy, but what could he say?"

"He didn't offer to come here?"

Tracy's nose wrinkled. "No, he didn't."

Bourne thought that odd. If Noah was so anxious to take possession of the Goya, why wouldn't he offer to complete the transaction at the hotel?

They had adjoining rooms with nearly identical views of al Mogran—the junction of the Blue and White Nile rivers—and a connecting door that locked from either side. The White Nile flowed north from Lake Victoria, while the Blue Nile flowed west from Ethiopia. The Nile itself, the main river, continued north into Egypt.

The decor in the room was shabby. Judging by both the style and the wear, it certainly hadn't been updated since the early 1970s. The carpets stank of cheap cigarettes and even cheaper perfume. Putting the Goya on the bed, Tracy crossed directly to the window, unlocked it, and pushed it up as far as it would go. The rush of the city was like a vacuum, sucking all the hums out of the room.

She sighed as she returned to sit beside her prize. "I've been traveling too much, I miss home."

"Where is that?" Bourne asked. "I know it's not Seville."

"No, not Seville." She pushed her hair back off the side of her face. "I live in London, Belgravia."

"Very posh."

She laughed wearily. "If you saw my flat—it's a tiny thing, but it's mine and I love it. There's a mews out back with a flowering pear tree that a pair of house martins nest in come spring. And a nightjar serenades me most evenings."

"Why would you ever leave?"

She laughed again, a bright, silvery sound that was easy on the ears. "I have to earn my way in the world, Adam, just like everyone else." Lacing her fingers together, she said more soberly, "Why did Don Herrera lie to you?"

"There are many possible answers." Bourne stared out the window. The bright lights illuminated the bend in the Nile, reflections of the city dancing across the dark, crocodile-infested water. "But the most logical one is that he's somehow allied with the man I'm trying to find, the one who shot me."

"Isn't that too much of a coincidence?"

"It would be," he said, "if I wasn't being set up for a trap."

She seemed to digest this news for a moment. "Then the man who tried to kill you wants you to come to Seven Seventy-nine El Gamhuria Avenue."

"I believe so." He turned to her. "Which is why I'm not going to be with you when you knock on the front door tomorrow morning."

Now she appeared alarmed. "I don't know whether I want to face Noah alone. Where are you going to be?"

"My presence will only make things dangerous for you, believe me." He smiled. "Besides, I'll be there, I just won't go in through the front door."

"You mean you'll use me as a distraction."

She was not only uncommonly smart, Bourne thought, but quick as well. "I hope you don't mind."

"Not at all. And you're right, I will be safer if I go in alone." She frowned. "Why is it, I wonder, that people feel the need to lie altogether?" Her eyes found his. She seemed to be comparing him with someone else, or perhaps only with herself. "Would it be so terrible if everyone just told each other the truth?"

"People prefer to remain hidden," he said, "so they won't get hurt."

"But they get hurt just the same, don't they?" She shook her head. "I think people lie to themselves as easily as—if not more easily than—they do to others. Sometimes they don't even know they're doing it." She cocked her head to one side. "It's a matter of identity, isn't it? I mean, in your mind you can be anyone, do anything. Everything is malleable, whereas in the real world, effecting change—any change—is so bloody difficult, the effort is wearying, you get beaten down by all the outside forces you can't control."

"You could adopt an entirely new identity," Bourne said, "one where effecting change is less difficult because now you re-create your own history."

She nodded. "Yes, but that has it own pitfalls. No family, no friends—unless, of course, you don't mind being absolutely isolated."

"Some people don't." Bourne looked beyond her, as if the wall with its cheap print of an Islamic scene was a window into his thoughts. Once again, he wondered who he was—David Webb, Jason Bourne, or Adam Stone. His life was a fiction, no matter in which direction he looked. He'd already determined that he couldn't live as David Webb, and as for Jason Bourne, there was always someone, somewhere in the world, hidden in the shadows of his forgotten former life, who wished him ill or wanted him dead. And Adam Stone? He might be called a blank slate, but that would be, in practice, untrue because the people who encountered this identity reacted to him—reacted to whoever the real Bourne was. The more he was with people like Tracy, the more he learned about himself.

"What about you?" she said now as she joined him at the window. "Do you mind being alone?"

"I'm not alone," he replied. "I'm with you."

She laughed softly and shook her head. "Listen to you, you've perfected the art of answering personal questions without revealing one iota of yourself."

"That's because I never know who I'm talking with."

She watched him for a moment out of the corner of her eyes as if trying to figure out the real meaning of what he'd just said, then she stared out the window at the two Niles winding their way through North Africa, like a story you read while falling asleep.

"At night, everything becomes transparent, or insubstantial." Reaching out, she touched their reflections in the window.

"And yet our thoughts—and why is it especially our fears?—are somehow magnified, taking on the proportions of titans, or gods." She stood very close to him, her voice lowered almost to a whisper. "Are we good or evil? What's really in our hearts? It's dispiriting when we don't know, or can't decide."

"Perhaps we're both good and evil," Bourne said, wondering about himself, about all his identities, and where the truth lay, "depending on the time and the circumstance."

Arkadin was lost in the star-dazzled Azerbaijani night. Starting promptly at five in the morning, he and his one-hundred-strong cadre of hardened soldiers had hiked into the mountains. Their mission, he'd told them, was to find the snipers hiding along their route and shoot them with the long-range paintball guns that looked and felt exactly like AK-47s that had been shipped at his request to Nagorno-Karabakh. Twenty members of the indigenous tribe, equipped with paintball sniper rifles, had secreted themselves along the route. When Arkadin had handed them out, he'd had to explain their use to men who thought them both amusing and idiotic. Still, within half an hour the tribesmen had become proficient with the pseudo-weapons.

His men had missed the first two snipers completely, so two of the hundred had been "killed" before they hunkered down and learned from their inattention and lapses in judgment.

This exercise had lasted all day and into the swiftly falling dusk, but Arkadin drove them on, deeper and deeper into the mountains. They stopped once for fifteen minutes, to eat their rations, then it was on again, climbing ever upward toward the clear, shining vault of heaven.

Toward midnight, he called a completion to the exercise, graded each man as to performance, stamina, and ability to adapt to a changing situation, then allowed them to make camp. As usual, he ate little and slept not at all. He could feel his body's aches and strains, but they were small and, it seemed to him, very far away, as if they belonged to someone else, or to a different Arkadin he knew only in passing.

Dawn had arrived before he stilled his feverishly working mind and, marshaling his energies, pulled out his satellite phone and punched in a specific set of numbers, connecting him to an automated "zombie" line that switched his call several times. With each switch, he was required to punch in a different code, which allowed him to continue the call. At length, after the last code was digested by the closed system at the other end of the line, he heard a human voice.

"I didn't expect to hear from you." There was no rebuke in Nikolai Yevsen's voice, only a faint curiosity.

"Frankly," Arkadin said, "I didn't expect to call." His head tilted up, he was staring at the last stars as they were banished by the pink and blue light. "Something has come to my attention I thought you should know."

"As always, I appreciate your thoughtfulness." Yevsen's voice was as harsh as a saw cutting through metal. There was about it something feral, a fearsome kind of power that was his alone.

"It has come to my attention that the woman, Tracy Atherton, is not alone."

"How is this information of interest to me?"

Only Yevsen, Arkadin thought, could convey a lethal stillness with the mere tone of his voice. In the course of his freelance career with the Moscow *grupperovka* he had gotten to know the arms dealer well enough to be exceedingly wary of him.

"She's with a man named Jason Bourne," he said now, "who is out for revenge."

"We all are, in one way or another. Why would he seek it here?"

"Bourne thinks you hired the Torturer to kill him."

"Where would he get that idea?"

"A rival, possibly. I could find out for you," Arkadin said helpfully.

"It doesn't matter," Yevsen said. "This Jason Bourne is already a dead man."

Exactly what I wanted to hear, Arkadin thought as he could not stop his mind from turning toward the past.

Approximately five hundred miles from Nizhny Tagil, when daylight had bled into dusk and dusk fell victim to night, Tarkanian drove toward the village of Yaransk to look for a doctor. He had stopped three times on the way, so everyone could relieve themselves and get a bite to eat. At those times, he checked on Oserov. The third stop, near sunset, he'd found that Oserov had peed himself. He was feverish and looked like death.

During the long drive at high speed over incomplete highways, rough detours, and suspect roads, the children had been remarkably quiet, listening with rapt attention to their mother spin tales—fabulous adventures and magnificent exploits of the god of fire, the god of wind, and especially the warrior-god, Chumbulat.

Arkadin had never heard of these gods and wondered whether Joškar had made them up for her daughters' benefit. In any event, it wasn't just the three girls who were held rapt by the stories. Arkadin listened to them as if they were news reports from a distant country to which he longed to travel. In this way, for him, if not for Tarkanian, the long day's journey into night passed with the swiftness of sleep.

They arrived in Yaransk too late to find a doctor's office open, so Tarkanian, asking several pedestrians, followed their directions to the local hospital. Arkadin was left with Joškar in the car. They both climbed out to stretch their legs, leaving the girls in the backseat, playing with the sets of painted wooden nesting dolls Arkadin had bought them during one of the rest stops.

Her head was partly turned away from him as she glanced back at her children. Shadows hid most of the damage done to her face, while the sodium lights drew out the exoticism of her features, which seemed to him a curious mixture of Asian and Finnish. Her eyes were large and slightly uptilted, her mouth was generous and full-lipped. Unlike her nose, which seemed formed to protect her face from life's tougher blows, her mouth exuded a sensuality bordering on the erotic. That she seemed quite unaware of this quality in herself made it all the more magnetic.

"Did you make up the stories you were telling your children?" he asked.

Joškar shook her head. "I was told them when I was a little girl, looking out at the Volga. My mother was told them by her mother, and so on back in time." She turned to him. "They're tales of our religion. I'm Mari, you see."

"Mari? I don't know it."

"My people are what researchers call Finno-Ugrik. We're what you Christians call pagans. We believe in many gods, the gods of the stories I tell, and the demi-gods who walk among us, disguised as humans." When she turned her gaze on her girls something inexplicable happened to her face, as if she had become one of them, one of her own daughters. "Once upon a time, we were eastern Finns, who over the years intermarried with wanderers from the south and east. Gradually, this mixture of Germanic and Asian cultures moved to the Volga, where our land was eventually incorporated into Russia. But we were never accepted by the Russians, who hate learning new languages and fear customs and traditions other than their own. We Mari have a saying: 'The worst your enemies can do is kill you. The worst your friends can do is betray you. Fear only the indifferent, because at their silent consent, treachery and death flourish!'"

"That's a bleak credo, even for this country."

"Not if you know our history here."

"I never knew you weren't ethnic Russian."

"No one did. My husband was deeply ashamed of my ethnic background, just as he was ashamed of himself for marrying me. Of course, he told no one."

Looking at her, he could see why Lev Antonin had fallen in love with her. "Why did you marry him?" he said.

Joškar gave an ironic laugh. "Why do you think? He's ethnic Russian; moreover, he's a powerful man. He protects me and my children."

Arkadin took her chin, moving her face fully into the light. "But who protects you from him?"

She snatched her face away as if his fingers had burned her. "I made certain he never touched my children. That was all that mattered."

"Doesn't it matter that they should have a father who, unlike Antonin, genuinely loves them?" Arkadin was thinking of his own father, either falling-down drunk or absent altogether.

Joškar sighed. "Life is full of compromises, Leonid, especially for the Mari. I was alive, he'd given me children whom I adore, and he swore to keep them from harm. That was my life, how could I complain when my parents were murdered by the Russians, when my sister disappeared when I was thirteen, probably abducted and tortured because my father was a journalist who repeatedly spoke out against the repression of the Mari? That was when my aunt sent me away from the Volga, to ensure I stayed alive."

Arkadin watched one of the girls playing in the backseat of the car. Her two sisters had fallen asleep, one against the door, the other with her head on her sleeping sister's shoulder. In the pale, ethereal light slanting in they looked like the fairies in their mother's stories.

"We must find a place soon to immolate my son."

"What?"

"He was born on the solstice of the fire-god," she explained, "so the fire-god must take him across into the death-lands, otherwise he will wander the world forever alone."

"All right," Arkadin said. He was impatient to get to Moscow, but considering his complicity in Yasha's death he felt he was in no position to refuse her. Besides, she and her family were his responsibility now. If he refused to take care of them, no one else would. "As soon as Tarkanian and

Oserov return we'll head out into the woods so you can find a suitable spot."

"I will need you to help me. Mari custom dictates a male's participation. Will you do this for Yasha, and for me?"

Arkadin watched the play of light and dark chasing themselves across the flat planes of her face as vehicles swept by, their headlights pushing back the oncoming night. He didn't know what to say, so he nodded mutely.

In the near distance, the spire of the Orthodox church rose up like a reproachful finger, in admonition to the world's sinners. Arkadin wondered why so much money was spent in the service of something that couldn't be seen, heard, or felt. Of what use was religion? he wondered. Any religion?

As if reading his thoughts, Joškar said, "Do you believe in something, Leonid—god or gods—something greater than yourself?"

"There's us and there's the universe," he said. "Everything else is like those stories you tell your children."

"I saw you listening to those stories, Leonid. They caught and held something inside you even you might not know about."

"It was like watching movies. They're entertainment, that's all."

"No, Leonid, they are history. They speak of hardship, migration, sacrifice. They speak of deprivation and subjugation, of prejudice and of our unique identity and our will to survive, no matter the cost." She studied him closely. "But you're Russian, you are the victor, and history belongs to the victor, doesn't it?"

Funny, he didn't feel like a victor, and he never had. Who had ever stood up and spoken for him? Weren't your parents supposed to be your advocates, weren't they supposed to protect you, not imprison you and abandon you? There was something about Joškar that touched a place inside him that, as she'd said, he hadn't known existed.

"I'm a Russian in name only," he said. "There is nothing inside me, Joškar. I'm a hollow man. In fact, when we place Yasha on the funeral pyre and light the wood I'll envy him the pure and honorable method of his dissolution."

She looked at him with her bourbon

eyes and he thought, *If I see pity in her face I'll have to strike her.* But no pity was evident to him, just a singular curiosity. He glanced down and saw that she was holding out her hand to him. Without knowing why, he took it, felt her warmth, almost as if he could hear the blood singing in her veins. Then she turned, went back to the car, and gently drew out one of her daughters, whom she deposited in his arms.

"Hold her like this," she directed. "That's right, shape your arms into a cradle."

She turned and stared up into the night sky where the first saltings of stars were becoming visible.

"The brightest ones come out first, because they're the bravest," she said in the same voice she used when telling her stories of gods, elves, and fairies. "But my favorite time is when the most timid appear, like a band of gossamer lace, the last decoration of night before morning comes and spoils it all."

Through this all, Arkadin held the slender-limbed child in his arms, his skin brushed by her diaphanous hair, her small fist already curled around one of his calloused forefingers. She lay within the heart of him. He could feel her deep, even breathing, and it was as if a core of innocence had been returned to him.

Without turning around, Joškar said softly, "Don't make me go back to him."

"No one is sending you back. What makes you say that?"

"Your friend wants no part of us. I know, I see how he looks at me, I feel his contempt burning my skin. If it weren't for you, he'd have dumped us at one of the rest stops and I'd have no choice but to go back to Lev."

"You're not going back to him," Arkadin said, hearing the sleeping girl's heartbeat close to his own. "I'll die before I let that happen."

This is where we part company," Bourne said to Tracy the next morning. As close as he could tell, they were five blocks from 779 El Gamhuria Avenue. "I told you I wasn't going to put you at risk. I'll make my own way into the building."

They had exited their *raksha* when El Gamhuria Avenue had become permanently blocked by a military rally that had attracted a huge, vocal crowd, gathered around a portable dais on which stood a pantheon of officers in khaki, dark green, and blue uniforms, depending on their rank. These officers, their freshly shaved faces shining in the sun, huge smiles on their faces, waved to the crowd as if they were genial uncles. With all the noise and confusion it was impossible to understand what they were shouting or celebrating. Nearby, on a side street, a manned tank, bristling with weaponry, hunkered like a fat tomcat licking its chops. They paid their fare and, skirting the agitated crowd, picked their way along the palm-lined avenue.

Bourne glanced at his watch. "What time do you have?"

"Nine twenty-seven."

"Do me one favor." Bourne adjusted his watch slightly. "Give me fifteen minutes, then walk directly to Seven Seventy-nine, go in through the front door, and announce yourself to the receptionist. Hold the receptionist's attention and don't let go until either Noah sends for you or he comes out to get you."

She nodded. Her nervousness had returned. "I don't want anything to happen to you."

"Listen to me, Tracy. I've told you that I don't trust Noah Perlis. I particularly don't like the fact that he wouldn't come to the hotel last night to complete the deal."

With him as a shield, she raised her dress to reveal a gun in a sleek holster strapped to a thigh. "When you're a transporter of precious objects, you can't be too careful."

"If Seven Seventy-nine Gamhuria has any kind of security, they'd find that," he said.

"No, they won't." She tapped the butt. "It's ceramic."

"Clever girl. I assume you know how to use it."

She laughed at the same time she gave him a withering look.

"Please be careful, Adam."

"You, too."

Then he walked off into the crowd, disappearing almost at once.

27

Seven seventy-nine El Gamhuria Avenue was a large, three-tiered structure of modernist lines constructed of chunky concrete and green-glass blocks. Above the first floor, the second and third stepped back, like a ziggurat. There was about the building the unmistakable feeling of a fortress, both in design and in intent, which the rooftop garden, whose treetops were visible from the street, did little to allay.

However, it was the garden that seemed most vulnerable to Bourne, who, immersed in the hectic street traffic, had quickly made two circuits of the building. There were, of course, entrances other than the gleaming wenge-wood front doors—two for deliveries, in fact—but they were both exposed and guarded.

A large truck was parked at one of these freight entrances, made humpbacked by the oversize refrigeration unit on its top. Bourne judged distances and vectors as he crossed the street, approaching the truck from the side facing away from the building. Two men were busy unloading large crates from the open back of the truck, overseen by a grim-looking security guard. Bourne made a mental note of everyone's position relative to the truck as he passed by.

Several hundred yards down the street, one of the city's numerous doorway lurkers leaned in the shadows, smoking languidly. He watched with bored suspicion as Bourne approached him.

"Tour?" he said in very bad English. "Best guide in all of Khartoum. Anything you want to see I take, even forbidden." His grin seemed like more of a yawn. "You like forbidden, yes?"

"How about a cigarette?"

The sound of his own language surprised the lurker so much he righted himself and his half-glazed eyes seemed to clear. He handed Bourne a cigarette, which he lit with a cheap plastic lighter.

"You like money better than you like standing in this doorway?"

The lurker nodded with a quick, disjointed bob of his head. "Show me a man who doesn't revere money and I'll mourn his death."

Bourne fanned out some bills and the lurker's eyes widened; the poor man couldn't help it, it was a reflex action. Bourne was willing to bet he'd never imagined possessing so much money.

"Certainly." The man licked his lips. "*All* the forbidden places in Khartoum will be open to you."

"I'm only interested in one," Bourne said. "Seven Seventy-nine El Gamhuria Avenue."

For a moment the man blanched, then he licked his lips again and said, "Sir, there is forbidden and then there is *forbidden*."

Bourne increased the number of bills he fanned out. "This amount will cover it, won't it." It wasn't a question; neither was it a statement. It was, rather, a command, which caused the lurker to twitch uncomfortably. "Or should I find someone else?" Bourne added. "You did say that you were the best guide in the city."

"That I am, sir!" The lurker snatched the bills and stuffed them away. "No one else in the entire city could get you in to Seven Seventy-nine. They are most careful about visitors, but"—he winked—"my cousin's cousin is a guard there." He pulled out a cell phone, made a local call, and talked rapid-fire Arabic. There ensued a short argument that seemed to concern money. Then the lurker put away his cell and grinned. "This is no problem. My cousin's cousin is downstairs now, while the truck you see there is unloading. He says it's an excellent time, so we go now."

Without another word Bourne followed him back down the street.

Checking her watch one last time, Tracy strode across El Gamhuria Avenue and opened the wooden front door. Directly inside was a metal detector overseen by two grim-faced guards, which she and the wrapped Goya went through without incident. This place didn't seem like the headquarters of any airline she'd ever encountered.

She walked up to the circular desk, as high and harsh looking as the exterior of the building itself. A young man with an unfriendly, angular face glanced up at her approach.

"Tracy Atherton. I have an appointment with Noah Per—Petersen."

"Passport and driver's license." He held out a hand.

She expected him to check her ID then hand the documents back to her, but instead he said, "These will be returned to you at the end of your visit."

She hesitated for just a moment, feeling as if she'd turned over the keys to her apartment in Belgravia. She was about to protest, but the man with the unfriendly face was already on the intrabuilding phone. The moment he cradled the receiver his demeanor changed. "Mr. Petersen will be down to fetch you momentarily, Ms. Atherton," he said with a smile. "In the meanwhile, please make yourself comfortable. There's tea and coffee, as well as a variety of biscuits on the sideboard against the wall. And if there's anything else you require, just ask."

She kept up a monologue of meaningless chatter, all the while taking in her surroundings, which seemed as oppressive in their way as the interior of a church. Instead of being dedicated to the glory of God, the architecture seemed to deify money. In just the same way churches—particularly those of the Roman Catholic religion—were meant to draw a reverence from the parishioner, to put him squarely in his lowly place vis-à-vis the divine, so the Air Afrika headquarters sought to intimidate and demean those penitents entering its portals who could not conceive of the half-a-billion-dollar cost of construction.

"Ms. Atherton."

She turned to see a slim man, handsome despite his hatchet face, with salt-and-pepper hair and an amiable demeanor.

"Noah Petersen." He smiled winningly and stuck out his hand for her to shake. It was firm and dry. "I put great store in punctuality as a human trait." He lifted a hand, indicating they should walk back the way he had come. "It says so much about an orderly mind."

He slipped a metal key-card in a slot,

and after a moment of clicks a red light turned green. He leaned on part of the wall, which turned out to be a door set flush with the massive concrete panels on either side. Inside, Tracy was obliged to put her package through an X-ray scanner, then they rode up to the third floor in a small elevator. Exiting, he took her down a corridor with twelve-foot mahogany doors. These doors had neither a name nor a number on them and, after negotiating several turns, she had the sensation of being in a labyrinth. Music was playing out of hidden speakers. Occasionally they passed a photo close-up of part of an Air Afrika plane with a half-clad model posing beside it.

The conference room into which he led her was decorated for a party, with colored balloons, the long table covered with a gaily striped cloth and groaning with a seemingly endless array of savory food, sweetmeats, and fruit.

"Having the Goya here at last is cause for celebration," Noah said, which was apparently all the explanation she was going to get. He pulled a slim briefcase out from under the striped cloth and, setting it on the one clear space on the tabletop, twiddled the combination lock and disengaged the snaps.

Inside, Tracy saw, was the cashier's check for the balance of her fee, made out to her. Seeing this, she stripped off the packing to reveal the Goya.

Noah barely glanced at it. "Where's the rest?"

She handed over the document of authenticity, signed by Professor Alonzo Pecunia Zuñiga of the Museo del Prado in Madrid. Noah studied it for a moment, nodded, and put it alongside the painting.

"Excellent." He reached into the attaché case and handed her the check. "I believe this concludes our business, Ms. Atherton." At that moment, his cell rang and he excused himself. His brows knit together. "When?" he said into the phone. "Who? What do you mean alone? Dammit, didn't I— All right, don't fucking move until I get there!" He cut the connection, his face dark.

"Is something wrong?" Tracy asked.

"Nothing that need concern you." Noah managed a smile through his annoyance. "Please make yourself comfortable here. I'll come and fetch you when it's safe."

"Safe? What do you mean?"

"There's an intruder in the building." Noah was already hurrying across the room to the door. "Not to worry, Ms. Atherton, it seems we already have him cornered."

We were picked up the moment we arrived in KRT," Amun Chalthoum said as he and Soraya drove into the city. KRT was the aviation acronym for the Khartoum International Airport, which had been appropriated by the Sudanese themselves.

"I saw them," Soraya said. "Two men."

"They were joined by two others." Chalthoum glanced in the rearview mirror. "All four of them are in a gray 1970s-vintage Toyota Corolla three car-lengths behind us."

"The men at the terminal looked local."

Chalthoum nodded.

"I find that odd, because no one locally knew we were coming to Khartoum."

"Not true." A small, secretive smile played about the Egyptian's lips. "As the head of al Mokhabarat, I was obliged to tell a superior I was leaving the country, if only temporarily. The man I chose to tell is the one I have suspected for some time of secretly undermining me." His eyes once again flicked to the image in the rearview mirror. "Now, at last, I have my proof of his treachery. Nothing will stop me from bringing one of these miscreants back to Cairo to denounce him."

"In other words," Soraya said, "we need to let them catch us."

Amun's smile broadened. "Catch up to us," he corrected, "so we can catch them."

The poker game had given up the ghost an hour ago, leaving the house off Dupont Circle redolent of the scents of men—and women—hard at play: cigar ash, leftover pizza, stale but honest sweat, and the ephemeral but powerful odor of money.

Four people draped themselves over purple velvet art deco sofas: Willard, Peter Marks, Police Commissioner Lester Burrows, and Reese Williams, whose house, surprisingly, this turned out to be. Between the four principals, on a low table, sat a bottle of scotch, a bucket half full of ice, and four fat old-fashioned glasses. Everyone else had packed up what was left of their poker stakes, if any, and had staggered home. It was just after twelve on a night without either moon or stars, the clouds so thick and low that even the lights of the district were reduced to murky smudges.

"You won the last hand, Freddy," Burrows said, addressing the ceiling as he reclined against the sofa's curled back, "but you haven't told me the consequences of seeing you after the final round of raises. I was tapped out, so you put in for me. Now I owe you."

"I want you to answer Peter's question about the two missing officers."

"Who?"

"Sampson and Montgomery," Marks provided helpfully.

"Oh, them."

The commissioner was still staring absently at the ceiling while Reese Williams, her legs curled up under her, watched the scene with an enigmatic expression.

"There's also the matter of a motorcycle cop shooting a man named Jay Weston, which caused the accident Sampson and Montgomery were dispatched to investigate," Marks continued. "Only there was no investigation; it was strangled."

Everyone in the room knew what "strangling an investigation" meant.

"Freddy," Burrows said to the ceiling, "is this also part of what I owe you?"

Willard's eyes were fixed on Reese Williams's unexpressive face. "I ponied up a ton of money for you to see me, Lester."

The commissioner sighed and finally relinquished his gaze from the ceiling. "Reese, you know you have a rather large crack up there."

"There are cracks throughout this house, Les," she said.

Burrows seemed to consider this for some time before saying to the other two men, "Be that as it may, there will be no cracks in the information shared here. Whatever I share with you gentlemen is strictly off the record, not for attribution, and however the hell else you want to say it." He sat up abruptly. "Bottom line: Afterward I will not only repudiate the statement, I'll go out of my way to prove it false and to run into the ground those who claimed I did say it. Are we clear?"

"Perfectly," Marks said, while Willard nodded his assent.

"Detectives Sampson and Montgomery are currently fishing on the Snake River in Idaho."

"Are they really fishing," Marks asked, "or are they dead?"

"Jesus Christ, I talked to them yesterday!" Burrows said heatedly. "They wanted to know when they could come home. I told them there was no rush."

"Lester," Willard said, "they're not in Idaho on your dime."

"Uncle Sam has deeper pockets than I do," the commissioner conceded.

Willard was watching emotions crossing like clouds across Burrows's face. "Precisely what piece of Uncle Sam?"

"No one told me, and that's the truth," Burrows grumped, as if no one told him anything of any real importance. "But I remember the representative's name, if that's of any help."

"At this stage," Willard said heavily, "anything might prove useful, even a pseudonym."

"Well, dammit, no one tells the truth in this town!" Burrows lifted an accusing finger. "And let me tell you two right now that no police officer of mine shot your Mr. Weston, of that I'm damn sure. I conducted my own investigation into that allegation."

"Then someone was impersonating

one of your police officers," Willard said calmly, "to point everyone in the wrong direction."

"You spooks." Burrows shook his head. "You live in your own world with its own rules. Christ, what a tangled web!" He shrugged, as if shaking off his consternation. "That name, then. The man who made the arrangements for my detectives said his name was Noah Petersen. That ring a bell, or was he just blowing spook smoke up my ass?"

Bourne had parted company with the lurker, as his cousin's cousin had first ensured that both truckers were inside the building, unloading crates, then furtively led the way into the building through the service entrance. Grabbing hold of the truck's rear door handle, he vaulted up, grabbing on to the rim of the top and rolling his body onto the truck's roof. By climbing onto the refrigeration unit, he was able to reach a concrete abutment on the building's facade, by which means he gained the setback along the second floor. Using the spaces between the concrete slabs, he picked his way farther up the building's side until he got to the third-floor setback, where he repeated the procedure until, reaching up, he levered himself over the parapet onto the tiled floor of the roof garden.

Unlike the architecture of the building itself, the garden was a delicate mosaic of colors and textures, perfectly manicured, fragrant, and shaded from the glaring sun. Bourne, crouching in a patch of the deepest shadow, breathed in the heady scent of lime as he studied the garden's layout. Save for him, the roof was deserted.

Two small structures were cleverly integrated into the garden's design: the door down into the building and, as he discovered, a toolshed for the staff who pruned the trees, plants, and flowers. He headed to the doorway, saw that it was protected by a standard circuit-breaker alarm. The moment he opened the door from the outside, the alarm would be triggered.

Backtracking to the toolshed, he took a pruner and a wire stripper to the parapet. There, at the crevice where it met the tiled floor of the roof, he found the wires that connected the garden's lights. Using the pruning shears, he cut off a six-foot length of wire. As he walked back to the doorway, he stripped the insulation off both ends.

At the door, he felt above for the alarm wire, stripping off two sections of the insulation and attaching the bare ends of the length of lighting wire he'd cut to the bare alarm wire. When he was certain the connections were secure, he cut the alarm wire midway between the jerry-rigged splices he'd made.

Cautiously, he opened the door only wide enough to slip inside. The splices had worked; the alarm was silent. He crept down the narrow, steep staircase to the third floor. His first order of business was to find Arkadin, the man who'd lured him here, so he could kill him. The second was finding Tracy and getting her out.

Tracy was standing by the window, looking out at the chaotic street, when she heard the door open behind her. Assuming it was Noah, she turned back into the room, only to confront a man with a shaved head, a goatee, black shot through with white, a ring of diamonds in the lobe of one ear, and a tattoo of a fanged bat on the side of his neck. With his wide shoulders, barrel chest, and thick legs, he looked like a wrestler or one of those mutant extreme fighters she'd seen once or twice on American TV.

"So you're the one who brought my Goya," the Bat-man said as he sauntered over to the table where the painting lay in all its grotesque grandeur. He had a way of walking, a rolling gait one saw only on musclemen and sailors.

"That's Noah's," Tracy said.

"No, my dear Ms. Atherton, it's mine," the Bat-man said in grating, thickly accented English. "Perlis merely bought it for me." He held the painting up in front of him. "It's my payment." His chuckle was like the gurgle of a dying man. "A unique prize for unique services rendered."

"You know my name," she said, moving toward the table with its platters and thick glass bowls of food, "but I don't know yours."

"Are you certain you want to know it?" He continued to examine the Goya with a connoisseur's practiced eye. And then, without allowing her space to answer: "Ah, well, then, it's Nikolai Yevsen. Perhaps you've heard of me, I own Air Afrika, I own this building."

"Frankly, I never heard of you or of Air Afrika. My business is art."

"Is that so?" Yevsen placed the Goya back onto the table, across which he faced her. "Then what are you doing with Jason Bourne?"

"Jason Bourne?" She frowned. "Who's Jason Bourne?"

"The man you brought here with you."

Her frown deepened. "What are you talking about? I came alone. Noah can vouch for that."

"Perlis is busy at the moment, interrogating your friend Mr. Bourne."

"I don't—" The rest of her words choked in her throat when saw a snub-nosed .45 in his left hand.

28

If your business is art," Yevsen said, "what are you doing with an assassin, a spy, a man with no scruples, no heart? A man who would put a bullet through your head as soon as look at you."

"But who's threatening to shoot me?" Tracy said. "You or him?"

"You brought him here to kill me." Yevsen had a face that conveyed brute force, blunt power. He was a man used to getting what he wanted from anyone, at any time. "I have to ask myself why you would do that."

"I don't know what you mean."

"Who are you working for? Really."

"I work for myself. I have for years."

Yevsen pursed his lips, which were thick as slabs of raw meat, and as ruddy. "Let me make this easy for you, Ms. Atherton. In my world there are only two kinds of people: friends and enemies. You have to decide which one you are, right now, this minute. If you don't answer truthfully I will put a bullet through your right shoulder. Then I'll ask again. Silence or a lie will only gain you a bullet through your left shoulder. Then I'll go to work on that beautiful face of yours." He waggled the gun at her. "One thing is certain, when I get through with you, you won't be a pretty sight." That ghastly chuckle again. "No Hollywood casting agents will come calling, that I can guarantee you."

"The man I'm with is Adam Stone, that's really all I know."

"See, the problem, Ms. Atherton, is that I'm not feeling it—the truth, I mean."

"That is the truth."

He took a step toward her so that he was pressed up against the far side of the table. "Now you've offended me. You think I'll believe you brought someone here without knowing anything about him but his name—which in fact isn't his name at all."

Tracy closed her eyes. "No, of course not." She took a deep breath and stared straight into Yevsen's coffee-colored eyes. "Yes, I knew his real name was Jason Bourne, and, yes, it was my job not only to bring Noah the Goya, but to ensure Bourne would get here."

Yevsen's eyes narrowed. "Why was Bourne sent here? What is he after?"

"Don't you know? You sent one of your Russian assassins, a man with a scar and a tattoo of three skulls on his neck, to kill Bourne in Seville."

"The Torturer?" Yevsen's face twisted in obvious disgust. "I'd sooner cut off my arm than hire that piece of filth."

"All I know is that he thinks the man who tried to kill him is here. The same man who must have hired the Torturer."

"That's not me. He's been given the wrong information."

"Then I don't understand why I was hired to make sure he got here."

Yevsen shook his head. "Who hired you to do this?"

"Leonid Arkadin."

Yevsen aimed the .45 at her right shoulder. "Another lie! Why would Leonid Danilovich hire you to ensure Bourne arrived here?"

"I don't know, but . . ." Gauging his response, noting the look on his face, caused her to make a delayed connection. "Wait a minute, it must have been Arkadin who told you I had Bourne with me. He must be the one who hired the Torturer, which means he must be here, lying in wait for Bourne."

"Being so close to death has made you desperate. At this very moment, Leonid Danilovich is in Nagorno-Karabakh, Azerbaijan."

"But don't you see, Arkadin is the only one who knew Bourne was with me."

"This is bullshit! Leonid Danilovich is my partner."

"Why would I make up a lie like that? Arkadin paid me twenty thousand in diamonds."

Yevsen recoiled as if he'd been struck. "Diamonds are Leonid Danilovich's signature—how he gets paid and how he pays. Damn him to hell, what's that lying sack of shit up to? If he thinks he can double-cross me—"

And at that moment Tracy saw Bourne sprinting down the hallway. Yevsen recognized the surprise in her eyes and began to turn toward the door, his .45 at the ready.

Noah Perlis's sense of triumph vanished as soon as he saw a Sudanese lurker and one of the guards that Yevsen's security personnel had cornered on the street level just inside loading dock A.

"What the hell is this?" he said in Sudanese Arabic. With a wave of his hand, he sent some of the security people out into the street to check for anyone else who had no business being on the block. Then he confronted the guard, quickly determining that he knew nothing. The chief of security—who had, by that time, joined him—fired the man on the spot.

Addressing the lurker, he said, "Who are you and what are you doing on these premises?"

"I . . . I lost my way, sir. I was talking with my cousin's cousin—the man who was just fired, which, I think when you hear my story, you'll agree is too harsh a punishment." The man kept his eyes lowered and his shoulders hunched in a pose of servility. "My cousin's cousin had to urinate, you see, but he didn't want to turn me away because I needed money to pay for my child's—"

"That's enough!" Noah slapped him hard across the face. "Do you think I'm some tourist you can gull with your idiotic stories?" He slapped the man again, harder this time, so that his teeth clacked together and he winced. "Tell me what you're doing here or I'll turn you over to Sandur." The chief of security grinned, showing black gaps between his teeth. "Sandur knows what to do with vermin like you."

"I don't—"

This time Noah's fist slammed into the lurker's mouth, spraying bits of teeth and blood onto the man's filthy shirt. "There's a full moon tonight, but don't count on seeing it."

The lurker had just launched into his story about being accosted by an American who wanted to get inside 779 El Gamhuria Avenue when the contingent of security people Noah had sent out into the street returned. One of the men leaned over and whispered something into his ear.

At once Noah grabbed the lurker and threw him into the arms of Sandur. "Here, take care of him."

"Sir, have pity," the lurker protested, "I don't deserve this, I swear I'm telling the truth."

But Noah was no longer concerned with the lurker or who had tried to gain access to the Air Afrika headquarters. An urgent sense of self-preservation had taken hold of him. He approached the glare of the loading dock and peered out from the shadows. Sure enough, as the security man had said, there was a minibus parked across the street. It was full of people—all male—which was what had raised a red flag for the guard. Then Noah saw the flash of metal—the muzzle of an AK-47—and his worst fears were confirmed. Someone was planning an imminent raid on the Air Afrika offices. He was so stunned he couldn't even think of who might have the knowledge and the wherewithal to attempt what most considered unthinkable.

But that wasn't the issue now. He needed to get away from ground zero before he was caught in the crossfire between Yevsen's mercenaries and the raiding party crowded into the Sudanese minibus across the street.

Bourne, combing the third floor of the building while keeping out of the way of both the staff and the security personnel, heard a deep, rough-edged voice coming from a large room ahead of him. When he heard Tracy's voice in the interval between the male voice's questions, he broke into a flat-out run because he was certain that she had been captured by Arkadin as the last bit of bait for him.

As he burst through the open doorway, he curled himself into a ball, rolling fast into the room then unfolding himself all in one smooth motion. He saw a burly man with a bat tattooed on the side of his neck turn and fire at him. He ducked, rolling toward the conference table laden with food. In that moment he saw Tracy pull her ceramic gun out of a thigh holster. He heard the report of another gunshot and launched himself, his body low and twisting, into the massive legs of the Bat-man, taking him down just as he fired at Tracy, who instinctively turned away. The bullet went low into one of the heavy glass bowls, sending shards exploding in all directions.

Bourne and Bat-man crashed to the floor with Bourne trying to wrest the .45 out of his left hand. The gun went off again, the bullet whining past Bourne's ear, rendering him temporarily deaf. Bat-man drove his right hand into Bourne's ribs, Bourne slammed his knuckles into Bat-man's jaw, then followed it with three quick chops with the edge of his hand to the side of Bat-man's neck. Using all his strength, his adversary inched the muzzle of the .45 toward Bourne's temple. Bourne drove it back, but three successive punches to the same spot on his rib cage caused him to suck in air and, all at once, the muzzle was aimed at his head. Bat-man bore down on the trigger with his left forefinger.

That was when Bourne found his shoulder wound. Driving his finger into the pulpy mass caused Bat-man to howl like a wolf at bay, and Bourne was able to slap the .45 out of his hand. But with a great heave of his body, Bat-man shoved Bourne off, lunged for the gun, and, grabbing it by its barrel, struck Bourne on the temple with the butt end. Bourne's head snapped back, bouncing off the floor, but Bat-man kept up the attack, already sensing victory. Bourne, his consciousness wavering, crawled away, as if seeking safety beneath the conference table. Bat-man grunted with each blow he delivered, rising up as he swung the heavy butt down again and again.

Bourne, feeling consciousness slipping further and further away into a red haze of agony, crawled the few more inches he needed to grab Tracy's ceramic gun, which was lying on the floor. With grim determination, he pointed it up at Bat-man and shot him point-blank in the face.

The air was filled with a storm of blood, bone, and bits of pink brain matter. Bat-man had reared up to deliver another titanic blow, but the force of the bullet arched his head and torso back and away. Then Bourne heard, as if through a ton of cotton wool, what sounded like a sack of wet cement hitting the floor.

For a moment, he lay on his back, one

leg raised, his heart pumping like a sprinter's at the finish line. Pain suffused him, radiating out from the bullet wound he'd sustained in Bali. His violent actions and the beating he had taken had a deleterious effect on his healing, just as Dr. Firth had warned. Just like after the second surgery, he felt like he'd been struck by a speeding train.

Then he breathed, and heard his blood singing the song of life in his inner ears. And then came the fiery touch of Shiva, removing the chill of death from his bones, as if this spirit—or, as Suparwita believed, god—had protected him once again, extending his strong hand to take Bourne's and bring him back fully into the land of the living.

All at once, hearing conflicting rounds of semi-automatic fire coming from the hallway, he twitched, stirred, and, rising on one elbow, groaned deeply. His head was swimming and he seemed afloat in blood—not his blood, Bat-man's, dead as yesterday's news, faceless, all but unrecognizable.

It was then, amid the semi-automatic fire that seemed both closer and more frenzied, that he looked around for Tracy.

She was lying on her side beyond the table.

"Tracy," he said, and then more urgently, "Tracy!"

Her right arm moved in response. He crawled painfully under the table, across the floor glittering with knife-like glass shards that tore into the heels of his hands and his shins.

"Tracy."

Her eyes stared straight ahead, but as he rose up into her field of vision, her eyes tracked him and a small smile lit her face.

"There you are."

He reached down, putting one arm beneath her shoulders, but when he moved to pick her up, her face contorted and she cried out.

"Oh, God—God help me!"

"What is it? What's the matter?"

She stared at him mutely, a web of pain clouding her eyes.

He lifted her torso as gently as he could, and that was when he saw the two large shards of glass sticking out of her back like dagger blades. Wiping the sweat off her brow, he said, "Tracy, I want you to move your feet. Can you do that for me?"

He looked at her feet, but nothing happened.

"What about your legs?"

Nothing. He pinched the flesh of her thigh. "Do you feel that?"

"What . . . what did you do?"

She was paralyzed. At least one of the glass spears had severed key nerves. And the other one? He moved, trying to get a better look at how deeply the glass was embedded. These were good-size pieces, six to eight inches long, he judged, and they were buried deep. He recalled Tracy turning away, then the bullet from Yevsen's gun slamming into the heavy glass bowl. The impact had acted like the detonation of a nail bomb, impaling her on two of the larger projectiles.

The thunder of the semi-automatic fire was very close now, though more intermittent.

"I've got to get you to a hospital," Bourne said, but as he tried to lever her from her half-sitting position she vomited a gout of blood, and he eased back, cradling her in his arms.

"I'm not going anywhere."

"I'm not going to let you—"

"You know it and I know it." Tracy's eyes were bloodshot, cratered with dark circles like deep bruises. "I don't want to be alone, Jason."

He held her as she relaxed back against him. "Why did you call me that?"

"Yes, I know your real name, I have from the moment I met you, which wasn't a coincidence. Keep still," she said, cutting him off, "I have things to tell you and there isn't much time." She licked her bloody lips. "Arkadin hired me to make sure you got here. Nikolai Yevsen, the man you just killed, told me that Arkadin is in Nagorno-Karabakh, Azerbaijan, why I don't know, but he isn't here."

So she'd been working for Arkadin all along. Bourne shook his head grimly at how well he'd been played. He'd been made to suspect her and then been given a perfectly plausible explanation as to why she'd lied about knowing the Goya was real. At that, he'd stupidly let down his guard. He saw Arkadin's hand in these delicate threads and admiration mingled with his anger at himself.

Tracy's eyes suddenly opened so wide

he could see the bloodshot whites all the way around. "Jason!"

Her breathing had become shallow and erratic. She tried to smile. "It's in our darkest hour that our secrets eat us alive."

He put two fingers against her carotid. Her pulse was weak and irregular. She was slipping away. All at once their conversation of last night came back to him—"*Why is it, I wonder, that people feel the need to lie altogether?*" she had said—and he knew absolutely that she had wanted to tell him then. *"Would it be so terrible if everyone just told each other the truth?"* Their entire conversation had been about her double life, and her inability to confess it to him. *"What about you?"* she had said. *"Do you mind being alone?"*

He struggled to understand the situation—to understand her—but all human beings were too complicated to be summed up by one thought, or even one string of thoughts. Once again, he was struck by all the myriad strands that went into the weave of a human life—Tracy's no less than anyone else's—perhaps more so in her case because, like him, she lived a double life.

Like Don Hererra and the Torturer, she had been part of Arkadin's spider's web, an attempt to manipulate him into doing—what? He still didn't know. But here was one of his enemy's pawns, lying still and dying in his arms. It was obvious now—and, in retrospect, last night—that she felt conflicted about the role Arkadin had hired her to play. Her ambivalence struck him like a blow to his stomach. She had fooled him but, as she had wondered last night, had she in the process been fooling herself? These were questions that went to the heart of his own dilemma: the not-knowing, the always being on the verge of another identity and, in consequence, losing the people around him. Death was always and ever around him, the other side of Shiva, who was the destroyer as well as the harbinger of resurrection.

All at once Tracy gave a great shiver in his arms, as if she were exhaling for the last time. "Jason, I don't want to be alone."

Her plaintive words thawed his icy heart. "You're not alone, Tracy." He bent over her, his lips touching her forehead. "I'm here with you."

"Yes, I know, it's good, I feel you around

me." She gave a sigh, akin to a cat's purr of contentment.

"Tracy?" He took his lips away so he could look into her eyes, which were fixed, staring at infinity. "Tracy."

29

It's coming through!" Humphry Bamber said.

"How much of it?" Moira asked.

Bamber watched the numbers scrolling across his screen as the download bar registered the illicit transfer from Noah Perlis's laptop.

"All of it," he said as the green bar reached the 100 percent level. "Now to get under the hood and see what's going on."

Her adrenaline was running high, and she lost patience with the minutes ticking off, pacing around the perimeter of his work space, which smelled of hot metal and spinning hard drives, the scent of money in the twenty-first century. The room was in the rear of the office, its dusky north light forming wan pools in between the shadows thrown by the stacks of electronic equipment, whose fans and motors whirred and hummed like a menagerie. The only two spaces on the walls not filled with instruments or shelves overloaded with computer peripherals, containers of blank DVDs, and USB and power cords of all lengths and descriptions, were taken up by a window and a framed photograph of Bamber at college in full football gear down in a three-point stance. He was even more handsome then than he was now.

When Moira's circuit of the room took her past the window, she paused, staring out across the street onto which the building backed. In the facing building, fluorescent lights were on, revealing an office filled with filing cabinets, hulking Xerox machines, and identical desks. Middle-aged people rushed back and forth, clutching files or reports the way a drowning man clutches a piece of driftwood. On the floor above that living death, she saw through high loft windows into an artist's atelier, where a young woman was throwing paint onto a massive canvas propped against a dead-white wall. Her concentration was so intense, lost within the vision she was trying to reproduce, that she appeared unaware of her surroundings.

"How are you coming?" Moira asked as she turned back into the room.

Bamber, concentrating as intensely as the artist across the street, needed a bit of prompting to answer. "A few more minutes and I'll know," he mumbled at last.

Moira nodded. She was about to continue her anxious perambulation when a sudden movement brought her attention back to the street. A car had drawn up near the end of the block and a man had emerged. Something about the way he moved set off alarm bells in her head. He had a way of turning his head in minute increments, as if he was looking at everything and nothing, that made the hair stir at the nape of her neck. When he reached Bamber's building, he stopped. Keeping close to the rear door, he took out a set of picks and inserted one, then another in the lock, until he found the right one to simulate the hills and valleys of the key.

Reaching down, Moira drew her Lady Hawk out of its thigh holster.

"Almost done!" There was a defiant note of triumph in Bamber's voice.

The door opened and the man entered the building.

Noah Perlis seems to be the nexus of this crisis," Peter Marks said. "He engineered Jay Weston's death, he pulled the rug out from under the Metro police, and he's infiltrated Moira's new organization and got her on the run."

"Noah is Black River," Willard said. "And as secretive and powerful as that band of mercenaries is, I very much doubt that even they have the muscle to accomplish all that without questions being asked."

"You don't think Perlis is behind this?"

"I didn't say that." Willard rubbed the stubble on his cheek. "But in this case I have to believe that Black River had major help."

The two men were facing each other in a brown tufted Naugahyde booth in a late-night bar, listening to a mournful Tammy Wynette song on the jukebox and the insistent growl of garbage trucks rumbling past. A couple of skinny whores were dancing together, having given up on the night. An old man with a shock of unruly white hair was on a stool, bent over his drink; another, who'd put the dollar in the juke, was dueting with Tammy in a passable Irish tenor, tears in his eyes. The smell of old booze and older despair clung to every bit of run-down furniture in the place. The bartender, one foot on the inside rail, was peering over his belly to read a newspaper with all the enthusiasm of a stoned student cracking open a textbook.

"From what I've gleaned," Willard continued, "Black River's major client now is the NSA, in the person of the secretary of defense, who has been championing them to the president."

Marks fairly goggled. "How d'you know all this?"

Willard smiled as he rolled his shot glass between his fingers. "Let's just say that being a mole inside the NSA safe house for all these years gives me a couple of legs up—even on the likes of you, Peter." He slid out of the banquette, went past the two whores, who both blew him a kiss. The juke was now playing Don Henley's

"The Boys of Summer," which appeared to make the Irish tenor weep all the harder as he sang along.

When Willard returned to the banquette it was with a bottle of single-malt. He filled his shot glass and topped off Marks's. "Before we go any further," he said, "I'm wondering why you haven't reported our startling information regarding Noah Perlis and Black River to the Arab."

"M. Errol Danziger is the new DCI," Marks said thoughtfully, "but I'm not sure I want to report anything to him, especially if the NSA is involved. He's Secretary Halliday's man through and through."

Willard took a sip of his single-malt. "So what are you going to do? Quit?"

Marks shook his head. "I love CI too much. It's my life." He inclined his head. "I'd ask the same of you: Are you going to quit?"

"Indeed not." Willard threw down some more whisky. "But I do plan to go my own way."

Marks shook his head. "I'm not following you."

Something had surfaced on Willard's face, a certain contemplative air, or perhaps his innate secretiveness was battling with an urge to recruit, because he said, "Did you know Alex Conklin?"

"No one knew Conklin—not really."

"I did. I don't say that as a boast, just hard fact. Alex and I worked together. I knew what he was building with Treadstone. I'm not certain I approved then, but I was much younger. I hadn't experienced the things Alex had. In any case, he confided all of Treadstone's secrets to me."

"I thought the Treadstone files were destroyed."

Willard nodded. "The ones the Old Man didn't shred, Alex did. Or that was his story, anyway."

Marks considered this for a moment. "Are you saying the Treadstone files still exist?"

"Alex, being Alex, had prepared a duplicate set of files. Only two people know where the files are stored, and one of them is dead."

Marks downed his single-malt then sat back, regarding Willard with care. "You want to reboot Treadstone?"

Willard refilled their glasses from the bottle. "It's already rebooted, Peter. I want to know whether you want to become part of Treadstone."

They've been here no more than forty-eight hours, possibly as little as twenty-four." Yusef, Soraya's agent in place in Khartoum, was a small man with skin the color of thoroughly cured leather. He had large, liquid eyes and very small ears, but he heard everything. He was one of Typhon's top agents because he was clever and resourceful enough to make use of the youth underground that had energized the city through its connection to the Internet. "It's the quicklime, you see. Whoever dumped them wanted them completely destroyed in a way that even fire couldn't accomplish, because the quicklime will eat away everything, including bone and teeth, that could be used to ID the remains."

Soraya had made contact with Yusef on the way in from the airport and, at Amun Chalthoum's urging, had set up a meet with him, despite the men following them—actually because of them. "These men have been sent by my enemies," Amun had said to her in the car. "I want them close enough so we can grab them."

Yusef had heard about the dead men from a young boy who'd come across the grave while he and some friends were exploring the Ansar forts near Sabaloga Gorge; the forts had once been used to attack the troopships on their way to relieve the British General Gordon and his exhausted men in 1885. The young boy and his friend lived in the adjacent village, but a network of kids in Khartoum soon learned of the discovery of the bodies in their Internet chat room.

After handing them a pair of Glocks and extra ammunition, Yusef had led the way about fifty miles north, through the desert with its harsh winds and brutal sun. They used two four-wheel-drive vehicles, as Yusef had advised, because the rough roads and the unreliability of Sudanese vehicles made traveling in just one foolhardy.

"You see how much of the men is left," Yusef said now, as they stared into the shallow pit that had been hastily dug in the packed-earth floor inside one of the old crumbling forts, "despite the quicklime."

Soraya waved away a cloud of flies as she crouched down. "Enough to see they've

"One dead, two wounded, not seriously."

"Who died?"

"Milinkov."

Karpov nodded. "Tragic, but the building is secured."

Bourne felt the fire of the slivovitz all the way down to his stomach. The growing warmth felt good, as if he'd regained solid footing.

"Boris," he said softly, "have your man take Tracy. I don't want to leave her."

"Of course." Karpov signaled to the medic, who lifted Tracy from Bourne's lap.

Bourne watched her as she was carried out of the conference room. He felt her loss, her struggle to come to terms with her duplicitous life and her sense of isolation, living half in the shadows of a world most people were unaware of, let alone able to understand. Her struggle was his struggle, and the pain she felt because of her life was one with which he was all too familiar. He didn't want to see her go, didn't want to let go of her, as if a part of him, suddenly found, had been ripped away just as abruptly.

"What is this?" Boris said, holding up the painting.

"It's a Goya, a previously unknown work of the famous Black Paintings series, which makes it virtually priceless."

Boris grinned. "I hope you don't covet this, Jason."

"To the victor belong the spoils, Boris. So Yevsen was your mission in Khartoum."

Karpov nodded. "I've been working in North Africa for months now, trying to track down Nikolai Yevsen's arms-smuggling suppliers, clients, and pipeline. And you?"

"I spoke to Ivan Volkin—"

"Yes, he told me. That old man has a soft spot for you."

"When Arkadin discovered that his attempt on my life had failed, he came up with another plan, which was to get me here. Why, I don't know."

With a quick glance over to the corpse lying on the other side of the room, Karpov said, "It's a mystery, one of many here. We were hoping to find both Yevsen's supplier and client list, but the hard drives on his remote servers appear to have been wiped clean."

"It wasn't Yevsen who did it," Bourne said. He rose, and Boris with him. "He was here with Tracy, he had no idea about your raid."

Boris scratched his head. "Why would Arkadin send you here, especially in the company of that beautiful young woman?"

"Pity we can't ask Yevsen," Bourne said. "Which begs the question: Who wiped Yevsen's servers clean? Someone made off with his entire network. It had to have been one of Yevsen's own men—someone high up who had the access codes to the servers."

"Anyone who ever dared move against Nikolai Yevsen wound up disappeared."

"As long as he was alive." Bourne, whose mind finally had identified enough of the silken strands to make sense of the spider's web, tilted his head and beckoned Karpov to walk with him. "But look at him now, he isn't a danger to anyone, including Arkadin."

Boris's countenance grew dark. "Arkadin?"

Together they walked down the corridor, manned now by Boris's military cadre, to the men's room.

"I'll have my medic check you out."

Bourne waved away his words. "I'm fine,

Boris." He was marveling at the scope of Arkadin's demonic genius.

Inside, Bourne went to the line of sinks and began to wash the blood and bits of glass off himself. As he did so, Karpov handed him a roll of paper towels.

"Think about it, Boris, why would Arkadin trick me into coming here—especially, as you said, with a beautiful young woman?" It pained Bourne to talk about Tracy, but as much as she was still on his mind, he had a mystery to unravel—and a deadly enemy to confront.

A light suddenly came on behind Karpov's eyes. "Arkadin was banking on you killing Yevsen?"

Bourne splashed tepid water over his face, feeling the small cuts and bruises stinging like nettles. "Or Yevsen killing me. Either way, he'd win."

Karpov shook himself like a dog coming out of the rain. "If what you theorize is true, he might have known of my raid. He wouldn't want Yevsen singing about him or anyone else. Dammit, I've seriously underestimated that man."

Bourne turned his blood-streaked face toward the colonel. "He's more than a man,

Boris. Like me, he's a graduate of Treadstone. Alex Conklin trained Arkadin, just like he trained me, to become the ultimate undercover killing machine, carrying out covert operations impossible for anyone else to accomplish."

"And just where is this devilish graduate now?" Boris asked.

Bourne wiped his face down with a fistful of paper towels. They came away pink. "Tracy told me before she died. Yevsen said he was in Nagorno-Karabakh, Azerbaijan."

"Mountain country, I know it well," Boris said. "I discovered the area was one of Yevsen's prime stopovers for the Air Afrika flights transshipping his illegal arms throughout this continent. It's home to a number of indigenous tribes—all of them fanatic Muslims."

"That makes sense." Bourne regarded his face in the mirror, taking stock of the damage, which was superficial but extensive. Whose reflection stared back at him? Tracy surely would have empathized with that question, no doubt having many times asked it of herself. "Ivan told me that Arkadin has taken over the Eastern Brotherhood, which means he's also the leader of their Black Legion terrorists. Maybe he's trying to branch out into Yevsen's multibillion-dollar business."

Then Bourne saw the Goya that Karpov had propped up against the tile wall. "Do you know a man named Noah Petersen, or Perlis?"

"No, why?"

"He's a senior officer in Black River."

"The American risk management company—also known as private contractors for your government—also known as mercenaries."

"Right on all three counts." Bourne led the way back out into the corridor, which stank of gunpowder and death. "Tracy was bringing the Goya to Noah, but I believe now it was actually a payment to Yevsen for services rendered. That's the only logical explanation for Noah being here."

"So Yevsen, Black River, and Arkadin are in something together."

Bourne nodded. "Did you or your men encounter an American when you raided the building?"

Karpov pulled a small walkie-talkie off its Velcro patch on his vest and spoke into it.

After the crackle of an answer had been received, he shook his head. "You're the only American in the building, Jason. But there's a Sudanese of questionable character who claims he was being interrogated by an American just before the raid began."

Perlis must have been lured away by Bourne's diversion with the lurker. Where had he gone? Bourne could feel himself approaching the center of the web, where the lethal spider patiently lay in wait. "And since Black River's main client is the NSA, there's a good chance it has to do with the ratcheted-up tension in Iran."

"You think Nikolai Yevsen is arming a Black River raiding party ready to invade Iran?"

"Highly unlikely," Bourne said. "The NSA can provide more than enough state-of-the-art armaments that Yevsen could never get his hands on. Besides, for that they wouldn't need Arkadin's help. No, the Americans have identified the missile that brought down the plane—it's Iranian, a Kowsar 3."

Karpov nodded. "Now it's starting to make sense. This Goya is payment to Yevsen for supplying the Kowsar 3."

At that moment, Karpov spotted one of

his men jogging along the hallway toward him. He stared at Bourne for a moment, then handed his commander a sheet of curling thermal paper—clearly a printout from a portable printer.

"Get Lirov," Karpov said as he scanned the document. "Tell him to bring his full kit. I want this man checked out from stem to stern."

The soldier nodded wordlessly and sped off.

"I told you I didn't need—"

Karpov held up a hand. "Hold on, you'll want to hear this. My IT man was able to salvage something from Yevsen's servers after all—apparently they weren't completely wiped." He handed Bourne the sheet of thermal paper. "Here are Yevsen's last three transactions."

Bourne did a quick scan of the information. "The Kowsar 3."

"Right. Just as we surmised, Yevsen acquired an Iranian Kowsar 3 and sold it to Black River."

Where are you going?" Humphry Bamber said, twisting around in his seat. "And why are you holding a gun?"

"Someone knows you're here," Moira said.

"Dear God." Bamber moaned and began to get up.

"Stay right there." Moira held him down with a firm hand. She could feel the chills running through him in waves. "We know someone's coming and we know what he wants."

"Yeah, me dead. You don't expect me to sit here and wait for a bullet in the back."

"I expect you to do what you've done before, help me." She looked down into his pinched face. "Can I count on you?"

He swallowed hard and nodded.

"Okay, now show me the bathroom."

Dondie Parker liked his work—almost too much, some said. Others, like his boss, Noah Perlis, appreciated the almost religious fervor with which he committed to his assignments. Parker liked Perlis. It seemed to him as if the two of them occupied the same gray space at the fringe of society, the place where both of them could make anything happen—the one with his command, the other with his hands and his weapons of choice.

After Parker got through the rear entrance to Humphry Bamber's building, he considered his life's work, which he privately likened to a polished wooden box filled with a collection of the most expensive and aromatic cigars. The climax of each assignment, the death of each target, lay in that box for him to revisit anytime he chose. To take out, one by one, smell, roll between his fingers, and taste. They took the place of military ribbons—medals of valor—commemorating actions necessary, as Noah had said to him time and again, to the welfare and security of the homeland. Parker liked the word *homeland.* It was so much more powerful, more evocative, more virile than the word *nation*.

Parker removed his shoes, tied the laces together, and, slinging them over his shoulder, climbed the stairs. When he reached the second floor, he went down the hallway to the far end, where a window overlooked the fire escape. Unlatching the window, he threw it open and climbed out, making his way up floor by floor, like a fly climbing a wall.

Noah Perlis had found Dondie Parker in one of the local ghetto gyms. Parker was part of a boxing club, the leading contender in the regional welterweight division. He was an exceptional boxer because he learned fast, had tons of stamina, and had found a way to channel his murderous aggression. On the other hand, he wasn't crazy about concussions and fractured ribs, so when Noah showed up and expressed an interest in him, Parker was only too happy to listen to his proposition.

To say that Dondie Parker owed Noah everything would not be overstating the case, a fact that was ever on Parker's mind, never more so than when, as now, he was carrying out an assignment that came directly from Noah. Noah reported to only one man, Oliver Liss, who was so far up the Black River food chain he seemed to be in another universe altogether. Parker was so accomplished that every now and then Oliver Liss would call him in and give him a personal assignment, which Parker carried out immediately and without telling anyone, including Noah. If Noah knew about these extracurricular assignments, he never said anything to Parker, and Parker was happy to leave those horrific sleeping dogs lie.

He'd reached the floor of Humphry Bamber's office. And now, after one more recheck of the building layout Noah had sent to his cell, he crept down to the other end of the fire escape, where he peered in a window. He saw all manner of electronic equipment, most of it up and running, so he knew Bamber had to be there. He untied his laces and slipped on his shoes. Then, taking out his jimmy-picks, he forced open the window with minimal difficulty. Drawing his custom SIG Sauer, he climbed through.

He turned as he heard the sound of someone urinating. Grinning to himself, he made his way toward the sound of urine striking porcelain. The only thing better would be to drill Bamber while he was on the throne.

The door was ajar and, peering in, he could see a wedge of light, Bamber spread-legged in front of the toilet. He could just make out a corner of the sink and, against the rear wall, the bathtub with a shower curtain of gaily dancing fish so cute he had to resist the urge to puke.

He peered into the space between the door and the jamb created by the hinges.

Seeing no one hiding behind the door, he nudged it open with his free hand while he leveled the SIG at Bamber's head.

"Hey, pussycat." His chuckle came from deep in his throat. "Noah says hello and good-bye."

Bamber flinched, just like Parker was expecting him to, but instead of turning to face him, he collapsed as if poleaxed. As Parker was goggling at him, the gaily dancing fish folded up like an accordion. Parker had a split-second look at a woman staring at him. He just had time to think, *Who the fuck is this? Noah didn't tell me*—when the eye of her Lady Hawk spit flame and he spun around in an ungainly pirouette from the bullet fracturing his cheekbone.

He screamed, not in pain or fear, but in rage. He emptied his gun, squeezing off shot after shot, but there was blood in his eyes. He didn't feel a thing—the burst of adrenaline and other endorphins made him for the moment immune to the pain. Ignoring Bamber, curled up in a fetal position under the toilet, he leapt at the woman—a woman, for chrissakes!—swinging the butt of his SIG at the curve of her chin. She retreated, only to slam against the tiled wall and slip on the treacherous curve of porcelain, falling to one knee.

Parker took another vicious swing at her with the SIG. She ducked away, but not before the front sight laid a gash across the bridge of her nose. He saw the glazed look come into her eyes and he knew he had her. He was just about to plant the thick sole of his shoe in her solar plexus when the eye of her Lady Hawk spat fire again.

Parker never felt a thing. The bullet exploded through his right eye and took off the back of his head.

30

You realize," Bourne said, brandishing the sheet of thermal paper as he and Boris Karpov clattered down the stairs at 779 Gamhuria Avenue, "that this information could have been left for you to find."

"Of course. Yevsen could have left it," Karpov said.

"I was thinking of Arkadin."

"But Black River is his partner."

"So was Yevsen."

The medic had done his best to patch up Bourne's face before Bourne shooed him away—at least he'd stopped the bleeding and administered a shot to prevent any possibility of infection.

"One thing about Arkadin, he's consistent," Bourne said. "What I've learned about the way he sets up operations is that he makes sure he has a stalking horse, a diversionary target whom he directs his enemies toward." He slapped the printout. "Black River could be his new stalking horse, the people he wants you to go after rather than finding him."

"The other possibility," Boris said, "is that he's knocking off his partners one by one."

They had passed through the lobby and out into the scalding afternoon sun, where traffic was at a standstill and passersby were gathering as each minute passed, gaping at Boris's heavily armed contingent.

"That brings up another question," Karpov said as they climbed into the minibus he'd commandeered and which had become his mobile headquarters. "How the hell does Arkadin fit into this puzzle? Why would Black River need him?"

"Here's a possibility," Bourne said.

"Arkadin's in Nagorno-Karabakh, a remote area of Azerbaijan that, as you said, is dominated by tribal chieftains, all fanatic Muslims—just like the Black Legion terrorists."

"How would the terrorists be involved?"

"That's something we'll have to ask Arkadin himself," Bourne said. "To do that we'll have to fly to Azerbaijan."

Karpov ordered his IT man to bring up real-time satellite pictures of the Nagorno-Karabakh region in order to figure the best route to the specific area Yevsen used.

The IT man was zooming in on the area when he said, "Hold on a second." His fingers blurred over the keys, shifting the images on the screen.

"What is it?" Karpov said with some impatience.

"A plane just took off from the target area." The IT man swiveled to another laptop and keyed into a different site. "It's an Air Afrika jet, Colonel."

"Arkadin!" Bourne said. "Where's the flight headed?"

"Hold on." The IT man switched to the third computer, bringing up an image similar to those on an air controller's screen. "Just let me extrapolate from the jet's current heading." His fingers danced some more over the keyboard. Then he swiveled back to the first laptop and an area of landmass filled the screen. The image pulled back until the IT man pointed at a place in the lower right-hand quadrant of the screen.

"Right there," he said. "Shahrake Nasiri-Astara, just off the Caspian Sea, in northwest Iran."

"What in the name of all that's unholy is there?" Karpov said.

The IT man, moving to the second laptop, plugged in the name of the area, hit the ENTER key, and scrolled through the resulting news stories. There were precious few, but one of them provided the answer. He looked up into his commander's face and said, "Three whopping huge oil fields and the beginnings of a transnational pipeline."

I want you out of here." Amun Chalthoum's eyes sparked in the semi-darkness of the old fort. "Instantly."

Soraya was so taken aback that it was a

moment before she said, "Amun, I think you're confusing me with someone else."

He took her by the elbow. "This is no joke. Go. Now."

She extricated herself from his grip. "What am I, your daughter? I'm not going anywhere."

"I won't risk the life of the woman I love," he said. "Not in a situation like this."

"I don't know whether to be flattered or offended. Maybe I'm both." She shook her head. "Nevertheless, we came here *because* of me, or have you forgotten?"

"I don't forget anything." Chalthoum was about to continue when Yusef cut him off.

"I thought you'd planned for these people to catch up to you."

"I did," Chalthoum said impatiently, "but I didn't count on getting trapped in here."

"Too late for regrets now," Yusef whispered. "The enemy has entered the fort."

Chalthoum held up four fingers, to let Yusef know how many men had been following them. Yusef gave a curt nod and gestured for them to follow him. While the men moved out, Soraya bent and, ripping off a piece of one of the men's shirts, scooped some quicklime into the makeshift sling.

As they reached the doorway, she said very clearly, "We should stay here."

They turned, and Amun looked at her as if she were insane. "We'll be trapped like rats."

"We're already trapped like rats." She swung the sling back and forth. "At least here we have the high ground." She gestured with her chin. "They've already dispersed themselves. They'll pick us off one by one before we can get to even one of them."

"You're right, Director," Yusef said, and Chalthoum looked like he wanted to swat him across the face.

She appealed to Chalthoum directly. "Amun, get used to it. This is how it is."

Three of the four men, having found shadowed nests for themselves, lay in wait, sighting down the long barrels of their rifles. The fourth man—the beater—moved cautiously from desolate room to ruined room, across abandoned sand-piled spaces without roofs. Always the wind was in his ears, and the grit of the desert in his nose and throat. Granules, shot by the wind, insinuated themselves inside his clothes and formed a familiar layer as they clung to his sweaty skin. His job was to find the targets and drive them into the crisscrossing lines of fire set up by his comrades. He was cautious, but not apprehensive; he'd done this work before and he'd do it again many times before old age made this life impossible. But he knew by then he'd have more than enough money for his family and even his children's families. The American paid well—the American, it seemed, never ran out of money, just as the fool never bargained down his price. The Russians, now—they knew how to drive a hard bargain. He'd sweated through many a negotiation with the Russians, who claimed they didn't have money, or, anyway, enough to pay him what he asked. He would settle on a price that made them all happy and then he went about the business of killing. It's what he did best, after all—the only thing he was trained for.

He'd secured more than half the fort and was frankly surprised that he'd not yet come upon even a sign of the targets.

Well, one of them was an Egyptian, he'd been told. He didn't like Egyptians, they smeared you with their honeyed words all the while lying through their teeth. They were like jackals—grinning as they tore the flesh off you.

He turned down a short corridor. When he was no more than halfway along, he heard the sound of the flies buzzing and knew, even though he failed to catch a whiff of rotting flesh, that there must have been a death up ahead of him, and quite recently, too.

Gripping his handgun more tightly, he continued down the hallway with his spine pressed up against one wall, squinting into the gloom. Here and there, sunlight fluttered and twittered like birds in a tree, where the ceiling or wall was cracked or even, in some places, broken open, as if by the hammering fist of a murderous giant.

The sound of the flies had become a hum, as of some great, nebulous creature that waxed and waned as it fed and drowsed. He paused, listening and, in his own unscientific way, counting their number. Something big had died in that room ahead of him, possibly more than one big thing. A human being?

He pulled the trigger of his handgun, the brief light-flare, the report, transforming the entire area. He was like a beast marking its territory, warning other predators of its presence, wanting to instill fear. If the targets were in that room, they were trapped. He knew that room—just as he knew every room in this and the other forts in the area. There was only one entrance and he was five steps away from it.

Then a figure shot out from the open doorway, and he squeezed off four accurate shots in rapid succession that made it dance and jerk.

It was Soraya who followed the dead American Chalthoum had heaved out of the doorway. Swinging her makeshift sling amid the hail of bullets, she let fly its load of quicklime into the face of the shooter. The instant the caustic calcium oxide struck his body fluids—the sweat on his cheeks and the tears in his eyes—a chemical reaction caused the blooming of a terrible heat.

The shooter screamed, dropped his gun, and instinctively clapped his hands to his burning face, trying to scrub off the substance. This only made matters worse for him. Soraya scooped up his gun and shot him in the head, putting him out of his misery, as she would a crippled horse.

Her low whistle brought Chalthoum and Yusef out of the burial chamber. "One down," she said. "Three to go."

Are you all right?" Moira stepped out of the bathtub and helped Humphry Bamber to stand.

"I think I ought to be asking you that question," he said, glancing with a shudder at the shattered head of the intruder. Then he turned and vomited into the toilet.

Moira turned on the cold water in the sink, drenched a hand towel, and placed it on the back of his neck. He took it and held it against the bridge of her nose as they left the bathroom.

She put her arm around his wide shoulders. "Let's get you back to somewhere safe."

He nodded like a lost little boy as they picked their way through the office. They were almost at the door when she glanced at the wall of computers.

"What did you find out? What's inside Noah's version of Bardem?"

Bamber broke away, went to the laptop hooked up to all the other equipment, and disconnected it. Closing it, he tucked it under his arm.

"If you don't see it for yourself, you won't believe it," he said as they hurried out of the office.

I'm not interested in Treadstone or what Alex Conklin was up to," Peter Marks said.

Willard appeared unfazed. "But you are, I assume, interested in saving CI from the Philistines." It was almost as if he'd anticipated Marks's response.

"Of course I am." Marks turned his empty glass over when Willard tried to fill it with the bottle's last round of whisky. "Do you have something in mind—something, I assume, to do with Black River's complicity in domestic murder, especially, goddammit, the DCI's death?"

"The DCI is M. Errol Danziger."

"Don't remind me," Marks said sourly.

"I have to. He's the eight-hundred-pound gorilla in CI's shop, and believe me when I tell you he's going to beat all you fine young gentlemen into banana paste if nothing's done to stop him."

"What about you?"

"I am Treadstone."

Marks stared bleakly at the older man. Whether it was all the single-malt he'd consumed or having his face pushed into reality, he felt sick to his stomach. "Go on."

"No," Willard said emphatically. "Either you're in or you're out, Peter. And before you answer, please understand that there's no backing out, no room for second thoughts. Once you're in, that's it, no matter the cost or the consequences."

Marks shook his head. "What choice do I have?"

"There's always a choice." Willard poured himself the last of the liquor and took a deep sip. "What there isn't—and this goes for me as well as for you—is an opportunity to look back. From this moment on, there is no past. We move forward, only forward, into the dark."

"Jesus." Marks felt a shiver run down his spine. "This sounds like I'm making a deal with the devil."

"That's very funny." Willard smiled and, as if on cue, produced a three-page document, which he spread on the table facing the younger man.

"What the hell is this?"

"Also funny." Willard placed a pen on the table. "It's a contract with Treadstone. It's non-negotiable and, as you can see in clause thirteen, nonrevokable."

Marks peered at the contract. "How is that enforceable? Will you threaten to take my soul?" He laughed, but it was too brittle to hold any humor. Then he squinted, reading one paragraph after another.

"Jesus," he said when he was finished. He looked at the pen, then at Willard. "Tell me you have a plan to get rid of M. Errol-fucking-Danziger or I'm out of here right now."

"Lopping off one head of the hydra will be useless because it will only grow another." Willard picked up the pen and held it out. "I will get rid of the hydra itself: Secretary of Defense Ervin Reynolds Halliday."

"Many have tried, including the late Veronica Hart."

"They all thought they had evidence that he was operating beyond the law, a well-trod path that Halliday knows far better than they did. I'm taking an altogether different route."

Marks looked deep into the other man's eyes, trying to judge his seriousness. At length, he took the pen and said, "I don't care what route we take as long as Halliday ends up being roadkill."

"Tomorrow morning," Willard said, "you'll need to keep that sentiment in mind."

"Is that a whiff of sulfur I smell?" But Marks's laugh was distinctly uneasy.

"I know this man." Yusef brushed the quicklime paste off the dead gunman's face with the tip of his boot. "His name's Ahmed, he's a freelance assassin who usually works for the Americans or the Russians." He grunted. "Now and again at the same time."

Chalthoum frowned. "Has he worked for the Egyptians before?"

Yusef shook his head. "Not to my knowledge."

"You don't use him, do you?" Soraya

was examining what was left of Ahmed's face. "I don't remember seeing his name on any of your reports."

"I wouldn't trust this scum to bring me a disk of bread," Yusef said with a curl of his upper lip. "In addition to being a professional murderer, he's a liar and a thief, always, even when he was a small boy."

"Remember," Chalthoum said with a grim look at Soraya, "I want at least one of them alive."

"First things first," she said. "Let's just concentrate on getting out of here alive ourselves."

He was still trying without success to brush the odors of quicklime and death off his clothes, but this business allowed Soraya to take the lead—which, again, was something he deplored. Ever since they'd arrived in Khartoum something had taken possession of him, a sense of protectiveness toward Soraya that clearly made her uncomfortable. Possibly it was being away from Egypt; he was in unknown territory, after all, and he knew only too well that he was most sure of himself in his own territory.

She heard him call softly to her but

resisted the urge to turn and look at him. Instead she moved steadily forward in a semi-crouch until she came to the first courtyard. There were positions to the left and right on either wall where snipers would have an excellent field of view. She fired a shot at each spot in turn, but there was no answering fire. That was it for the shooter's .45, so she dropped it and took out the Glock that Yusef had given her. After double-checking that it was loaded she moved out across the expanse of the grim-looking courtyard, keeping to the shadows thrown by the walls. Not once did she look back, trusting that Amun and Yusef were not far behind her and would provide cover if she got into trouble.

Moments later the second, central courtyard, larger and more intimidating than the first, presented itself. Again she fired shots at the likely sniper positions, again without any result.

"There's only one more," Yusef said. "It's smaller, but because it's at the front there are more places to defend it."

Soraya saw at once that he was right,

and that no matter what they did they'd never be able to reach the parapets on either wall without being shot dead.

"What now?" she said to Amun.

Before he could think of a reply, Yusef said, "I have an idea. I knew Ahmed all his life, I think I can imitate his voice." He looked from Chalthoum to Soraya. "Shall I give it a shot?"

"I don't see how it can hurt," Chalthoum said, but Yusef didn't move until Soraya nodded her assent.

Then he brushed by ahead of her and, crouching in the shadowy mouth where the corridor debouched onto the courtyard, he raised his voice. It wasn't his voice, but one neither of them had heard before.

"It's Ahmed—please, I'm hurt!" Nothing but echoes. He turned to Soraya. "Quick!" he whispered. "Give me your shirt."

"Take mine," Chalthoum said with a glower.

"Hers will be better," Yusef said. "They'll see it's the female's."

Soraya did as he asked, unbuttoning her short-sleeved shirt and handing it over.

"I've killed them!" Yusef called in Ahmed's voice. "See here!" Soraya's shirt fluttered onto the cobbles of the courtyard like a bird settling onto its nest.

"If you've killed them," a voice came from their left, "come out!"

"I can't," Yusef replied, "my leg is broken. I've dragged myself this far, but I've fallen and I can't take another step! Please, brothers, come fetch me before I bleed to death!"

For a long time nothing happened. Yusef was about to shout again when Chalthoum cautioned silence.

"Don't oversell it," he whispered. "Be patient now."

More time passed, it was difficult to say how much since in their situation time was bent like taffy, minutes seeming like an hour. At length, they discerned movement on their right. Two men could be seen making their way down to the ground. They moved cautiously, keeping their sides toward the mouth of the hallway. The third man—the one who had queried Yusef—was nowhere in sight. Clearly, he was covering them from his hidden position on the left.

Chalthoum motioned silently to Yusef, who lay down and moved slightly so that the two men could see that one leg was drawn up under the other. Soraya and Chalthoum retreated several steps into the gloom.

"There he is!" one of the men cried to the man covering them—who was, it appeared, their leader. "I can see Ahmed! He's fallen, just as he said!"

"I don't see any other movement," the leader's voice floated down from the parapet. "Go get him, but make it quick!"

Running in a semi-crouch, the two men approached Yusef.

"Hold it!" their leader said, and they obediently squatted on their hams, their rifles laid across their thighs, their avid eyes on their fallen comrade.

There was movement from the left as the leader abandoned his eyrie, clattering down stone steps to the courtyard.

"Ahmed," one of the men whispered, "are you all right?"

"No," said Ahmed. "The pain in my leg is terrible, it's—"

But he'd said enough at close range for the other man to move back a pace.

"What is it?" his companion said, aiming his rifle into the mouth of the hallway.

"I don't think that's Ahmed."

That was when Chalthoum and Soraya, Glocks firing, moved out on either side of Yusef. The two crouching men were struck immediately, and Chalthoum kicked their weapons away from where they lay sprawled on the ground. The leader, scurrying to find cover where there was none, fired off-balance and Chalthoum went down with a grunt.

Soraya, running, aimed and fired at the leader, but it was Yusef, from his prone position, who shot the leader in the chest. The man spun around and fell. At once Soraya veered toward him.

"Check Amun!" she called to Yusef as she stooped, picking up the leader's rifle. He was writhing, bleeding from his right side, but he was breathing. The bullet hadn't punctured a lung.

She knelt down beside him. "Who hired you?"

The man looked up at her and spat in her face.

A moment later she was joined by the two men. Amun had been shot in the thigh, but the bullet had gone through and the wound, Yusef said, looked clean. He'd tied off the area above the wound with a makeshift tourniquet made from her shirt.

"Are you all right?" she said, looking up at Chalthoum.

He nodded in his usual dour way.

"I've asked him who hired him," she said, "but he's not talking."

"Take Yusef and see about the other two." Chalthoum was staring intently at the fallen leader.

Soraya knew that look of determination. "Amun . . ."

"Just give me five minutes."

They needed the information, there was no question about that. Soraya nodded reluctantly and, with Yusef, walked back to where the other two men lay near the mouth of the hallway. There wasn't much to see. Both had taken multiple shots to the abdomen and chest. Neither was alive. As they gathered up the rifles, they heard a muffled cry that, in its inhumanity, sent shivers down their spines.

Yusef turned to her. "This Egyptian friend of yours, he can be trusted?"

Soraya nodded, already sick at what

Amun was doing with her consent. There was silence then, except for the desperate voice of the wind, keening through the abandoned rooms. After a time, Chalthoum returned to them. He was limping badly, and Yusef handed him a rifle to lean on.

"My enemies had nothing to do with this," he said in a voice that had not been changed one iota by what he'd just done. "These men were hired by the Americans, specifically a man known ridiculously as Triton. Mean anything to you?"

Soraya shook her head.

"But these might." She saw four small rectangular metal objects swinging from a length of cord. "I found these around the leader's neck."

She examined them when he handed them over. "They look like dog tags."

Amun nodded. "He said they came from the four Americans who were executed back there. These bastards murdered them."

But she had to admit the tags weren't like any she had ever seen. Instead of carrying name, rank, and serial number, they were laser-engraved with what looked like—

"They're enciphered," she said, her heart beating fast. "These might be the key to proving who launched the Kowsar 3, and why."

Book Four

31

Leonid Danilovich Arkadin roamed the passenger area of the Air Afrika flight that had been sent for him and his cadre in Nagorno-Karabakh. He knew their destination was Iran. Noah Perlis was certain that Arkadin didn't know the specific site, but Noah was wrong. Like many Americans in his position, Noah believed himself smarter than those who weren't American and able to manipulate them. Where Americans got that idea was something of a mystery, but having spent time in DC, Arkadin had some ideas. America's smug sense of isolation might have been shaken by the events in 2001, but not its sense of privilege and entitlement. When he'd been there, he'd sat in district restaurants, eavesdropping on conversations as part of his Treadstone training. But at the same time he'd listen to the neocons—men of power, substance, and influence who were convinced that they had the keys to how the world worked. For them, everything was childishly simple, as if there were only two immutable variables in life: action and reaction, both of which they understood completely, and for which they planned. And when the reactions were not what their brain trust had anticipated—when their plans blew up in their faces—instead of admitting their error, in a tide of amnesia they redoubled their efforts. To him, it was madness that turned these people deaf and blind to real events as they unfolded.

Perhaps, he thought now, as he checked and rechecked the readiness of his men and their equipment, Noah was one of the last of his kind, a dinosaur unaware that his age was ending, that the glacier that had been forming on the horizon was about to plow him under.

Just like Dimitri Ilyinovich Maslov.

She has to go back," Dimitri Ilyinovich Maslov said, "she and the three girls. Otherwise there will be no peace with Lev Antonin."

"Since when does a shit-kicker like Antonin dictate to you," Arkadin said, "the head of the Kazanskaya *grupperovka*?"

Arkadin had the sensation that Tarkanian, who stood by his side, had winced. The three men were surrounded by sound, amplified to an earsplitting level. In the Pasha Room of Propaganda, an *elitny* club in downtown Moscow, there were only two other men—both Maslov's muscle. All the other attendees—of which there were more than a dozen—were young, long-legged, blond, busty, gorgeous, and sexually desirable, which pretty much defined them: *tyolkas* all. They were clothed—or, more accurately, semi-clothed—in provocative outfits, whether miniskirts, bikinis, see-through tops, plunging necklines, or completely backless dresses. They wore high heels, even the ones in bathing suits, and plenty of makeup. Some reluctantly returned to their high school classes each day.

Maslov stared hard at Arkadin, assuming that like everyone else he confronted, he could intimidate him just by a look. Maslov was wrong, and he didn't like being wrong. Ever.

He took one step toward Arkadin, which was an aggressive step, though not a threatening one, and his nose wrinkled. "What's that fire smoke I smell on you, Arkadin, are you a fucking woodsman on top of everything else?"

Five miles from the Orthodox cathedral, Arkadin had taken Joškar into the dense pine forest. She was cradling Yasha in her arms and he was holding an ax he'd drawn out of the trunk of her car. Her three daughters, sobbing hysterically, trailed along behind the adults in single file.

When they'd left the parked car, Tarkanian had yelled after them, "Half an hour, after that I'm getting the fuck out of here!"

"Will he really leave us here?" she asked.

"Do you care?"

"Not as long as you're with me."

At least, that's what he thought she'd said. She'd spoken so softly that the wind had taken her words almost as soon as they were out of her mouth. Wings fluttered by overhead as they tramped beneath the swaying pine branches. Once they crunched through the thin crust, the snow was soft as down. Overhead, the sky was as woolly as Joškar's coat.

In a small clearing she set her son down on a bed of snowy pine needles.

"He always loved the forest," she said. "He used to beg me to take him to play in the mountains."

As he set about finding felled trees, deadwood, and chopping it up into foot-long logs, Arkadin remembered his own all-too-infrequent trips to the mountains around Nizhny Tagil, the only place where he could take a deep breath without the oppressive weight of his parents and his birthplace withering his heart and sickening his spirit.

Within twenty minutes he had a bonfire going. The girls had stopped their sobbing, their tears freezing like tiny diamonds on their ruddy cheeks. As they stared, fascinated, into the building flames, the frozen tears melted, dripping from their rounded chins.

Joškar delivered Yasha into his arms while she said the prayers in her native language. She held her daughters close to her as she intoned the words, which gradually became a song, her strong voice lifted through the pine boughs, echoing into the thick clouds. Arkadin wondered if the fairies, elves, gods, and demi-gods she had invoked in her stories were somewhere close, watching the ceremony with sorrowful eyes.

At length, Joškar instructed Arkadin on what to say when she placed Yasha onto the funeral pyre. The girls were crying again as they watched their brother's little body being consumed by the flames. Joškar said a final prayer, and then they were done. Arkadin had no idea how much time had passed, but Tarkanian and the car were still waiting for them when they broke out of the tree line and returned to civilization.

I made a promise to her," Arkadin said.

"This fucking baby factory?" Maslov scoffed. "You're stupider than you look."

"You're the one who risked two of your men—one of them totally incompetent—to bring me back here."

"Yes, you shithead, not you and four civilians who belong to someone else."

"You talk about them as if they're cattle."

"Hey, fuck you, bright boy! Lev Antonin wants them back, and that's where they're going."

"I'm responsible for her son's death."

"Did you kill the little fucker?" Maslov was fairly shouting now. The muscle had been drifting closer and the *tyolkas* were doing their best to look in another direction.

"No."

"Then you're not responsible for his death. End of fucking story!"

"I made a promise that she wouldn't be sent back to her husband, she's dead scared of him. He'll beat her half to death."

"What the fuck does that mean to me?" In his fury, Maslov's mineral eyes seemed to shoot sparks. "I have a business to run."

Tarkanian stirred. "Boss, maybe you should—"

"What?" Maslov turned on Tarkanian.

"Are you gonna tell me what I should do, too, Mischa? Fuck you! I asked you for something simple: Bring this kid back from Nizhny Tagil. And what happens? The kid beats the shit outta Oserov and you come back like a fucking pack mule with a shitload of problems I don't need." Having effectively silenced Tarkanian, he turned back to Arkadin. "As for you, you better get your fucking head screwed on right, bright boy, or I'll send you back to the shithole you crawled out of."

"They're my responsibility," Arkadin said levelly. "I'll take care of them."

"Listen to him!" Now Maslov was shouting. "Who died and made you boss? And whatever gave you the crooked idea that you have a say in anything that happens here?" His face was red, almost swollen. "Mischa, get this motherless fuck out of my sight before I rip him apart with my bare hands!"

Tarkanian dragged Arkadin out of the Pasha Room and took him over to the long bar on one side of the main room. A stage, lit up like it was New Year's Eve, featured a tall nubile *tyolka* with very little on, who spread her mile-long legs to a beat-heavy song.

"Let's have a drink," Tarkanian said with forced joviality.

"I don't want a drink."

"It's on me." Tarkanian caught the bartender's eye. "Come on, my friend, a drink is just what you need."

"Don't tell me what I need," Arkadin said, his voice suddenly raised.

The absurd argument carried on from there, escalating enough so that a bouncer was summoned.

"What seems to be the trouble?" He might have been addressing both of them but, because he knew Tarkanian by sight, his eyes were firmly fixed on Arkadin.

With a venomous glare, Arkadin reacted. He grabbed the bouncer and slammed his forehead against the edge of the bar with so much force that nearby drinks trembled and the closest ones tipped over. Then he kept slamming it until Tarkanian managed to pull him off.

"I don't have a problem," Arkadin said to the stunned and bleeding bouncer. "But it's clear you do."

Tarkanian hustled him out into the night before he could do any more damage.

"If you think I'm ever going to work for

that pile of dogshit," Arkadin said, "you're sorely mistaken."

Tarkanian held up his hands. "Okay, okay. Don't work for him." He guided Arkadin down the street, away from the club's entrance. "However, I don't know how you're going to make a living. Moscow is a different—"

"I'm not staying in Moscow." Breath, condensing in the chill, was shooting out of Arkadin's nostrils like steam. "I'm going to take Joškar and the girls and—"

"And what? Where will you go? You have no money, no prospects, nothing. How will you feed yourselves, let alone the kids?" Tarkanian shook his head. "Take my advice, forget about those people, they belong to your past, to another life. You've left Nizhny Tagil behind." He peered into Arkadin's eyes. "That's what you've wanted all your life, isn't it?"

"I'm not letting Maslov's people take them back. You don't know what Lev Antonin's like."

"Maslov doesn't care what Lev Antonin's like."

"Fuck Maslov!"

Tarkanian rounded on him. "You really

don't get it, do you? Dimitri Maslov and his kind own Moscow lock, stock, and vodka. That means they own Joškar and her girls."

"Joškar and the girls aren't part of his world."

"They are now," Tarkanian said. "You dragged them into it."

"I didn't know what I was doing."

"Well, that's clear enough, but you have to face facts: What's done is done."

"There must be a way out of this."

"Really? Even if you had money—say, if I were stupid enough to give you some—what would it accomplish? Maslov would send his people after you. Worse, considering how you provoked him, he might come after you himself. Trust me when I tell you that's not what you want for them."

Arkadin felt like pulling his hair out by the roots. "Don't you understand? I don't want them going back to that fucker."

"Have you considered that it might be the best outcome?"

"Are you out of your mind?"

"Look, you yourself said that Joškar told you Lev Antonin promised to protect her and her children. You know what she is, and the girls have her blood. If her secret gets out she'll never be able to have a normal life among ethnic Russians. Face it, you can't protect them from Maslov, but they'll be safe enough back in Nizhny Tagil, where no one is going to say a word against her for fear of her husband. And listen, she's smart enough to tell him that she and the kids were abducted to ensure your safe passage. Chances are he won't lift a hand to her."

"Until the next time he's drunk or depressed or just in the mood for a little fun."

"That's her life, not yours. Leonid Danilovich, I'm talking to you as one friend to another. This is the only way. You managed to escape Nizhny Tagil; not everyone can be so fortunate."

The fact that Tarkanian was telling the truth only made Arkadin angrier. The problem was he didn't know what to do with that anger, so he began to turn it inward. More than anything, he wanted to see Joškar again, he wanted to hold her youngest girl in his arms again, to feel her warmth, her heartbeat. But he knew that it was impossible. If he met with her again, he'd never be able to let her go. Maslov's people would surely kill him and the family would be shipped back to Lev Antonin anyway. He felt like a rat in a maze with no beginning and no end, only an eternal race chasing his own tail.

This was Dimitri Maslov's doing. At that moment he vowed that no matter how long it took he'd make Maslov pay: Death would come to him only when he'd been systematically stripped of everything he held dear.

Two days later he watched from the shadows across the street—Tarkanian at his elbow, either for moral support or to drag him back if he got any ideas at the last minute—as Joškar and the three girls were led into a large black Zil. Two of Maslov's muscle were with them, plus the driver. The girls, bewildered, allowed themselves to be stowed in the car as docilely as lambs to the slaughter.

For her part, Joškar, with hands on the car's roof, one foot already inside, paused and looked around for him. As she did so, Arkadin saw not the look of despair he had been expecting, but rather an expression of infinite sadness, which tore through him like phosphorus, burning his insides as black as Yasha's flesh. He'd deceived her, broken his promise.

In his mind he heard her voice as if she were calling to him now: *"Don't make me go back to him."*

She'd believed in him, trusted him, and now she had nothing.

She ducked down, and he lost sight of her. The car door slammed, the Zil drove off, and he had nothing as well. This was brought home to him in an even more vicious fashion when, six weeks later, Tarkanian informed him that Joškar had shot her husband to death, then turned the gun on her children and herself.

32

Shahrake Nasiri-Astara at last! Noah Perlis had been to many exotic destinations in his time, but this area of northwestern Iran wasn't one of them. In fact, apart from the stark towers of the oil wells and the attendant petroleum particulates, it was so ordinary looking it could have been somewhere in rural Arkansas. However, Noah had no time to be bored. An hour ago, he'd received a call from Black River informing him that Dondie Parker, the man he'd sent to kill Humphry Bamber, had failed to check in as he should have following the completion of his assignment. To Noah, this meant two things: One, Bamber was still alive, and, two, he'd lied about getting away from Moira, because there was no way he could have survived Dondie Parker on his own. Extrapolating from these hypotheses brought him to another hypothesis of vital and immediate importance to him: the possibility that the newest version of Bardem was poisoned in some way he'd never be able to discover.

Lucky for him his innate paranoia forced him to back up everything, even his computer. No point in letting his enemies know he was on to them. He'd shut down the laptop on which Bamber had uploaded the poisoned software and switched to his fully loaded second laptop, which was still running the previous version of Bardem.

He sat inside a canvas tent on a camp chair, much as he imagined Julius Caesar had sat, mapping out his successful military campaigns, centuries ago. Instead of a map of Gaul hand-drawn by Greek cartographers, he had a handmade software program analyzing this oil-rich part of the world running on his laptop. Caesar, a brilliant general in any age, would have understood instantly what he was up to, of that he had no doubt.

He had three scenarios running simultaneously on Bardem, all of them different in small but crucial ways. Much depended on how the Iranian government responded to the incursion—if they found out about it in time. That was the issue, really: timing. It was one thing to be on Iranian soil, quite another to start a military operation on it. The point of Pinprick was its small footprint, hence its name. Did an elephant even feel a pinprick? You could be sure it didn't. Unfortunately, Noah couldn't be as certain that the Iranian government wouldn't feel Pinprick until Arkadin's force of twenty men had established their beachhead and begun redirecting the oil pipeline.

Because the objective of Pinprick had always been the oil in the Iranian fields here in Shahrake Nasiri-Astara. There was nothing else of value here, militarily or otherwise. That was what was so brilliant about Danziger's plan—the seizure of these rich oil fields under the cover of a larger military incursion by America and a sizable coalition of allies in response to Iran's alleged act of war against the United States and, indeed, all civilized nations. If the Iranians could shoot down an American passenger jet over Egyptian airspace, what would stop them from downing the jets of other nations that opposed their nuclear program? This had been the cornerstone of the president's argument to the United Nations, one that had proved so compelling that it had eaten through all the knee-jerk pacifistic, foot-dragging bullshit that usually infested the international body of navel-gazers and do-nothings.

Through his machinations, Iran had been proven to be a true outlaw nation in the eyes of the world. So much the better for everyone. The country's regime was a menace; if the rest of the world needed a bit of goading to get off their fat backsides and take matters into their own hands, well, that was the way of the world. One of Black River's specialties—one that set it apart from any other private risk management firm—was its ability to alter facts to create a reality that could be molded to a client's wishes. This was what Bud Halliday had asked of Black River, why the NSA was paying it a fortune through one of many blind trusts that could in no way be traced back to the secretary or anyone at NSA. So far as any paper trail was concerned—there was always a paper trail, electronic or otherwise, that was a given—Black River's client was Good Shepherd Holdings, PLC, on the Inner Hebrides island of Islay, which, if anyone cared to make the trek, consisted of a three-room office in a drafty stone building, where three men and a woman wrote and managed insurance policies for local distilleries throughout the islands.

As for the democratic indigenous group Halliday so heartily touted to the president, it and the meetings its leaders had with Black River personnel were a part of Pinprick. In other words, they were a figment of Danziger's imagination. Danziger had argued that the creation of the indigenous group was vital both to get the president moving further in the direction of war and as a reason to shovel virtually unlimited funds to Black River, to cover the massive expenditures for its partners: Yevsen, Maslov, and Arkadin, all of whom were paid by Good Shepherd.

One of Perlis's men entered the tent to

tell him that Arkadin's plane would be arriving within fifteen minutes. Perlis nodded, silently dismissing him. He had disliked using Dimitri Maslov, not because he felt he couldn't trust him, but because it galled him that he needed Maslov to deal with Yevsen. Worse, Maslov had brought in Leonid Arkadin, a man Perlis had never met, but whose curriculum vitae in the shadow world of wet work was both impressive and worrying. Impressive because he'd never failed to successfully complete an assignment; worrying because he was a wild card—in his own way, eerily similar to the late Jason Bourne. Both men had proved themselves unreliable at taking orders and sticking to the game plan they'd been given. They were both master improvisers, certainly an element in their success, but also a nightmare for anyone attempting to handle them.

Thinking of the Russians caused him to consider the raid on Nikolai Yevsen's headquarters in Khartoum. He hadn't stayed around to find out who had staged it or what had happened, instead racing safely to the airport, where a Black River light transport was waiting for him just off the runway. When he'd tried to contact Oliver Liss, he'd gotten Dick Braun instead. Braun was another of the triumvirate who had founded Black River, but Perlis had never reported to him before. Braun wasn't happy, but then he already knew that the raid had been staged by a contingent of the Russian FSB-2 that, it turned out, had been on the trail of Yevsen's business for over two years. Noah also learned that Yevsen had been killed in the raid, a mildly surprising turn of events, but one that he, unlike Braun, welcomed. As far as he was concerned the arms dealer's death meant one less partner, one less potential security problem to deal with. He could neither fathom nor condone Braun's white-hot fury at Dimitri Maslov's displeasure. So far as Noah was concerned, the head of the Kazanskaya *grupperovka* was just another money-hungry Russian thug. Sooner or later he'd have to be dealt with—not that he said this to his boss; such a comment would only further inflame the situation. What neither he nor Braun knew was the identity of the American who had infiltrated the Air Afrika building immediately prior to the FSB-2 raid. It was too late to think about what the American might have wanted.

Unfortunately for Noah, Braun was fully briefed and, before Noah could ask him where Liss was, Braun asked him for an update on the situation with Humphry Bamber, to which Noah replied that Bardem was as secure as it had ever been.

"Does that mean he's been terminated?" Braun said bluntly.

"Yes," Noah lied, not wanting to get into that thorny issue on the cusp of Pinprick's operational phase. He killed the call before Braun could interrogate him further.

Briefly, he felt a stab of concern at Oliver Liss's continuing absence, but right now he had more pressing problems, namely Bardem. Running the three scenarios again gave him a probability success rate of 98 percent, 97 percent, and 99 percent. The main military incursion, he knew, was going to take place on two pincer-like fronts: on the borders with Iraq and Afghanistan. One was far to the south, the other clear across the country, in the east. All three scenarios were the same, except in two crucial details: how long Perlis and his team had to secure the oil fields and redirect the oil pipeline before the besieged Iranian military got wind of what was happening, and what shape their military would be in once they became aware of the oil field takeover. Still, by that time Halliday would have diverted the American forces set to rendezvous with the nonexistent indigenous group to provide support and lock down the area.

Someone else entered the tent. Anticipating a progress report on Arkadin's flight, he glanced up and started, suddenly certain that it was Moira. His heart racing and adrenaline pumping through him, he realized that it was only Fiona, another member of his elite team who had accompanied him here. Fiona, a redhead with fine features and porcelain skin heavily laced with freckles, looked nothing like Moira, and yet Moira was who he'd seen. Why was she still on his mind?

For many years he'd believed that he could not feel anything other than physical pain. He felt nothing when his parents died, or when his best friend in high school was killed in a hit-and-run accident. He remembered standing in burnished sunshine, watching his coffin being lowered into the ground, staring at the epic breasts of Marika DeSoto, their classmate, and wondering what they felt like. It was easy for him to stare at Marika's breasts because she was crying; all the kids were crying, apart from him.

He was certain there was something wrong with him, some missing element or essential connection to the outside world that allowed everything to pass him by like two-dimensional images on a movie screen. Until Moira, who had somehow infected him like a virus. Why would he care what she was doing, or how he had treated her when she was under his command?

Liss had warned him about Moira or, more accurately, his relationship with her, which Liss had termed "unhealthy." *"Fire her and fuck her,"* Liss had said in his usual economic style, *"or forget her. Either way, get her out of your head before it's too late. This happened to you once before, to disastrous results."*

The problem was that it was already too late; Moira was lodged in a place inside himself even he couldn't get to. Other than himself, she was the only living person who seemed three-dimensional, who actually lived and breathed. He desperately wanted her near him, but had no idea what he'd do when she was. Whenever he confronted her now he felt like a child, his ferociously cold anger hiding his fear and insecurity. Possibly one could say he wanted her to love him, but being unable to love even himself, he had no clear conception of what love might consist of, what it would feel like, or even why he should desire it.

But of course, at the throbbing core of him he knew why he desired it, why, in fact, he didn't love Moira or even the thought of her. She was merely a symbol of someone else, whose life and death threw a shadow over his soul as if she were the devil or, if not the devil, then surely a demon, or an angel. Even now she had such a perfect hold on him that he could not even speak her name, or think of it, without a spasm of—what? fear, fury, confusion, possibly all three. The truth was that it was she who had infected him, not Moira. Terrible truth be known, his rage at Moira in the form of this unwavering vendetta was really a rage against himself. He had been so certain that he'd hidden the thought of Holly away forever, but Moira's betrayal had cracked open the receptacle in which he stored her memory. And just this memory caused him to touch the ring on his forefinger with the same trepidation a cook might use to test the handle of a burning hot saucepan. He wanted it out of his sight, he wished, in fact, that he'd never seen it or learned of it, and yet it had been years in his possession and not once had he taken it off for any reason. It was as if Holly and the ring had fused, as if, defying the laws of physics or biology or whatever science, impossible as it might seem, her essence remained in the ring. He looked down at it. Such a small thing to have defeated him so utterly.

He felt feverish now, as if the virus were advancing to another, terminal stage. He stared at the Bardem program without his usual concentration. *"Just remember this last bit of advice, mate,"* Liss had said to him. *"More often than not, women are the downfall of men."*

Was it all coming apart, was there nothing but loss in the world? Thrusting the laptop aside, he stood and strode out of the tent into the alien atmosphere of Iran. The architectural spiderwebs of the oil rigs circled the area like prison towers. The sound of their pumping filled the oily air with the low, steady rumble of mechanical animals prowling around their cages. The screech and clang of outmoded trucks shifting ill-maintained gears punctuated the afternoon, and the smell of crude was always in the air.

And then, above it all, came the scream of the jet engines as the Air Afrika plane appeared like a silver tube against the hazed and mottled blue of the sky. Arkadin and his men were moments away from landing. Soon the air would be thick with tracer fire, explosions, and shrapnel.

It was time to go to work.

Please tell me this is a joke," Peter Marks said when he and Willard walked into the Mexican restaurant and saw the man sitting alone at the rear banquette. Apart from this figure, Marks and Willard were the only customers in the place. The room smelled of fermented corn and spilled beer.

"I don't make jokes," Willard said.

"That really sucks, especially right at this moment."

"Don't ask me to do better," Willard said with some asperity, "because I can't."

They were in a part of Virginia unknown to Marks. He had no idea a Mexican restaurant would be open for breakfast. Willard raised an arm, a clear invitation for Marks to head on back. The man sitting alone was dressed in an expensive bespoke charcoal-blue suit, a pale blue shirt, and a navy tie with white polka dots. A small enamel replica of the American flag was pinned to his left lapel. He was drinking something out of a tall glass with a sprig of green growing out of the top. A mint julep, Marks would have thought, except that it was seven thirty in the morning.

Despite Willard's pressure, Marks balked. "This man is the enemy, he's the fucking anti-Christ as far as the intelligence community is concerned. His company flouts the law, does all the things we can't do, and gets paid obscene amounts of money to do them. While we slave away in the shit-filled belly of the beast, he's out there buying his Gulfstream Sixes." He shook his head, stubborn to the last. "Really, Freddy, I don't think I can."

"Any route that leads to roadkill—weren't

those your words?" Willard smiled winningly. "Do you want to win this war or do you want to see the Old Man's dream flushed into the NSA recycle bin?" His smile turned encouraging. "One would think that after serving all this time in, as you say, the shit-filled belly of the beast, you might crave a little fresh air. Come on. After the first shock, it won't be so bad."

"Promise, Daddy?"

Willard laughed under his breath. "That's the spirit."

Taking Marks's arm he steered him across the linoleum tiles. As they approached the banquette, the solitary man seemed to appraise them both. With his dark, wavy hair, wide forehead, and rugged features, he looked like a film star; Robert Forster came immediately to mind, but there were bits and pieces of others, Marks was certain.

"Good morning, gentlemen. Please sit down." Oliver Liss not only looked like a film star, he sounded like one. He had a deep, rich voice that rolled out of his throat with controlled power. "I took the liberty of ordering drinks." He lifted his tall, frosty glass as two others were set down in front of Marks and Willard. "It's iced chai with cinnamon and nutmeg." He took a swig of his drink, urging them to do the same. "It's said that nutmeg is a psychedelic in high doses." His smile managed to convey the notion that he'd successfully tried out the theory.

In fact, everything about Oliver Liss exuded success to the most exacting degree. But then he and his two partners hadn't built Black River from the ground up on trust funds and dumb luck. As Marks sipped at his drink, he felt as if a nest of pit vipers had taken up residence in his abdomen. Mentally, he cursed Willard for not preparing him for this meeting. He tried to dredge up everything he'd read or heard about Oliver Liss, and was dismayed to discover that it was precious little. For one thing, the man kept out of the limelight—one of the other partners, Kerry Mangold, was the public face of Black River. For another, very little was known about him. Marks recalled Googling him once and discovering a disconcertingly short bio. Apparently an orphan, Liss was raised in a series of Chicago foster homes until the age of eighteen, when he got his first full-time job working for a building contractor. Apparently the contractor had both contacts and juice, because in no time Liss had begun working in the campaign of the state senator, for whom the contractor had built a twenty-thousand-square-foot home in Highland Park. When the man was elected he took Liss with him to DC, and the rest was, as they say, history. Liss was unmarried, without family affiliations of any kind, at least not that anyone knew about. In short, he lived behind a lead curtain not even the Internet could pierce.

Marks tried not to wince when he drank the chai; he was a coffee drinker and hated any kind of tea, especially ones that tried to masquerade as something else. This one tasted like a cupful of the Ganges.

Someone else might have said, *Do you like it?* just to break the ice, but it seemed Liss was uninterested in icebreaking or any other form of conventional communication. Instead he directed his eyes, the same deep shade of blue as the background of his tie, to Marks and said, "Willard tells me good things about you. Are they true?"

"Willard doesn't lie," Marks said.

This brought the ghost of a smile to

Liss's lips. He continued to sip his vile chai, his gaze never wavering. He seemed not to have to blink, a disconcerting asset in anyone, especially someone in his position.

The food came, then. It appeared as if Liss had ordered not only their drinks but their breakfast as well. This consisted of buttered fresh corn tortillas and scrambled eggs with peppers and onions, drenched in an orange chile sauce that just about incinerated the lining of Marks's mouth. Following the first incautious bite, he swallowed hard and stuffed his face with tortillas and sour cream. Water would just spread the heat from his stomach to his small intestine.

Graciously, Liss waited until Marks's eyes had stopped watering. Then he said, "You're quite right about our Willard. He doesn't lie to his friends," just as if there had been no gap in the conversation. "As for everyone else, well, his lies seem like the soul of truth."

If Willard was flattered by this talk, he gave no indication. Rather, he contented himself by eating his food as slowly and methodically as a priest, his expression Sphinx-like.

"However, if you don't mind," Liss continued, "tell me something about yourself."

"You mean my bio, my curriculum vitae?"

Liss showed his teeth briefly. "Tell me something about yourself I don't know."

Clearly, he meant something personal, something revealing. And it was at this precise moment that Marks realized that Willard had been in discussions with Oliver Liss before this morning, perhaps for some time. *"It's already rebooted,"* Willard had said to him, referring to Treadstone. Once again he felt blindsided by the quarterback of his own team, not a good feeling to have at a meeting with the import of this one.

He shrugged mentally. No use fighting it, he was here, he might as well play out the string. This was Willard's show, anyway, he was just along for the ride. "One week shy of my first wedding anniversary I met someone—a dancer—a ballet dancer, of all things. She was very young, not yet twenty-two, a good twelve years my junior. We saw each other once a week like clockwork for nineteen months and then, just like that, it was over. Her company went on tour to Moscow, Prague, and Warsaw, but that wasn't the reason."

Liss sat back and, drawing out a cigarette, lit it in defiance of the law. *Why should he care?* Marks thought acidly. *He* is *the law.*

"What was the reason?" Liss said in an oddly soft tone of voice.

"To tell you the truth, I don't know." Marks pushed his food around his plate. "It's a funny thing. That heat—one day it was there, the next it wasn't."

Liss blew out a plume of smoke. "I assume you're divorced now."

"I'm not. But I suspect you already knew that."

"Why didn't you and your wife split up?"

This was what Liss's information couldn't tell him. Marks shrugged. "I never stopped loving my wife."

"So she forgave you."

"She never found out," Marks said.

Liss's eyes glittered like sapphires. "You didn't tell her."

"No."

"You never felt the urge to tell her, to confess." He paused reflectively. "Most men would."

"There was nothing to tell her," Marks said. "Something happened to me—like the flu—then it was gone."

"Like it never happened."

Marks nodded. "More or less."

Liss stubbed out his cigarette, turned to Willard, and regarded him for a long moment. "All right," he said. "You have your funding." Then he rose and, without another word, walked out of the restaurant.

It's the oil fields, stupid!" Moira slapped her forehead with the palm of her hand. "Good God, why didn't I see that all along, it's so damn obvious!"

"Obvious now that you know everything," Humphry Bamber said.

They were in Christian Lamontierre's kitchen, eating roast beef and Havarti cheese sandwiches on sprouted-wheat bread Bamber had made from the well-stocked fridge, washed down with Badoit, a French mineral water. Bamber's laptop was on the table in front of them, Bardem up and running through the three scenarios Noah had inputted into the software program.

"I thought the same thing the first time I

read Israel Zangwill's *The Big Bow Mystery.*" Humphry Bamber swallowed a mouthful of sandwich. "It's the first real locked-room mystery, although others as far back as Herodotus in the fifth century BCE, believe it or not, toyed with the idea. But it was Zangwill who in 1892 introduced the concept of misdirection, which became the touchstone for all stories of so-called impossible crimes from then on."

"And Pinprick is classic misdirection." Moira studied the scenarios with mounting fascination and dread. "But on such a massive scale that without Bardem no one would be able to figure out that the real reason for invading Iran was to confiscate their oil fields." She pointed at the screen. "This area—Noah's target area, Shahrake Nasiri-Astara—I've read a couple of intelligence reports about it. At least a third of Iran's oil comes from there." She pointed again. "See how small a geographic area it is? That makes it both vulnerable to an assault by a relatively small force and easily defendable by that same small force. It's perfect for Noah." She shook her head. "My God, this is brilliant—demented, horrific, unthinkable even, but decidedly brilliant."

Bamber went and got another bottle of Badoit out of the fridge. "I don't understand."

"I'm not yet certain of all the details, but what's clear is that Black River has made a deal with the devil. Someone high up in the US government has been pushing for us to do something about Iran's fast-progressing nuclear program, which threatens to destabilize the entire Middle East. We—and other right-minded governments—have been making noises in the correct diplomatic channels for Iran to cease and dismantle its nuclear reactors. Iran's response has been to thumb its nose in our faces. Next, we and our allies tried economic embargoes, which only made Iran laugh because we need their oil, and we're not the only ones. Worse, they have the strategic option of closing down the Straits of Hormuz, which would have the effect of shutting down oil shipments from all the OPEC nations in the region."

She got up and put her plate into the

sink, then returned to the table. "Someone here in Washington decided that patience was getting us nowhere."

Bamber frowned. "And?"

"So they decided to force the issue. They used the downing of our airliner to go to war against Iran, but they're also apparently running a side mission."

"Pinprick."

"Exactly. What Bardem is telling us is that under the chaos of the ground invasion, a small cadre of Black River operatives—with the full consent of the government—is going to take over the oil fields in Shahrake Nasiri-Astara, giving us far more control over our economic destiny. With this Iranian oil, we'll no longer have to kowtow to the Saudis, the Iranians, Venezuela, or any OPEC nation, for that matter. America will be oil-independent."

"But the oil field land-grab is illegal, isn't it?"

"Duh. However, for some reason that doesn't seem to be concerning anyone at the moment."

"Well, what are you going to do now?"

That was, of course, the billion-dollar question. In another time, another place she would have called Ronnie Hart, but Ronnie was dead. Noah—she was quite certain it was Noah—had seen to that. She missed Ronnie now, more than ever, but the selfish reason for her emotion shamed her, and she turned away from the acknowledgment. That's when she thought of Soraya Moore. She'd met Soraya through Bourne, and liked her. That they'd shared a past hadn't bothered her in the slightest; she wasn't the jealous type.

How to get in touch with Soraya? Opening her cell, she called CI headquarters. The director, she was told, was out of the country. When she told the operative that her call was urgent, he told her to wait. A little over sixty seconds later, he was back on the phone.

"Give me the number where Director Moore can reach you," he said.

Moira recited her cell phone number and cut the connection, fully expecting that her request would be promptly lost in the maze of paperwork and requests that must constantly flood Soraya's electronic in box. She was therefore stunned when her cell phone rang ten minutes later, showing an OUT OF AREA logo on her tiny screen.

She put the cell to her ear. "Hello?"

"Moira? It's Soraya Moore. Where are you? Are you in trouble?"

Moira laughed in relief to hear the other woman's voice. "I'm in DC and yes, I've been in trouble, and out. Listen, I have some news for you." Quickly and methodically, she started at the beginning, outlining what she knew about Jay Weston's murder—and what she was now certain was Steve Stevenson's murder—as well as what she knew of Ronnie Hart's death. "It all boils down to this software program Noah Perlis commissioned." She went on to describe what Bardem did, how she had obtained a copy of it, and what it had revealed about Black River's plans to confiscate the Iranian oil fields.

"What I can't figure is how such a complex plan could have been hatched after the terrorist attack on the airplane outside Cairo."

"It wasn't," Soraya said. "I'm currently in Khartoum and here's why." And she told Moira what she and Amun Chalthoum had discovered regarding the Iranian Kowsar 3 missile and the four-man American cadre that had smuggled it over the Sudanese border into Egypt. "So you see it's bigger even than Black River and elements inside the government. Even Noah couldn't have gotten to Nikolai Yevsen without the help of the Russians."

Now Moira understood why no one was concerned about the illegality of the oil field land-grab. If the Russians were in on Pinprick they would deflect world opinion in the right direction.

"Moira," Soraya said now, "we found the four men outside Khartoum. They were shot once in the head, execution-style, and their bodies dumped in with quicklime. But we managed to salvage something odd from each of them. They look like dog tags, only the writing on them is enciphered."

Moira felt her heart thumping hard in her chest. "They sound like the tags Black River gives to its field personnel."

"Then we could prove it was Black River personnel who fired that missile. We could avert this ill-advised and self-serving war."

"I'd have to see them to make sure," Moira said.

"I'll overnight them to you," Soraya said.

"My pal here tells me he can expedite the shipment so you'll get the tags tomorrow morning."

"That would be fantastic. If they are what they seem to be, I can get them processed in hours. I'll just have to make sure they're delivered into the right hands."

"That wouldn't be CI," Soraya said. "There's a new director, M. Errol Danziger. Though his appointment hasn't yet been officially announced, he's already taken over—and he's Secretary Halliday's man." She took a breath. "Listen, do you need protection? I can have some of my people to wherever you are within twenty minutes."

"Thanks very much, but the way things are going the fewer people who know where I am, the better."

"Understood." There was another, longer pause. "I've been thinking a lot about Jason recently."

"Me, too." Moira was thinking how happy she was that Jason wasn't a part of all this. He needed his time to heal, both physically and mentally. Being a hairbreadth from dying wasn't something you got over in a few weeks or even months.

"There's a lot about him to remember."

Half a world away, Soraya was thinking she'd call Jason and update him just as soon she concluded this conversation.

"You and I share that, don't we?"

"Don't forget about him, Moira," Soraya said just before she rang off.

33

Arkadin, alighting from the Air Afrika jet, despised Noah Perlis on sight. For that reason, he was at his most cordial when he, at the head of his twenty-man cadre, met with the Black River operative. At the same time, he was trying his best to ignore the eerie similarities between this section of Iran and Nizhny Tagil, with its sulfurous stench, the particulate-filled air, the ring of oil wells that seemed so much like the guard towers on the high-security prisons surrounding his home city.

The rest of Arkadin's contingent was still

in the plane, where they were looking after the pilot and navigator, as they had the entire flight, to make sure they didn't warn anyone about the larger-than-normal cargo. At a prearranged signal, the men would come pouring out of the belly of the plane, not unlike the Greek warriors who had been taken inside the impregnable walls of Troy in the wooden horse.

"It's good to meet you at last, Leonid Danilovich," Perlis said in passable Russian as he gripped Arkadin's hand. "Your reputation precedes you."

Arkadin smiled his most welcoming smile and said, "I think you ought to know Jason Bourne is here—"

"What?" Perlis looked as if the world had dropped away from him. "What did you say?"

"—or if he isn't here yet, he soon will be." Arkadin kept the smile on his face even as Perlis tried to yank his hand away from the death grip Arkadin had on it. "It was Bourne who infiltrated the Air Afrika building in Khartoum. I know you must have been wondering who it was."

Perlis appeared to be struggling to

understand what Arkadin was up to. "That's nonsense. Bourne is dead."

"On the contrary." Arkadin jerked back hard on Perlis's trapped hand. "And I ought to know. I shot Bourne in Bali. I, too, thought he'd died, but, like me, he's a survivor, a man with nine lives."

"Even if all this is true, how would you know Bourne was in Khartoum, let alone at the Air Afrika building?"

"It's my business to know these things, Perlis." He laughed. "Now I'm being coy. Actually, I sent Bourne on a course expressly designed to lead him to Khartoum, to the Air Afrika building, to—and this is most important of all—Nikolai Yevsen."

"Yevsen is at the heart of our plan, why would you do such an idiotic—"

"I wanted Bourne to kill Yevsen. And that's precisely what he did." Arkadin's smile spread all the way up to his eyes. *This arrogant American looks good with all the blood drained from his face,* he thought. "I have all of Yevsen's computer files—all his contacts, clients, and suppliers. Not that that's a wide circle of people, as you can imagine, but by now they've all been informed of Nikolai Yevsen's death. They've also been told they'll be dealing with me from now on."

"You—you're taking over Yevsen's business?" Despite what he'd just heard, Perlis couldn't stop himself from laughing in Arkadin's brutal face. "You have delusions of grandeur, my friend. You're nothing but an uneducated, low-IQ Russian hood who's inexplicably come into some good luck. But in this business good luck will get you only so far, then it's time for the professionals to take you out."

Arkadin resisted the urge to turn the American's face into bloody pulp. That time would come, but first he required an audience for what he was about to do. Still holding on to Perlis's hand, he thumbed open his cell phone and sent a three-digit text message. A moment later the belly of the Air Afrika jet seemed to split open with the remaining eighty men in Arkadin's private army.

"What's this?" Perlis said, as he watched his own personnel being overpowered, disarmed, thrown to the ground, where they were systematically bound and gagged.

"It isn't only Yevsen's business I'm taking over, Mr. Perlis, it's these oil fields. What's yours is now mine."

The Russian Mi-28 Havoc combat helicopter carrying Bourne and Colonel Boris Karpov, two of his men, as well as a two-man crew and a full complement of weapons, banked low over the Iranian oil fields in Shahrake Nasiri-Astara, and immediately they saw the two planes—one the Air Afrika jet Karpov's IT man in Khartoum had tracked here, the other a Sikorsky S-70 Black Hawk painted matte black but with no markings: Black River transport.

"According to my intel in Moscow, the American-led allied forces have not yet crossed over into Iranian territory," Karpov said. "We may still have time to avert this catastrophe."

"If I know anything about Noah Perlis, he's sure to have made contingency plans." Bourne, peering down at the swiftly changing terrain, was mulling over everything Soraya had told him. At last he had all the pieces of the puzzle, save one: Arkadin's angle. He had to have one, Bourne was as certain of that as he was of anything in this delicately constructed spider's web.

And there was the spider, he thought, as the Havoc swept down like a bat out of hell, passing directly over the figures of Arkadin and Perlis. As Karpov directed the pilot to land, Bourne felt the deep throbbing pain in his chest wound, returning like an old enemy to dog him. Ignoring it, he tried to work out what was going on. Five men and one woman were lying facedown on the ground, trussed like suckling pigs ready for the rotisserie. Bourne counted a hundred heavily armed men in camo uniforms that were clearly not American military issue.

"What the fuck is happening down there?" Boris had just now switched his attention to the same scene that absorbed Bourne. "And there's that fucker, Arkadin." He clenched his fist. "How I want his nuts in a sling, and now by God I'll have them."

By this time the Havoc had come under small-arms fire and the pilot, sitting in his raised cabin in the rear, was taking evasive maneuvers, the two TV3-117VMA turboshaft engines whining in response. Neither Bourne nor Karpov was particularly concerned by the semi-automatic fire, since the Havoc was outfitted with an armored cabin able to withstand the impact of 7.62 and 12.7mm bullets as well as 20mm shell fragments.

"Are you all set?" Karpov asked Bourne. "You look ready for anything, just like an American should." And he laughed tonelessly.

The weapons man yelled a warning. Looking to where he was pointing, they saw one of the men slide a Redeye missile into its launcher, and his compatriot swing it up onto his shoulder, aim it at them, and pull the trigger.

The moment Arkadin saw the Redeye rammed home into its launcher, he delivered a vicious uppercut to Perlis's jaw and, releasing his hand as the American went down, ran toward the man who was about to fire at the Havoc. He shouted for the man to stop, but it was useless, the noise of the helicopter rotors was too loud. He knew what had happened. His men had seen the Russian combat Havoc and had reacted instinctively against an enemy.

The Redeye shot into the air, detonating

against the Havoc's fuel tanks. That was a mistake because the Havoc's tanks were insulated with polyurethane foam to protect them from being set on fire. Plus, any rents in the tanks themselves were instantly closed with latex in the self-healing covers. Even if the blast had ruptured one of the fuel lines, which seemed likely because the Havoc was at a low altitude when it was hit, the fuel feed system operated in a vacuum, which prevented the fuel from leaking into areas where it could be ignited.

In the aftermath of the hit, the Havoc swung back and forth like a disoriented insect; then what Arkadin feared most happened: two Shturm anti-tank missiles streaked out from the underbelly of the wounded Havoc toward the surface. The resulting detonations took out three-quarters of Arkadin's cadre.

Bourne, thrown face-first against a bulkhead, felt the explosion of pain in his chest radiating out into his arms. For an instant he thought the trauma to his wound had caused a heart attack. Then he got himself under control, mentally tamped down on the pain, and, extending a hand, pulled Karpov off the deck of the Havoc. Smoke drifted into the cabin, which made it more difficult for him to catch his breath, but it wasn't immediately clear whether it was from damage the helicopter had sustained or from the shallow craters on the ground where the Shturms had struck.

"Set this bucket down, and I mean now!" Karpov ordered over the racket of the engines.

The pilot, who had been battling the controls ever since they were hit, nodded and they descended vertically. The moment they made contact with a bone-rattling jar, Karpov wrenched the door open and dropped to the ground. Bourne followed him with a grimace of pain. His breath was hot in his throat. Both of them ran, crouched over, under the aircraft's wind-sweep, until they were outside the circumference of the rotors.

What they came upon was hell on earth. Or, rather, war. In the air, the virile whoosh of the missiles had been exhilarating, especially as retaliation for the first strike, but here on the ground, without the cool detachment of a God's-eye view, all was devastation. Great mounds of black earth, scorched and smoking as if from the pits of the underworld, half-covered random bits and pieces of bodies, as if some insane creature had decided to improve on the human form by first dismantling it. The stench of roasted flesh mingled with the foul odors of excrement and exploded ordnance.

To Bourne, the scene had the nightmarish quality of Goya's half-mad Black Paintings come to life. When so much death presented itself, when all was horror in every direction, the mind interpreted it as surreal in order not to go mad.

The two men spotted Arkadin at the same time and took off after him. The problem was that the pain in Bourne's chest was growing in size and heat. Whereas only moments before it had seemed to be the size of a pinball it now seemed larger than a fist. It seemed, moreover, to have encompassed his heart. As he went down on one knee, he saw Karpov vanish into a plume of black, oily smoke. He couldn't see Arkadin, but what was left of his cadre was engaged with the Iranian oil field guards in a pitched hand-to-hand battle for every inch of territory that hadn't been turned into an infernal pit. As for the Black River operatives, none that he could see remained alive, having been either killed in the missile attack or executed by Arkadin's forces. All was chaos.

Bourne forced himself to his feet, staggering past the bodies into the curling smoke that reached up into the sky. What he encountered on the other side was not encouraging. Boris lay on the slope of one of the craters, one leg at an unnatural angle underneath the other. White bone shone through. Standing astride him was Leonid Danilovich Arkadin. In Arkadin's hand was a .38 SIG Sauer.

"You thought you could fuck me up, Colonel, but I've waited a long time for this moment." Arkadin's voice could just be heard over the screams and the harsh, rat-a-tat sounds of weapons of war. "And now my time is here."

He turned abruptly, facing Bourne, and a slow smile spread across his face as he squeezed off three shots in a tight triangle into Bourne's chest.

34

Bourne was blown back off his feet by the concussion of the bullets striking him. Searing pain racked him; he must have passed out for a moment, because the next thing he knew Arkadin had climbed up to the lip of the crater, looking down at him with an odd expression that might have been pity or even disappointment.

"Here we are," he said as he walked toward Bourne. "Karpov isn't going anywhere and Perlis's men are dead, if not buried. They're both dead men. So now it's just you and me, the first and last Treadstone graduates. But you're on the verge of death as well, aren't you?" He crouched down. "You are complicit in Devra's death and I made you pay, but there's something I want to know before you die. How many more graduates are there? Ten? Twenty? More?"

Bourne could barely speak, he felt paralyzed. There was blood all over the front of the jacket Boris had given him.

"I don't know," he managed to get out. Breathing was more difficult than he'd expected, and the pain was incredible. Now that he was in the center of the web, now that he had found the clever spider who crouched there spinning his intricate strands, he felt helpless.

"You don't know." Arkadin cocked his head to one side, mocking him. "Well, here's what I know and, unlike you, I don't mind sharing. I imagine you think I hired the Torturer, but nothing could be farther from the truth. Why would I hire someone to do something I'm itching to do myself? Doesn't make sense, does it? But here's what does make sense: The Torturer was hired by Willard. Yes, that's right, the man who remade you in Bali, after you somehow survived a bullet to the heart. How did you manage that, by the way? Never mind. In a moment, when you're dead, it'll be irrelevant."

Ordnance—mortars perhaps—from the Iranians came whistling through the sky, detonating at two different flanking points not a hundred yards away. Arkadin never flinched or even blinked. He merely waited for an abatement of the screaming.

"Where was I? Oh, yes, Willard. Here's another news flash for you: Willard knew I was alive and that I was the one who'd pulled the trigger in Bali. How did he know? The typical Treadstone way, he interrogated the man I hired to make sure you were really dead. He called me on my own man's cell, can you believe the balls on that fuck!"

Not far away, aircraft engines whined into life. The Black Hawk's rotors started spinning. Now Bourne knew where Perlis had gone.

"I imagine you're wondering why he didn't tell you? Because he was testing you—just like he was testing me. He wanted to see how long it would take you to find out about me because he already knew how long it took me to find out about you." Arkadin sat back on his heels. “Clever little fucker, I’ll give him that.

“Well, now that we’ve gotten to know each other a little better, it’s time to end it. There’s only so much time I can spend with my doppelgänger without getting sick to my stomach.”

He got to his feet. “I’d make you crawl, but I’m quite sure in your condition you can’t manage it.”

That was when Bourne rose up as if he’d returned from the dead, and lunged at him.

Arkadin, in shock, raised the SIG and fired. Once again Bourne was knocked off his feet, once again he rose to one knee and then to his feet.

“Good Christ!” Arkadin said. His eyes harbored a hunted and dangerous look. “What the fuck are you?”

Bourne reached out and grabbed at the gun. At precisely that moment, a shot rang out, spinning Arkadin around. Blood leaked from a wound in his shoulder. He shouted, struck out at Bourne, then fired off two shots at Boris Karpov who, despite his broken leg, had crawled up the side of the charred crater. Arkadin's SIG clicked hollowly; the magazine was empty.

The Black Hawk lifted off and, swinging around, began a raking fire of machine-gun bursts at the remaining members of Arkadin's cadre. It made no difference to the Black River gunner aboard the helicopter that Arkadin's men were still engaged with the Iranian guards—both were being systematically mowed down.

Throwing the useless SIG into Bourne's face, Arkadin raced toward what remained of his men. Bourne took three steps after him and fell to his knees. His heart felt as if it was about to burst. Despite the Kevlar vest and packets of pig blood Karpov had insisted he put on under his jacket, the impact of the four shots Arkadin had fired at him had torn open his original wound. He could barely catch his breath.

The Black Hawk was swinging around for another run at the men on the ground, but now Arkadin had slammed a missile into the shoulder launcher. Bourne knew that it was imperative for Arkadin to protect what was left of his cadre—without them, there was nothing he could do here. He couldn't hold the oil fields by himself. His only chance now was to bring the Black Hawk down.

With an extreme force of will, he rose and loped toward a tangle of dead soldiers. Picking up an AK-47, he aimed it at Arkadin and pulled the trigger. The magazine was empty. Throwing it aside, he wrenched a Luger from a holster on one of the soldiers, checked that it was loaded, and ran toward where Arkadin stood, spread-legged, the rocket launcher on his right shoulder.

Bursts of machine-gun fire from the Black Hawk tracered through the air as Bourne ran and squeezed the Luger's trigger, forcing Arkadin to fire the missile at a run. Possibly the launcher had sustained damage or else the missile itself was defective because it missed the helicopter. Without breaking stride, Arkadin tossed aside the launcher and, with almost the same motion, ripped a submachine gun out of a fallen soldier's grip. He fired at Bourne on the run, forcing Bourne to scramble for cover. Arkadin kept firing until the clip ran out, then Bourne was up and running, though he could scarcely catch his breath. He fired, still on the run, but

Arkadin was lost in a plume of dense black smoke. Above their heads the Black River helicopter lifted away in the direction of the oil wells.

There were no Black River personnel left alive that Bourne could see, and Arkadin's cadre lay strewn on the smoking ground. Bourne ran into the smoke and immediately his eyes began to tear; his breath felt ragged in his throat as his lungs labored. In that moment he sensed something coming at him from out of the swirling blackness, and he ducked, but not quite in time.

Arkadin's two-handed blow caught him on the shoulder, spinning him around. For the moment, the Luger was useless, and Arkadin delivered a punch to the side of Bourne's head, staggering him further. Bourne felt as if both his head and his chest were about to explode, but when Arkadin lunged for the Luger, he struck out with the barrel, flaying open a long bloody wound on Arkadin's cheek, so deep he could see bone.

Arkadin reeled backward into the thick black pall, and Bourne squeezed off the Luger's last three rounds. He careered through the smoke, searching for his foe, coming at last out of the plume. He turned in all directions, but Arkadin was nowhere to be seen.

All at once he was on his knees, felled by the pain in his chest. His head hung down, the agony all-encompassing. In his mind he saw the fire creeping through him, threatening to consume him, and he thought of what Tracy had said as she lay in his arms, dying: *"It's in our darkest hour that our secrets eat us alive."*

And then in the center of that fire a face appeared—a face made of fire. It was the face of Shiva, the god of destruction and resurrection. Was it Shiva who lifted him to his feet? He'd never know, because one moment he was on the verge of collapse, the next he stood swaying on his feet.

And it was then that he saw Boris lying at the edge of the crater, his head covered in blood.

Ignoring his own pain, Bourne dug his hands under Karpov's armpits and hauled him up. Then, with the tracers buzzing through the air overhead, he dipped his knees and threw Boris over his shoulder.

Gritting his teeth, he began to pick his way past the dead and the dying, the still-smoldering remnants of human beings, toward the Russian helicopter.

Several times, he was forced to stop either by the hail of machine-gun fire or by the pain that gripped his heart like a vise cinched so tight he could scarcely breathe. Once, he went down on one knee, and the blackened hand of a soldier—of which side it was impossible to tell—grabbed at the fabric of his trousers. Bourne tried to brush it away, but the fingers stuck to him like glue. All around him half-shattered faces seemed to turn to him, shrieking in the silent agony of their death throes. They were all the same now, these victims of violence that was always, at heart, senseless. Their allegiances were rendered irrelevant by chaos, blood, and fire, erasing not only their humanity but also their beliefs—that one thing that drove them, whether it be politics, religion, or simply money. They were all jumbled together under a lowering sky filled with the ashes of their compatriots and their enemies.

Finally, he peeled the soldier's grip off him and, rising unsteadily, continued on his agonizing journey over the blasted landscape. Visibility was now an issue, what with the oily smoke that choked the already filthy air. As if in a dream, the Russian helicopter seemed to fade in and out of focus, to be at first near at hand, then thousands of yards distant. He ran, stopped, crouched over, panting, then ran on again, feeling like Sisyphus rolling the boulder up the hill but never getting to the top. His goal still seemed a mile away, and so he kept on, one foot in front of the other, stumbling and loping with his ungainly burden, zigzagging through the zone of death this mini-war had produced. And at last, lungs bursting, eyes tearing, he saw Boris's men pour out of the shelter of the helicopter to meet him and their fallen commander. They took him off Bourne's numb shoulder, and he fell to his knees. Two of Boris's men lifted him to his feet and fed him water.

But more bad news awaited him here. Boris's crew had been forced to abandon the Havoc, which had been rendered inoperable by the missile strike. Bourne, looking around while he tried to regain his breath, directed them to the Air Afrika jet, sitting idle three hundred yards away.

They encountered no one around the jet or on the gangway. The door gaped open. Inside, they discovered why: The crew had been bound and gagged, presumably by Arkadin and his cadre. Bourne gave the order to free them.

They lay the colonel down on the floor of the Air Afrika jet and the medic crouched over him, beginning his examination.

After five anxious minutes, when he tested and probed, he looked up at Bourne and the men hovering around. "The leg is a simple break and is no problem," he said. "As for his wound, it could have been worse. The bullet grazed the side of his head, but didn't crack the skull. That's the good news." His hands continued to work on his fallen commander. "The bad news is he's got a serious concussion. Pressure is building in his brain; I'm going to have to relieve it by drilling a small hole"—he pointed to a spot on Boris's right temple—"just here." He took a closer look at Bourne and clucked his tongue. "Still and all, I can only do triage. We need to get him to a hospital as quickly as possible."

Bourne went up front and gave the Air Afrika pilot and navigator orders to take them back to Khartoum. At once, they began their pre-flight checklist. The engines came on one by one.

"Please strap yourself in," the medic said when Bourne returned. "I'll see to you as soon as I've got Colonel Karpov's condition stabilized."

Bourne was in no condition to argue. He collapsed into a seat, stripped off his jacket and the spent packets of pig blood Arkadin's bullets had ripped open. He said a silent prayer to the spirit of the pig who'd given its life to spare his own, and could not help seeing in his mind's eye the great carved pig at the pool in Bali.

He unstrapped the Kevlar vest and buckled up, but his gaze never left Karpov's prone form. He looked deathly pale, there was blood all over him, and for the first time in Bourne's spotty memory he looked truly vulnerable. Bourne found himself wondering whether he'd looked like that to Moira after he'd been shot in Tenganan.

As they began to roll down the runway, he had the presence of mind to call Soraya on his sat phone and tell her what happened.

"I'll get to General LeBowe, who's commanding the allied forces, and tell him to stand down," Soraya said. "He's a good man, he'll listen. Especially when I tell him that by tomorrow morning we'll have enough hard evidence to prove it was Black River, not Iranian terrorists, who fired the Kowsar 3."

"A lot of people in the US government are going to have egg on their faces," Bourne said wearily.

"With what we have, I'm hoping more than egg for some of them," Soraya said. "Anyway, it wouldn't be the first time and it sure as hell won't be the last."

He heard three huge blasts from somewhere outside. Looking through the Perspex window he saw Perlis's parting gift: the Black Hawk had fired missiles into each of the wells. They were now all on fire. Doubtless this was his way of ensuring that, even if he survived, Arkadin wouldn't get his hands on them.

"Jason, you told me Colonel Karpov will be okay, but are you all right?"

Bourne, sitting in the cabin of the jet that was just now airborne, had no idea what to say.

How many times do you have to die, he thought, *before you learn how to live?*

The moment Moira ripped open the package Soraya had sent her and pulled out the titanium tags, she knew she had the last piece of physical evidence to take Noah and Black River down. The tags were Black River, all right. After she had decoded them, had gotten the names and serial numbers of the four operatives, she took the tags and Humphry Bamber's laptop with Bardem to the only person she knew she could absolutely trust: Frederick Willard.

Willard accepted her evidence with a controlled amount of glee and, it seemed to her, a curious equanimity that spoke of a degree of foreknowledge. In due course Willard presented the evidence against Black River to a multiplicity of sources, to ensure the evidence would not somehow be deliberately mislaid or otherwise disposed of.

Soraya and Amun Chalthoum returned to Cairo. Despite the fact that Soraya's people had gathered compelling evidence on the identity of Chalthoum's enemy, it was not a happy time for them personally. Soraya knew that he'd never leave Egypt, that he felt comfortable only in his homeland. Besides, he still had political battles to fight here, and she knew that even if she hadn't helped him, he'd never run away from them. She also knew that she'd never leave America to live here with him.

"What are we going to do, Amun?" she said.

"I don't know, *azizti*. I love you in a way I've never loved anyone in my life. The thought of losing you is unbearable." He took her hand. "Move here. Live with me. We'll get married and you'll have babies and we'll raise them together."

She laughed and shook her head. "You know I wouldn't be happy here."

"But think how beautiful our children will be, *azizti*!"

She laughed again. "Idiot!" She kissed him on the lips. She'd meant it as a friendly kiss, but it turned into something else, something deeper, something ecstatic, and it lasted a long time.

When at last they broke apart, she said, "I have an idea. We'll meet once a year for a week, a different place each year, or wherever you wish."

He looked at her for a long time. "*Azizti,* there is nothing else for us, is there?"

"Isn't this enough? This has to be enough, you must see that."

"I see very clearly." He sighed and held her tight. "We'll make it enough, won't we?"

Three days later the Black River scandal hit the Internet and newswires with the force of a hurricane, overshadowing even the disbanding of the allied forces on Iran's borders, which had already been parsed to death by the news media's talking heads.

"This is it," Peter Marks told Willard, "both Black River and Secretary Halliday are going down."

He was surprised when Willard gave him an inscrutable look. "I hope you're not eager to back out of our deal, princeling."

That cryptic remark became clear when, hours later, Secretary of Defense Bud Halliday held a press conference condemning Black River's role in what he termed "a stupefying abuse of power that goes so far beyond the parameters of the company's stated mission that steps are being taken to dismantle it. I've spoken personally to the attorney general, who confirmed to me that both civil and criminal charges are at this moment being prepared against members of Black River, including the principals. I want to make perfectly clear to the American people that the NSA hired Black River in good faith on the basis of that organization's assurances that they had met with and had come to an agreement with leaders of a pro-democracy group inside Iran. Documentation was provided as to dates, times, names of the principals, and issues discussed, all of which I have turned over to the attorney general as evidence against Black River. I want to assure the American people that at no time did I or anyone in the NSA know that this was a total fabrication on the part of Black River. To that end, a blue-ribbon panel is at this moment being created to investigate the entire matter. My pledge to you today is that the perpetrators of this unthinkable plot will be punished to the full extent of the law."

Not surprisingly, no link was ever discovered between the NSA, let alone Halliday himself, and Black River other than the one he publicly described. And to Marks's astonishment, the principals charged by the attorney general were Kerry Mangold and Dick Braun. Nowhere was there a mention of Oliver Liss, the third member of Black River's triumvirate.

When Marks asked Willard about this, he received the same inscrutable look, which sent him scrambling to Google stories on Black River. What he discovered, after an exhaustive search, was a small article buried in *The Washington Post* of several weeks back. It seemed that Oliver Liss had tendered his resignation without notice from the company he had helped found "for personal reasons." Try as he might, Marks could find no mention anywhere of what those personal reasons might be.

That's when Willard, with a Cheshire Cat grin, told him there weren't any.

"I trust you're ready to start work," Willard said, "because Treadstone is back in business."

35

On a magnificent sunny day in Bali when May had just begun to bud, Suparwita arrived at the sacred temple of Pura Lempuyang. Not a cloud was in the sky as he climbed the dragon staircase and passed through the carved stone portal to the second temple high on the mountainside. Mount Agung, clear, completely free of clouds, and blue as the Strait of Lombok, rose up in all its splendor. Then, as Suparwita made his way toward a group of kneeling penitents, a shadow fell across the stones and he saw that Noah Perlis was waiting for him.

"You don't look surprised." Perlis wore

his Balinese sarong and T-shirt as uncomfortably as a drug addict wears a suit.

"Why would I be surprised," Suparwita said, "when I knew you would return?"

"I had nowhere else to go. Back in the States I'm a wanted man. I'm a fugitive now, that's what you wanted, isn't it?"

"I meant for you to be an outcast," Suparwita said. "The two are not the same."

Perlis sneered. "You think you can punish me?"

"I have no need of punishing you."

"I should have killed you when I had the chance, years ago."

Suparwita regarded him with his large liquid eyes. "It wasn't enough that you killed Holly?"

Perlis appeared startled. "You have no proof of that."

"I don't need what you call proof. I know what happened."

Perlis took a step toward him. "Which is what, exactly?"

"You followed Holly Marie Moreau back here from Europe. What you were doing with her there I can't presume to know."

"Why not?" The sneer hadn't left Perlis's face. "You claim to know everything else."

"Why did you follow Holly back here, Mr. Perlis?"

Perlis kept his mouth shut, then he shrugged as if feeling that it no longer mattered. "She had come into possession of something of mine."

"And how did that happen?"

"She stole it, goddammit! I came back here to retrieve what was mine. I had every right—"

"To kill her?"

"I was going to say that I had every right to take back what she had stolen. Her death was an accident."

"You killed her without purpose," Suparwita said.

"I got it back from her. I got what I wanted."

"But of what use was it? Did you ever crack its secret?"

Perlis remained silent. If he knew how to mourn, he would have done so already.

"This is why you've come back here," Suparwita said, "not just to Bali, but to the very spot where you murdered Holly."

Perlis suddenly experienced a flicker of anger. "Are you a policeman now as well as a holy man or whatever it is you call yourself?"

Suparwita produced the ghost of a smile that held nothing for Perlis to cling to. "I think it's fair to say that what Holly took from you, you yourself stole."

Perlis went white. "How could you possibly . . . how could you possibly know that?" he whispered.

"Holly told me. How else?"

"Holly didn't know that, only I knew it." He tossed his head contemptuously. "Anyway, I didn't come here to be interrogated."

"Do you know now why you came?" Suparwita's eyes burned so brightly their fire was scarcely dimmed by the sun.

"No."

"But you do." Suparwita raised an arm, pointing to the bulk of Mount Agung rising in the stone archway.

Perlis turned to look, shading his eyes from the glare, but when he turned back Suparwita had vanished. The people were still at their endless praying, the priest was absorbed in God alone knew what, and the man beside him was counting his money in a mesmerizingly slow, even rhythm.

Then, as if without his own volition, Perlis found himself walking toward Mount Agung, the carved stone gate, and the top of the stairs where, years before, Holly Marie Moreau had been sent to her death.

Perlis awoke with a shout of false denial trapped in his throat. Despite the air-conditioning of his room, he was sweating. He had bolted to a sitting position from a deep sleep or, more accurately, from the deep dream of Suparwita and Pura Lempuyang. He felt the pain around his pumping heart that always accompanied the aftermath of these dreams.

For a moment, he couldn't recall where he was. He'd been on the run ever since he'd ordered the Iranian oil fields set on fire. What had gone wrong? He'd asked himself that painful question a thousand times and finally, he was left with one answer: Bardem had failed to predict this outcome because of the introduction of two almost identical variables outside the million parameters with which it had been programmed—Bourne and Arkadin. In the world of finance, the appearance of a game-changing event that no one was anticipating was called a Black Swan. In the hermetic world of esoteric software programmers, a circumstance outside the parameters that crashed the program was called Shiva, the Hindu god of destruction. For one Shiva to appear was rare enough, but two was unthinkable.

Days and nights had passed as if in one of Perlis's dreams; often now he was unsure as to which was a dream and which waking life. In any event, nothing seemed real anymore, not the food he ate, the places in which he stayed, the shallow sleep he managed to snatch. Then yesterday he'd arrived in Bali, and for the first time since the Black Hawk lifted off from the ruins of Pinprick, something changed inside him. His work at Black River had been his family, his comrades—he was able to see nothing beyond its parameters. Now, without it, he had ceased to exist. But no, it was far worse than that, because come to think of it, for all the time he'd worked at Black River, he'd made himself cease to exist. He'd reveled in all the roles he'd had to play because they took him further and further away from himself, a person he'd never liked or had much use for. It was the real Noah Perlis—pathetic weakling that he was, not heard from since his childhood—who had fallen in love with Moira. Joining Black River was like donning armor, a protection against the weakling full of feelings that lurked like a spineless wretch inside him. Now that he no longer had Black River, he'd been stripped of that armor, and his little pink mewling self was exposed. A switch had been thrown, from positive to negative, and all the energy that used to come to him was flowing out of him.

He swung his legs out of bed and walked to the window. What was it about this place? He'd been to many paradisiacal islands in his time—spots strewn all across the globe in diamond-like glitter. But Bali seemed to throb against his eyes with an ethereal presence. He was a man who did not believe in the ethereal. Even as a child, he'd been pragmatic. He had spent virtually his entire adult life isolated, without family or friends; a situation entirely of his own making, since both friends and family had the habit of betraying you without even knowing it. Early on in his life, he'd discovered that if you felt nothing you couldn't get hurt. Nevertheless, he had been hurt, not only by Moira.

He showered and dressed, then went out into the moist heat and the glare. The sky was precisely as cloudless as it had been in his dream. In the far distance, he could see the blue bulk of Mount Agung, a place of eternal mystery to him, and of fear, because it seemed to him that something he didn't want to know about himself dwelled on that mountain. This thing—whatever it was—drew him as powerfully as it repelled him. He tried to regain some semblance of equilibrium, to push down the emotions that had erupted inside him, but he couldn't. The fucking horses had bolted from the stable and without the iron discipline of Black River, without his armor, there was no getting them back in. He stared down at his hands, which shook as violently as if he had the DTs.

What's happening to me? he thought. But he knew that wasn't the right question to ask.

"Why did you come?" That was the right

question, the one Suparwita had asked him in his dream. From what he'd read on the subject all the people in your dreams were aspects of yourself. This being so, he had been asking himself the question. Why *had* he returned to Bali? When he'd left after Holly Marie's death he was certain that he'd never return. And yet, here he was. Moira had hurt him, it was true, but what had happened with Holly had hurt him most of all.

He ate a meal without tasting it, and by the time he had reached his destination, he could not have said what it was. His stomach felt neither full nor empty. Like the rest of him, it seemed to have ceased to exist.

Holly Marie Moreau was buried in a small *sema*—cemetery—southwest of the village where she'd been raised. As a rule, modern-day Balinese cremated their dead, but there were pockets of people—original Balinese like those in Tenganan, those who weren't Hindu—who did not. Balinese believed that seaward-west was the direction of hell, so *sema* were always built—when they were built at all—to the seaward-west of the village. Here, in the south of Bali, that was southwest. The Balinese were terrified of cemeteries, certain that the uncremated bodies were the undead, wandering around at night, being raised from their graves by evil spirits, led by Rudra, the god of evil. Consequently, the place was utterly abandoned—even, it appeared, by birds and wildlife.

Thick stands of trees were everywhere, casting the *sema* in deepest shadow, so that it seemed lost in the inky blues and greens of a perpetual twilight. Apart from one grave site, the place had a distinctly unkempt aspect that bordered on the disreputable. This particular grave site bore the headstone of Holly Marie Moreau.

For what seemed an eternity, Perlis stood staring at the slab of marble engraved with her name and dates of birth and death. Beneath the impersonal information was one word: BELOVED.

As with whatever was waiting for him on Mount Agung, he felt an inexorable pull and repulsion toward her grave. He walked slowly and deliberately, his pace seemingly dictated by the beat of his heart. All at once, he stopped, having glimpsed, or thought he glimpsed, a shadow darker than the others flit from tree to tree. Was it something or nothing, a trick of the crepuscular light? He thought of the gods and demons said to inhabit *semas* and laughed to himself. Then he saw the shadow, more clearly this time. He could not make out the face but saw the long, streaming hair of a young woman or a girl. *The undead,* he told himself, as a continuation of the joke. He was quite close to Holly's grave, practically standing on top of it, and he looked around, concerned enough to draw his gun, wondering if the *sema* was as deserted as it appeared.

Making up his mind at last, he went past the gravestone, picking his way through the trees, following the direction of the girl-shadow he'd seen, or thought he'd seen. The land rose quickly to a ridge, more heavily forested than that of the *sema.* He paused at the crest for a moment, unsure which way to go because his view was obstructed by trees stretching away in every direction. Then, out of the corner of his eye, he saw another flicker of movement, and he turned his head like a dog on point. Only a bird, perhaps? But cocking an ear, he heard no birdsong, no rustle of leaves in the underbrush.

He pushed on, following the flicker, walking sure-footedly down into a steep-sided ravine filled with even thicker stands of trees.

Then, up ahead, he saw her hair flying, and he called her name though it was foolish and completely unlike him.

"Holly!"

Holly was dead, of course. He knew that better than anyone else alive, but this was Bali and anything was possible. He began to run after her, his legs and heart pumping. He ran between two trees and then something slammed the back of his head. He pitched forward into blackness.

Who knew her better," said a voice in his head, "you or me?"

Perlis opened his eyes and, through the pain dizzying him, saw Jason Bourne.

"You! How did you know I'd be here?"

Bourne smiled. "This is your last stop, Noah. The end of the line."

Perlis glanced around. "That girl—I saw a girl."

"Holly Marie Moreau."

Perlis saw his gun lying on the ground and lunged for it.

Bourne kicked him so hard, the crack of two ribs echoed off the tree branches. Perlis groaned.

"Tell me about Holly."

Perlis stared up at Bourne. He could not keep the grimace of pain off his face, but at least he didn't cry out. Then a thought occurred to him.

"You don't remember her, do you?" Perlis tried to laugh. "Oh, this is too good!"

Bourne knelt down beside him. "Whatever I can't remember you're going to tell me."

"Fuck you!"

Now Perlis did cry out as Bourne's thumbs pressed hard into his eyeballs.

"Now look!" he commanded.

Perlis blinked through eyes streaming with tears and saw the girl-shadow climbing down from one of the trees.

"Look at her!" Bourne said. "Look what you've made of her."

"Holly?" Perlis couldn't believe it. Through watering eyes he saw a lithe shape, Holly's shape. "That isn't Holly." But who else could it be? His heart hammered in his chest.

"What happened?" Bourne said. "Tell me about you and Holly."

"I found her wandering around Venice. She was lost, but not in the geographic sense." Perlis heard his own voice thin and attenuated, as if it were being transmitted through a poor cell connection. What was he doing? That switch had been thrown, the energy flowing out of him, just like these words he'd kept inside himself for years. "I asked her if she wanted to make some quick money and she said, Why not? She had no idea what she was getting into, but she didn't seem to care. She was bored, she needed something new, something different. She wanted her blood to flow again."

"So you're saying all you did was give her what she wanted."

"That's right!" Perlis said. "That's all I ever gave anybody."

"You gave Veronica Hart what she wanted?"

"She was a Black River operative, she belonged to me."

"Like a head of cattle."

Perlis turned his head away. He was staring at the girl-shadow, who stood watching him, as if in judgment of his life. Why should he care? he wondered. He had nothing to be ashamed of. And yet he couldn't look away, he couldn't rid himself of the notion that the girl-shadow was Holly Marie Moreau, that she knew every secret he had chained in the prison of his heart.

"Like Holly."

"What?"

"Did Holly belong to you, too?"

"She took my money, didn't she?"

"What did you pay her to do?"

"I needed to get close to someone, and I knew I couldn't do it myself."

"A man," Bourne said. "A young man."

Perlis nodded. Now that he'd embarked on this path he seemed to need to keep going. "Jaime Hererra."

"Wait a minute. Don Fernando Hererra's son?"

"I sent her to London. In those days, he wasn't yet working in his father's firm. He frequented a club—gambling was a weakness he couldn't yet fight. Even though he was underage, he didn't look it, and no one challenged his fake ID." Perlis paused for a moment, struggling to breathe. His left arm, underneath his body, moved slightly as he tried to ease his suffering. "Funny thing, Holly looked so innocent, but she was damn good at what I'd sent her to do. Within a week she and Jaime were lovers, ten days after that she moved into his flat."

"And then?"

Perlis appeared to be having an increasingly difficult time catching his breath. He continued to stare, not at Bourne, but at the girl-shadow, which seemed to him all that was left of the world.

"Is she real?"

"It depends what you mean by real," Bourne said. "Go on, what did Jaime Hererra have that you wanted Holly to steal?"

Perlis said nothing, but Bourne saw him curl the fingers of his right hand, pushing them into the leafy forest floor.

"What are you trying to hide, Noah?"

Perlis's left hand, which had been lying under him, swung out, a switchblade biting through Bourne's clothes into the flesh of his side. Perlis began to twist the knife, trying to find a way through muscle, sinew, and bone to one of Bourne's vital organs. Bourne struck him a horrific blow to the head, but Perlis, with a burst of superhuman strength, only plunged the knife in deeper.

Bourne took Perlis's head between his hands and, with a powerful twist, snapped his neck. At once, the life force ebbed and Perlis's eyes grew dim and all-seeing. There was a bit of foam at the corner of his mouth, either from his excessive effort or from the madness that had begun to infect him at the end of his days.

Gasping, Bourne let his head go and drew out the blade from his side. He started to bleed, but not badly. He grabbed Perlis's right hand and dug the fist out of the dirt. One by one, he opened the fingers. He'd expected there to be something held against the palm—whatever it was that Perlis had taken back from Holly—but there was nothing. Circling his index finger, the one he'd been so anxious to hide, was a ring. It was impossible to slip off, so Bourne used the switchblade to cut off the finger. What he held up into the emerald and sapphire light was a plain gold band, not unlike ten million wedding rings all around the planet. Could this be the reason Perlis had killed Holly? Why? What might have made it worth a young woman's life?

He turned it over and over, tumbling it between his fingers. And then he saw the writing on the inside. It went all the way around the circumference. At first he thought it was Cyrillic, then possibly an ancient Sumerian language, long-dead and forgotten except by the most esoteric specialists, but in the end the characters were unfathomable. A code, then, surely.

As Bourne continued to hold the ring aloft, he became aware of the girl-shadow approaching. She stopped a number of paces away, and because he could see the fear on her face, he rose with a grunt of pain and walked over to her.

"You've been very brave, Kasih," he told the Balinese girl who had led him to the bullet casing in the village of Tenganan, where he'd been shot.

"You're bleeding." She pressed a handful of aromatic leaves she had gathered to his side.

He took her hand and together they began their trek back to her family compound at the top of the terraced rice paddy not far from Tenganan. His free hand pressed the poultice of herbs to his fresh wound, and he could feel the blood coagulating, the pain receding. "There's nothing to be afraid of," he said.

"Not when you're here." Kasih threw one last glance over her shoulder. "Is the demon dead?" she asked.

"Yes," Bourne said, "the demon is dead."

"And he won't come back?"

"No, Kasih, he won't come back."

She smiled, content. But even as he said it, he knew it for a lie.